The Blue Girl Murders

THE BLUE GIRL MURDERS

A Mystery

In Turbulent Baltimore in 1966

By

Dan Riker

Happy Valley, OR

2015

2

ISBN-10: 1517637406

ISBN-13: 978-1517637408

First Trade Paperback Edition

Cover photo credit www.123RF.com

In memory of my late wife, Janis Ahalt Riker, (1944-2014),
my lover, my best friend, a wonderful mother to our daughter,
Cary, and the finest person I ever have known, who gave me
the idea for the solution to this mystery.

The Blue Girl Murders Soundtrack

Went to a dance, lookin for
romance
Saw Barbara Ann, so I
thought I'd take a chance
 - The Beach Boys, <u>Barbara
Ann</u>

And the sign said, "The
words of the prophets are
written on the subway
walls
And tenement halls"
And whispered in the
sounds of silence
 - Simon & Garfunkel, <u>The
Sounds of Silence</u>

Silver wings upon their
chest
These are men, America's
best
One hundred men we'll
test today
But only three win the
Green Beret
 - Barry Sadler, <u>The Ballad
of the Green Berets</u>

We all live in a yellow
submarine,
a yellow submarine, a
yellow submarine
 - The Beatles, <u>Yellow
Submarine</u>

When a man loves a
woman
Can't keep his mind on
nothing else
 - Percy Sledge, <u>When A
Man Loves a Woman</u>

Mustang Sally, think you
better slow your mustang
down.
 - Wilson Pickett, <u>Mustang
Sally</u>

I'm pickin' up good
vibrations
She's giving me excitations
 - The Beach Boys, <u>Good
Vibrations</u>

Wild thing, I think I love
you
But I wanna know for sure
 -The Troggs, <u>Wild Thing</u>

These Boots Are Made for
Walking
 - Nancy Sinatra, <u>These
Books Are Made for
Walking</u>

I'm gonna wait 'til the
midnight hour
That's when my love comes
tumbling down
 -Wilson Pickett, "<u>In the
Midnight Hour</u>"

What a drag it is getting old
- The Rolling Stones, Mother's Little Helper

Try to see it my way
Only time will tell if I am right or I am wrong
While you see it your way
There's a chance that we may fall apart before too long
- The Beatles, We Can Work it Out

Two Girls for Every Boy
- Jan and Dean, Surf City

When I was twenty-one, it was a very good year
-Frank Sinatra, It Was a Very Good Year

This is a man's world
But it wouldn't be nothing, nothing without a woman or a girl
He's lost in the wilderness
He's lost in bitterness
-James Brown, It's a Man's Man's Man's World

But I would not feel so all alone
Everybody must get stoned.
- Bob Dylan, Rainy Day Women

Things they do look awful c-c-cold (Talkin' 'bout my generation)
Yeah, I hope I die before I get old (Talkin' 'bout my generation
- The Who, My Generation

She takes just like a woman, yes she does
She makes love just like a woman, yes she does
And she aches just like a woman
But she breaks just like a little girl.
- Bob Dylan, Just Like a Woman

Well I love that dirty water
Oh, Boston, you're my home
- The Standells, Dirty Water

Even think I`ll go to prayin`
Every time I hear `em sayin`
That there`s no way to delay
That trouble comin` every day
- "Trouble Every Day, From "Freak Out," Frank Zappa's first album

Chapter One

The First Murder

It was the Sunday before Valentine's Day in 1966. Because the mayor of Baltimore ordered snow cleared from alleyways inside the complex of empty downtown warehouses, they found Candy Barlow before she completely defrosted.

The "Blizzard of 66" had dropped a foot of snow on the city two weeks earlier, and bitter, below-freezing temperatures remained until Friday. A story in *The Sun* on Saturday alleged that because large piles of snow blocked the alleys, the fire department would be unable to control any fire that occurred in the old wooden buildings where the homeless frequently sought shelter, and it would spread to major buildings nearby.

So, on Mayor Theodore McKeldin's orders, Bobby Pardoe and his crew used two Bobcats and a front-end loader to clear snow piles as tall as twelve feet and to load the snow into dump trucks. The trucks took it to a dock four blocks away and dumped it into the harbor. Temperatures soared into the 50s that Sunday afternoon for the first time since December, making it a sloppy job.

Darkness approached. Bobby Pardoe looked at his watch and swore. Almost five o'clock, too late to take his wife to dinner at the famous and popular German restaurant, Haussner's. That was supposed to be an early Valentine's Day gift, so they could avoid a larger crowd, and longer line on Monday. Pardoe and an assistant supervisor, Tim Roberts, stood in one of the alleys, smoking cigarettes and watching the crew finish.

"Why the fuck didn't they dump all the snow in the harbor when they cleared the streets around here?" Roberts said

"They probably didn't think leaving this snow around the empty warehouses would be a problem," Pardoe said.

"They were right," Roberts said. "No one could have gotten in here to start any fires, anyway."

Two Baltimore City Police patrol cars drove down the alley toward them and stopped about ten feet away. Two uniformed officers got out of the first one and waved. Pardoe recognized one of them, a red-faced sergeant in a uniform that fit a little too tight.

"Sergeant O'Malley, it's good to see you on this fine day," Pardoe said. "Did the Mayor send you down here, too?"

"Some asshole did, I guess it could have been the Mayor. Whoever it was got on our new acting Police Commissioner and being a General, he knows how to give orders. My orders are to make sure these fucking rattraps are locked up tight. We don't want these precious relics to be burned down before we have a chance to tear them down. This is Brian Cushman. Brian, meet Bobby Pardoe. He's one of the guys responsible for the streets being full of potholes."

"Fuck you, too," Pardoe said. "These smell like rattraps, also. One of the guys says there is a rank odor coming out of the door that's open in that building in the next alley." Pardoe pointed toward the east. "Even the aroma from McCormick's couldn't cover it up."

"That old spice plant sure does make downtown smell good, doesn't it?" O'Malley said. "We'll get that door closed and locked. You see any others open?"

"We haven't noticed any others, but we haven't checked them all, either."

"We will," O'Malley said. "Looks like you're about done. Can I bum a couple cigarettes? I left my pack in the station."

"Sure," Pardoe said. After taking one cigarette out, he handed the pack to O'Malley. "Keep the pack, I've got another one in the car."

"Thanks," O'Malley said. They both lit up.

"So how is General Gelston?" Pardoe said. Three weeks ago Governor Tawes appointed Major General George Gelston, the Adjutant General of the Maryland National Guard, as acting Police Commissioner of the City of Baltimore. Since the police force of Baltimore was created by the state legislature in 1867 it has been a unit of the state government, not the city's, and the Governor appoints its chief, the Police Commissioner. A study by the International Association of Chiefs of Police released in January described Baltimore's police department as among the most corrupt, and most incompetent, in the U.S. That report led to the forced resignation of the top two officials of the police department. As head of the National Guard, Gelston previously demonstrated firm leadership and a natural ability to manage crises, particularly racial conflicts.

"He's changing things and also made it plain that anyone who resists will be history," O'Malley said. "I think he's for real. He's improving the department, and while I hate to admit it, it's about fucking time."

"Well, I guess we ought to get out of your way, so you can carry out those orders," Pardoe said. He and Roberts walked south to Pratt Street where their cars were parked.

Built adjacent to the downtown waterfront to replace buildings destroyed in the Baltimore Fire of 1904, the wood and brick buildings housed seafood and produce markets until the early 1960s. Since the markets had moved out to the suburbs, the old buildings were scheduled for demolition. Their large sliding garage-like doors were sealed shut and padlocked. Metal panels long ago replaced the broken glass in the conventional doors.

O'Malley and Cushman walked down the alley toward the warehouse with the open door. Cushman went in first, his flashlight turned on. O'Malley heard him cough. "Christ, what a stink," he said. "It smells like a dead rat."

O'Malley followed him in, also with his flashlight turned on. The odor was sickening.

"It must be a bunch of them," he said.

There were two rooms, separated by a partition across the middle that was open at the top and at both ends. The room where they entered once upon a time had been a loading area, with a large sliding garage door that locked from the inside, and a loading dock at the far end. O'Malley walked over to the partition, and the smell got much stronger. He choked, and stepped back.

"That's not a rat," he said. Pointing to the far wall, he said to Cushman, "Go around that way. I'll take this side."

They circled carefully around the partition quickly flashing their lights around the room until they saw the counter and found the source of the smell.

Lying on the counter was the bluish naked body of a thin but big-breasted woman. Her decapitated head sat upright on the counter about two feet away in a pool of blood, her blonde hair spread out behind it. Her blue eyes stared into space from a blue face. While Cushman choked and threw up, O'Malley stepped closer, and then saw that the blue color on her face and body was paint.

Chapter Two

Nick Prescott, UPI Baltimore Bureau Manager

Shortly before five o'clock Monday morning, Nick Prescott drove through the center of downtown Baltimore on nearly empty St. Paul Street, glistening from melting snow. He felt good because he loved starting the day before almost everyone else. He turned on WCAO and heard that week's number one song, Nancy Sinatra's "These Boots Are Made for Walking," which he hated, so he switched to WITH, which was playing "Barbara Ann" by the Beach Boys. He sang loudly along with the song, and tapped the steering wheel of his 1964½ Mustang.

He turned left onto Pratt Street and headed towards the *News American* newspaper building four blocks away at Gay Street. He noticed police cars parked on the left side of the street next to the empty warehouses that faced the waterfront and the dock of the tourist attraction, the *USF Constellation*, a naval warship dating to the early 1800s, and bright lights shining in one of the alleys between the buildings.

With Gay Street one-way south, Nick drove around the block and came back west on Lombard before turning onto Gay and parking in a small lot across from the newspaper. He bought the final edition of *The Sun* from a box on the corner, went into the newspaper building and took the elevator to the third floor. He wore what could pass for the uniform of a journalist, a brown leather jacket, a light blue Brooks Brothers shirt, tan chinos and brown loafers. He kept a tie and a sport coat at work for the times they were needed.

He waved at a couple of the men on the city desk in the middle of the large room with offices around the sides, and which already reeked of cigarette smoke. He passed the glassed-in room of AP, UPI and Hearst teletype machines clattering away with stories for afternoon newspapers. He went to the small office that housed the Baltimore bureau of United Press International located off a hall that led to the newspaper's photo department, library and cafeteria.

A stained olive green metal and glass eight-foot high partition, with an open area of several feet above it to the high ceiling, separated the UPI bureau from the *News American's* radio and television department. It made the small, cluttered, wire service bureau seem larger. Pages of letter-size newsprint containing phone numbers of important people, newspaper, radio and television subscribers, police departments and government agencies were taped to the wall below the windows.

Nick scanned the clipboard of the bureau's copy from Sunday, glanced quickly through *The Sun*, marked several stories to rewrite, and then called the dispatcher at the Baltimore City police department to find out what that police activity he saw nearby was all about. After a year of working the morning shift, he knew the dispatchers of the City, county and State Police.

"Morning, Nick, nothing much today," the sergeant said.

"Driving in, I saw a bunch of patrol cars by the warehouses on Pratt, just a block from here," Prescott said. "Anything to that?"

"There was a report last night of a body found in one of those buildings," he said, "let me check." He was back on the phone a minute later.

"All we have here is that a body of a woman was found in one of those buildings, apparently a homicide. We don't have any other details. Homicide has it now, so you'll have to talk to them."

Nick called the number for homicide, but was told the detectives on that case were out. He left a message.

Then he went over to the weather bureau's teletype machine, one of four receive-only teletype machines on one side of the small office, collectively generating a racket that sometimes made it hard to hear the telephone ring. A telephoto transmitter and receiver sat on a desk next to the teletype machines. Ancient typewriters, each equipped with a (UP) button, sat on the two other desks in the office, his desk and the desk they called the "slot" desk, used by whoever was in charge of the shift's news report. The typewriters dated to many years before Scripps-Howard's United Press and

Hearst's International News Service merged to form UPI in 1957.

Nick tore the zone weather forecasts for Maryland and Delaware from the weather wire and went to the broadcast wire teletype transmitter. He sat in front of that a machine that dated from the World War I era, and arranged the forecasts and the newspaper stories he had marked for rewriting into broadcast stories. He would do that on the teletype transmitter after typing the weather forecasts.

He lit a Pall Mall, took a couple of puffs, and put the butt on the edge of the machine that was burned black from generations of previous cigarettes, and began typing his rewrites, doing what was known in wire service lingo as "punching." His typing generated signals that punched various combinations of five holes in a 1-inch wide yellow tape, a different combination for every letter and symbol. He could only tell by feel, or by looking at the tape, if he had made a typo. If he did, he would have to back up the tape, erase everything back to the point of the error, and retype. After a year of this he seldom made any mistakes that went out on the wire.

The bureau transmitted its stories to three dozen radio and television stations in Maryland, Delaware, the District of Columbia and Northern Virginia on the half hour. Promptly at 5:30 the national wire stopped. Nick threw a switch, starting the tape through the transmitter. Those stories he transmitted comprised most of that morning's six o'clock local newscasts for the UPI subscribers.

He turned on the radio and tuned it first to WCAO, that did its news at five minutes before the hour. News director Frank Luber did the newscast that morning but had nothing Nick didn't. He then tuned to the two stations that had both the UPI and AP broadcast wires, first WCBM and Jack O'Rourke, and then WBAL, and the melodious voice of Galen Fromme, the dean of Baltimore newscasters. On the half hour he would check WFBR, an AP only station. All four stations had aggressive news departments, but like most Monday mornings, stale news from the weekend comprised most of their newscasts.

The telephone began ringing a few minutes later. Because of a contest Nick started when he became bureau manager, newsmen with UPI subscriber radio stations in Maryland and Delaware now called in more stories every morning than ever before. If Nick used their story, the station's call letters would appear at the bottom of the story and the newsman would receive a few dollars at the end of the month. Those with the most each month received an extra payment. Nick divided Maryland and Delaware into regions so that there would be more competition and more winners. As soon as the phone stopped ringing, he ran down the hall to the cafeteria and got a cup of coffee and a doughnut. Coming back he ran into Bob Bradley, one of the *News American's* police reporters.

"There's an interesting murder a couple blocks over," Bradley said. "I'll drop a carbon by in a little while."

"Thanks," Nick said. He wasn't surprised that Bradley had the story and he didn't. The *News American's* three police reporters were legendary for their knowledge and sources, and their regular crime column was said to be the paper's most popular feature.

He loved the hectic pace of the morning shift. Big name newscasters read his stories as if they were their own. Nick took no journalism courses in college. They weren't offered at Johns Hopkins where he had been a political science major. He learned broadcast news from working part-time at WCBM where news director Fred Neil taught him how to write tight and bright broadcast copy, and showed him how a first class news operation should run in a highly competitive environment. He learned quickly and discovered he had a talent for broadcast writing, but his Western Pennsylvania nasal accent would keep him from being a newscaster. Instead UPI hired him, with a strong recommendation from Neil, one of the most important UPI subscribers in the region.

The Baltimore bureau provided local and regional news, weather and sports to the regional broadcast subscribers and also covered stories of national, or international interest. AP and UPI competed intensely. UPI editors in New York kept track on a daily basis of which service's stories were used by the newspapers that had both services. Losing the "logs" to the AP very often was not good for a UPI bureau manager's future.

Nick had just been promoted to bureau manager late in December and it was not normal practice for the bureau manager to work a shift, but one of the bureau's reporters was in Annapolis covering the Maryland Legislature. The AP had a bureau in Annapolis. UPI did not. That reduced the

Baltimore staff to three, including Nick, to cover 13 shifts a week - 5 AM to 11 PM Monday through Saturday, and 11 AM to 8 PM on Sunday - until the legislative session ended on March 31. So for three days during the week Nick worked the early shift. It was his work on this most important shift during the past year that gained him his promotion.

When he had learned that the previous bureau manager was being transferred, Nick had applied for the job, but, at the age of 22, did not expect to get it. However, his Division New Editor, Norm Braun, summoned him to Pittsburgh for an interview. Braun was known for being stern and demanding, but also very fair. He told Nick that a number of UPI's radio station customers in Maryland had spoken favorably of him and had recommended he be promoted.

"But you will be one of the youngest bureau managers we've ever had," Braun said. "In fact, the only younger one we can think of was David Brinkley, and he was fired. So don't think for a minute that you will be excused for fucking up just because you are so young."

With that encouragement, Nick took charge of a bureau that had not been highly regarded, nor was it a significant contributor to company revenues. Unlike the AP, which was a member cooperative owned by its subscribing newspapers, UPI was a private company that was supposed to make a profit, which it had not done for quite a few years. Budgets were ridiculously tight, but having no money to spend was no excuse for a bureau not being competitive with the AP.

He wasn't sure how he was going to do it, but Nick vowed to himself to improve the bureau's reputation and its revenue. In six weeks in the job he had reformatted the way the bureau did its stories for broadcasters and had begun that contest among the UPI subscribers to have more stories called to the bureau. The result had been a dramatic improvement in the news report.

The token $20.00 a week raise from his second year union scale salary of $112.00 per week did not make up for not getting overtime anymore, but he didn't care. He liked being in charge, and working whatever hours he wanted, usually about 60 a week. For most of his young life Nick often had found himself put in charge of things, or he just assumed command. He didn't think of himself as a natural leader, but he frequently discovered he could figure out how to do things better than most other people, and most other people were

16

content to have someone else take responsibility for getting things done, or be blamed when they weren't.

With a $75 a month apartment near the Hopkins Homewood campus, and only three other bills, a student loan on which he paid $50 a month, his car payment of $85.00, and his $20 a month telephone bill, he had enough money left from his paycheck to take his girlfriend, Joan Holland, a junior at Goucher College, to dinner, a movie, or a concert, once a week. They spent a lot of time talking to each other by telephone on the other days.

They started dating two years ago, and he was madly in love with her and wanted to marry her when she graduated in 1967. Even though she said she loved him, and despite their very passionate relationship, she had other ideas. Joan lived with her parents in suburban Towson, and she said she didn't want to go from her parents' house to a husband's house. She wanted to live on her own for a while. A European history major at Goucher, she wanted to go to graduate school and become a college professor.

Her ambitions conflicted with his hope of becoming a foreign correspondent for UPI, possibly a war correspondent in Vietnam, and then maybe on an assignment in Europe. While not a natural linguist, he read French, and could speak enough to get around. He took a year of beginning Chinese, and he had learned some Vietnamese from a language book. He had considerable difficulty with the tonal nature of both Asian languages, but a fraternity brother from Taiwan provided some coaching. He told himself he still had time to work things out with Joan, but some tension currently existed because she told him last week she didn't think he understood her point of view. Nick's stomach hurt when he thought of the possibility of losing her. He was going to see her that night and was worried. However, the hectic pace of his work kept him from thinking about her all the time. He would try to figure out what to say during his drive out to Towson.

Shortly before eight o'clock, Bradley brought in a carbon of his story on the murder. The police identified the murdered woman as Candy Barlow, a stripper in one of the clubs on Baltimore's infamous "Block," a five-block section of strip bars and clubs on Baltimore Street just two blocks north of the *News American*. Much of the Block's recent fame came from the stripper, Blaze Starr, owner of its best-known business, the "Two O'Clock Club," and her affair with Louisiana politician Earl Long. The Block also included the Gayety burlesque theatre, a large all-night pool hall where the unwary could be hustled by serious pros, and a variety of retail establishments selling goods not generally available elsewhere in the city.

Barlow had not been seen since January 29. The strip club filed a missing persons report with the police on Feb. 1. The police checked her apartment and found no evidence of her planning to leave town. Her possessions seemed to be intact.

Bradley said the medical examiner's preliminary report said her body showed no signs of rape or trauma, other than the fact that her head was cut off. It was a very clean cut, done by a very sharp blade. The ME said the freezing of the body after the murder, and its partial defrosting before its discovery made it impossible to determine the time of death. He tentatively concluded that she died instantly from the decapitation.

"Oh, by the way, Detective Maury Antonelli mentioned he had a message from you," Bradley said. "He asked me to fill you in. He's young, but I think a real comer. He got himself in trouble early on for saying too much about a case, so he's a little skittish about talking to reporters he doesn't know well. I told him you were OK, but he probably won't call you back unless you call again, and keep this in mind about him. He doesn't like to be quoted."

Bradley then gave Nick a flier from the strip club that had a picture of the young woman, Candy Barlow, very pretty, a Marilyn Monroe/Jayne Mansfield type, very buxom, with long, blonde hair. Nick took the flier, put a caption on it, and set it up on the photo transmitter. He would call the UPI pictures bureau in Washington after his story was ready. They then could activate the transmitter when they wanted the photo to go onto the network.

"She had big hair and it was all hers," he said. "So were her tits. The guy who did this was very careful. The Crime Lab techs haven't found any prints at the scene. The ME didn't find any body fluids. He chopped off her head with something very sharp, like a butcher knife, or cleaver."

Nick called the homicide department and left another message for Antonelli. He wanted to establish a relationship so he did not have to be completely dependent on Bradley. This story had the potential to make the national wire. Lucien

Carr, UPI's brilliant and legendary "night editor," the editor in charge of UPI's national news report for morning newspapers, almost certainly would be on the phone to Nick some time this morning. Carr, a close friend of Jack Kerouac and Allen Ginsberg, the "Lucien" mentioned affectionately in Ginsberg's poem, "Howl," served a prison term in the early 1950s for killing a homosexual who had stalked him. He loved bizarre and gory crime stories, and this one qualified on both grounds. Nick wanted to be prepared to answer the questions he surely would have.

Nick made one of his regular trips to the city desk at 10:45 to pick up carbons of local stories that the city editor, Eddie Ballard, kept for him on a spike. Haze from cigarette smoke hung around the busy city desk. Nick noticed a blonde woman in a short skirt and figure-hugging red top sitting at a desk in a previously vacant office along one side of the room behind the city desk. She reminded him of the Barlow girl whose photo he had just seen, but looked even better, more refined. She seemed to be unpacking several boxes.

"A little more detail on that murder for the 9 star edition, kid," Ballard said, "but not much else." Even after a year, Nick thought, Ballard still didn't know his name, because he never called him anything other than "kid."

"Who's that?" he said to Ballard, motioning his head towards the blonde in the office.

"Susan Fanning," he said, "you heard of her?"

"No, I don't think so," Nick said.

"She's a feature writer for the Hearst Headline Service, writes stories for the Sunday papers. She's won some awards. She was just transferred here from Boston."

"What kind of stories does she do?"

"From what I was told, just about anything she feels like doing," Ballard said, with an expression in his eyes that told Nick he was less than happy about that, reflecting his well-known disdain for anyone he considered a prima donna.

The phone rang as Nick walked into the bureau and found Dewey Coughlin reading the stories from the sports wire as he usually did every morning. As Nick walked past Dewey to answer the telephone, he smelled the stink of his Gauloise cigarettes.

"Detective Antonelli here, I'm returning your phone call," the voice said on the phone, with a tone of someone doing something he really didn't want to do.

"Thanks for calling me back," Nick said in as sincere and polite a tone as he could muster. "I know you're busy. I just wanted to confirm some facts and get an update, if there is one."

"What facts?"

Nick went through the details that Bradley gave him. Antonelli confirmed them.

"Do you have any suspects?"

"If I did, I wouldn't say," Antonelli said. "Shit, I didn't mean it to sound like that. I don't want you to report that we don't have any suspects."

"No problem," Nick said. "I'm curious about whether there is anything about this case similar to any other recent murders or rapes?"

"Why do you ask?"

"It just doesn't sound like any murder I've heard of, the chopping off of her head, Isn't that a lot more than strange?"

"It definitely is," Antonelli said. "We've checked all the open cases we have for the past couple of years, and we've asked the FBI for some help in trying to find out if this has happened elsewhere. It's too soon to know anything about that."

Nick asked if Barlow's family had been notified.

"I talked to her mother this morning," Antonelli said.

"Do you think it would be possible for me to talk with her by phone?" Nick said.

"She took it very hard," Antonelli said. "She was going to try to get here later today, so I don't think you can reach her."

"If she does get here, I'd really like to talk with her. From what I heard from Bradley, her daughter was a really nice girl. I'd like to know more so I can write more about her."

"I'll think about it," Antonelli said. Nick realized what that meant and didn't push it.

"I think this is going to be a national story," Nick said. "I may need to ask some more questions later. Will you be there?"

"Maybe, I don't know," Antonelli said. "If I'm not, leave a message. I'll call you back."

"Thanks," Nick said, and they hung up.

Dewey hung around while Nick was on the phone. Nick first met Dewey during the fraternity rush season of his freshman year at Hopkins when Dewey presided over a small fraternity of wealthy geniuses, he being the smartest among them. Dewey built his legend on the campus by attending classes off and on for nine years without getting a degree, periodically flunking out when he became bored. He made the school's College Bowl team, only to be dropped because the competition occurred after one of the times he flunked out.

Dewey came from an old Baltimore society family that, except for him, had died out. He inherited the family house in the city's exclusive Guilford section, but denied being wealthy, at least wealthy by the standards of the wealthy. He had the society look: sandy-brown hair, gray-blue eyes, a slight bend to his nose, and a relaxed, self-confident personality. When Nick met him at Hopkins he drove a Morgan sports car, often with a pretty girl in the passenger seat.

Though he failed to persuade Nick to join his fraternity, which closed later for lack of membership, Dewey remained friendly, and introduced Nick to Joan, a friend of one of his girlfriends. They double-dated several times until Dewey moved on to another girl. He seldom kept a girlfriend for more than a few months. Nick and Joan remained friends with Dewey, who occasionally invited them to his house to show off his considerable cooking skills, and the well-stocked wine cellar he inherited from his father.

Dewey took a job as a supervisor in the circulation department of the *News American* at the beginning of the year. He organized the loading of packages of newspapers onto the right trucks for delivery to boxes and to distribution points for home delivery. It seemed like odd work for him, but he said he liked it because it paid well and it gave him time to pursue his other interests. He told Nick that he needed income because his father's estate, after the inheritance taxes were paid, did not have much available cash, his house was in need of many repairs, and he didn't want to sell stocks while the market was trending down.

Dewey took one course at Hopkins early in the morning, one late in the day and two at night. These would be his last courses at Hopkins. The University informed Dewey they were giving him a BA degree, and also, if he completed his thesis, a Masters degree as well.

Almost every day he brought the first edition of the afternoon *News American* up to the UPI bureau and hung around, reading the wires, and chatting until Nick chased him out.

"That the detective working the murder of that stripper?" he said.

"Yes."

"Anything new from what's in the paper? Do they have any idea who did it?"

"If he does, he wouldn't tell me," Nick said. "I was just trying to make sure that if something breaks with the case that we get a call. Apparently he doesn't like to talk to the press."

"So this really is a national story? You weren't bullshitting him?"

"I sent a story to New York this morning and it got on the "B" wire, but I think now that I have more information it may make the "A" wire this afternoon," he said, adding, "Dewey, I've got to get back to work."

"Me too, see you later," Dewey said.

Almost at that moment the phone rang.

"I like the story of the headless stripper," the gravelly voice spoke through the phone, and Nick recognized it as Lu Carr. "But I want more detail."

He then peppered Nick with questions. What more do you have on her? Have you talked to her family? What are they saying at the strip joint? He seemed satisfied with what Nick had found out so far, but he said he needed more for the story to make the "Sked," the summary of major stories that opened the morning newspaper cycle every afternoon. He also mentioned a recent *Time* article about Baltimore's "Block."

Nick found the *Time* issue in the *News American's* library. The magazine reported that the scandal in the Baltimore police department and the resulting cleanup of the department probably would not result in a cleanup of the "Block," which the article described as the city's "Casbah."

Of course, Nick was quite familiar with the Block. He and others in the UPI bureau often went to the large newsstand on the Block because it was the closest place to get the first edition of the morning *Sun*, which came out around nine o'clock at night. It also was a good place to get out of town newspapers. Almost anything went on the Block. Barkers stood outside the clubs and bars loudly and passionately extolling the virtues of their performers to everyone walking by. It was colorful and risqué, but almost entirely free of violent crime.

No substantial interest in shutting down the Block existed in the community. To the contrary, as intimated in the *Time* article, a certain amount of community pride in the Block seemed to exist despite its flagrant violations of numerous laws. Baltimore did not have a large religious community concerned about sin so long as it was confined as it was.

Nick called the strip club and talked with the manager. Bradley talked with a several employees of the club and gave Nick some quotes. Nick focused his story on Barlow's reputation as a nice girl who sent money home to her family. His story made the sked and ran with very few changes.

Nick left the bureau at 4 PM and got on an elevator with Susan Fanning. She smiled at him and he introduced himself.

"You seem very young to be a bureau manager," she said, "and I mean that as a compliment. UPI is a tough place to work. I worked in the Boston bureau for a summer while I was in college."

"Thanks," Nick said. "I'm enjoying it. Why did you come to Baltimore? Boston seems like a more exciting city."

She looked away for a second, and Nick sensed he had struck a nerve. She impressed him with classic looks that don't show age. He thought she had to be 30, or a little older, but she looked younger. With her light blonde hair contrasting against her black coat and red blouse, she was even more of a knockout close up, and in the tight confines of the elevator he could smell her perfume, but didn't know enough about perfumes to recognize it. It had a light, seductive odor that seemed to soften but emphasize her striking appearance. He felt an immediate attraction, tightness in his chest, and slight perspiration. He hoped it didn't show.

"I think a lot is going to happen here this year, with the big push for desegregation and the political situation. I think there will be some good stories to write."

"Well, I hope so," Nick said, as they crossed Gay Street to the parking lot. "If I can be of any help, just let me know. The city room didn't seem to give you the warmest reception."

"Oh, you noticed," she said. "Thanks. It's probably natural. I was sent here. They didn't have a choice. I just have to prove myself again. It's nothing I can't handle, but I appreciate the offer, and I may take you up on it." She smiled as she got into a Pontiac GTO with Massachusetts plates.

"This is a hot car," Nick said. "One of my fraternity brothers got one as a graduation gift, last year and he was the envy of the house."

"Well this one was a man's car," she said, "but it's mine now. Would you like a ride?"

"I would, but I can't right now. I have an appointment and I'm already late."

"Maybe tomorrow," she said, and she spun the tires as she accelerated out of the parking lot.

Nick now felt guilty for being attracted to her. He was on his way to his date with Joan at Goucher College in Towson to give her a Valentine's Day card. Susan immediately impressed him as the kind of woman he thought Joan would become: independent, self-confident, and intimidating to many men; the kind of woman he admired, the kind he wanted for his wife.

On Saturday, after going to see *Dr. Zhivago*, they again argued over their competing ambitions. On Sunday night, when he talked to her by phone and invited her to a Valentine's Day dinner with him, she declined, saying she was behind on a paper and had a test on Tuesday. She agreed to meet him for coffee in the college snack bar. That was what had worried him. It was out of character. He didn't believe her story about the paper and the test. She was a straight-A student who never ran behind on papers and didn't have to cram for tests. Something else was going on and he was afraid she was going to break off their relationship.

In the drive out to Towson, which took about 20 minutes, he rehearsed what to say if she really was going to break things off. He thought about other possibilities. Nick generally was very good under pressure, in emergencies and handling breaking news stories. He never panicked. The more pressure, the calmer he would be. Except when it came to relationships. He really wasn't sure how to deal with personal crises, with the problems of another person, even someone he loved. It wasn't that he didn't care. He cared deeply but he had trouble expressing his feelings. He had little experience with close relationships. He wanted them. He desperately wanted Joan. He was not going to give up on her very easily, but he wasn't sure how to keep her.

He feared they would break up if one of them didn't give in, and the thought of losing his best friend made him desperate. He didn't know what to do. He didn't have anyone to turn to for advice. His lonely and bitter mother, who lived in a Pittsburgh suburb, never liked any of his girlfriends and had her own problems. His father, a mid-level executive with

U.S. Steel, died young from a heart condition, and his mother never remarried. He had a younger brother still in high school, too young to provide any useful advice. His closest friends from college, several of his fraternity brothers, were in the Army and in Vietnam, where he probably would have been if he had passed the Army physical. But he had lost too much vision from his left eye, hit by a baseball his freshman year. So this was a problem he needed to solve by himself, and he was trying.

He met her in Goucher's snack bar shortly before 5:00 PM. She smiled, but her eyes had a serious look. Nick now felt some panic and he began to sweat. He felt a huge pang in his stomach. It was different from what he felt when he was in that elevator with Susan Fanning. This was fear. They sat at a corner table, away from other students, and he lit her cigarette, then his. He decided to take the initiative. He gave her the Valentine's card. Inside the card he had written, "I love you because of who you are, and who you will be, and I will love you and follow you wherever you go."

She read it and tears showed in her eyes. She took his hand and leaned over the table to kiss him. "Is the dinner invitation still open?' she said.

Nick felt a lump in his throat. "You bet," was all he could get out.

Nick drove north on York Road to Johnny Unitas' Golden Arm restaurant in Timonium, which earlier in the day he had verified would be open. They told him they were not going to be closed on one of their bigger nights of the year. Arriving early, they were able to get a booth before it became crowded. Unitas was away, somewhere warm, but Nick was recognized because he had interviewed the quarterback at his restaurant twice during the past season. No one asked for IDs when he ordered glasses of white wine to start, and a decent Bordeaux with their steaks, which was good thing since Joan was three months shy of her 20th birthday.

Joan exuded beauty, with light brown hair, blue eyes, classic features and a nice figure, but it was her intelligence that made Nick want to marry her. Now one of the top students at Goucher, one of the nation's best women's colleges, she thrived on competition. Her often-challenging personality excited him. Her quick, and sometimes sarcastic, wit complimented his less sophisticated and gentler sense of humor. He loved being with her, and he wanted her to be the mother of his children. Now was the time to say that.

"You are the most remarkable young woman I have ever known," Nick said.

"And you've known a lot?" Joan said with a smile.

"Well, no, but I've always known what kind of woman I wanted to marry and you are the one. I've wanted someone who would be my partner, someone with whom I could talk forever and never be bored. You are smart. You have a wide range of interests. You have a sense of adventure. You want to go places. We are alike, but we also are complimentary. You are shy. You are not a self-promoter. I am not shy and I just got myself promoted. We can help each other. We can have a lot of fun together. And we could have great kids."

"I think you are right about all of that," Joan said. "I love you for most of the same reasons except I also love your body. You didn't say anything about mine."

"I thought I already had shown great appreciation for it," Nick said.

They laughed.

"But there are differences," Joan said. "I know you have trouble seeing things the way I do. I know you believe in women's liberation. From what you have told me, you were raised to believe in it."

"That's true," Nick said. "It never occurred to me when I was a kid that women didn't work. My mother worked all the time."

"Well, how did she take care of you?"

"We stayed at my aunt's house a lot of the time when I was little," Nick said. "When I was older, I looked after my brother."

"But you can see how hard it is for a married woman to have a career," Joan said. "What if there isn't an aunt to take care of the kids? And there isn't one for me. What happens to my career when you get transferred? What if I want to take a great job somewhere else? My mother is very unhappy and a lot of it is due to the fact that she never had a life outside the home. I don't want to be like her. How do we resolve this?"

Joan's eyes sparkled as she talked. And as always, she drew people to her. Strangers sometimes blurted their deepest secrets to her as if she were a long lost close friend. Right then, the waiter fell under her spell. He wanted to keep refilling her wine glass, or to find something else he could do for her. Nick put a stop to the waiter's fawning by insisting he would pour the wine.

"You've made another conquest," Nick said with a laugh.

"I wasn't trying to," she said.

"You can't help it," Nick said. "You had me entranced the first time we met, on that blind date that Dewey arranged. I love you. I want to be with you all the time." He reached his right hand across the table and took her left hand. She put her right hand over the two.

"I love you very much," she said. "And I want to be with you all the time, as well, despite everything I've said about my hopes for a career."

"The Beetles are right," Nick said, looking at her intently, and seriously, "we can work it out. You just have to see it my way." Then he smiled, and they both laughed. "We are going to work it out," Joan said. "I don't know how yet, but I know we will."

He felt good. Progress had been made. He wished he could take Joan back to his apartment, but they had to settle for some passionate making out and fondling in his car before he drove her home.

Driving back into the city he scanned the radio stations for news. They had nothing about the murder of Candy Barlow. There were so many murders in Baltimore that seldom did one stay in the news through a day. As Joan's father said, "When I was a kid, a murder was front page news. Now you have to look inside to find out how many there are each day." Nick was used to murder stories, and seldom felt much emotion about them. But this one was different. It had touched him. He felt sad about it and wondered what kind of person could have done such a thing.

He then sang along softly with "The Sounds of Silence" on the radio, and forced his mind to wander too much more pleasant thoughts about the two beautiful women who had brightened his day.

Chapter Three

Baltimore Homicide Detective Maury Antonelli

He walked down a dark tunnel towards a blinding light. He passed the light and stepped into a room. A blue naked body of a woman lying on a table came into focus. His eyes fixed on her large breasts for a moment before looking at the rest of her headless body. Her head sat upright on the table a foot from her body, her face streaked with blue, her long blonde hair spread out on both sides and behind, some tips colored the dark reddish-brown of blood. Her open blue eyes stared at him, imploring: Why?

At that point Detective Maury Antonelli woke suddenly, dripping with sweat. The nightmares kept occurring every night, even two weeks after the murder. Of the more than a dozen murders he investigated in the past year, his first year as a homicide detective, none bothered him like this one.

Antonelli joined the police force at the age of 18, right out of high school. He spent five years as a patrolman, winning several commendations. He went to the University of Baltimore at night, and hoped he eventually could go to law school. He was from a large Italian family, and his father, Sergio - known as Serge because he was a sergeant in the Army in World War II - owned one of the best-known restaurants in the city's "Little Italy" neighborhood, "Antonelli's Family Restaurant." His father also was active in local Democratic Party politics.

Serge served as a gunner on an American bomber in England during World War II, and there he met and married Maury's mother, a half-Jamaican beauty who, Serge told his family in Baltimore, was Sicilian. In the two photos Maury had of her, she certainly looked like she could have been Sicilian. She died in a V-2 attack on London in 1944. At the time, his father, whose plane had been shot down over Germany, was hiding from the Nazis after safely parachuting out of the burning plane.

Serge killed several German soldiers while escaping into France and eventually running into Patton's advancing army.

The Silver Star he received made him a hero back in Baltimore's Little Italy, although he never would talk about it.

Serge brought Maury back from London after the war, and married a girl from a Baltimore Italian family. She adopted Maury, and then had four children of her own. His father did not tell him the truth about his mother until he was 21, and even after that Serge continued to keep it secret from everyone else in the family.

Maury did not want to keep it secret, but understood why his father did, and to avoid great distress in the family, he had not told anyone else. There was a great deal of prejudice against Negroes among the people with whom he grew up, particularly his stepmother's family. While his skin had a little different hue from that of other members of his family, Antonelli appeared to be no darker than them. At slightly over six feet, with a lithe, muscular build, he did not have the stocky build of his father, but he did have his father's slightly sorrowful-looking brown eyes, with big eyebrows. His hair represented the most noticeable difference. It was darker and curlier. After his father told him about his mother he recalled an incident involving his hair from many years earlier.

When he was around six years old his father took him to a barbershop where a barber said he had "nigger hair." His father took one of the barber's straight razors and held it to his throat, threatening to slit it. Known to have a temper and for being "a little pink" in his political beliefs, this incident burnished Serge's reputation. Maury never heard that word used in his presence again.

Serge would not tolerate racist remarks or attitudes in their house. He had more liberal views on most issues than many in the community, and his attitudes greatly influenced Maury, who grew up as the "liberal" of his generation of the family. Many were surprised that he had become a policeman, rather than a politician.

Maury grew up in the restaurant, but always wanted to be a detective. His performance as a patrolman, and influential family political connections, helped him get the transfer to homicide a year ago. Even though he was the youngest detective, he quickly made a name for himself by solving several tough cases with considerable analytical skill, and enormous self-confidence. Some already called him "Sherlock."

He was in a squad with four other detectives, headed by Detective Sergeant Brad Jenkins, a 25-year cynical veteran who seemed to enjoy Antonelli's enthusiasm and intelligence. He became a mentor and Antonelli eagerly absorbed his knowledge.

The Crime Lab determined that Candy Barlow was painted blue with tempera paint while still alive. Traces of a sedative and of LSD were found in her body, but too much time had passed to determine when they might have been ingested, and what part they might have played in her death. Antonelli was the prime on the case because, having the least seniority, he was working the Sunday night shift, usually the quietest night of the week, when the call came in.

Almost immediately, the bizarre nature of the murder inspired Jenkins to organize a much larger force of detectives and uniformed officers to do an inch-by-inch search of the grounds inside and outside the old warehouse. Crime lab technicians used vacuums inside to try to find every bit of possible evidence. Satisfied that the crime scene investigation was under control, Antonelli shifted his focus to the victim.

Barlow came to Baltimore a year ago to make money and had hopes of getting into more serious show business. The other strippers at the bar, as well as the bartenders and bouncers, all said she was a sweet young thing, who just happened to make her living showing off her magnificent body. She didn't hook. She didn't do drugs. She was polite to her elders, and well liked by her co-workers. She sent money home to her dirt-poor family in West Virginia.

"She was a nice, clean kid, a natural blonde with beautiful hair and fantastic boobs," the manager of the strip club said. "I can't understand why anyone would want to kill her."

The more Antonelli found out about her, the more angry and frustrated he became. He was determined to find out why she was killed, and by whom. He choked up when he looked at her neat little apartment in a new building on Charles Street, the photos of her family, and her small number of modest possessions that included one very worn teddy bear.

There were five other strippers who worked with her, two of them college girls who only worked part-time on the weekends and did not know Barlow very well. It was different with the three other fulltime strippers who worked regularly with Candy. All three were good-looking young women in their mid-20s, none as stunning as Candy. All three also provided extra services, but Antonelli heard everyone say that Barlow did not.

It was the general practice for the strippers to mix with the customers in between performances. If a customer wanted to be alone with one of the strippers, or with his own date, there were curtained booths in the rear of the club that were available for an extra fee. What services the girls provided, also for an additional fee, were a matter of private negotiation. All three strippers had arrest records, but no convictions.

One of the women, Janey Williams, was open about it.

"A blowjob, occasionally something more, and the charges get dropped," she said. "No one really wants to prosecute us. I think the clubs pay good money to make sure we're not. People in the city like the Block. They don't want us given a hard time. It's really that the guys just don't want to pay for it."

"But Candy never was arrested?" Antonelli said.

"No, because she wouldn't do anything that would get her arrested," she said. "She just did her act. She would have a drink with a guy, but nothing more. The guys wanted more. They were after her all the time. She could have made a lot more money if she'd given them what they wanted."

"Can you think of anyone in particular who pursued her more than others?" he said.

"There are about a half-dozen guys that are more or less regulars here, and they tried all the time. It became a joke. A couple of them started begging her at the end of her dance. She would smile, shake her boobs at them, laugh and walk off. It drove them crazy."

Between the women and the club's manager, Antonelli had the names of ten men. In the next three days all ten were interviewed. As it turned out, only two were at the club on the night of her disappearance, and both had perfect alibis. Each spent the night with one of the other strippers. The rest also had good alibis, particularly since the blizzard came in the next day, and they were snowed in.

Antonelli went to the strip club every evening, except Sundays, for two weeks, watching the customers, looking for the one who didn't fit. Other than Friday and Saturday nights, the club usually was more than half empty. There always were groups of visiting Japanese businessmen, in their suits, white shirts and ties. The girls loved them. They were polite and did nothing more than look, buy the girls over-priced drinks, and leave good tips.

There were a handful of regulars who came just to drink and watch. To keep them coming every night, the club gave them substantial discounts on their liquor purchases. There were assorted tourists, and walk-ins, of various kinds who usually only stayed for one show.

Then there were the guys who wanted more than just a view. There were at least two or three every night, sometimes more. They were watched closely, and, with the help of the club and the girls, who were assured by Antonelli that he would ignore any vice violations, they were identified and checked out.

It was an eye-opening experience for someone raised in a strict Italian Roman Catholic family, where if a boy even thought about having sex with a neighborhood girl, he was as good as engaged to her. And unless he accidentally got a peek at one of his sisters, magazines provided the only views of naked women. The only sexual experience Antonelli had before he moved out of his parents' home was on his 16th birthday when the waiters in the family restaurant paid for a high-class call girl to give him lessons.

Antonelli visited some of the strip clubs in the past, but he knew very little about that world. He discovered that in some ways it was not all that different from his father's restaurant. They both appealed to senses, just different ones. The attraction of his father's restaurant was its great food. The attraction of the strip club was beautiful naked girls. Most of the profits in both businesses came from the sale of liquor. The employees in both businesses formed a sort an extended family.

The strip club manager's wife was in charge of the girls, including their costumes, makeup, and routines. She conducted rehearsals in the morning. The girls' dressing room was open, and employees walked in and out randomly. Antonelli blushed every time he went in and encountered the girls partially, or completely naked. They were perfectly willing to sit and talk with him without putting anything on. One made a point of carefully putting on and taking off the pasties that were required by law to cover her nipples, while grinning at his embarrassment.

Two of the girls lived in an apartment on the second floor, where they entertained over-night customers. Nudity and sex were as routine in this business as pasta and Chianti were in the restaurant.

The bartenders were the operating managers, controlling the flow of the business, keeping an eye on everyone. The bouncers were the "cops," screening the customers at the door and quickly ejecting anyone inside who got too far out of line. One of them always was nearby if a customer took one of the girls to the back room. They protected the girls and were liberally rewarded with their affections. Antonelli wondered how they missed with Barlow. They seemed very upset by her murder, and had no explanation for what happened. He questioned them at length and carefully checked each of their alibis.

Barlow did her three shows on that Friday night, the last one at midnight. She left the club shortly before 1 AM, as usual, through the rear door that opened to an alcove in the alley behind the building where she parked her car, a four-year old Ford Fairlane 500. Her car was found three days after he body was found, parked in a downtown multilevel garage. Her missing clothes and purse were found in the trunk, with $500 in cash in an envelope, from the tips she got that Friday night.

Antonelli believed the killer was waiting for her in the alley, where he over-powered her, possibly injecting her with the drugs later found in her body. He then drove her car to the parking garage, where he moved her to another vehicle, and from there went to the abandoned warehouse. Upon re-examination, Crime Lab techs determined that the large sliding door in the building where she was found had been opened recently. A few small drips of motor oil found on the grimy floor also were determined to be of very recent vintage.

Antonelli now knew the "how" of her murder. He did not know the why. The painting of her body intrigued him. He kept that fact from the news media. He recalled reading something about human sacrifices and blue paint in a Sun story about a recent exhibit of Mayan art at the Baltimore Museum of Art. He went to the museum, located in Wyman Park, adjacent to the Johns Hopkins Homewood campus in the north central part of the city and learned from the curator that the exhibit ended in January.

The curator told him that one aspect of the exhibit featured the mystery of the unique "Mayan Blue" paint. He gave Antonelli the catalog from the exhibit, which explained that the blue color, similar to a mix of sky blue and royal blue, with a slightly chalky hue, was produced by the Mayan priests from a combination of indigo plants and clay cooked in large pots over burning incense. The blue in murals found in Mayan ruins hundreds of years old, illustrated in the catalog, appeared to be as bright as new. It seemed immune to age and to fading, but no one knew why.

The Mayan priests painted the bodies of people who were to be sacrificed by beheading, or by the cutting out of their beating hearts, or, most commonly, by being thrown alive into deep wells. A 14-foot layer of the blue pigment was found in the excavation of the pit at a famous site where human sacrifices occurred for hundreds of years.

Antonelli did not know what to make of the painting of her body, and her decapitation. While similar to a Mayan sacrifice, it seemed absurd to him that it was intended as a human sacrifice. He thought it was far more likely that the killer could have seen the museum display and, to confuse the police, staged the murder to look like a human sacrifice. He believed the motive for the killing lay elsewhere.

The museum provided Antonelli with copies of the exhibit materials, lists of contributors to the exhibit, and people who signed up for memberships during the time of the exhibit. No names on the lists matched any names provided by the strip club owner. He and other detectives then began the tedious and time-consuming task of checking the backgrounds of each person on the museum lists.

While gruesome and tragic, the murder of Barlow did not cause a public outcry, nor did it gain any priority on the long list of unsolved homicides. It was Maury's case, and before long the others dropped off it. A new murder to solve occurred almost every night, and sometimes more than one.

Antonelli knew that most murders were simple and solved quickly. Some were complete mysteries and never solved. The odds of a murder being solved diminished significantly as time passed. Time was passing on this case, but he couldn't let go. He was thinking about it almost all the time.

He couldn't get the image of that dead girl out of his mind. The eerie and unusually cold-blooded nature of her murder, without any obvious motive, frightened him. Jenkins said he could not recall any murder like this. He called it a "thrill killing," and he said he thought it could happen again.

Maury didn't think she was killed for the thrill of it. It was too carefully planned and executed, and it didn't appear to him to be an act of pleasure, or hatred. He did think Jenkins was right that it could happen again. And because of that thought, the nightmares continued into March when they finally subsided.

By the middle of March he had three more homicides to investigate. When he could find the time he continued to check names on the list he got from the Museum, but no one pressured him about the Barlow murder. There were others the brass viewed as more important.

Chapter Four

Susan Fanning

T.S. Eliot may have described April as the cruelest month, but as Nick drove to work and observed the explosion of color downtown, he thought that in Maryland it is the most beautiful month. Spring goes off like an alarm clock at the beginning of the month with flowering cherry trees, forsythias and daffodils. Towards the end of the month come the dogwoods, azaleas and tulips that bloom sometimes into the middle of May.

And best of all, as far as he was concerned, April is the start of the baseball season. The Orioles look like a competitive team. New outfielder Frank Robinson hit home runs in each of the Orioles' first three games, leading them to a 4-1 record in the first week of the season.

Nick covered the Oriole home opener on Friday the 15th, when they lost to the Yankees, and the game on Sunday when they won, mostly because of three errors by 20-year old shortstop Bobby Murcer, who the Yankees were hoping would be the replacement for Tony Kubek.

With the balmy weather came an improvement in Nick's relationship with Joan, but it didn't occur because of the weather. It happened because Nick decided he had to tell her about Susan.

March had been tough. Joan was in a foul mood for much of the month, but even though she blamed it on school, Nick knew there was more to it. Goucher had a trimester system and the second semester ended in mid-March. In each ten-week trimester, the girls took three courses, each meeting four days a week. She had term papers in two courses and she struggled with the third course, a physics course with a lab, she took as an elective and now greatly regretted doing. As exams approached, Joan became more remote. They only saw each other once during the two-week period around exams, although they did talk by telephone every day. They put off discussing their major issue, and that kept things tense.

Nick saw much more of Susan during the month than he did of Joan, not only because she worked on the same floor as the UPI bureau, but also because he was the only friend she had made so far in Baltimore. She still was getting the cold shoulder from many in the newspaper despite having written several feature stories that almost everyone grudgingly admitted were quite good.

Susan asked him to help her become better acquainted with the city, and that included several dinners she paid for at well-known restaurants he usually couldn't afford. He kept her away from Danny's, where he occasionally took Joan. When she wanted to learn how to crack crabs, one of Maryland's most famous customs, she said someone had recommended Thompson's Sea Girt House. He diverted her to Obrycki's. The son of the owner of Thompson's was one of Joan's high school classmates.

She let him drive the GTO, and while he showed her interesting areas of Baltimore, she talked of her frustrations of working in a city where she had no roots, and, except for Nick, no friends. He learned that she was twenty-seven, only five years older than him. She desperately wanted to return to Boston, and went there several times recently, the last time for an interview at the Boston Globe as a possible replacement for a columnist they were considering dropping.

Never before had he been so friendly with a sophisticated and beautiful woman like Susan. While he liked her, and enjoyed her company, their friendship caused him increasing anxiety. He feared how Joan would react when she found out, as eventually she would, about their friendship, and how much time they spent together.

Even though greatly attracted to her, and he sensed the attraction was mutual, Nick did not intend to have a sexual relationship with Susan. He knew that even a brief affair with Susan would destroy his relationship with Joan. He never cheated on any girlfriend. It was a matter of honor, and pride to him. He wasn't about to start. So, within a short time, when he felt the desire rising to a dangerous level, he told Susan about Joan.

That seemed to have the desired effect. She made no advances on him and they never were alone together in either's apartment. She never kissed him on the lips, but there were times when he thought just one move on his part would change everything. That feeling slowly subsided and by the end of March their relationship seemed to have stabilized to something like brother and sister. That was when he sought her advice on how to resolve the conflict with Joan.

He wanted to know what it was like to be a professional woman, and why Joan was so averse to marrying and having a family. His mother did not bring him up to believe that a woman's place was in the home. She always worked, but she also had a home and children. He really didn't know if she would have worked had his father lived, but he suspected she would have. He thought it was possible to balance work and family.

One night at the elegant Chesapeake Restaurant, where they were having crab cakes and drinking expensive Pouilly Fuisse, Susan put it to him bluntly.

"What if you had to take a few months off to have a baby?" she said. "What would that do to your career?" He admitted that it would be nearly impossible for him to do what he was now doing.

"What if you are working in the bureau alone," she said, "and you get a call from school that your child is sick, and Joan is out of town? What do you do? These are questions that women who have careers and children always have to deal with. What kind of careers do you think they can have?"

"I think I see what you are saying," Nick said, "but I don't see how it gets resolved happily. Either both people have careers that are not very demanding so they can share the child rearing and other responsibilities, or one gives in. Either way it isn't fair."

"That's right," she said. "It isn't. It can't be."

"Is this why you are not married?" Nick said.

"In part, but I also had an affair with a married man," she said. "At first it was just a fling, but it became much more than that, at least for me. As it turned out it wasn't for him. That's why I'm here in Baltimore."

Nick heard the rumors that had spread around the *News American*. Susan's exile from Boston came after the promotion of her lover to a senior position at the *Herald-American*. Their relationship had become too open, and too much of an embarrassment. Furthermore, the man's wife, who had all the money in the family, gave him an ultimatum.

She confirmed the rumors.

"When he called me into his office the last time, and told me what was going to happen, I took his keys to this car. I told him to send me the title, or else."

"Or else, what?" Nick said.

"I don't know," she said. "It was a bluff, but it worked. I got the title. It was the closest I could get to cutting off his balls."

"Did it make you feel better?" Nick said.

"Not really, but it gave me some satisfaction," she said. "I'll never feel better about what happened. It hurts, but I'm dealing with it."

"Do you think you will get married some day? Have a family?"

"I don't know. I might get married sometime, but I like my freedom. I don't want to give it up."

"Even to be with someone you truly love and really want to be with?'

"I haven't met someone like that," she said. "Maybe that might change my mind, but right now, I doubt I'll meet anyone like that."

It was after that conversation that he decided to tell Joan about Susan.

Third trimester classes started for Joan, putting her in a much better mood. She no longer fretted over the "B" she received in physics, the first grade lower than an "A" she had received since the first semester of her freshman year. She also did not take another physics course, opting instead for an elective in philosophy. Nick thought she should be a college professor. She loved school, and thrived on it. She could be a great teacher.

He took her to a Phil Ochs concert, and then to Sabatino's in Little Italy. They both loved the concert, and talked about Ochs' antiwar songs, and the increasing amount of antiwar sentiment. She was further along in her opposition to the war than Nick. He had questions in his mind, but did not feel right opposing a war in which his closest friends were fighting. Although it wasn't his fault, he still felt guilty that his left eye prevented him from passing the Army physical, and being with his friends in Vietnam.

They both ordered the Veal Francese, a Sabatino specialty, and after drinking some Chianti, he decided the time had come.

"I have a new friend I would like you to meet," he said. "She's given me a lot of good advice that I want to share with you."

"She?"

"Her name is Susan Fanning," he said. "She's a feature writer for the Hearst Headline Service. She was transferred from Boston to Baltimore in February."

"And what kind of advice has she given you?" Joan said.

Nick proceeded to tell Joan what Susan had told him about the problems a career woman faces if she has a family.

"She really has helped me understand the unfairness of it," Nick said, "and how hard it is for ambitious career-oriented people."

"And does she have a solution?"

"No. Basically there is no solution that doesn't involve sacrificing something," Nick said. "We have to find ways of balancing things. When you are having children, I have to be the principal income-provider. Later, maybe I cut back and devote more time to the family, while you pursue a career.

"In order for a relationship like ours to work we both have to give, and we both have to respect the other," Nick said. "And how we do that is something we work out together.

"I think you should go to graduate school and get that Ph.D.," Nick said. "It may mean we are separated for periods of time, or we live in two places. I think you would be a great teacher, and having that Ph.D. would put you in a position to get a position in a college, and still have children. It really is an ideal career."

"And I was thinking that I should postpone it," she said.

"I really think that would be a mistake," Nick said. "I still want us to get married, but I think we should hold off having children so you can get that degree."

"And what if UPI sends you to California and I'm in school in Boston?" she said.

"We'll figure that out," Nick said. "I don't have to stay with UPI. I'd like to, but it isn't as important as you getting your Ph.D."

Joan was quiet for a few moments.

"Tell me more about Susan," she said. "What is she like? How old is she?"

Nick laughed. "She's 27, and she is very attractive, and very smart," he said.

"Are you attracted to her?"

"Certainly," Nick said. "When you see her, you'll understand. But it's not like how I'm attracted to you. I've never had a friendship with a woman like this. It truly is just a friendship, maybe something like having a sister."

"Really?" Joan said somewhat sarcastically. "Why haven't you told me about her sooner? Maybe, I'd better meet her."

Nick felt himself blushing, and Joan laughed.

"I think I need to keep a closer eye on you."

They began seeing each other more frequently than once a week and the relationship grew more passionate. Nick had less time for Susan. He hoped she would make some other friends. He intended to arrange a meeting between Susan and Joan, but didn't do it.

He and Joan went to see the movie, "Thunderball," on the last Saturday of the month, and afterwards he bought Harleyburgers from the carryout on 32nd St. on the way to his apartment.

Inside his apartment, Nick put the bag of burgers on the counter and turned to the refrigerator to get them something to drink. Joan stopped him and put her arms around his hips. Nick grew hard immediately. Joan unzipped his pants and slipped her hand inside. He put his right hand under her blouse and then under her bra where he began caressed her hard nipples. He glanced toward his bed in the next room.

"I want you now," said Joan with emphasis on the "now," and they headed for the bed.

After they made love, he reheated the Harleyburgers in his oven. They ate them while sitting naked on his bed, and that aroused them both again. This time she was on top.

Chapter Five

A Missing Society Couple

Nick heard about the missing college students from Joan when she called him on Monday night. Karen Billingsley, a student at the College of Notre Dame and member of a prominent Baltimore society family, disappeared Saturday night with her date, Rory Crawford, a Johns Hopkins student from a socially and politically influential South Carolina family. They had gone to a party at Rory's fraternity house on St. Paul St., only two blocks from Nick's apartment. They were last seen walking outside the fraternity house.

Karen, who lived in a dorm at Notre Dame instead of her family's Ruxton home, did not return to the campus Saturday night. The school notified her parents on Sunday and they contacted the police. Rory did not return to his room in the fraternity house. As of Monday both still were missing.

Joan heard this from a lifelong friend and neighbor, Connie Del Gavio, also a Notre Dame student, who had gone to the fraternity party with her boyfriend, and who had been interviewed by the police earlier in the day.

Nick called Rory's fraternity house, and talked with the fraternity's president who he knew casually. Jack Bryce confirmed that Rory was missing and that police were there most of the day, interviewing the brothers, and searching his room.

"Everybody had a lot to drink," Bryce said. "You remember what these parties are like." Yes, Nick said, he certainly did.

Fraternities provided most of the organized social life available to the all-male undergraduate school of Johns Hopkins, as well as housing for more than two hundred upperclassmen. Located off campus, in houses in the neighborhoods to the east and north the Homewood campus, they operated with virtually no regulation, or supervision, by the university, nor did city authorities pay much attention to them. The police ignored their open violations of the liquor laws. To insure good relations, Nick's fraternity always invited the neighborhood beat patrolman to their parties. Some fraternities, like Bryce's, were notorious for heavy drinking and raucous parties.

"There were about seventy-five here, and it got pretty hot inside the house, so a lot of people went outside," Bryce said. "I remember seeing Rory and Karen walking through the house, heading towards the front door, probably around 10 PM. One of the brothers apparently was in Rory's room with a girl, and I think they went outside to wait. That was the last time I saw them. However, a couple of brothers saw them outside in front a short time later, walking on the sidewalk towards 30th St. where he parked his car. Apparently they didn't go to his car because the police found it locked with no sign of anything of theirs inside."

"Were they dating each other regularly, or was this a casual date?" Nick said.

"It wasn't their first date, but they haven't been dating very long. Rory was really hot for her. She's a knockout. She sure looked good Saturday night, and ready, if you know what I mean. I think he was pretty pissed about not being able to get into his room."

"I bet," Nick said. "I wonder if they just shacked up some place?"

"That's what I think," Bryce said. "There's that little motel down on Charles Street that some of the guys use. I wouldn't be surprised if they are there, or some place like that, or even eloped. As I said he really had the hots for her, and he has plenty of money. They could have gone to the airport and flown somewhere. He'd do things like that."

"Still, in any case, they would have taken his car," Nick said.

"I guess that's right."

"Why would they walk out along the street if they weren't going to his car?"

"I supposed they might have been meeting somebody?"

"Who might that be?"

"Well, you know, somebody who they might get something from."

"I get it," Nick said. "Is there much of that going on?"

"Some, not a huge amount, but more than last year when you were here."

"And was Rory into that?"

"Maybe. I don't want to say any more than that, you understand?"

"Did the cops ask about this?"

"No, not when they talked to me. I don't think the subject came up."

"And he didn't have anything in his room?"

"No, thank God."

Chapter Six

Dewey Meets Susan

WCAO played, for at least the sixth time that Tuesday morning, Barry Sadler's "Ballad of the Green Berets," the hottest song in the country, as the Vietnam War, now involving nearly 300,000 American soldiers, continued to escalate. Defense Secretary McNamara denied the U.S. was running out of bombs.

While already tired of the song, it did make Nick think about his fraternity brothers in Vietnam and wonder how they were doing. He thought about how much he would like to be a war correspondent, and maybe write stories about a couple of the guys. He knew at least two of them were in combat units, and he worried about them. The casualty lists that were transmitted on the B wire seemed to be longer every day.

After confirming with the police that Rory and Karen still were missing, he typed a story about the missing couple and handed the top copy from his carbon set to Marsha Golding, who was writing stories on the broadcast wire transmitter. He wrote it as a straight missing person story, with the emphasis on the social prominence of both. He did not write anything about the possible drug connection. Golding proceeded to punch the story into teletype tape for the next "split" of local news.

Nick hired her from a weekly newspaper in the Washington area three weeks ago as the first woman to work in the Baltimore UPI bureau. A perky brunette, with large, almost electric-like violet eyes, only a little over five feet tall, and fairly thin, she looked younger than her 25 years. Brassy, profane, and quick-witted, she quickly proved to be a very good reporter, although she struggled to learn to write in broadcast style.

Nick made her read her copy out loud to him, telling her that if she took a breath in mid-sentence she would be fired.

At first she believed him, and she got red-faced reading some long sentences. But she learned quickly. He liked her, and so did the UPI clients and several of the reporters at the News American.

Nick saw Bob Bradley in the hall and waved him in, giving him a copy of his story. It became the lead local story in the paper that day, and a scoop for the *News American* over the *Evening Sun*.

Dewey Coughlin came in to check on the condition of Jan Berry, of Jan & Dean fame, who was nearly killed in an auto accident earlier in the month when he suffered a serious brain injury. Dewey was a big Jan & Dean fan, and had a huge collection of surfer music. During one of the times when he was out of school, he decided to become a surfer. He went to Southern California and hit all the beaches, and while surfing he suffered a bruise to his brain when his surfboard hit him in the head.

Since Jan's accident, Nick, who knew of Dewey's interest, regularly rolled up and saved the yellow teletype paper from the A and B wires so that Dewey could see all the stories about Jan's accident and condition.

"I'm worried about him," Dewey said today. "It's very hard to recover from a brain injury. I've never told you this, but I never fully recovered from mine. I still have some problems from time to time. Recently, it's been worse."

"How so?" Nick said. "You don't seem to have suffered any physical problems. At least, if you have, it isn't obvious."

"I didn't lose any mobility," he said. "I was lucky, but I've been getting some terrible headaches, not very often, but almost unbearable when they happen. I've blacked out a couple of times for several hours."

"What does your doctor say?"

"Doctors are assholes," Dewey said. "They don't know what the fuck is going on. I'm trying some experimental drugs, but so far they haven't seemed to help except for short periods of time."

Just then Susan walked by the bureau, headed towards the cafeteria, and smiled at Nick. Dewey noticed.

"You know her?"

"Yes, we're friends," Nick said.

"What about Joan?'

"Really, we're just friends," Nick said,

"No guy is just friends with a woman who looks like that," he said. "But if you insist, then I'd like to meet her."

"You don't know who she is?" Nick said. "How did you miss her?"

"I haven't missed her," Dewey said. "I've had some other things on my mind. But I'd like to meet her."

It suddenly occurred to Nick that Susan and Dewey might be a good match. If nothing more, Dewey might enjoy taking her around the city. It certainly was worth a try.

"OK, I'll introduce you," Nick said. "Let's go down to the cafeteria."

Dewey and Susan hit it off as soon as the subject of Jan and Dean and surfing came up.

"I did a feature on the surfing culture for Hearst," Susan said. "I interviewed Jan and Dean and a bunch of others. I even tried surfing, but I wasn't very good at it."

Nick thought of what she might have looked like on a surfboard. He suspected Dewey was having similar thoughts. Dewey had not taken his eyes off her since he introduced them.

"Do you like their music?" Dewey said.

"I love it, but it seems to have faded away," she said.

"I bet I've got the greatest collection on the East Coast," Dewey said. "Come to my place and I'll show you, and I'll play you some pieces you probably have never heard. How about Friday night?" Then, before she could answer, he said to Nick, "And why don't you and Joan come as well? You can assure Susan that I am a good cook."

Susan arched her eyebrows a little with a mischievous look in her eyes.

"He's a great cook," Nick said to Susan. "And he has a very interesting house."

"Well, that's a good endorsement, OK, I'll come," Susan said.

"I'll have to check with Joan," Nick said to Dewey, "but if she is available, I'm sure we'll come. I've wanted Joan and Susan to meet. I'm working the early shift Saturday morning. We just won't be able to stay late."

As they were walking back towards the bureau, Dewey said quietly to Nick, "You're a brave man," and then laughed.

When Nick called Joan later, she didn't hesitate about going to Dewey's house and meeting Susan. "It's about time," she said.

Chapter Seven

Another Blue Girl Murder

A small package addressed to "Detective Maurice Antonelli, Homicide," arrived in the Homicide department Wednesday morning. Its return address had no name, just a number on Lee Street, just south of the downtown McCormick Spice Co. plant. Inside there were two human ears.

Antonelli, Jenkins, and two dozen detectives and tactical police officers descended on the Lee Street address about as surreptitiously as an army could. They kept chatter off the police radios to prevent the news media from hearing what they were doing. Slumlords were being pushed out of this area to make room for reconstruction. Many of the dilapidated houses in the neighborhood that dated to the 1840s sat empty, waiting for demolition. Poor black families still occupied a few, but all of the houses in this block appeared to be empty.

They found the front door nailed shut, but the rear door that opened to the kitchen was slightly open. Entering the kitchen they were greeted by an unmistakable putrid odor nearly all of them had previously encountered.

From the wallet in his pants pocket, they quickly identified the body lying on the floor in the kitchen as Rory Crawford. What the rats and other creatures did to him did not disguise that he died from a slit throat, and that both ears were cut off.

Not finding Karen Billingsley on either the first, or second floor, they headed for the basement stairs under the front stairway. A choking stench greeted them when they opened the door to the stairway. Two patrolmen ran from the room and threw up outside. Antonelli looked at Jenkins, who just shrugged.

"You want me to go first?" he said. "It's no big deal."

"No, I'll do it," Antonelli said, attempting to ignore his churning stomach. It took all his willpower to keep his breakfast down. He clenched his teeth and headed down the stairs, one hand holding a handkerchief over his nose and mouth, and the other holding a flashlight. Jenkins followed him, also holding a handkerchief over his nose and mouth, but, being more suspicious by nature, he held his .38 in his other hand.

Antonelli did not anticipate the effects of the warm weather and depredations of various creatures from the basement's dirt floor attracted by the blood. What he saw on the table in the basement took his breath away, and he almost lost it.

Just like the Barlow murder, Karen's body and face were painted blue, although most of the blue was gone from what was left of her. Her decapitated head was upright next to the body, her blonde hair spread out behind her head, just like Barlow's. But, unlike Barlow, she had no eyes left to look at him. There had not been freezing conditions to preserve the body, or the head, or to restrain the activities of the wildlife. Given the state of her, it would be difficult to tell if she had been abused in any other way before she died.

Antonelli was the primary detective on this case, as with the Barlow case, and that put him in charge of the crime scene. He ordered the area sealed off and requested a team of Crime Lab techs, and priority by the medical examiner. He had to move fast. His investigation of the Barlow murder had slowed because of more immediate events, and a lack of any particular priority given the murder of a stripper. He had not finished going through all the names the Museum of Art had provided. Solving these murders now would be a much higher priority. Because of the decapitation, their link to the unsolved Barlow murder would become public knowledge.

He told all those present to stay off the radios. He did not want this discovery to leak out before he had a chance to get more information. He still hoped to keep secret the painting of the bodies.

Jenkins took on the task of telling the families. He also asked for additional detectives from other squads to help interview residents in the area. The Southern District was contacted and asked to identify any officers who might have driven through the neighborhood on patrols Saturday night and Sunday morning.

It only took 45 minutes for the additional detectives, and the Crime Lab and ME teams to arrive.

"We have to go over every inch of the house, especially the basement, as well as this area," Antonelli said. "If the killer so much as left a single hair behind, we have to find it." The Crime Lab techs vacuumed the basement and first floor of the house. A team of patrolmen and detectives slowly walked the perimeter of the house, collecting every piece of trash.

Other teams checked every house in the neighborhood, and interviewed every resident they found. No one heard or saw anything, or that's what they said. Antonelli desperately hoped to find some physical evidence that might prompt some eyewitness accounts.

He pulled aside a deputy medical examiner who had just arrived.

"I don't know how he managed to get the two of them into this house, especially the girl into the basement, but I wouldn't be surprised if he drugged them, and he might have used something unusual. The Barlow girl had traces of a sedative and LSD in her. So check these two very carefully."

Then he saw Bob Bradley drive up, and realized that he had not been able to squelch the reporter's sources.

Nick, with Bradley's help, had an exclusive for more than an hour on the finding of the bodies; long enough to win the morning newspaper logs on Thursday by a lopsided margin, and to give UPI's broadcasters in Maryland a major scoop over those who just had the AP. The "Headless Stripper murder" story became "the headless blondes murders."

Chapter Eight

Dewey Coughlin

Dewey Coughlin lived alone in the elegant two-story white stucco and stone house he inherited from his parents. When Nick first met Dewey, he lived in his fraternity house, just three blocks from the Hopkins campus. He moved to the family home two years ago after his parents died. The turn-of-the-century house, renovated by his parents in the 1950s, sat back from North Charles Street on a wooded lot surrounded by ancient boxwoods, azaleas and rhododendrons in need of pruning. Positioned sideways on the lot, its three-car garage faced the driveway and the street.

Nick stopped behind Susan's GTO parked in front of an open garage door. He and Joan found Dewey and Susan inside the garage, looking at the old Morgan sitting on blocks.

"Are you ever going to get that running again?" Nick asked. "If you let it sit out here much longer, it's going to get termites."

"Termites?" Susan said.

"It has a wood frame," Dewey said, laughing. "It's made of ash, but it's not going to get termites. It's got some engine problems and I'll get it running again some time."

Two other vehicles were in the garage, a Ford Country Squire of uncertain vintage, and what appeared to be a brand new Ford Bronco.

"Is this new?" Nick said. "I don't remember seeing it before."

"I just got it," Dewey said.

When they went inside Dewey poured them glasses of white wine, which Nick thought tasted expensive, but Dewey didn't say anything about it. Nick made a note of its name, Le Montrachet, which he later discovered from his wine book to be one of the world's most expensive white wines. The house was much different from what Nick remembered from his last visit, more than a year ago. There were more antiques, art, sculpture, and clutter. Dewey had somewhat bizarre taste. He liked modern, ancient and primitive art and mixed the three throughout the house.

The house itself, in many ways, was an architectural monstrosity. Dewey's father was a collector of architectural details from old buildings and houses in the city. One of his clients at Alexander Brown was a prominent architect who knew when important buildings were being torn down or renovated. Dewey's father scoured them for interesting features he could incorporate into his house. Almost every door in the house was unique. There were antique window frames, elaborate carved arches between rooms, and a large collection of smaller architectural details.

Since the deaths of his parents, Dewey had made his own changes in the house. He converted the large living room into a library and office, with overflowing floor to ceiling bookcases, stacks of books and papers on the floor, folders and papers on a table in the middle of the room, a worn leather chair and table by the fireplace at one end of the room, and a cluttered desk at the other end. Nick believed the old and muted Oriental rug that covered much of the hardwood floor had to be quite valuable.

Dewey proved Nick right about his cooking. Dinner consisted of a beef rib roast, no doubt a prime rib, Nick thought, with creamy mashed potatoes, carrots with a brown sugar, peas flavored with tarragon, and a salad of Bibb lettuce, tomatoes and Bermuda onion slices, followed by a cheese course and crème brulet with rich dark coffee. This time Dewey did talk about the wine he served, a Beaulieu "Private Reserve," which he said his father, who had a large wine collection, believed to be America's best red wine.

Dewey was a charming host, regaling them with stories about his various bouts with Hopkins over his incredibly inconsistent performances, and some of his traveling experiences, which included Southern California surfing, and several archaeological expeditions in the American Southwest and in Mexico. He also had been to Europe several times, as well as to archaeological digs in North Africa, Egypt and the Middle East.

Dewey said he began his Hopkins career as a pre-med, but over the course of the years, had taken courses in most of the disciplines. His BA would be in Liberal Arts and his MA in

Anthropology. He said he might go to Boston to get a Ph.D. at Harvard, but he said that after learning that Susan graduated from Radcliffe, so Nick could not be sure he was serious. Dewey did not disguise his infatuation with Susan and clearly tried to impress her. Nick could not tell if he succeeded. Susan smiled frequently, but said little.

At one point during the course of the conversation, Dewey said he signed up for ten courses one semester, getting A's in five and F's in the other five.

"Why didn't you just drop the courses you didn't like?" Susan asked.

"It was too much trouble," Dewey said. "I wasn't getting along with my advisor, a snobbish ass who had to approve the drops. He had resisted agreeing to my schedule, and I didn't want to go back to him and have him think he was right. So I just decided to drop them unofficially, and get a different adviser the next semester."

"How did you manage to sign up for that many courses?" Joan said. "I couldn't do that at Goucher.

"You can do just about anything you want at Hopkins if you can make a good enough argument," Dewey said. "Besides I had a 4.5 average the previous semester. I had three of the five point H grades that semester and three As. Not a large number of people ever did anything like that."

"What's a H grade?" Susan said.

"It's an honors grade, a grade above an A," Dewey said. "There are so many brilliant students at Hopkins that it became a way of distinguishing almost genius-like work from just A level work. However, a lot of people don't like them because they devalue the A grade, which in many courses is almost as hard to get as an H. There's talk the H grade may be abolished."

"I think I only knew three other guys who ever got Hs," Nick said, "and I don't think any of them ever got more than one."

"Well, there were others," Dewey said. "I had a couple of fraternity brothers who got more than I did."

"So what happened with your fraternity?" Susan said.

"We were so small that the cost of membership became too high," Dewey said. "The house needed a lot of work. We got cited, and we weren't allowed to have anyone live there. We didn't have the money to repair it, so we shut it down."

"I remember the house was not in very good shape," Nick said. "What happened to it?"

"We still have it," Dewey said. "As I get some contributions from the alumni I am having it renovated. Once it's fixed up, we'll sell it and divide the proceeds among the alumni who contributed to the repairs."

When the conversation naturally drifted to the murders that week, Dewey became very serious. The murders were the biggest story in the city. *The Sun* published extensive stories about the Billingsleys, one of Baltimore's more prominent society families. Gen. Gelston announced the formation of a special team of homicide detectives to investigate the case, with Maurice Antonelli in the lead.

"Karen's father is a securities analyst and he worked with my father at Alexander Brown," Dewey said. "My parents were very close with her parents. I danced with her at the Bachelor's Cotillon three years ago. She was a beautiful girl. It's very sad."

The four of them talked about the many questions being raised by the kidnappings and murders, especially how one person managed to get the two of them into the abandoned house.

"Maybe he had an accomplice," Susan said.

"The police haven't found any evidence of that," Nick said, "but then, they apparently don't have much evidence of any kind. The girl seems to have been the target, but they say she wasn't molested, just decapitated. That's very odd."

"It could be some kind of ritual," Dewey said. "Maybe the ritual doesn't permit them to be molested."

"What kind of ritual is like that?" Susan asked.

"Human sacrifice rituals sometimes are like that," Dewey said.

"You mean this is some kind of religious thing," Nick said.

"It could be," Dewey said. "Human sacrifice has been practiced for thousands of years, and still happens occasionally."

"That's really sick," Joan said. "I read about Aztec sacrifices - thousands of them at one time."

"They may have been the most excessive, but almost every ancient people did human sacrifices, including the Greeks, the Celts, the Indus cultures, and all the Meso-American cultures, including the Mayans and Incas as well as the Aztecs," Coughlin said. "Their religions included many deities representing forces of nature, such as rain.

"The Mayans performed human sacrifices over a much longer period of time than the Aztecs, but not in as huge numbers at one time, or in one place. The Mayans also sometimes beheaded their victims in sacrifices. Most of the time they either cut their hearts out while they still were beating, or they threw them alive into deep pits.

"Most of the Mayan sacrifices were to the rain god," he said. "It wasn't always as tropical in that part of the world as it is now. And there are no rivers on the Yucatan peninsula so water always was a problem. About the time their civilization peaked, it was a much warmer than it is now. That was the time when Greenland was green and was settled by the Vikings. There were droughts in the American Southwest, Mexico and Central America. The end of that period is about the time when some of the ancient Indian cultures in the American Southwest disappeared. Some anthropologists believe the sudden decline of the Mayans, which started around 1100 AD, was due to drought, as well as to wars caused by over-population."

"Is this one of your areas of interest?" Nick said.

"It's my Masters thesis," Dewey said. "My thesis is an analysis of high Mayan culture based on digs that I was on a few years ago."

"We don't know a lot about the Mayans, do we?" Joan said.

"We're learning more very rapidly now," Dewey said. "The problem is that there is no Rosetta Stone, like there was in Egypt, to help us translate their language, which like the Egyptian, used hieroglyphics. They were the only literate people in Meso-America and they had thousands of books. They kept records of everything. They dated everything. They had an amazingly accurate calendar. But the Spanish burned just about every book they could find. They thought they were the works of the Devil."

"Wonderful," Nick said. "They destroyed the records of a culture probably more advanced than their own."

"In many ways it was," Coughlin said, "but it was very primitive in other ways. It was highly organized and they had magnificent architecture and art. They were great engineers and artists, but not great inventors, or innovators. For example, they didn't use the wheel, or draft animals. Their culture was dominated by an incredibly complex religion. It really stymied development of new ideas. They also had virtually no contact with peoples from other parts of the world to bring in new ideas.

"Some of their texts did survive, including their creation myth," he said. "They have a flood in their mythology just like most cultures in the world. More writing is being found in excavations. They not only wrote books, they also wrote on walls, on stones, and on statues. Translating what they wrote is going to take time, and some luck. There have been some recent breakthroughs, and maybe in a few years we'll know a lot more. One of the more interesting recent theories is that they were descendants of one of the lost tribes in the Book of Mormon."

"Really?" Joan said. "That sounds very far-fetched."

"Oh, it probably is," Coughlin said. "There was an article published a few years ago making some comparisons between descriptions in the Book of Mormon and what we know of the Mayans from archaeology. There is more work underway now. I doubt it will prove out, but it has spurred more activity at Mayan sites, which is good."

"So maybe somebody is copying Mayan sacrifices," Susan said. "It sounds weird, but there are a lot of weird people around."

"I've got some photos I took when I was in Mexico," Dewey said. "I'll show you after dinner."

As promised, he showed them some photos of wall paintings, some of which depicted human sacrifices. His finished thesis of almost 500 typewritten pages sat on the table.

"I started work on this about six years ago, but I lost interest for a while," Dewey said. "I got back to work on it last fall after visiting the Yucatan again.

"I'd like to publish it as a book, but I think I need more illustrations and more photos. It will have to wait until I can go back down there, maybe in a month or two."

They listened to his surfing music for much of the rest of the evening, singing along with "Surf City." Susan and Joan split off from the two men for a while and went into the library where they engaged in a half hour of intense talk. Dewey gave Nick a tour of parts of the rambling house he had not seen before.

One of the rooms had been Dewey's parents' bedroom, and it appeared that Dewey had not changed it. A hand-tinted photograph of a stunningly beautiful young blue-eyed blonde hung on one wall. Dressed in a white gown and holding a bouquet of flowers, she looked very familiar. Nick could see that there was a strong resemblance between her and Susan, but there also was a resemblance to someone else. He just couldn't remember who.

"Is that your mother?" Nick said.

"Yes, it's the photograph of her from the 1928 Bachelor's Cotilllon, when she was a debutante," Dewey said. "My father loved that photograph. He had it colored. He married her in 1931 when they both graduated from college. He went to Hopkins and she went to Goucher. He devoted his life to her, and eventually she killed him."

"What do you mean?"

"My mother was mentally ill," Dewey said. "It probably was a form of depression, maybe more than that. She had episodes of extreme narcissism and exhibitionism. She was very self-centered. It didn't manifest itself until she had children. I don't know exactly when people began to realize something was wrong, but certainly it was not long after I was born, in 1934. There was a bit of a scandal. I don't think I ever heard the full story. All I know is that soon after my birth she spent some time at Sheppard Pratt, part of the time when Zelda Fitzgerald was there.

"I never really had a mother," he continued. "She spent most of my childhood either in a facility, a luxury facility like Sheppard Pratt of course, or away at various resorts or spas, or in foreign countries. My father spent a lot of the family fortune on her," he said. "My sisters, my brother and I were raised by nannies. I never got to know her until much later, and I never was close to her. In fact, I hated her.

"In recent years, some of the new drugs helped and she was able to live at home," Dewey said. "She never was happy, however, and the narcissism returned. When she thought her looks were gone - and believe me, they weren't - she still was stunning - she went into deep depression. That eventually led to her suicide about two and half years ago. She was 58. Two months later my father dropped dead of a heart attack. She killed him, just as sure as anything. She wouldn't let him be free of her."

60

"My God," Nick said. "I never knew any of that. I'm so sorry."

"It's not something I like to talk about except with close friends," Dewey said.

Nick had not previously thought of himself as a close friend of Dewey's, and was surprised to learn that Dewey considered him one.

"And you lost your brother and sisters as well?" Nick said.

"One sister to Polio, another in a plane crash, and my brother in Korea, right at the end of the war, only two weeks after he was sent there, right out of OCS. I am the last surviving member of the family."

"Your family goes way back and, for a long time was one of the most prominent society families, wasn't it?"

"From the beginning," Dewey said. "Two of my ancestors were founders of the Cotillon here in Baltimore in the 1790s. It is the second oldest in the country, after Charleston's. And, of course, ours is distinctive because we spell it without an "i.""

"Really?" Nick said, smiling. "Is that important?"

"Probably not," Dewey said. "None of it really is that important anymore."

"We have a society in Pittsburgh," Nick said, "but Baltimore's is a lot bigger and more traditional."

"Oh, yes, and it is hard to buy your way into the Baltimore society. It happens, but mostly family heritage is what is important."

"It's so funny," Nick said. "Almost everyone who came here definitely was not society. Many were criminals, or fugitives. Some were speculators and adventurers. But the people with real power stayed home, back in England."

"We created our own class system," Dewey said. "I think it's just human nature. We have to find ways to classify ourselves, to rank ourselves against others."

"I think that happens when people are secure enough that they don't have to worry about important things anymore, like making a living and feeding a family." Nick said.

"There's probably some truth to that," Dewey said.

"And you go to those debutante balls every year?" Nick said.

"I haven't been to one since that one where I danced with Karen. My mother committed suicide not long after that, and then my father died. I just don't have much interest in it anymore. Even though it still is very big, and very exclusive, I think it's going to fade in the coming years. The world is changing, and I think the influence and importance of society will diminish. Wealth is becoming more important than family and tradition."

They walked through the house and headed for the patio.

"Do you belong to any of those exclusive clubs I hear about," Nick said.

"All the important ones," Dewey said. "My father made sure I was a member, and I used to go to them a lot with him. Sometimes he would take me golfing at the Baltimore County Country Club course, which, if you don't know, is a great course. I haven't gone to any since his funeral."

"Are you still friends with other members of the Cotillon?" Nick said.

"Not really. I'm not sure I really ever was. I think they outgrew me, and maybe shunned me to some extent, because I stayed in school so long. It's good that I'm getting out of school. It's time for me to do something with my life. First, however, I have to cure these fucking headaches."

"So they are really bad?"

"They come and go, but it seems they are getting worse."

"You really need to see a top doctor," Nick said. "There are a lot at Hopkins. You shouldn't be trying to do this by yourself."

"I've been to six doctors in the past year, all of them Hopkins docs, and none of them helped me," Dewey said. "They don't know what's wrong. One of them even said he thought it was psychosomatic, that there is nothing wrong. Another got me to see a shrink. I think nearly all of them believed I inherited my mother's insanity. And, I guess I can see why. But the shrink said he thought my problem was physical, not mental. One doctor wants to do exploratory surgery. I really don't want someone poking around in my brain.

"So, I'm sort of out of options with the medical profession. I'm trying other things," he said.

"But nothing's working?"

"Not yet, but I keep trying different combinations. Sometimes I get a little relief, Last weekend I felt better for a while. Now I'm having some trouble again."

"Let me know if things get real bad again," Nick said. "Don't go through it alone."

"I really appreciate that, I really do," Dewey said. "Tell me a little more about Susan. I'm surprised she's still single."

"I don't think getting married is high on her agenda," Nick said. "She's very career-oriented, and she's a rising star. I don't think she's looking to have a close relationship right now, but she could use some friends. I seem to be the only one she's made in Baltimore."

"And she really is only a friend? I find that hard to believe," Dewey said.

"Believe it. That's really all we are, and have been," Nick said. "I'm in love with Joan. I'm not going to fuck up my relationship with her by fucking someone else."

"I'd like to be her friend," Dewey said, "maybe more that that. I haven't seen anyone like her in a long time."

"There aren't many like her," Nick said. "You can start by taking her sight-seeing, to places she hasn't seen yet. Also, she likes to go out to dinner, but not by herself. Other than me, she really doesn't have any friends here with whom to do things like that. She's fun, and she's interesting."

"I certainly can do that, I'd enjoy that," Dewey said. "I'll ask her out."

They sat on the patio, with the door open so they could hear the music, smoked cigarettes and drank coffee. The women returned a few minutes later. Dewey served another round of coffee. At eleven o'clock Nick said he and Joan had to leave. Susan left at the same time. Nick noticed that Dewey could not hide his disappointment about that.

"He certainly is a very unusual person," Joan said as they drove out of Dewey's driveway. "I've known him for three years and I still don't know what to make of him."

"I don't either," Nick said. "He's brilliant, but he's got some problems. He's had a much tougher life than we knew and things are not good for him now." Nick then told Joan what he had learned from Dewey about his parents and his headaches.

"Susan is intrigued by him, but she's also a little wary," Joan said. "She's not used to people as odd as he is. She's not quite sure what to make of him."

"He's going to ask her out." Nick said. "We'll see what happens. So what else did you and Susan talk about, or shouldn't I ask?"

He was about to make the turn onto St. Paul Street, but out of the corner of his good right eye he caught her smiling.

"I think I am lucky that you are not a few years older," she said. "Susan likes you. She thinks you are someone I should not let get away, even if it means that I can't do everything else that I want to do."

"That's a little surprising, considering I don't think she has much use for men in general," Nick said, "and she has put her career ahead of relationships."

"She's had a lot of bad experiences," Joan said, "but she thinks you are different."

"How so?"

"Well, she was circumspect, but I think she's lonely and misses having a relationship. She knows you are attracted to her and, as I said, she likes you. Under most circumstances, and with most men, there would have been only one outcome from that combination."

Nick thought, *I'm not most men*, but he didn't say it.

He glanced at her and smiled. She laughed.

"She realizes that you wouldn't have a relationship with her because of me. She thinks that is pretty unusual for a man, any man, at least in her experience, and I can see why. She is very attractive, and, I suspect when she wants to be, she can be very seductive, very hard to resist."

"I haven't seen that side of her, but it wouldn't make any difference," Nick said.

Joan didn't say anything more about that subject, but they had an especially passionate time in his bed until the early morning hours. By he time he returned from taking her home, he had to go to work.

Chapter Nine

The Suspect, Victor Blodgett

Maury Antonelli wondered what his life would be like if he had a wife and family, what would happen to them when he had to work around the clock like he had been doing since Wednesday. Here on a Saturday morning when, if he had a family, he would want to spend it with them, he and Detective Rollie Meador were on 36th Street in the Hampden neighborhood looking for a student from the Maryland Institute College of Art who specialized in painting blue female nudes.

With the help of six other detectives assigned to now what the Department called "The Blue Girl Case," the checking of names provided by the Museum of Art was completed. The Museum provided their membership list, and identified members who subscribed during the Mayan exhibition. There were three people who aroused some suspicion, but chiefly Victor Blodgett, who became a prime suspect when a detective saw one of his paintings at the Maryland Institute, a full frontal nude of a young blonde woman, painted with a blue color very close in hue to the blue used on the two dead girls.

In addition, a 1962 dark blue Buck was registered in his name. A resident of a house on 30th Street, just around the corner from Crawford's fraternity house, told police that she saw a couple get into a dark colored Buick in front of her house about 10:30 PM on Saturday night. Her description of the couple matched that of Crawford and Billingsley. She could not see the driver of the car, and she did not see the license plate, but she recognized the car as a Buick because she had owned one. She said she thought it was either a 62 or a 63.

His driver's license and car registration provided an address in Hampden, an apartment in one of the neighborhood's turn of the century stone houses originally built for workers in one of the plants and factories that once lined Jones Falls Valley. Now most were divided into apartments occupied by students and young singles.

When Blodgett did not respond to his doorbell on the front of the house, Antonelli pressed another, and a scruffy young man, dressed in dirty blue jeans and a grimy t-shirt, and having a strong body odor, came to the door. He said Blodgett worked part-time at the nearby Noxzema chemical plant, and would not be back until late in the afternoon. Now in the process of changing their name to Noxell, the company was the maker of the famous "Cover Girl" cosmetics, and one of the few industries in the valley still thriving. Antonelli remembered that one of their best-known products was packaged in a dark blue jar.

After the young man closed the door, Meador, using two fingers to squeeze his nose to shut out the odor, said, "Doesn't that kid have a mother? I wonder if Blodgett is just like him? Let's take a look at his place."

"We don't have a warrant," Antonelli said.

"So what?" Meador said. "You think anyone's going to give a shit, especially if he's our guy?"

Not having a warrant had seldom been a problem in high profile cases like this in the past. There were several highly publicized cases in recent years when Baltimore police violently raided the homes of suspects without warrants, without any repercussions other than some citizen outrage. Despite the highly publicized complaints of the violation of their rights, the suspects were convicted, and sent to prison.

"There's a case the Supreme Court is about to rule on that could change everything, the Miranda case," Antonelli said. "It has to do with the rights of suspects, and what we can do to them. I don't think it has anything to do with search warrants, but I think we should be very careful that we don't do something now that might raise questions by the time our case gets to trial. We could fuck things up."

"You may be right," Meador said, "but you better hope this creep we just talked to didn't give us a bunch of bullshit. You better hope he's not upstairs warning Blodgett right now."

"Let's stake out the place, and wait for Blodgett," Antonelli said.

Blodgett showed up at 4:25 and, dressed in blue jeans, a blue work shirt, white sneakers and a light jacket, he did look a little more respectable than his housemate. He also didn't stink. In fact, he was a fairly handsome young man, but styled his hair to try to make himself look tough, Antonelli thought, reminding him of some of the guys he knew in Little Italy. He caught up to him on the porch of his house and flashed his badge.

"We have a few questions we would like to ask you," he said.

"What about?" he said, with a look of wariness.

"I think maybe it would be better to do this inside, unless you'd like to ride downtown with us," Antonelli said.

"You guys with Vice?"

"Homicide, why'd you ask about Vice?"

"You're not here to bust me for drugs?"

"No, we're investigating some murders," Antonelli said.

"Well, I haven't killed anyone, and I need to piss, so let's go inside," Blodgett said. He had large dark brown eyes, but seemed to have trouble making eye contact, and didn't look at them when he added, "I can't imagine why you would want to talk with me."

Blodgett had two rooms on the second floor and shared a hall bathroom and small kitchen in the rear, with two other rooms made into a separate apartment. His apartment consisted of a small bedroom on one side, and a larger room facing the front with large, uncurtained windows. Sparsely furnished with an old sofa, a broken recliner, a table and a black and white television, it barely met the minimum requirements of comfort. Much of the space contained painting equipment, supplies and materials. Canvasses were stacked against the wall. There were several easels and a number of boxes, some of which obviously contained paints and artist supplies, He had no storage cabinet or shelves. The linseed oil smell was strong.

There were several paintings of blue naked girls on one side of the room.

"I hope you're not a smoker," Antonelli said. "You could set off quite a fire in here."

"No, I don't smoke in here," Blodgett said. "It doesn't always smell this bad. I dropped a bottle last night and it spilled all over the place."

"We're investigating the murders this week of Rory Crawford and Karen Billingsley," Antonelli said. "One of our contacts said you might know something about them."

"Who said that?" Blodgett said.

"Confidential," Antonelli said.

"Well, it's a fucking lie. I never heard of those people until I read about them in the paper," Blodgett said. "I don't know anything about their murders."

"I'm curious about those paintings of the blue girls," Antonelli said. "Where'd you get that idea? It seems pretty odd. And what is that shade of blue?"

"It's my attempt to copy Mayan blue, but it didn't work with these paintings. The blue isn't quite right. My best one is hanging down at Maryland Institute. That color is deceptively difficult to copy."

"Why the Mayan blue?"

"I saw this exhibit at the Museum of Art last fall, and part of it was about the human sacrifices the Mayans did. I'm in a course that uses live nude models. I thought it would be cool to paint them in blue, like the Mayans did their sacrifice victims. The Museum had this depiction of a naked woman painted blue about to be sacrificed. I'm just doing them nude and blue, and I think it's kind of original. I haven't tried to sell the paintings because it took a while to get the blue just right. I might try to sell the one I'm showing at Maryland Institute. What does this have to do with a murder investigation?"

"Well, there are some similarities in the murders to human sacrifices," Antonelli said. "So we're checking out everything that is remotely similar, including paintings of blue naked women. We'd like to know a little more about your whereabouts this past week, beginning with Saturday night. Where were you on Saturday night?"

Blodgett hesitated for a moment.

"I was downtown, at a bar I know," he said.

"The name of the bar?"

When Blodgett named it, Antonelli recognized it as a strip bar on the Block. It was one block away from the bar where Barlow worked. But when asked if he knew Barlow, Blodgett said he didn't, that he never had been to her bar.

"But you were down there on the Block admiring some more female bodies?"

"Yeah, there's a girl there who does some modeling for me, privately, you know," he said. He then pointed to one of the blue girl paintings. "That painting over there, on the right, that's her."

"Did you spend time with her on Saturday night?"

"I saw her, but she was busy," Blodgett said. "She said she couldn't come back to my place that night, so I left a little early, before 10 PM."

"What did you do then?"

"I came home, went to bed. I was tired," Blodgett said. "I work hard on Saturdays."

"Anyone see you come home?"

"I don't know. People sort of keep to themselves around here," he said.

They continued to question Blodgett for another half hour, but heard nothing incriminating. They got the name and address of the stripper who posed for him. They talked to two other people who lived in the house. No one saw Blodgett come home on Saturday night. No one would say they saw him on Sunday. Blodgett had no alibi for the time of the kidnapping and for the rest of the night Saturday and Sunday morning.

Antonelli and Meador sat in their car and talked it over.

"We need to get more background on him," Antonelli said. "He doesn't strike me as a killer, but I don't like coincidences. He's also probably lying about not even being aware of Barlow. I don't know how he could have missed her."

"He could have driven from the Block to 32nd Street in time to have been there around 10:30 to pick them up, like that lady told us," Meador said.

"We'll get a photo of him and show it to the friends of Crawford and Billingsley," Antonelli said, "as well as to everyone at the strip club."

"Let's see if we can get a search warrant based on what we have so far," Antonelli said. "I especially want to check out his car."

They served the warrant on Sunday morning, and spent four hours going through his meager belongings piece by piece. They took samples of his paints, dusted the entire apartment for fingerprints, and used magnifying glasses to try to find every loose human hair. They vacuumed his car after dusting it carefully for fingerprints.

They found twenty-four foil packets of marijuana and a dozen of cocaine in a metal box in a kitchen cabinet. He said he bought them for his own use. Antonelli didn't want to screw up his possible murder case against Blodgett by charging him with drug possession. So he left the packets in the box in the cabinet.

They found nothing that linked him to the murders. He answered questions from Antonelli and Meador for several hours without showing any signs of guilt. He provided them with names of people who showed interest in his paintings. With no solid evidence he was released without any charges.

Chapter Ten

Hearst's Old City Room

The name on the door made Nick think about the golden days of journalism, when newspapers competed for readers who had no other source of news. Before radio and television, every major city had several newspapers, and powerful chains of newspapers influenced national and international events. Etched in the smoked glass of the door was "W.R. Hearst." It seemed hard to believe that 50 years ago the great William Randolph Hearst, often blamed for fomenting the Spanish-American War, might have been in that office, barking orders to the editors in the now vacant city room.

At midday on Tuesday the week following the murders of Crawford and Billingsley, Nick stood in what once had been the city room in the old section of the *News American* building that dated to early in the century. He just unloaded 200 rolls of the bureau's news report in a small storeroom on the fifth floor, behind the elevators. The only "official" copy of the news stories that the Baltimore bureau transmitted over the local broadcast wire was the bureau's copy of its daily transmissions. If any lawsuits or subpoenas ever were filed against UPI involving a story transmitted from the Baltimore bureau over the local broadcast wire, the bureau would have to produce its copy of the story in question. Each day's transmissions were kept on a clipboard until the end of the night shift when the night staffer rolled it up and put it in a metal bookcase by the door. The shelves were overloaded, and having some time that morning, Nick decided to clear them.

The *News American's* publisher and general manager, along with supporting staff, occupied the executive offices in the north section of the fifth floor, facing Lombard Street. The south end contained what once had been the city room. Although completely empty and dark because the power to that section was shut off, Nick could see ghostly outlines of the desks on the dusty floor, and no longer operating pneumatic tubes, once used to send copy to the composing room, hanging from the ceiling. One corner was walled off into the office with the door that he had just noticed.

Nick visualized what the room might have looked, and sounded like, when Hearst ruled his empire. In his mind's eye he saw editors yelling at reporters, and copy boys racing around, and Hearst stomping out of the office to berate an editor. He almost could smell the newsprint, the sweat, and the cigarette smoke. The city room now on the third floor still had some of the character, but no longer the glory and romance, of that earlier time.

Nick thought how the emergence of radio and television caused several waves of consolidation and mergers. The *News American* resulted from several mergers of newspapers, including one that dated to the 18th Century. Only a few cities like Baltimore still had competing newspapers. *The Sun*, with an illustrious past of famous journalists and Pulitzer Prizes, remained one of the few American newspapers still operating its own bureaus in major cities in the U.S., and in a number of foreign countries. Because of its own stable of reporters, *The Sun* did not subscribe to UPI's services. That was a constant frustration to Nick, and the reason why the Baltimore UPI operation was not larger and more important.

The *News American* was UPI's largest and most important subscriber in the state. It was the industrial city's blue-collar paper, and as such, it competed reasonably well against *The Sun's* duller afternoon paper, the *Evening Sun*, which was denied the benefit of its morning sibling's national and international staff. The *News American* also had the rights to a number of the most popular comic strips, and *Parade Magazine*, which helped to keep its Sunday paper viable, despite *The Sun's* far greater circulation. There's a lot to achieving success in the newspaper business beyond the city room, Nick thought.

In his reverie in the silent room, Nick noticed a change in the smell he was imagining, an odor that didn't belong. It took him a few moments to realize that it was the strong odor of Dewey's cigarettes, and as he realized that, Dewey's voice startled him from behind by saying what he had been thinking.

"If you imagine the desks in place, this looks just like it might have in 1920. Hearst only came here now and then, and half the time he was here, he probably was chasing whores, but that office had to be maintained for him. He was the man. There hasn't been anyone like him in the newspaper business since. Maybe that's why newspapers are dying."

Nick spun around. Dewey was just three feet behind him, holding a newspaper, slightly smiling.

"I didn't realize you knew so much about the newspaper business," Nick said, when he was able to speak.

"It's become a new interest," Dewey said, "and when I get interested in something, I have to learn all I can about it."

"Of course," Nick said. The shock had worn off, and now he could joke with Dewey. But Dewey was in a serious mood.

"Have you ever thought about the economics of the newspaper business, about the enormous expense of publishing a newspaper, and the huge economic benefits a newspaper brings to a city?" Dewey said.

"Not really," Nick said.

"Well, look around this building," Dewey said. "Look at all the complex equipment, all the people employed to make it run, to get the information, sell the ads, organize the classifieds, compose, print, and deliver it. Think of all the different skills that are required to publish and distribute a newspaper. Hundreds of people make their livings from it. Businesses all around the city depend on their ads in it. A newspaper is a major enterprise. A huge amount of capital is expended to deliver a package of words and pictures printed on newsprint. It's actually pretty amazing."

"Yes, I guess it is," Nick said.

"Newspapers are the record of our existence as a species, almost every aspect of it, every day, and dated so that if you want to know what happened on a specific day, what we humans were doing on that day, all you have to do is find a newspaper from that day," Dewey said.

"Look at today's paper," he said, holding up a copy. "Let's see what it says about us."

"There are two stories that I think present the perfect irony that people in the future will see about this time. There's one story about us increasing the bombing of North Vietnam because they are refusing to give up. Ho Chi Minh says they will fight forever to free their country.

"Then there is a story about the candidates in the Democratic gubernatorial primary in September, illustrating our exercise of our democratic rights that we had to fight to get, just like the Vietnamese. We don't see it that way, but people in the future will see it, especially after we have lost the war, and Ho Chi Minh is presiding over a unified Vietnam."

"You really think they can defeat us?"

"Absolutely. We haven't got a chance," Dewey said. "We've been on the wrong side since we double-crossed Ho after World War II. In return for him helping us against the Japanese, we agreed to support his goal of an independent Vietnam. Instead, we let the French go back in, and then, when they couldn't defeat him, we stupidly got involved. We're blinded by him being a communist when we should have known that he is an ardent nationalist. He just wants his country free from foreign domination, all foreign domination. And, believe me, it will happen."

"It's going to take a while," Nick said.

"Yes, and we're wasting our money, and even worse, the lives of our men," Dewey said. "It's a crime, but I digress. Look what else is in the paper.

"One copy of a general newspaper gives you get a snapshot of our culture, today," he said, opening to another page. "Here's an ad by the discount store Korvette's. They have a sale on diamond rings. If you're planning to get engaged to Joan, here's a good chance to get a ring cheaper."

Nick smiled. That wasn't a bad idea, he thought.

"Then," Dewey continued, "Hutzler's has an ad for swim suits. Those in the picture are pretty modest, but they say they have the new bikinis. I wonder if we could get Susan and Joan to go there and model the bikinis for us?" He said, and then laughed.

"And here is Jack Luskin wanting to sell you a color television at the lowest price ever. See, it's only a matter of time. We'll all be glued to our color televisions, and not reading newspapers.

"Towards the back are the official records of our lives, all in agate type. Here are the engagement announcements, including a picture of a pretty girl. She, or her parents, will clip this out, and it will find its way into a scrapbook that someone in the future will see, with the date. This newspaper captures this moment for her, forever. What else can do that?

"Then, there are the wedding announcements, the birth announcements, and finally, the death notices. Who's going to publish these when the newspapers are gone? Will we still care enough about each other to bother? Maybe there'll just be periodic governmental announcements that 425 babies were born in Baltimore in April, and 370 people died, but without names. People will just be statistics. In this document, this newspaper, our lives as individuals are recorded. They mean something to somebody. Do you have any idea what it feels like to mean nothing to no one?"

"I don't," Nick said.

"I do, and that's where we all are headed," Dewey said, "and it is against human nature. Man always has wanted life to have meaning. Individuals always have wanted the things they do with their lives to mean something to others.

"Did you know that those Mayan paintings I showed you were dated and signed by the artists? They wanted the future to know what they had done, who they were, and when they did it. They were doing for their culture what newspapers do for ours.

"Look at all the various kinds of information contained just in this newspaper, a record of this day in the history of humans. What will do this for us when newspapers are gone?"

"What makes you think they will disappear?" Nick said.

"It's inevitable," Dewey said. "Look at what television has done to them already. In a very few years we've managed to get the mass of the population to sit and do one thing all together - watch television shows. It is so convenient to have information fed to us over the tube, but mostly to be anesthetized by silly comedy and crime shows. It is far more work to read a newspaper, or a book. Color TV is just the beginning. It will only get worse as technology finds even more convenient ways to entertain us. What you see in this room is what you will see on the third floor in a few years."

"That's a depressing thought, Dewey. What's gotten into you?" Nick said.

"It's just the way I think things will go," he said. "It certainly isn't the way I would like them to go. When I discovered Hearst's old office up here, it really got me to thinking. There's a great view from in there. Come, let me show you."

Dewey opened the door to the Hearst office. The view over Baltimore's harbor was spectacular. There was a huge dark wood desk and chair, a credenza built into one wall and an empty bookcase attached to another, but they were not dusty like everything else on the floor. Dewey sensed what Nick had observed.

"Apparently they built this office around the desk," Dewey said. "It's far too big to get through the door. I've sort of adopted this office as my getaway when I'm at work and there's nothing to do. I've taken to coming up here, sitting at the desk, and thinking. It's very peaceful."

"Have you thought about Susan since the dinner on Friday night," Nick said.

"I'm taking her to dinner tonight, to Tio Pepe's," Dewey said.

"That's great," Nick said. "That's one I haven't taken her to. You two should have a good time."

He had been to the Spanish restaurant for a couple of business lunches, and he liked it. He intended to take Joan there, but the right occasion had not presented itself.

"Why don't you and Joan join us?" Dewey said.

"Truthfully, I can't afford it," Nick said. "I'm just barely covering my expenses right now."

"I understand," Dewey said. "The drop in the stock market is really putting a crimp in my wallet as well."

"Dewey," Nick said, "there's no comparison between my circumstances and yours. I don't own any stocks. I live from paycheck to paycheck."

"But you have something I fear I never will have," Dewey said.

"What's that?"

"You have the love of a woman Actually I think you might have the love of two women, but, whatever, it's something I really never have had. Sex I've had. I've had a lot of sex, but never real love. You have that. I'd give up a lot to have it."

Chapter Eleven

Changes in the Police Department

The murders of Crawford and Billingsley, and the gruesome sight of her body did not cause Antonelli's nightmares to return. They didn't have to. The deaths, and the images of the two girls, were in his mind all the time now. They also didn't have much time to return because he wasn't sleeping very much.

The artist was a lousy suspect. Antonelli knew it, but it was important to have a suspect. They wanted this killer caught, and there were eight detectives now working the case, without any progress, despite public statements to the contrary. Two two-man teams of detectives were interviewing every acquaintance of Crawford and Billingsley they could find. Two others were interviewing people in the Hopkins neighborhood, going door to door, trying to find someone who saw something.

Lieutenant Joseph Rauch, one of the most senior officers in Homicide, with many decorations and a great record, now headed the investigation. Technically they still were Antonelli's cases, and Rauch deferred to him on most matters, leaving him in charge of day-to-day investigations. Antonelli had high regard for Rauch except for the fact that he was a racist.

Gen. Gelston had ended open racism in the police department. Racist remarks to Negro officers no longer were tolerated. Calls for assistance from Negro neighborhoods no longer could be ignored. Gelston ended the practice of restricting Negro police officers to walking beats, not allowing them to ride in patrol cars. He ordered the police to wear nametags on their uniforms, similar to those on military uniforms. It had the immediate impact of personalizing and humanizing the police.

He also brought into the police department the Negro who had integrated the state's National Guard, and gave him that rank of Major, in charge of community relations. Major William "Box" Harris immediately started a program to recruit Negroes for the police department.

This was all good news to Antonelli could see that with Major "Box" Harris now in the department, opportunities for blacks were going to open up, and that having already established a good record - despite being unable to solve the Blue Girl murders - he could become a leader in the change. But, he feared that Rauch would block him if he knew about his Jamaican heritage, and would limit his activity on the blue girl case. Rauch, who came from a Southern-leaning blue-collar family from East Baltimore, made no secret that he had little use for Negroes, but he was smart enough to be subtle in his prejudice, and thus dangerous.

Antonelli also had to be concerned about his father. He knew that some of the family would ostracize him, and that would hurt and anger his father.

Obsessed with the blue girl murders, Antonelli had lost weight and smoked more than he ever had before. Convinced that he had missed something, he believed he could solve the crimes if he just worked a little harder.

They didn't have the resources to keep Blodgett under surveillance, but Antonelli checked on him every few days, and on a Saturday night, tailed him when he visited the Block. He liked a girl who used the name Candy Kane on the stage, but whose real name was Karen Winston. She was a big breasted bottle blonde with the twangy accent of her Southwestern Virginia origin. She did three strip acts every night, and was available in between for brief oral sexual encounters, as well as for the rest of the night, afterwards. She also liked Blodgett, and liked modeling for him. She was proud of her body and liked to show it off. She would go back to his apartment with him if she didn't have a john after her last show.

"He's a sweet guy," she told the police. "He treats me with respect. He's not a killer."

Chapter Twelve

Dewey Wants to Buy a Newspaper

"When a man loves a woman
Can't keep his mind on nothing else"
- Percy Sledge, When a Man Loves a Woman

Nick and Susan drove into the parking lot across from the News American at the same time on Wednesday morning. Susan waved and smiled. Nick walked over to her.

"How was Tio Pepe's?" he said.

"It was great," Susan said. "I loved it. I want to go back there, soon."

"And Dewey, how are you getting along with him?" They were about to cross the street, but Susan stopped, and looked at Nick.

"I like him," she said. "He's different, that's for sure, but very interesting, and maybe the most interesting man I've ever met."

"So you're going to keep seeing him?"

"Sure," she said. "I don't think I've ever met anyone who knows as much about as many different things as he does."

"Nor have I," Nick said. "Just yesterday I found out that he has been learning about the economics of the newspaper business."

"Yes, that's because he's thinking of buying a newspaper," Susan said.

"You're kidding," Nick said. They were standing outside the entrance to the paper, but not moving towards it. "Any particular one?"

"There's a weekly for sale in Carroll County that he says he can afford," Susan said. "He says he would prefer a daily.

He'd like the one in Annapolis, but it would take more money than he has right now. He's looking at some others, also."

"Where would he get the money for any? He's always telling me that he doesn't have a lot of money."

"He has a lot of assets," she said. "His father bought all kinds of things and held on to them. Nick said he still is finding property his father bought, like a share in an island off the coast of Maine that he just found out about. It's worth a bundle. He owns ranch land in Montana, a farm in Iowa, a condo in Florida, even an apartment in London. He also has a house in Rehoboth Beach. It had been rented to a family for years, and they recently moved out. He's having it renovated. When it's ready, he wants me to go down there with him on a weekend to look at it."

"Are you going to do that?"

"We need to get a little better acquainted before I'd do that," Susan said. "I'd feel better about it if you and Joan came along. Apparently it's a big house."

"I don't know," Nick said. "We haven't done anything like that. I think her parents might give her a very hard time."

"Certainly they know the two of you are serious?" she said.

"Yes, but we're discreet. Her parents are old-fashioned, but they also have common sense and good manners. They like me. I think they want us to get married. They don't ask a lot of questions, and we avoid doing things that might make them feel like they should."

"Why don't you get her a ring?' Susan said. "Then, they'll care a whole lot less about what the two of you are doing."

"Have you and Dewey been conspiring?"

"What do you mean?"

"He made the same suggestion yesterday. He showed me an ad for diamond rings."

She laughed.

"No," she said. "The subject hasn't come up. It's a coincidence, but maybe one you should pay attention to."

When Dewey came into the bureau later in the morning, Nick asked him if he was serious about buying a newspaper.

"Maybe," he said. "I don't want to run one by myself. I'd have to have a partner, maybe a couple. After all, the only business I've ever run was my fraternity, and that didn't turn out too well. While I write a lot, I am not an editor."

"Do you have anyone in mind?"

"I think Susan would make a great Executive Editor, don't you?"

"Dewey, is this something you really want to do, or are you thinking that you can snare Susan by buying her a newspaper?"

"That idea crossed my mind," Dewey said. "What's wrong with it? What else do I have to do with my money?"

"So all that crap you threw at me yesterday about newspapers was just bullshit," Nick said.

"Hell no," Dewey said. "I believe every word I said. But I probably wouldn't have thought about the idea of owning a newspaper if I hadn't met Susan. If things work out, I'll owe you big time."

"Maybe I could open your Paris bureau." Nick said, smiling. "I read French, and I speak it de facon acceptable."

"Seriously, you'd do that? You'd do that for me?" Dewey said, looking very earnest. Then his face changed and he laughed. "She must have told you about the Paris apartment."

"No, she mentioned a London apartment," Nick said. "You have one in Paris, also?"

"I guess I didn't mention that one to her," Dewey said. "It was my mother's place in Paris. She lived there for quite a few years at various times. It's managed by an agency there. My father wouldn't go near it, and I've never been there. I don't want it. I probably should sell it."

"Before you go much further with this newspaper idea, you probably should develop your relationship with Susan a little more," Nick said.

"I intend to," Dewey said. "It's all I think about. I wish I could take her to Mexico with me, but she's taking her vacation in Boston and it overlaps mine."

"When are you going?

"Around the beginning of June, before it gets too hot down there," he said. "We won't see each other for almost the entire month."

"So I guess you'll be spending as much time with her this month as you can," Nick said.

"You bet," he said, and he walked out.

Chapter Thirteen

A Weekend in Delaware

Nick and Joan planned to go to a movie on Saturday afternoon and then out to dinner, but Nick had another idea. After they left her house, he drove towards the shopping center where the Korvette's was located.

"Where are we going?" she said.

"I want to make a little stop at Korvette's," he said. He pulled the car over to side of the road, where parking was allowed. He turned to her.

"We've talked about getting married, but we've never talked about getting engaged. I want to buy you a ring. I want us to be engaged. We don't have to set a date to get married. All we are doing is telling each other, your parents, and everyone else, that we intend to get married, when we both are ready, sometime - we don't have to say when - after you graduate. I love you, and I can't think of a better way of showing it."

She looked down for a few moments, and when she looked up, at him, her eyes were moist. A tear ran down a cheek.

"I'd love to be engaged," she said. He brushed the tear off her cheek and they kissed, and then kissed again. She smiled radiantly, and sort of bounced in her seat. "Let's do it. I can hardly wait to tell my parents. They'll be so happy."

Nick didn't know much about engagement rings, and realized when the sales clerk began showing them, that many were far more expensive than anything he could afford. He started to worry about how he would tell Joan that he couldn't afford the one she picked out. It would not be an auspicious way to start the engagement.

He soon realized that Joan either had read his mind, or simply was more practical than he had given her credit for being. She didn't hesitate to tell the clerk that she wanted something simpler, and less expensive, quite a bit less expensive.

She picked out a ring that had pretty diamond of modest size surrounded by very small diamonds. It was attractive and elegant without being gaudy. It was below the limit on his charge card and he felt enormous relief and exhilaration when he gave his card to the clerk and the charge was approved.

As she predicted, her parents were ecstatic. Her mother cried. Her father shook Nick's hand, and hugged him, and them offered him a cigar. They sat on the deck in the rear and smoked the cigars while Joan talked with her mother.

Nick had lunch on Monday with Dewey and Susan at Burke's, a hangout for some of the *News American* people, where he told them about his engagement. After they congratulated him, and boasted of having some of the credit, Susan said, "Now you can join us in Rehoboth."

"I thought the two of you were going off in opposite directions, Dewey to Mexico and you to Boston," Nick said.

"We're going to do it on the last weekend of the month, as a kickoff to our vacations," Dewey said.

"It's good to see the two of you getting along so well," Nick said.

"Yes, we have gotten to know each other much better," Dewey said.

Susan just smiled.

Nick could feel himself blushing.

Susan and Dewey laughed.

"You have to come with us," Dewey said. "The house is designed to provide plenty of privacy when you want it. From what my agent says, the renovations will be done in about a week. It will be great. It's two blocks from the boardwalk. It should be a lot of fun "

"We'll try not to embarrass you too much," Susan said.

Nick realized she was teasing him, and he laughed.

"OK, I'll talk to Joan," Nick said.

Joan figured out a way to tell her mother without having a problem. Her father, as she expected, was fine. So she told Nick she went shopping for some clothes for the occasion, "mostly for the bedroom." That confirmed Nick's guess that even though Joan might have not reached her 20th birthday, she understood they weren't going to the beach to spend a lot of time sightseeing and baking in the sun. The purpose of this weekend was sex, a lot of sex.

He and Joan regularly had sex, but they never had spent a night together, to say nothing of an entire weekend. His anticipation grew with the thought of spending it in a beach house with two older, more experienced people, who were lonely and hungry for love. He felt good that he had put them together.

They drove to Rehoboth Beach on Thursday, May 26, in Dewey's Ford Bronco. WCAO was featuring Bob Dylan's new album, "Blonde on Blonde," with songs like "Rainy Day Woman" and "Just Like a Woman." Nick thought that even though they weren't going to be smoking pot, those Dylan songs somehow seemed appropriate for this weekend. They planned to return on Monday. Dewey wanted to beat the weekend traffic both ways. The weather on the last weekend of May historically ranged from wet and chilly to hot and humid. This year it was in-between, with cool rain in the forecast. Even if they had wanted to, they would not be spending much time on the beach.

The wood-shingled one story house seemed ideal for its purpose. It consisted of three sections. The main section contained the kitchen, dining room, utility room and a large combination living room/family room with a vaulted ceiling that opened through sliding glass doors in the rear to a screened-in deck. A large stone gas-fired fireplace dominated the left wall of the room, and three leather sofas were grouped around it, separated by a deep-pile rug. Large pillows were stacked by the hearth.

There were two wings on the left side, accessed by doors on each side of the fireplace. Each wing contained a large bedroom equipped with a king-size bed, a much smaller bedroom, and a bathroom with a large walk-in shower. The wings wrapped around a fully enclosed deck, partially open to the sky, with a hot tub, a sauna, a table and lounge chairs, a bar equipped with a small refrigerator, and a fireplace on the other side of the one in the family room, its flue sharing the chimney structure. The deck area only could be accessed from the two bathrooms, each of which was stocked with fluffy towels and terrycloth bathrobes.

Dewey told them he had completely remodeled the house, leaving only the stone fireplace in the family room from the original interior. The house smelled of fresh paint, new wood, new carpeting, and cleaning materials. They opened the windows to air it out.

After quickly unpacking, they went to a small shopping center nearby where they stocked up on food and liquor, and bought two carryout pizzas. Dewey also had a case of wine he brought from his wine cellar. The kitchen not only had a new stove, dishwasher and refrigerator, it also had a glass-doored wine cooler.

After sitting at the kitchen table to eat the pizza, they moved to the family room. Dewey started the fire, and poured glasses of a Beaujolais he purchased at the local store. They chatted for about an hour, but Nick felt some tension in the air. Susan broke through it by announcing she was going to take a shower.

"Dewey," she said, "why don't you join me, so we can let them have some fun by themselves." Everyone laughed, partially in relief. The serious sex was about to begin. Soon, both showers were occupied.

He had watched Joan take a shower in his apartment, but his shower was too small to accommodate both of them. This one was large enough for two, and had seating on both ends. They took turns washing the other, massaging and stimulating. Nick was so stimulated that he wasn't sure he would make it to the bed, and get the Trojan on in time. He did, but he came too quickly. Using one hand to knead a breast, and the other to explore and massage her vagina, he brought Joan to climax. They hugged and dozed for about 45 minutes and then made love again, this time more leisurely, more erotically, with her finishing on top, his hands on her breasts as they gently bounced up and down with her motions.

"I love you so much," Joan said, after lying down beside him. "Being here with you is the most exciting thing I've ever done."

"Me, too," Nick said. "I just love looking at you, touching you, just being with you. And it is different being away from the apartment, from work, and not having to take you home."

"Especially that," she said.

After making trips to the bathroom, they noticed that it was chilly in the room. They pulled up the covers, snuggled together and went to sleep.

His body clock at work, Nick woke up at 5:30 A.M. He loved getting up early anyway, and after laying in bed for a few minutes listening to Joan sleep, he got out of bed, put on a pair of jeans, a t-shirt and some boat shoes, and left the room.

He found Susan sitting at the kitchen table, reading Harper's, with the smell of percolating coffee filling the air. Even with her hair askew and no makeup, she still was stunning, maybe even more so in the thin red kimono she was wearing.

"I thought I was the only morning person among us," he said.

She looked up and smiled. "I like to get up just as the sun is coming up. I've done it for years."

"I assume Dewey is still asleep?"

"Yes, I think he'll sleep late. We drank quite a bit, among other things. What about Joan."

"Sleeping soundly."

She arched her eyebrows mischievously and then gave him what he thought had to be her most seductive look, and it certainly was that.

"Well, alone at last," she said, moving in such a way that the kimono separated in front exposing the center part of her chest down to her stomach, but not quite uncovering all of her breasts. It was enough to make Nick's heart jump, and to cause an erection.

He took a deep breath to calm himself. Before he could say anything, she laughed, and closed the kimono.

"I shouldn't have done that, but you are so much fun to tease," she said. "You get red as a beet, and, it might be my last chance to do so."

"Why is that?"

"You probably won't embarrass so easily after we get you and Joan into that hot tub."

"When are you planning that?" Nick said, as he poured two cups of coffee.

"I think maybe this afternoon. It's supposed to rain and it would be a fun indoor activity."

Nick put the cups on the table and sat down.

"It wouldn't be the first time for me," Nick said. "One of my fraternity brothers at Hopkins had one. A bunch of us boys and girls were in it several times. Have you had much experience in them?"

"Not a whole lot," she said. "The first time I was in one I was doing a story on an institute a lot like the Esalin Institute. They copied some of Esalin's practices, including the use of hot tubs. So all these high-powered business executives were made to get naked together in the hot tubs. I didn't find it very interesting, probably because they weren't very interesting, and, to be truthful, sex wasn't part of it. A hot tub is a lot more fun when sex is part of it."

"Well, we won't have to worry about that here," Nick said. "This whole weekend is about sex. As far as I know, Joan's never been in one. I'm sure she's never been in one under circumstances like this. I don't know how she'll react to it."

"I think she'll be fine," Susan said. "She'll look better than I do now. Things are starting to sag a little."

"Oh, really," Nick said. "It will be fun to compare." This time she blushed, and he laughed.

"I really want to talk to you about Dewey," Susan said.

"You two seemed to be getting along very well," Nick said, with an emphasis on the "very."

"On that level, yes," she said. "He's a great sex partner. He's very skillful and considerate. Like everything else that interests him, he is very knowledgeable about lovemaking. If we could keep our relationship on that level, but otherwise not so intense, it would work for me. But it won't work for him.

"He's infatuated with me," Susan said. "He wants to marry me. He wants to buy me a newspaper. He just wants me in every sense of the word. Its like he wants to possess me, almost to the point of smothering me with his affection. I don't want that. Even worse, it frightens me a little. I fear he has some psychological problems resulting from his terrible relationship with his mother. I assume you know about that?"

"I know something of it," Nick said. "I saw a picture of her in his parents' bedroom. He told me a little. You do look a lot like her."

She took a sip of coffee and when she put the cup down, her kimono gaped open again, almost entirely exposing her left breast. This time it didn't appear purposeful. She pulled it closed without comment. Her eyes had a faraway, deep-in-thought, expression.

"I know, and that worries me," she said. "He could be looking for the mother he never had. I'm not that person. In addition to all that, I think he has a medical problem."

"You mean the headaches?" Nick said.

"Yes," she said. "I think they're getting worse. I wonder if he might have a tumor. One of the doctors he saw also thought that was possible, and wanted to take a look. He won't agree to that. I think he should do it."

"So do I," Nick said, "but you can't tell him anything. He gets very emotional."

"I know," she said. "The only time we've had a fight so far was when I tried to persuade him to go back to that doctor. He scared me. For a fraction of a moment I saw something in his eyes - almost like a completely different, and very hostile, personality - that I hadn't seen before, and haven't seen since. He apologized profusely, and has been super sweet since then. But he still won't agree to go back to that doctor."

"I guess we need to keep working on him," Nick said.

"I'm glad you said that," she said. "I need your help with him, not only because of his health, but also because I am going to hurt him very deeply."

"When you go back to Boston," Nick said.

"Yes," she said. "I intend to go back to Boston, one way, or another, and I don't want him coming with me. I'm interviewing for three different jobs in two weeks when I am there. The job I really want is that columnist job with the Globe, but it probably won't be open until the fall. If I get a really good offer from one of these interviews, I may take it. I need to get out of Baltimore."

"That's going to be very hard on Dewey," Nick said. "You are the first person to come along in a long time, maybe ever, who he believes really cares about him."

"I do care about him," she said. "I really do. I just don't want to take care of him. Do you understand? I fear he is someone who needs a lot of care. I just can't do that. I'm not looking for someone to take care of me, either. I want someone as my mate who is my equal and who views me as an equal, someone strong and independent, but also loyal and loving. That's probably unrealistic, but it's the way I feel."

"I hope you find someone like that," Nick said. "I think they're around, but maybe not always obvious."

"You are one," she said. "Joan is lucky to have you."

"And I, her," Nick said.

And just then, Joan came in the family room, dressed in white slacks and a light yellow pullover. She looked radiant to Nick, immediately lifting his spirits, which were dampened by the conversation with Susan.

"Good morning," she said brightly. She smiled and bent over to kiss Nick. Nick noticed the smell of toothpaste on her breath, and that she wasn't wearing a bra. She sat in the chair next to him.

"That's a gorgeous kimono," she said to Susan.

"Thank you," Susan said. "I got it on a trip to Hong Kong. That's a great place to shop if you ever get the chance. I guess I should check on my roommate. He probably wouldn't want me to let him sleep with everyone else up. I'll take him some coffee."

She poured a cup of coffee, and left.

Nick got Joan a cup, and a second for himself.

"So how did you sleep?" he said.

"Wonderfully. How about you?"

"Like I would like to sleep every night, with you beside me," he said.

She kissed him again.

"What are we doing today?" she said.

"Susan wants us to get us all in the hot tub," Nick said. "Are you up to that?"

"I assume we won't be wearing any swim suits," she said.

"That's right, we'll all be bare-assed nekkid," he said, imitating a hick accent.

She laughed.

"That could be sexy," she said, "even more so if it was just the two of us."

"That would be special," Nick said. "Although with Dewey so fixated on Susan, I'll be the only one paying attention to you."

"Susan will be paying attention," Joan said. "She'll be comparing me to herself. No matter how hard she tries to suppress it, and I honestly think she is sincere about suppressing it, she still is attracted to you, and she wants you to be attracted to her."

"Yes, I know," Nick said. "I see that, also. And you are right. She already has compared herself to you. She says you'll look better because she is beginning to sag, and she's right." He reached under her pullover and fondled her left breast.

"There's no sag here," he said. He rubbed her nipple and it hardened.

"That kimono didn't hide much," Joan said. "She's really built, and I didn't see much sag, did you?"

Nick smiled.

"I'm sure you'll compare very favorably," he said, giving her breast a squeeze before withdrawing his hand.

The trick was to get into the water first so that the heat would discourage the erection he knew he would get as soon as he saw the women. So when the four of them gathered around the table on the deck, in their terry cloth bathrobes, Nick didn't hesitate. "Let's go in first," he said to Dewey, who seemed to understand. He nodded. They dropped their robes by the edge of the hot tub and stepped into the hot water.

"I think it's hot enough to take care of things," Nick said to Dewey.

"For the moment anyway," he said. Nick had never noticed Dewey's muscles. They didn't bulge. His body wasn't distorted, but it was very muscular, very taut. He also saw several scars.

"You must work out," Nick said.

"Every day," Dewey said.

Susan and Joan looked at each other.

"It's show time," Susan said. She walked a few feet towards the hot tub, and let her robe fall open on one side, exposing a breast. She turned her back and slid her arm out of the robe on that side, and then let the robe drop, showing her naked backside. She winked at Joan, and slowly turned around at the edge of the hot tub and spread her arms, giving the men a close up and full view of her front. She then stepped into the water.

Nick smiled and looked at Dewey, and was surprised that Dewey was not smiling. His eyes appeared very dark and distant. His face had a serious look, but then it changed, and he smiled broadly.

"I don't think I can compete with that," Joan said. She walked over to the hot tub, dropped her robe and stepped in, sitting down beside Nick, who put his arm around her shoulder. Dewey did the same with Susan.

"To us," Nick said, raising a wine glass. "To us," they responded.

Nick thought watching those two beautiful naked women walk over to the tub and step into it was the most erotic experience of his life. Susan most definitely was a natural blonde. Her pubic hair was very light, contrasting with Joan's. However, their skin tones were almost the same: very pale. Susan's breasts were larger than Joan's, and magnificently shaped, even though they did sag some. Joan still had her teenage figure, smaller and firmer breasts not drooping at all, with her nipples erect and hard. Seeing both of them had exactly the effect Nick thought it would, even in the hot water.

Susan was right. Nick probably was not going to blush anymore around her. When the heat of the water finally got to them, they got out, dried off, and sat naked in front of the fireplace, which kept the outside damp air from penetrating. They drank wine and Dewey, as usual, took the lead as the storyteller. This afternoon he told them about visiting Casablanca, and looking at Roman ruins in North Africa. Susan lay down with her head on his thigh. He told another story while fondling her right breast.

"How did you get those scars?' Nick asked Dewey.

"Various places," he said. Pointing to a jagged one just below his right kidney, Dewey said, "This one I got in a knife fight in a bar in the Yucatan. It took about 30 stitches."

"What about the other guy?" Nick said.

"You can't stitch up a slit throat," Dewey said.

"What?" Susan said. "You killed him?"

"Didn't want to, but it was him, or me. Everyone said it was a fair fight. They didn't charge me. They just told me that I better get out of that area before the guy's friends found me."

"This round mark on my left side is from a bullet wound," he said. "On one of the digs down in the Yucatan we had to scare off a gang that was coming in at night after we quit for the day and stealing anything that was portable. We wound up in a firefight. Several of us were wounded. We killed several of them, and the rest ran away and didn't bother us anymore."

"I didn't know that archaeologists carried weapons," Joan said.

"We hired some of the local police for security," Dewey said. "They gave us some guns, but they did most of the shooting."

"That gives us a little different image of you," Nick said. "You really are an adventurer, not just a story teller."

Joan snuggled against Nick, who did everything he could to try to avoid getting an erection, and then tried to hide it by putting a towel over his lap. After Susan started fondling his penis, Dewey leaned back to show off a prodigious erection. Susan turned around and took it in her mouth. Nick whispered to Joan, "let's go to the bedroom." He didn't want to watch them have sex, nor have them watch him and Joan. Susan was moving to get on top of Dewey, with her back to them, as they left. Moments later Joan was in the same position over him.

About an hour later Nick wanted some coffee. The wine, the heat, and the sex had given him a slight headache. He and Joan went into the family room. Dewey was puttering around in the kitchen, looking very relaxed, very happy. Susan had not yet come out of their bedroom.

Seeing Dewey like this, and knowing what Susan was planning, made Nick feel pangs of sadness and anger, sadness for Dewey, anger with Susan.

Dewey smiled. "That was a lot of fun, wasn't it?" Before Nick could answer, he looked at Joan, and added, "I've never seen two more beautiful young women, have you?"

"No, never," Nick said.

"I've never seen two better looking guys," Joan said. They all laughed.

"What are you up to now?" Nick said.

"Getting prepared for dinner," he said. "Just making sure we have the right implements. I found a place that has steamed crabs. I'll pick them up at six, along with some crab cakes and some salads. Meanwhile, I'll get everything else ready."

The dinner was a little tense. Nick thought Susan sensed his unhappiness with her. She barely spoke to him, and avoided eye contact. She was affectionate to Dewey and friendly to Joan. Joan picked up on Nick's mood, and later, when Susan and Dewey were in the kitchen, asked him about it.

"What's bothering you?" she said. "You've been quiet all evening."

"Nothing you've done," Nick said. "It's something else. I'll tell you later."

When they were in bed, Nick told her what Susan had told him that morning, and how he felt after seeing Dewey's response to her that afternoon.

"I'm feeling very ambivalent," he said. "I think she shouldn't be leading him on like she is. He's insanely in love with her, and he is going to get terribly hurt. On the other hand, she's giving him something he's never really had, a period of true happiness. You can see what a difference it makes in him. Whatever illness he has - and I am sure there is something wrong - seems to be suppressed by his feelings of love."

"She should find a way to let him down slowly," Joan said. "It would be cruel for her to break it off suddenly."

"I'm hoping she doesn't get a job offer when she is in Boston," Nick said. "I hope she has to wait for that columnist job. That way, maybe the passion can ebb a little. Maybe it won't be so painful for Dewey, although I think it will be bad no matter when it happens, or how it happens."

When Nick got up at 6 the next morning, he found Susan in the kitchen, sitting at the table with a cup of coffee, looking out the window. She was wearing a silk robe that, while thin, covered her completely. She looked at him, smiled slightly and said hello. Her eyes betrayed distress. He poured a cup of coffee for himself and sat in the chair across the table from her.

"You are really pissed with me, aren't you?" she said.

"Yes, I am," Nick said.

"Is it because of the hot tub, or Dewey and I having sex in front of you, or is it something else?"

"I enjoyed the hot tub, and I didn't mind you and Dewey going at it," he said. "Far from it. Joan and I were turned on, but didn't want to be spectators. We left because I find the intimacy of being alone with my partner far more erotic than performing in front of others. I'm certainly not upset about any of what you did then. I'd be happy for us to do it again before we leave.

"What is bothering me is what you did to Dewey, knowing what you are planning to do to him later. It is cruel. You are a very beautiful and sexy woman, and when you really turn it on, like you did yesterday, you can drive almost any man crazy with desire. You now have Dewey so obsessed that the pain you will cause will be ten times greater than it might have been. And while it's none of business, Dewey wasn't using a condom. What if you get pregnant? What will happen then?"

She was looking down at the table. She looked up at him. Tears were forming in the corners of her eyes.

"I know," she said. "I went too far with Dewey. I already had gone too far with him before we came here. He is the best lover I've ever had. Like I said yesterday, if I could keep it as that kind of relationship, I wouldn't think of breaking it off. I just don't think he will accept that. And normally he does use a condom. I told him it was OK not to use one this weekend because my period will start on Tuesday. My cycle is exactly the same every month, and has been for nearly 15 years. So I'm past any risk of pregnancy this month."

"Why don't you give him a chance," Nick said. "Right now he will give you anything you want. If you convince him that he can only keep a relationship with you by limiting it, he might do that. As long as he believes that you really care for him, I think he'll do just about anything you want."

"I'll try that," she said. "But I still am going back to Boston, I just don't know when, yet. But whenever it is, he can't come with me. He can visit me. I can visit him. But we're not living together. We're not getting married."

"He might accept that," Nick said. "Much will depend on what kind of arrangement you devise, and whether he suspects it is just a way to get rid of him."

"I don't want you angry with me," she said. "I want to keep you as a friend. I don't want to be cruel to Dewey. I like him. Yesterday wasn't just new for you and Joan. I've never made love to a man in front of another couple before. I didn't know I was an exhibitionist. I enjoyed doing it. But partly, I enjoyed it because I was doing it with Dewey."

Chapter Fourteen

Antonelli Solves a Murder and Frets About his Heritage

Most of the white men in jackets and ties seen in the Negro sections of Baltimore usually were either bill collectors, or insurance salesmen, only occasionally homicide detectives. Everyone Antonelli and Meador talked to expressed surprise that the police were in their neighborhood.

"You seriously investigating the Palmer killing?' the liquor store clerk asked. "We've had three dozen murders in this neighborhood in the past few years, and half the time no detective paid any mind."

"Things are changing," Antonelli said. "I'm sorry about the past, but I can tell you this one is being investigated, and any more also will be. This isn't a one time thing."

"Bout time," the clerk said.

"Now, we've heard that Willie Palmer was in here just a few minutes before he was shot," Antonelli said. "Is that true?"

"It's true," the clerk said. "Stood right there, bought a bottle of Johnny Walker. Paid cash. He always bought one bottle of Johnny Walker on Friday nights. He'd say he worked hard all week and this was his reward to himself. People say he was a real good mechanic."

Willie Palmer, a 34-year old auto mechanic, lived with his wife and two children in a two-story rowhouse, on which he had a mortgage, two blocks from the liquor store. His murder occurred on Friday night, May 27, at the other end of the block where the liquor store was located. He was stabbed to death. His wallet, his wedding ring, his watch and the liquor were taken. The murder was logged in on Saturday morning, but no detective was assigned to it. Along with three other violent deaths of Negroes over the weekend, it wasn't even listed as an active case on the blackboard.

A red-faced Lt. Rauch came out of a meeting with the Captain late Monday morning carrying a sheet of paper and four manila folders. Without saying anything he added a name to the lists of cases of four detective teams. Under Jenkins he wrote "Willie Palmer." He handed a file folder to Jenkins and said, "Solve this one quickly and you'll be in good with the Captain," he said. He dropped the other three folders on the desks of three other detectives who weren't in the office at that time. Jenkins handed the folder to Antonelli.

"You need a case to close," he said. "Do this one and it will count double. Take Meador with you as the secondary."

By Thursday afternoon, the folder had become a loose-leaf binder. Antonelli and Meador interviewed the victim's family, his co-workers, and dozens of people in the neighborhood. They had photographs and a forensics report. They thought they had reconstructed the crime, and had a good idea of the identity of the killers, two local toughs who had reputations for shaking down people in the neighborhood. The liquor store clerk had told them the two were in his store when Palmer bought the Johnny Walker, and left right after he did. Antonelli was certain there were witnesses to the murder, but no one wanted to talk to the police. Because murders like this almost never were investigated to any extent, to say nothing of being solved, Antonelli suspected the killers could be tripped up easily.

He found what he was looking for in the second pawnshop they checked, just five blocks away, Palmer's watch and wedding ring. They got the names, addresses, and descriptions of the two who pawned them, and they matched the descriptions given by the liquor store clerk. They arrested Robert Woods at the apartment and found his partner in a bar a short time later. Woods and Williams shared a two-room apartment in the basement of a decrepit rowhouse, infested with roaches and rats, which by never cleaning their place, they made no effort to discourage. The police search team found an empty bottle of Johnny Walker and a brown paper bag containing a receipt from the liquor store, dated the 27th. It only took a couple of hours to get the two to confess to try to avoid the death penalty.

The *News American* made the arrests the centerpiece of a feature about the results of Gelston's changes in the police department, with photos of Antonelli and Meador. The thrust of the feature was that Negro neighborhoods now could expect responses from the police, and results. Gelston sent handwritten notes to both Antonelli and Meador, congratulating and thanking them.

The investigation of this murder opened Antonelli's eyes to the Negro culture of Baltimore, something he knew very little about. He discovered that it was as complex as the white culture, with the same kinds of movers and shakers, some very public, some very private. Thousands of middle class Negro homeowners were as concerned about law and order as the whites, and very angry that they did not get the same kind of protection from the police as did the white neighborhoods. When he and Meador knocked on a door of one of these homes, they almost always got an earful before the homeowner answered any questions.

For the first time Antonelli realized how large and powerful the Negro population of Baltimore had become, and what the implications of that were for the future.

A week later he received a phone call from Major Harris, inviting him to lunch the next day at the Center Club, a club located atop the recently constructed One Charles Center high rise in downtown Baltimore.

Until two months ago Antonelli had never been to a private club in Baltimore. Since the murders of Crawford and Billingsley, he had interviewed men in several clubs that catered to Baltimore's society. The Center Club did not have the exclusivity of the old society-oriented clubs. Its membership was a broad cross section of the business and political leadership of the city, white and black, Catholic, Protestant and Jewish. Its contemporary design also differed rather dramatically with the older, traditional clubs, and the view of the city and the harbor from the large windows at the top of Charles Center was unparalleled.

After ordering drinks and lunch, Harris congratulated Antonelli, and told him how important what he had done was to race relations in the city. He then dropped the bombshell.

"There are going to be great opportunities on this police force for Negro officers, great opportunities to rise to the top ranks," he said. "Even being part Negro like you are means something."

It was a shock to Antonelli to hear himself referred to as part Negro.

"How did you know that?" Antonelli said. "I've only known it myself for three years, and I haven't told anyone. My father is the only other one who knows, and he hasn't told anyone."

"I have been doing routine background checks on many of our younger officers as part of my job to identify future leaders. It's in your father's Army record, his marriage to your mother, your birth, her death. She was listed as being from Jamaica, and a Negro. When I look at you I suspect she was only part Negro. Are you ashamed of being part Negro? Is that why you haven't told anyone?"

"I'm not ashamed of it," Antonelli said, "but if I had told anyone I never would have gotten into Homicide. My family would have ostracized me. I was raised in an old fashioned Italian Catholic family. That's my culture. I certainly wouldn't fit in the Negro community. I don't have anything in common with Negroes except some genes. I hope you aren't offended by that."

"No, I'd be surprised if it were any other way," Harris said. "It makes your performance in Homicide, which is very outstanding, especially for someone so young, all that more important. It shows that Negro blood in you did not make you less competent, less intelligent, less able to operate in the white world. There still are many people who believe Negroes are inherently inferior. You help to prove that untrue."

"I'm not sure I agree," Antonelli said. "I could argue just as easily that because I have so much white blood, the Negro part of me couldn't hurt me. I don't believe that, but others could. What I know is that no Italian girl I know would ever have anything to do with me if she knew about my Jamaican heritage. And probably most Catholic girls who would be acceptable to my family would feel the same way. My father told everyone my mother was Sicilian, and no one ever has questioned that."

"I can tell that she wasn't Sicilian just by looking at you," Harris said. "I guess I shouldn't be surprised that your family accepted what he said. Most of them probably don't know many Negroes, and they probably wouldn't want to believe anything else."

"True on both points," Antonelli said. He told Harris the story of the barber, and his father's attitude about race.

Harris laughed.

"He sounds like a good man, a hell of a guy to get away with that," he said.

"He is," Antonelli said. "You should come to the restaurant. Come as my guest. I'd like you to meet him."

"I'll do that, but I want your promise to think about what I've told you. I'm going to keep an eye on you. There are going to be opportunities for promotion before long. You could be a strong candidate."

"See, Major," Antonelli said, "I think I should be a strong candidate regardless of who my mother was. Isn't that the bottom line? Do you really want race to be a determining factor? It always has been, and look what has happened. You can't go the opposite direction."

"No, and I don't want that, either," Harris said, "but we're going to have Negro officers in command positions in this police force very soon, and eventually we want the force, from top to bottom, to look like the people of Baltimore."

"That means it's going to be half Negro," Antonelli said.

"That's right, some day it will be," Harris said. "And probably we'll have Negro Police Commissioners. But to do that, we have to have Negroes trained for leadership positions. They have to get experience in command positions. We have very few on the force now, and we'll take some chances with some of them. With you we are taking no chances because you already are proven. You can move far ahead on this force."

"If I am known as part Negro, or if I continue to be known as 100 per cent Italian from Little Italy?"

"Truthfully, I hope it can be either way, but our need is to expand Negro leadership in the police force. No one would expect you to be anything different from what you are now. It's just that for many different reasons, it would be good if people knew."

"I agree that it would be good if people knew," Antonelli said, "but only if it meant no difference to them. That's what would be truly good, that it didn't matter.

"I've given this a lot of thought," Antonelli continued. "I'm getting interested in a young woman. I haven't told her. I think I should, but I fear I'll lose her. Even worse, then other people may find out. It could wreck my relations with my family, and kill my father. I'm not about to take that risk right now."

"I understand," Harris said. "I appreciate your candor and thoughtfulness. I can see why you have such a good reputation."

Two weeks later, a reorganization of Homicide was announced. Two new teams of detectives were created, both reporting to Lt. Rauch. Antonelli was promoted to Detective Sergeant to head one of the teams of five detectives.

Antonelli fretted about Maria Conseco, the girl he believed he wanted to marry. She came from Cuba with her family just before Castro took over. Her parents came from Cuba's upper middle class, but they were not wealthy, especially since they lost their property in Cuba when they fled.

She would be twenty-one in the fall, but was slightly ahead of him in college. One of those stunning-looking Spanish Cubans, Maria had very white skin, very dark hair, with fine features, and a great figure.

Maria's parents operated a travel agency that specialized in Caribbean and Latin American vacations, especially to high-end resorts and islands. She worked in the family business fulltime and went to college at night. Maria spoke excellent English with a cultured accent.

They took two courses together, and during this semester he took her to movies and dinners several times. As devout Catholics her parents were very protective. While they had done nothing more than kiss at the end of each evening, there was good chemistry between them. Antonelli sensed real passion in her, and the promise of an adventurous relationship. His instincts, which he had grown to trust, told him she was the one.

He carried on a debate with himself whether he should tell her about his mother. If he didn't, she might never find out, but there was that small chance that she would, and he didn't know what the consequences would be if she did. One part of him wanted to tell her to test her. If it caused her to break off with him, it would be fortuitous. He did not want to be married to a racist. The great risk, as he told Harris, was that she then would reveal his secret to others.

He also thought that even if she was not a racist, if she didn't find out until after they were married she might be terribly hurt that he didn't trust her. That alone might destroy their relationship. Most of what he had learned about Cubans he had learned from Maria. Generally, they were not racists. For the most part, predominantly black and predominantly white Cubans lived together in relative harmony, especially since much of the elite, the mostly Spanish upper class, left the country when Castro took over.

Harris had forced Antonelli to think, but he still could not reach a conclusion. He could not reach what he thought was the right answer. In such situations, he believed that two possible options existed, depending on the circumstances. Under some circumstances bold action was the right approach, doing something that caused other things to happen, and then reacting to what happened. In other circumstances, the best thing to do was to wait, to let things percolate, and to think. That was what he wanted to do now. However, he feared that he didn't have a lot of time to sort things out.

Chapter Fifteen

Nick's Prospects Improve

The middle of June seemed like the middle of summer. The temperature routinely topped 90, and the city braced for racial trouble. The Congress of Racial Equality (CORE) made the city one of its "target" cities, and brought in professional staff. Bars that earned more than 50 per cent of their profits from the sale of liquor were exempt from the City's public accommodations ordinance, and, as a result, there were many "white only" bars in the city. They became a target of CORE for desegregation.

The extreme right-wing National States Rights Party (NSRP) added to the tension by holding "white power" rallies in the city. Charismatic twenty-year old Joseph Carroll led the Baltimore NSRP, delivering firebrand speeches that mixed populism, racism, patriotism and paranoia, and further inflamed the already tense situation. When Nick, who had studied modern German history at Hopkins, first heard Carroll he thought of the young Adolph Hitler stirring up German nationalism in Munich in the 1920s. Carroll's crowds were larger each time he spoke.

The murder rate rose with the temperatures, overwhelming the larger number of Homicide detectives. Every detective in Antonelli's new team now had at least two murders to investigate. He did not have the time he hoped he would to concentrate on the Blue Girl murders. He still did weekly reports on them, but now there was little to say. Intensive investigations of the backgrounds of the victims, and interviews with their friends and associates have produced no new suspects.

His relationship with Maria has grown into a real romance. He knew he was going to have to tell her about his background, but he kept putting it off. Watching the racial tensions grow in the city, along the number of murders, most of which are occurring in the Negro sections of the city, he wondered whether being part Negro would have any impact on his effectiveness. Would people be more willing to talk with him if they knew? How would they know? He thought it would be interesting to see whether an obvious Negro detective would be more effective than the white ones.

Joan just finished the trimester at Goucher and will be working downtown as an intern at the mutual fund company, T. Rowe Price. On a whim, she signed up for an interview at Goucher for the position. The company recently expanded into funds that specialized in natural resources, as well as in geographic areas. She won the position by impressing them with a paper she wrote on the economic background of exploration. The summer job, which involved working in a small group focused on investment opportunities in developing countries, carried with it the possibility of permanent employment following graduation. With her working downtown, Joan and Nick now will be able to see each other even more frequently.

With his success in covering the headless blondes murders, and in building a stronger staff, Nick's reputation has soared both locally, and inside UPI, where management views the small Baltimore operation as a way station for talented personnel, a training post, not somewhere to spend a career. Just last week, his boss in Pittsburgh raised the possibility of a promotion to run a larger bureau within the Eastern Division some time later in the year.

This rattled Nick. He wants to get ahead, but maybe not in management. He thinks that as a reporter he might have more career opportunities, and a better chance of working out a happy arrangement with Joan. He still wants to go overseas and Joan has agreed to go with him if that happens. He told his boss that his first choice is to go overseas, and he pointed out his language skills and extensive knowledge of world history and current affairs. His boss said that UPI had far greater needs at the moment for people like him in the domestic operations.

UPI was supposed to be a profit-making company, but, from what Nick heard, there was no prospect of one in the foreseeable future. Being recognized as a rising talent inside UPI by people whose skills and personalities awed him made Nick feel like he did when he was initiated into his college fraternity. There was a bond among UPI people, as if they were members of a religious movement, or a special fraternity. Being increasingly important in UPI now meant a great deal to Nick. He was torn between his belief that he would be better off, personally, by focusing on reporting, and the idea that if he advanced in UPI management he could help the company become more successful.

Nick loves his life. He has come a long ways in the year following his college graduation. His successes, in his job, and with Joan, have matured him, and given him greater self-confidence. He is more aware of the impact he has on others, that he is a natural leader who is respected far more than the normal 22-year old. He is eager to take on more responsibilities and more challenges. He feels a little guilty because he is excited by the rising tensions in the city, the prospect of more exciting stories to cover.

Tonight Nick and Joan are at Antonelli's Family Restaurant in Baltimore's Little Italy, celebrating a nice pay raise Nick unexpectedly received. The Division Manager, who had visited the bureau two weeks earlier, sent him a note saying that since he was the only bureau manager in the division who didn't ask for a raise, he was getting one.

This is their first visit to Antonelli's, which Nick knows is owned by the father of that detective. The prices are good and the atmosphere is friendly and casual. Little Italy, located just east of downtown Baltimore, has a tough Negro neighborhood to its North that extends up to the Johns Hopkins Hospital area, and the rapidly changing historic Fells Point neighborhood to its east. It is a unique community of several hundred Italian families living in formstone-surfaced brick rowhouses amid numerous Italian restaurants and businesses.

Their conversation naturally drifts to Susan and Dewey because both soon will be back from their trips.

"I'm concerned about how Dewey is going to react when Susan tries to cool down their relationship," Nick said, "which I know she is going to do. I have a feeling he is going to come back eager to take their relationship to a higher level, just the opposite of what Susan wants."

"Poor Dewey," Joan said. "He is such a nice guy, in many ways a real innocent. He is going to get hurt. Susan is beautiful and charming, and, from what we saw in Rehoboth Beach, a good sex partner, but I am not sure she is capable of love, and all that goes with it. Even if she were capable of loving, I don't think she wants it right now. She doesn't want to give up that much of herself."

"I have felt that way about her since I first met her," Nick said. "Hidden behind her beauty is a heart of stone. Dewey is blind to this. He sees her as the idealized woman he dreamed up some time in the past, his idea of the perfect woman for him, and he isn't looking as her, and understanding her as a real person."

"Have you told him that?"

"No, I didn't really figure that out until after he left," Nick said. "I don't know if I can get him to understand."

Chapter Sixteen

Dewey at the Maryland Club

Dewey Coughlin returned from his two-week trip to Mexico. As testimony to his time in the Mexican sun, his face and arms were much more tan than they were before he left. Even with the deeper color, he didn't look healthy. He had lost weight, and he said his headaches were getting worse.

He brought a folder of photos to the bureau. They included several of depictions in Mayan hieroglyphics and drawings of human sacrifice, and of one of the pyramid-like structures where they were performed.

Dewey seemed even worse the next day. He invited Nick to lunch.

"I'll take you to the Maryland Club," he said.

The dining room in the large building at the corner of Charles and Eager Streets, furnished with traditional dark mahogany tables and chairs, was nearly empty when Nick and Dewey arrived.

"Hello Mr. Coughlin, very good to see you, it's been a while," said the man who greeted them inside. When they were seated an ancient Negro waiter came over, and said almost exactly the same thing to Dewey.

"Winston, it's wonderful to see that you still are here," Dewey said. "Winston was our waiter the first time my father brought me here."

"Yes sir, I remember that occasion," he said.

The menu was simple and they both settled for a crab cake and a small salad.

As Dewey filled out the card, Nick took out his notebook to write down some observations. Dewey stopped him.

"Nothing is allowed on the tables, no papers, no notebooks," he said. "You'll have to remember what you were planning to write."

"It's an impressive building," Nick said.

"There are private meeting rooms and other facilities on other floors, and private bedrooms for members and guests," said Dewey. "It is one of the most important clubs in the State. It goes back to the period of the Civil War. A nephew of Napoleon, or someone like that, founded the club. I'm not really sure. But today, most of the prominent and powerful from society and the financial community are members."

"How many members does it have?" Nick said.

"I don't know. I don't think they give out that information," Dewey said. "As I told you, it was my father who tried to bring me into this world, and made me a member of the Cotillon, and all these clubs. I never had much interest in any of it, and once he died, I just pulled away from it. I have my own interests, which brings me to the purpose of this lunch. I need some help with Susan."

"How so?"

"Well, when I left for Mexico, I thought our relationship had really blossomed. It certainly seemed to be solid when we were in Rehoboth Beach, didn't it?"

"It would be hard to argue otherwise," Nick said with a laugh, "especially after the afternoon in the hot tub."

"Yes, that's what I mean," Dewey said.

"It was hard for me to call her while I was in Mexico, although I did get a couple of short calls through. It wasn't until Sunday night when I finally got a chance to talk to her at length that I became concerned."

Nick knew some of what was coming. Susan went to Boston a week after Dewey went to Mexico, and was not due back until next week. Susan called him twice to talk about Dewey, and he had a long conversation with her the night before.

"I guess you know she has some job interviews this week," Dewey said. "She really wants to go back to Boston. That would be OK with me, but she doesn't want me to go with her."

"I thought it was just that she doesn't want to live with someone," Nick said.

"Yes, that's what she says, but I sense it is more than that, and I'm worried," Dewey said. "I don't want to lose her. She means almost everything to me. I'll do anything for her."

"Maybe you are pushing her too fast," Nick said, "and she is just pushing back some. She doesn't want to be dominated by a man, any man, even someone to whom she is attracted like you. She wants her relationship to be less intense, and focused more on simple things."

"Like sex," Dewey said. "She likes the sex with me."

"That's true, she does," Nick said. "She told me that you are a very good lover."

Dewey smiled. "Yes, she's told me the same thing. Isn't it weird, but we have a relationship the reverse of the normal. Usually it is the man who just wants the sex, but no entanglement. Here it is the woman. That's what it boils down to. She's happy to spend time with me for pleasure, to go to nice restaurants, to talk about interesting things, and, mostly, to have really good sex."

"My God," Nick said, "What else do you want?"

"I want a family. I want someone I can love, and who truly loves me. I really haven't had any of that in my life," Dewey said. "And she is perfect. I doubt I'll ever find anyone else like her."

"She's not perfect, you just think she is," Nick said. "I can see why. She is beautiful and intelligent, a lot of fun to be with, in addition to being an adventurous sexual partner. But you haven't looked inside her. You don't know her as a person.

"I consider her a close friend, other than Joan, the only other woman close friend I've had, and I think I know her pretty well," Nick said. "I like her, but I would not want to be in love with her. She isn't a giving person. The closer you try to get to her, the more she is going to resist. She can't be what you want her to be, and she can't help that.

"She doesn't want someone draining her energy and emotions," Nick said. "She was quite content being 'the other woman' in that relationship she had in Boston. She had no intention of breaking up the man's marriage. She didn't want that kind of commitment. The man's wife was not so tolerant, nor was her employer. They probably didn't understand her, either."

Dewey sat silently for a few moments.

"Maybe I can help her overcome her past," he said. "I can give her security and love. I'll never cheat on her. I even would be willing to live apart part of the time."

"She wants to do it on her own," Nick said. "She doesn't want someone to take care of her. She also doesn't want to take care of someone else. She doesn't want that kind of mutually dependent relationship, even if arises out of love. It's too bad for her, but it is the way she is."

"Her first priority is her career," Nick continued. "You have to understand that about her. She's not looking to settle down with anyone. She doesn't want to be a mother and raise a family."

"I know that, but I'm having a hard time understanding it," he said. "I know she's had some bad experiences with other men, but I'm different."

"Dewey, you being the nice guy you are doesn't change how she feels. I don't think there is much you can do about it. As much as you think she is the one for you, she doesn't think there is any one person for her, and it is not nearly as important to her that there ever be such a person as it is to you."

"So you're warning me that I might get hurt," Dewey said.

"You could if you don't understand and accept her point of view," Nick said, "and tailor your relationship accordingly."

"Just some fancy dinners and good sex afterwards, maybe an occasional weekend like the one we had in Rehoboth Beach?" Dewey said.

"Exactly," Nick said. "If you take that approach with her, I think you can keep a relationship with her."

"I can get about the same thing from a high class call girl," Dewey said. "I want more than that. I need more than that."

"What you need is not compatible with what she needs," Nick said. "At least not right now. Look, she's on the verge of becoming a big name journalist, maybe a syndicated columnist. She's not going to let anything get in the way of that, especially a complicated personal life."

Dewey's mood seemed to change. His eyes had a distant look in them, more intense, more obtuse.

"I appreciate your concern, Nick," he said, "but I think things are better between us than you do. I think I can win her over. She may want to get out of Baltimore, but I don't think she wants to get away from me. I'm not going to let her."

"Hey," Nick said, "I've done my job as your friend." Then, holding up his glass in the form of a toast, he said, "You've been warned."

Chapter Seventeen

General Gelston Thwarts a Potential Racial Confrontation with Police

Nick covered various demonstrations almost every night, one night a sit-in by CORE at a local bar, another night a rally by the NSRP. CORE scheduled its national convention in Baltimore beginning on July 1. In a run-up to the convention it increased the desegregation pressure on the city. Efforts to get the Baltimore City Council to change the ordinance to forbid racial discrimination were unsuccessful. The 21-member council had only two black members, even though more than half of the city's population was black. While the Mayor was a liberal Republican, an entrenched Democratic Party white-dominated machine controlled city politics.

Walter Brooks, the local leader of CORE, decided on Thursday, June 16, to block downtown afternoon rush hour traffic with a demonstration. He, and about 50 demonstrators, sat down on Franklin Street, stopping traffic on the city's busiest westward one-way street. Brooks alerted the media in advance, and a large contingent of print and broadcast reporters and photographers waited for the confrontation with police.

Nick found Stuart Epstein, a classmate from Hopkins and now a CORE organizer, and his girlfriend, Rachel Kohn, sitting in the middle of Franklin Street. Whites comprised about half of the good-natured crowd of demonstrators. They joked about getting arrested and being shown on the early evening newscasts.

Epstein introduced Nick to Brooks, who had been a teacher before he became a fulltime organizer for CORE. He impressed Nick as a natural leader, with an apparent easy-going manner that masked great intensity.

"We're making it happen," Brooks said. "It won't be long, and there'll be no more segregation in this city."

About that time, Maj. Gen. Gelston, still the acting police Commissioner, arrived with a contingent of senior police officers. Instead of ordering the demonstrators to be cleared, Gelston and his contingent stood on the sidewalk, watching, smoking cigarettes and chatting among themselves. Nothing was done to stop the protest.

It was hot in the middle of the street, and after about a half hour some of the CORE members started complaining. "What the fuck is he up to?" Brooks said, pointing at Gelston. "He's supposed to arrest us. That's the whole idea." Gelston continued to ignore the protestors. Traffic continued to back up. After a few more minutes, Brooks, whose face now dripped with sweat, got up and walked over to Gelston. Nick followed.

"Isn't it illegal to block traffic like this without a permit?" he said.

"Sure is," Gelston said.

"Usually folks who do this get arrested and hauled away," Brooks said.

Gelston looked at his watch and said, "And in time for the early newscasts."

"That's right," Brooks said. "But you're not going to do it, are you? You're not going to arrest us?"

"No, you're welcome to sit there as long as you want," said Gelston, who could make himself look like the kind of military officer no one wanted to cross, lean and tough, with a glint in his eyes that could be intimidating. Nick decided it really was an indication of a very good sense of humor.

Gelston had much experience with civil rights conflict. He first encountered it as the head of the Maryland National Guard in Cambridge, on Maryland's Eastern Shore, in 1963. He proved to have considerable skill in defusing racial tensions. Major "Box" Harris stood next to Gelston while he talked with Brooks. He smiled when Gelston added, "We're just here to make sure that no one else interferes with your peaceful demonstration."

Brooks looked at Gelston for a couple of moments. The General's expression didn't change.

"You son of a bitch," he said, and then laughed. Gelston's eyes sparkled, and he let a small smile escape. Harris grinned.

Brooks turned around and walked back to the protestors. There would be no carrying off of protesters by the police today, nothing that would lead the evening newscasts. He waved to them to get up. A few minutes later traffic was flowing again.

Nick returned to his car, parked on a side street, to call the bureau. Because of the prospect of civil unrest, Nick had a mobile radiotelephone installed in his car and a large antenna now sprouted from the rear of his Mustang. He shared a frequency with a number of other users and it operated like an old-fashioned party telephone. If someone else was using their phone, their conversation could be overheard.

He picked up the phone, and it had a clear line. He called in his story:

"A possible confrontation between civil rights protestors and Baltimore police was avoided this afternoon when police refused to arrest a group that blocked a major downtown street."

He then drove to Charles Center and parked in the underground garage. Joan began her summer job this week at the mutual fund company T. Rowe Price, located there, and they were having dinner in the restaurant at the new hotel next door that was part of the first stage of a planned rebuilding of downtown Baltimore.

Joan said she found the work interesting and challenging.

"The people are very smart, and it is intense, but they are nice," she said. "It's been fun so far."

Joan knew about Nick's lunch with Dewey, but Nick had not said anything about him for several days.

"Anything new with Dewey," she said.

"I haven't seen him," Nick said. "Susan hasn't heard from him, either. I guess I better check on him. He didn't look good the last time I saw him. His headaches were worse."

Chapter Eighteen

A White Riot in Patterson Park and Another Blue Girl Murder

Joe Carroll delivered his best firebrand racist and anti-Semitic speech yet to a crowd of several hundred white people on a hot Friday night in Baltimore's Patterson Park, a day after the traffic-blocking sit-in by CORE in downtown Baltimore. The crowd rapidly grew larger as the working class people in the neighborhoods around the park came out of their un-air-conditioned rowhouses.

Accompanied by J.B. Stoner and Connie Lynch from the national headquarters of the party, Carroll stood in front of a display of at least a dozen of the party's flags, a red thunderbolt inside a white circle superimposed over a Confederate flag. Several NSRP members stood to the side wearing armbands with red thunderbolts.

Nick immediately thought of the swastika armbands worn by Nazi organizations in Germany and the irony of this neo-Nazi, racist rally occurring only a few hundred yards from Hampstead Hill, at the other end of the Park. In 1814 an American force of 10,000 dug in on that hill and successfully held off a British land attack in the "Battle of Baltimore." At the same time Francis Scott Key, inspired by watching Ft. McHenry in the Baltimore Harbor hold off the British naval attack, wrote "The Star Spangled Banner."

The hate-filled rhetoric of Carroll, Stoner and Lynch appalled Nick, but it clearly resonated with many in the crowd. When the speeches ended many surged out of the Park and towards a nearby Negro neighborhood.

Nick ran to catch up with the teenagers who were leading the charge across the invisible borders that separated the white and Negro neighborhoods. The white crowd violated the age-old custom of each ethnic group respecting the territory of the others. He saw several white youths attack some young

Negroes. Some Negroes threw rocks in response. A number of fistfights erupted between Negroes and whites.

Dozens of police who had been kept out of sight suddenly appeared, and started making arrests. The fights ended quickly and the crowd rapidly dispersed. Nick found himself in the middle of a menacing crowd of black teenagers, some of them bleeding. When he told them he was a reporter they began yelling about the whites coming into their neighborhood.

"They're not supposed to cross that street," one said.

"This is our neighborhood," another said. "They know that. We don't bother them. They're not supposed to bother us."

Nick had parked on other side of the Park so he used a payphone to call the story into the bureau, but the call went unanswered. Instead of waiting for the night staffer to return from wherever he was, Nick called UPI's general news desk in New York and dictated a story. The Baltimore riot story moved as an "Urgent" on the UPI national wire under his byline. The expected hot summer of racial unrest had arrived, but unexpectedly, it was whites, rather than Negroes, who ignited it.

A short time later Nick learned that Gelston ordered the arrests of the rally speakers on "Inciting to Riot" charges. Carroll and Lynch were taken away in handcuffs, but Stoner left before he could be arrested. Nick found Gelston just outside the Park at a police command post, angry, and clearly worried that the attack by the whites on the Negro neighborhood would cause retaliation.

"We've got CORE coming to town for their convention and these people start this," he said. "We could have this city on fire if we're not careful. Oh shit, that's off the record. Don't quote me."

Nick didn't quote Gelston, but he updated his story reporting that city officials were worried that the white racist rallies and violence might lead to an uprising by the city's Negroes. As a result, the city promised to be very tough on the white agitators. The inciting to riot charges could result in serious prison time.

The riot diverted attention away from something else that went on that evening at the other end of Patterson Park. In 1892 the city's park commissioner, Charles Latrobe, had a

Victorian pagoda built on Hampstead Hill. It provided a panoramic view of the harbor and the entire city, and for many years was a very popular attraction. It fell into disrepair and was closed to the public in the 1950s. Sometime during the evening of the riot someone broke into the pagoda. A park attendant noticed the jimmied door on Saturday morning.

Out of curiosity he went inside and climbed the circular stairs that led to a landing three stories up. There he saw the body, the blue naked body of a young woman. Next to it was her head, standing upright, with her blonde hair spread out behind it and her eyes staring out over the city.

Chapter Nineteen

Antonelli Visits Her Family

Antonelli and Meador arrived at the Pagoda before any other members of the homicide team assigned to the "Blue Girl" case. Antonelli had the area blocked off and secured before members of the medical examiner and Crime Lab teams, and the other "Blue Girl" homicide team members, including Lt. Rauch, arrived. The lieutenant organized a team of detectives and patrolmen to walk the grounds, looking for physical clues. Another team was sent into the nearby neighborhood to look for witnesses.

This murder now made the "Blue Girl" murders the overwhelming priority of the Department leadership. It wasn't long before there was a colonel on the scene. He wanted to go into the Pagoda and see the body, but Antonelli wouldn't let him. As the primary detective on the case, Antonelli controlled the crime scene. He politely told the colonel that no one could go inside until the Crime Lab and Medical Examiner teams completed their work.

"This is the freshest crime scene we have had with these murders, and we need to go over it with a microscope," he said. "If the killer so much as left one of his hairs in there, we'll find it."

The colonel said he understood, although it appeared to Antonelli that he was pissed. Meador whispered to him, "He's embarrassed. Detective Sergeants don't usually give orders to Colonels."

The girl's clothes and purse were found under a stair inside the Pagoda, revealing her name, Laurie Waslewski, and her address, a basement apartment in a formstone rowhouse a block from the park. Antonelli and Maedor went to the address and Waslewski's roommate, Carol Rouse, answered the door, and burst into tears when the policemen told her what had happened.

"She was a wonderful girl," Rouse said. "Everyone loved her. Who could do such a thing?"

She told them that Waslewski was a receptionist at the Walters Art Gallery. She took a bus to and from work from a bus stop just two blocks away. Carol spent Friday night with a boy friend and did not return to the apartment until late Saturday morning. She assumed that Laurie already had gone somewhere when she returned.

"I figured she had gone shopping, or over to her parents," Carol said.

"What about spending a night with a boyfriend like you did?" Antonelli said.

"She wouldn't do that," Carol said. "She was very proper. Her parents were very strict."

She then gave them the names and address of Waslewski's parents. They also asked her for the names she knew of any of Waslewski's boyfriends, as well as other people with whom the murdered girl had much contact.

"She didn't have any regular boyfriends," Rouse said. "I can give you the names of some boys I know she dated and some other friends." She wrote some names on a pad, tore off the page and gave it to Antonelli. Antonelli and Meador left to go to Waslewski's parents' house.

Laurie Waslewski, whose grandparents came from Poland, was a 20-year old beauty, a natural blonde with ample breasts and hips, very fair and clear skin and deep blue eyes. She wasn't thin, but probably was as thin as she ever would have been. Both of her parents were heavy.

Talking to Laurie's parents made Antonelli feel like he thought he might feel if he were telling his father and stepmother that his sister had been killed. Their lives seemed very similar to his family's.

Their two-story brick rowhouse with dormered rooms on the third floor, reminded Antonelli of his family home in Little Italy. A photo of President Kennedy hung on one wall, and one of the Pope on another. An RCA color television in the living room looked quite new. More and more television shows were being broadcast in color, but color TVs were expensive. Only a couple million homes had them.

A framed Bronze Star citation awarded to the father in 1945 sat on the mantle of the fireplace, with the medal displayed next to it. George Waslewski, a paratrooper dropped into France on D-Day, was in nearly continuous combat until the end of the war.

Waslewski, a stocky man with a big head and bushy hair, was a steelworker at Sparrows Point. He sat on his sofa with his left arm around his wife, Karen, a sad look of resignation on a face that Antonelli thought had seen much. He comforted Karen, but showed very little emotion himself. When Antonelli asked him about the medal, Waslewski responded almost exactly the way his father did. He didn't want to talk about it beyond saying that it was a medal for being lucky, that lots of other guys deserved it more than he did.

Laurie's mother, Karen, had a small home business making stained glass decorations of various kinds that were displayed in the living room of their small house and showed she had a fine, artistic touch. She had blue eyes and blonde hair, and clearly once had been as attractive as her daughter. Now, she was heavy, well over 200 lbs., and moved slowly with considerable effort, she said, because of arthritis. She was very emotional and cried at length before composing herself and talking at length about her daughter, who she adored.

"We didn't want Laurie to move out of our house," she said. "It wasn't right, but Laurie had a mind of her own, and she had a responsible job. But maybe things would have been different..."

"When did you talk with her last?" Antonelli said.

"On Wednesday," she said. "She was here for dinner with us."

"Did she say anything about boyfriends, or dates, or other people she was having contact with?"

"She never talked about boys," Karen said. "She did talk about some of the important people she met at The Walters, at some of their events."

"Anyone in particular?"

"I can't think of anyone right now," Karen said. "I'll try to remember. It's hard right now."

Mr. Waslewski said very little until Antonelli asked if any of the family had gone to the rally in the park the night before. His eyes sparked as he sat up on the sofa, looked right at Antonelli and pointed his index finger at him.

"Those bastards," he said. "They're nothing but Nazis. They're not good Americans. They're the enemy. They're bad for the country. You see those armbands they wear. That's just like what the Nazis wore. You know how many Polish people they killed? Millions. Some of them were relatives of ours. No, we wouldn't go to their rally, not once we saw what they were."

"What about Laurie?" Antonelli said. "Might she have stopped by there on her way home from work?"

"No, I don't think so," Waslewski said. "Hell, I don't know. Maybe she did. These kids, they don't feel the way I feel. They don't know what it was like, what those people really are like. So maybe. I don't know. It doesn't make any sense..."

The two teenage children still at home included another good-looking blonde, Annette, and a boy, George, Jr., who looked a lot like his father. They had been brought up properly, Antonelli thought, because they were polite and had good manners while they answered questions. The son went to the rally without telling his father, but he said he left before the riot began. He did not see his sister there.

"What did you think of the rally?" Antonelli asked him.

"It didn't make me feel very good," George said. "There was too much hate. That doesn't help us. We need some help. Things are tough around here. There are a lot of people out of work. People are worried about their neighborhoods and the value of their homes. For most people it's all they have. Something needs to be done. But what these people say will just make it worse. That's why I left."

"Good for you," Antonelli said. "You're right. We don't need that kind of talk here."

"But there are a lot of people around here who don't agree with me," George said. "They might follow these people if they show they can do something."

"I think that all they can do is shout hate," Antonelli said. "If you listen closely to what they actually are saying, they don't have any plan that will do any good. Tell your friends to think past their rhetoric. Ask them to tell you what it is they can do that will do some good. They won't be able to do that. Then they'll understand that these people are bad."

"I hope so," George said.

"What are you going to do after high school?" Antonelli said. George was going into his senior year.

"Dad would like me to go to college. I have decent grades - not great - but good enough for Maryland, and I did well on the PSAT," he said. "But I want to go into the Army."

"You want to be a paratrooper like your father?"

"I don't know, maybe, but I don't think we're doing a lot of that now. Maybe something like AirCav. I'd like to go to Vietnam before it's over."

"Well, it's far from over," Antonelli said. "It's probably going to get tougher there. I'm in the National Guard. We might get sent there eventually."

"I thought that Guard was the way to avoid the draft," George said.

"It's one of the ways. Being a cop is another. So I guess I've got myself covered," Antonelli said, with a laugh. But the truth was he never thought of either as a way of avoiding Vietnam. Sometimes, before the "Blue Girl" murders, he gave serious thought to volunteering. He felt a tug to be with those hundreds of thousands of young men of his generation.

Antonelli knew, because he was one of them, that the sons of these men like Waslewski and his own father, the heroes of World War II, had enormous shoes to fill, and that many struggled with it. At first, Antonelli, like many others, believed the Vietnam War was the chance for the sons of the heroes to be heroes themselves, to show that they were made of the same stuff as their fathers. He could see that young Waslewski had those feelings. But he also believed it was not going to turn out that way. It was not the "good war" their fathers experienced.

Antonelli thought the Waslewski's were a happy and well cared-for family. He and Meador both were deeply touched. As they walked down the street they talked about the family's reaction to Laurie's murder, and to the closeness and honesty of their household.

"This is not something that should happen to such people," Meador said. "This is bad. Our guy is branching out. He's becoming more aggressive. We've got to get the bastard. He's going to keep doing this. At least now we know it's not that artist."

"How so?" Antonelli said.

"This girl wouldn't have walked across the street with Blodgett, someone she didn't know," Meador said. "I don't think her parents would have let her out of their sight if they weren't confident she could handle herself properly. She wouldn't associate with someone like Blodgett. She could have her pick of many guys of much better character, and no doubt, with much better prospects.

"So our guy is someone a girl like Laurie would be attracted to, probably a solid citizen, or a person of some authority. That's the only kind of person she would follow into some place like that Pagoda. I don't think it could have happened any other way. Too many people might have seen him carrying her. She went in there on her own. Bank on it.

"He's not a creep like Blodgett," Meador continued. "He's someone we would never suspect. Hell, he might even be a cop, or pretend to be one. She probably would have liked a good-looking cop, a figure of authority like her father. A cop would have blended right in here last night. There were a couple of hundred here because of that rally, and the riot afterwards."

The Medical Examiner's staff had just finished when Antonelli and Meador returned to the Pagoda. Laurie's body and head were gone. A Crime Lab tech, Mike Robbins, was giving a preliminary summary to Lt. Rauch and two of the other detectives. One of the patrolman said the colonel had left.

"He probably didn't want to make a greater fool of himself," Meador said.

The Crime Lab vacuumed the entire interior of the Pagoda and thoroughly dusted it for fingerprints, finding only one set, which from their questioning, they knew to be those of the attendant who found the body. "This guy is very careful," Robbins said, smiling slightly, "but not quite as much this time."

That got everyone's attention.

"How so?"

We found a couple of thumb tacks that he used to hold black plastic in place around the openings to keep anyone from seeing light inside here," Robbins said. "There appears to be a partial print on one of the thumb tacks. They are awfully hard to handle through gloves. He also used a blue cloth, and it snagged. We have some fibers. There also are some drippings from what probably was a candle. There is some spilled paint. I think he hurried this along and was afraid to take as much time cleaning up afterwards."

"How long will it take to analyze what you found?" Antonelli said.

"It all depends, but we should have some preliminary information in a day or so," Robbins said. "This guy is a neat-nick. He folded her clothes like he was her mother. Nothing is missing from her wallet, including the 100 dollars in cash she had, and her paycheck."

"So you'll be going over those clothes very carefully, I assume," Antonelli said.

"With a microscope. If he left any hairs or prints, we'll find them," Robbins said.

"What did the ME's guy say about the body?" Antonelli said.

"He said it looks just like the others. There isn't the decomposition, so he thinks he'll learn more from the autopsy. We'll know later what drugs he used on her, but I'd bet they will be the same as the others."

Antonelli turned to Meador. "Let's go to the Morgue. I want to be there for the autopsy."

Just then, Antonelli saw Bob Bradley from the *News American* approaching. He had talked his way past the patrolmen who were supposed to keep the public and the news media away from the scene. Antonelli did not recognize the young man with him.

Chapter Twenty

The First Meeting of Antonelli and Prescott

Without having to work shifts in the bureau, Nick has more time to spend on reporting, and Saturday morning he covered the arraignment of Carroll and Lynch on charges of inciting to riot, an action not previously taken against political or civil rights speakers in Maryland. Free speech advocates already were accusing Gelston of acting unconstitutionally.

After they were freed on bond, Carroll and Lynch told reporters in front of the courthouse that they would continue to lead rallies, and would fight the inciting to riot charges as an infringement of free speech.

Nick filed a story on the internal wire to New York for Sunday newspapers shortly after noon. He also wrote a version for the state broadcast wire. Bradley stuck his head in the door at 1:45.

"There's been another murder of a girl with her head chopped off," he said. "I'm heading out there. Want to come?"

So Detective Antonelli saw Nick walking with Bradley toward the Pagoda. Even though they had talked on the telephone several times, they had not met.

Bradley introduced Nick and he and Antonelli shook hands.

"Are we the first reporters here?" Bradley said.

"So far as I know," Antonelli said, "at least the first to get past our barriers."

"What can you tell us?"

"Not a whole lot," Antonelli said. "I only have a couple of minutes. I'm headed for the autopsy."

He gave them a summary of the murder, including the decapitation, but again leaving out the blue paint on her body. He gave them her name and address.

"So it is the same MO?" Bradley said.

"There are many similarities," Antonelli said.

"This time you were able to identify the victim right away," Nick said.

"Yes, because we found her ID at the scene," Antonelli said. He did not mention her clothes, or the fact that her wallet had some cash and her paycheck.

"Could this be some kind of cult rite, or religious rite?" Nick said.

"We don't know, we really don't," Antonelli said. "It's certainly different from anything we've ever seen."

Antonelli and Meador arrived at the Morgue just in time for the autopsy of Laurie Waslewski. Dr. William Paul performed it, talking to the detectives as he went through each step. Antonelli has seen six autopsies in the past year. Meador many times that in his six years in Homicide, but it never got any easier, and this one was very tough.

Paul concluded that she died instantly from the decapitation. He found no other trauma to her body, and no sexual molestation.

"Only one drug was in her system, a powerful tranquilizer that was injected into her left arm. "Interestingly, there are two punctures from needles, but only one drug in her system. He may have injected her twice, maybe the first time to get control of her, and the second time to knock her out.

"So there was no LSD in her system, like there was in the others?" Antonelli said.

"There doesn't appear to be," Paul said, "but the concentration of the tranquilizer is greater. Unlike the other victims, she probably was unconscious when she was killed. We can't know for sure that the others were awake because of the condition of the other bodies, but I am fairly certain that was the case. With the LSD in their systems, they probably had no idea what was going on."

"He probably didn't give her that second injection until they were inside the Pagoda," he said. "Otherwise he would have had to carry her in. She was a big girl, five feet ten inches and 135 lbs. and it would have been a real task to carry her in there, to say nothing of the attention it would have drawn."

He estimated the time of death between 9:00 PM and midnight the night before.

"The Crime Lab took a sample of the paint, but I'll bet it is exactly the same as what was used on the other girls," Dr. Paul said. "It looks the same."

Paul said her body would be completely cleaned of the blue paint and everything that came off her would be put under microscopes. We'll then put her back together so she will look OK for her funeral."

When Antonelli returned to police headquarters, he was called into a meeting with Gen. Gelston. All the members of the "Blue Girl" team were present. Rouch and Antonelli did most of the talking. Antonelli reviewed the first two cases, and Rouch presented what was known about the latest one, supplemented by Antonelli's report on the autopsy.

Antonelli concluded.

"I know it seems very weird, but I swear these women were treated with some respect. There is no evidence of fear, or terror. There's no mutilation of the bodies. The victims weren't tortured, or forced to bear pain. There's no evidence that these are pleasure killings. They aren't sexual or sadistic. I don't know what they are. No one I've talked to has any idea what's going on."

Gelston was serious, but not panicky. He did not berate, or criticize, the officers. He listened to them, asked only a few questions to clarify some points, but not to challenge their presentation. He thanked them for their efforts, and then met privately with the Lieutenant, and his Captain.

The only thing the team heard from that meeting was that six more veteran officers from other departments were going to be assigned to the case. Lieutenant Rouch stopped by Antonelli's desk.

"You did a good job in there, thanks," he said. "The General was very impressed. However, he says that we've got to make some progress quickly. Otherwise, he's going to have to ask the FBI to come in to help. They've already been in touch with him and are ready to step in. We know what that will mean."

"The fuckers will take over," Antonelli said.

"That's right. We don't want that."

"No sir, we don't," Antonelli said. "We're going to solve these murders."

Nick's story of the third "headless blonde" murder hit UPI's national A wire for newspapers and the broadcast wire at 5 PM. Television crews descended on Patterson Park and the East Baltimore neighborhood. It led both the early and late evening newscasts.

Neighbors spoke freely about what a wonderful girl she was. There were some cries of outrage that the police had not caught the killer before now. Some people charged that it was retaliation by Negroes for the attacks on them Friday night.

The Waslewski family refused to appear on television, but did provide a photo of their daughter. Her looks were remarkably similar to those of the other two victims. Nick had the *News American's* photo lab put together a three-photo grouping that he then transmitted over the UPI Newspictures network. It was published by dozens of newspapers on Sunday.

Chapter Twenty-One

The Headless Blonde Murders Become the Blue Girl Murders

The murder of Laurie Waslewski caused the "headless blonde murders" to explode into a major national story. Out of town reporters began arriving on Sunday, and by midday Monday they besieged police headquarters, demanding a news conference, hungering for more detail.

Despite warning everyone involved in the investigation to avoid reporters, the most valuable piece of information withheld from the media so far, the blue painting of the bodies, leaked to The New York Times. Their Tuesday story reported that detail along with more details of the post mortems than previously had been released, including the fact that the girls were not raped, or physically abused. There was furor in the Department all the way up the line, although Gen. Gelston was sanguine about it, saying, "It was bound to leak out sooner, or later."

The beheadings, the bodies being painted blue, and the lack of physical, or sexual abuse were the subject of considerable speculation. Homicide detectives were inundated with phone calls and demands for interviews. The team of detectives investigating the murders operated in a fish bowl, with reporters following them as they searched for evidence and witnesses. Rauch called Antonelli into his office.

"I want you to move your team out of here. I've made a deal with the Southern District. It's usually fairly quiet there. They're going to give you their interrogation room. Take the files and get down there. Do it so the reporters don't know what you are up to. You've got to get on this case and make some progress. You can't do it in this fucking circus."

Nick did very well in the logs during the first couple of cycles, but the New York Times story caught him off-guard. The revelations in the Times story made it the hottest and raciest story in the country. Lu Carr was on the phone to him Tuesday morning, urging him to trump the Times in some way. He remembered the dinner at Dewey's house and the discussion of human sacrifices. He had not seen Dewey since they had lunch, but he was back on Monday, and again on Tuesday, looking better and wanting Nick and Joan to go out with him and Susan.

"I went to a doctor who wants to take a look inside my head," Dewey said. "He thinks I might have a tumor. First, I am going to have to have some tests and some x-rays. Those are in the process of being scheduled. He gave me some really good pain medication, so I'm feeling much better."

"I'm really glad you're doing something," Nick said. "Have you talked with Susan?"

"I talked to her last night," Dewey said. "I'm trying to see it her way, but I could use some help, and support. Maybe it would help some if you and Joan were with us more often. How about dinner at my place on Friday?"

"I think that would be fine," Nick said. "Of course, I'll have to check with Joan. In return, I need some help with these headless blonde murders."

"This is the second one I knew," Dewey said. "It's horrible."

"How did you know Laurie Waslewski?"

"I'm a member of the Walters. I go to events there fairly frequently," Dewey said. "Hell, I tried to get her to go out with me, but she wouldn't. She was nice about it, but she said I was too old for her. How can I help?"

"The New York Times is reporting today that the bodies of the girls were painted blue. I have a call into the detective who is handling the murders, but he hasn't returned it. This revelation makes these murders appear to be similar to Mayan sacrifices, doesn't it?"

"Maybe," Dewey said. "It would be interesting to compare the blue colors. When you come to the house on Friday, I'll show you some blue powder from one of the Mayan sites where they did human sacrifices for hundreds of years."

"I can't wait until then to do my story," Nick said. "New York is all over me, wanting me to come up with something the Times doesn't have."

"Do you have the Times story?" Dewey said.

"Over here," Nick said. He walked to his desk, picked up the Times, and handed it to Dewey.

Dewey sat down and read it.

"I don't know why this is being done," he said. "There's nothing in the story that tells us the purpose, but this sure seems like someone mimicking some aspects of Mayan human sacrifices. They painted their victims blue. They did not abuse them. In fact, women were protected from sexual abuse beforehand. They believed that life continued on another plane after what we know as death, and that the sacrifice was a noble act. They treated their victims with respect even though they sometimes inflicted great pain upon them.

"The two most common forms of human sacrifice were ripping the still beating heart of the victim out of their chests, or throwing them alive into a pit. It was from one of those pits that I got the blue powder. They also decapitated some. They often did it by cutting off their heads from the front, which is the fastest and least painful way of decapitating someone. They used very sharp knives made of obsidian."

Nick rapidly took notes as Dewey went on about Mayan culture and religion.

"I'd like to use some of your photos in a story I'm doing about Mayan human sacrifices. Can you lend me some?"

"Sure, I'll bring in a batch tomorrow," Dewey said.

"Great," Nick said. "I hate to say this, but even though I know you are an expert, you aren't a name expert. I need to talk to someone with some credentials who I could quote in my story."

"I understand," Dewey said. "There are several professors I know who I am sure would love to be quoted. One just published a book on the Mayans. He'd love some publicity."

"Give me their names," Nick said. Dewey took a sheet of paper and wrote down four names.

Nick spent the afternoon making phone calls to the people on Dewey's list. As Dewey said, they were happy to talk to him. All four confirmed what Dewey said, that there were similarities between the murders and Mayan human sacrifices. They also expressed skepticism that they actually were human sacrifices.

Dr. John Ramos, a professor of anthropology at Harvard, and the author of the recently published book, was the most adamant.

"At most, these are attempts by someone to copy the Mayan human sacrifices," he said. "The actual rites of the ceremonies are not known. The codexes that might have contained that information did not survive the Spanish conquests, so far as we know.

"What we know, which is nothing more than some of the basic elements, we know from paintings and drawings," he said. "I have read nothing in the New York Times story, and you have told me nothing else, that indicates the killer did anything more than what is commonly known."

"I understand the Mayan language still is spoken in some areas of Mexico and Guatemala," Nick said.

"Yes, it is widely spoken," Ramos said. "I speak it. Our mutual friend, Dewey Coughlin, speaks it. Many of us who work in that area speak it. Many of the Mayans there don't speak Spanish."

"Is it possible that knowledge has been passed by the oral tradition?" Nick said.

"Certainly," he said. "It not only is possible, it definitely happened, but I think the time lapse since the last Mayan human sacrifices occurred is too great for much knowledge to have passed."

"When was that?"

"We don't know exactly, but to give you some perspective, the Mayan civilization collapsed during the time of the Norman conquest of England, Eloise and Abalard, and the Crusades, in the period of the 11th and 12th centuries. Some cities survived on a much lesser scale much longer, even into the 19th Century, but so far as we know now, human sacrifices ended well before the Spanish arrived in the 16th Century. That's too long ago for any detailed knowledge to have passed down to us orally."

"So you don't think it is likely that the killer could do a full Mayan sacrificial ceremony?" Nick said.

"I think it would be impossible," he said, "but with some knowledge, and some imagination, he could make it appear that he did."

Nick again tried to reach Detective Antonelli, but his calls were not returned. He wrote his story that evening, in which he compared what now was publicly known about the murders to what little was known about Mayan human sacrifices. He quoted Ramos and others as saying that while the killings resembled the Mayan human sacrifices, they almost certainly were not real ceremonies. He raised the question whether the blue painting, and other elements of the killings that were similar to the Mayan rites, simply were done to hide his real purpose, and to confuse the police.

With three pictures Dewey provided him, Nick's story led the UPI reports for Thursday morning and afternoon newspapers, and received widespread play on the front pages of many newspapers, including the *News American*. That prompted Antonelli to return his calls Thursday afternoon.

"I'm sorry I didn't call you back sooner," Antonelli said. "We've been working almost around the clock interviewing people, trying to identify possible suspects, or witnesses."

Antonelli sounded tired and rushed.

"Have you had any luck?" Nick said.

"On the record, we're making progress," Antonelli said. "Off the record, not so much."

"I called you originally to ask you about the human sacrifice angle that I wrote about," Nick said. "I wanted to ask if you had considered the possibility that they were human sacrifices, or were intended to look like them?"

"I saw your story," Antonelli said. "We have considered that possibility. You didn't mention the Museum of Art's Mayan exhibition during the winter. There were some photographs of drawings of human sacrifices, somewhat like the ones in your photos."

"I didn't know there was one," Nick said. "When was it?"

"It ran from November through January," Antonelli said.

"So it ended just at the time of the Barlow killing?"

"That's right." Antonelli said. "Some coincidence, isn't it?"

"There are people who don't believe in coincidences. Are you one of them?" Nick said.

Antonelli laughed. "Let's say I usually am skeptical of them, and from my experience there usually are reasons to be skeptical."

"So the killer may have seen this exhibit and gotten the idea," Nick said. "That doesn't explain why he picked blue-eyed blondes."

"No, and we don't have an idea, either, at least not yet."

"Is it possible that there are multiple killings to disguise just one of them? By that I mean the killer wanted to kill one, but for some reason believed he had to do the others to throw you off his scent."

"I have no way of knowing," Antonelli said abruptly. "I wish I did. I've got to get going, but I wonder if it might be possible to get copies of those photos. The reproduction in the paper isn't very sharp, and I'd like to be able to see the details better."

"I got them from a friend who just took them in Mexico," Nick said. "I'll ask him."

Chapter Twenty-Two

The Pretty Girl and the Policeman

Of course Antonelli had considered the possibility that two of the murders were done to confuse, or to cover up one of the others. He also thought it was possible that all three were done to cover up one that had not yet occurred. He tried to consider every possibility, but it was getting harder to think. He had not slept much since the Waslewski murder.

When he moved his team into the Southern District interrogation room on Tuesday, he brought along some clothes and toiletries, a sleeping bag and an air mattress. He only had slept since then when he couldn't keep his eyes open any longer. The Blue Girl murders were killing him as well. He feared that unless he solved these murders soon, his career in homicide would be finished.

Detectives were sent out to interview all of Laurie Waslewski's friends whose names had been provided by the family and her roommate, including men who recently had dated her. Detectives went through the neighborhoods of Patterson Park, and the area around the Lee Street address, to try to find someone who saw something. Antonelli and Meador interviewed the employees and management of Walters.

They asked almost everyone at the Walters the same set of questions: Did they know of anyone with whom she had a conflict? Did anyone seem to be paying an unusual amount of attention to her? Did she complain about anyone? Did they notice anything unusual about her, or involving her, recently?

No suspects were identified.

"As you probably can imagine, Laurie was an attraction as our receptionist," said the museum's curator, "but she was quite proper and, I think, very selective. Most of the men who approached her were quickly disappointed."

They were given a copy of the membership list of the Walters. It was quite long, and contained the names of many of the city's most prominent people. They compared that list to the Museum of Art's. Many of the names were the same. They began the process of checking the alibis of hundreds of people.

It was late Friday afternoon when Walter Ostrowski told the detectives about the pretty girl and the policeman.

Detective Mike Finch had a hunch. He decided to walk from Laurie Waslewski's bus stop to the Pagoda at about the same time she did it the previous week. He stopped and questioned every person he saw along the way. Ostrowski was sitting on a park bench just inside the park only about twenty feet from the sidewalk.

"I stop by here every Friday afternoon, to get out of the house when my wife is vacuuming. I don't like the noise," he said.

"Yes, I saw a very pretty girl last week. She had long blonde hair," he said. His description of her clothes matched what Waslewski was wearing.

"She was walking with a policeman," Ostrowski said. "She was very close to him. He was holding her arm. No, I couldn't hear anything they were saying. He looked like those other policemen who were around last week, when those people held that rally in the park and caused all that trouble. He had a hat and was wearing sunglasses. Yes, he was white. He was about normal height, only a couple of inches taller than the girl. She was a tall girl. She had a nice figure. Honestly, I noticed more about her than I did the policeman."

Antonelli now believed he knew how the killer got close to all the victims. Disguised as a patrolman he would not have raised suspicion in the alley on the Block. There always were patrolmen in that vicinity. He could have flashed a badge at Crawford and Billingsley and told them to get into his car. And now, it appeared he got Waslewski to go into the Pagoda with him. Antonelli still wondered how exactly he did that, what he might have said. But, at least, they now had something. He was going to try very hard to make sure this piece of information did not leak. It was not going into any report that circulated beyond his team.

Antonelli thought a lot about what Nick had said to him. He again went back over the information they had collected about each of the victims. He read the post mortem reports on each. He didn't find anything, but he called the medical examiner.

"When you did the tox screens on Crawford and Billingsley, did you find any evidence of any recreational drug use, any marijuana, cocaine, etc?"

He put Antonelli on hold and came back after about two minutes.

"A tiny trace of what our tech thought was mescaline was found in Crawford, but he questioned his own finding. Mescaline is a very scarce drug, seldom seen around here. There was nothing in Billingsley. Based on how far it had gotten into his system our tech thinks the mescaline was ingested at least 24 hours earlier."

The murder of Crawford had bothered Antonelli all along. From reading about Mayan human sacrifices he knew that not only were men sacrificed, they may have been the majority of sacrifice victims. He had wondered why Crawford was killed the way he was, just a garroting with a sharp wire. Now he wondered if it was possible that Crawford was the real target, and that the killings of the girls were done to draw attention away from his murder.

Antonelli went to Crawford's fraternity house late in the afternoon on Saturday. He hoped he might find some members staying there for the summer. He found four young men in t-shirts and shorts, playing cards, and drinking beer in the front room. None of them lived in the house during the regular school year, but they all knew Crawford.

"Do any of you know if he used illegal drugs of any kind?"

Silence.

"Don't worry, I'm not vice, I'm trying to track down a piece of the puzzle. You could really help me."

"Yeah, he did some pot and, I think maybe some coke," one said. "None of us was a close friend. That's about all I know." The others nodded but didn't say anything.

"Do you know if he had any close friends who might know a little more?" Antonelli said.

"His best friend was Carl Hodges," one of the others said. The name did not ring a bell. It wasn't on Antonelli's list.

"He is a fraternity brother?"

"He's an alum," the boy said. "He graduated last year, but he and Rory were real close. I think he was Rory's 'big brother.'"

"Is he around?" Antonelli said.

"I haven't seen him recently, but the last I heard he was living with a girl by the name of Betsy in her apartment on Calvert Street. I don't know the number, but I can tell you which house it is. It is the third one from this end, on this side, in the thirty-one hundred block.

With the temperature at 90 degrees at 5:30 PM, it was sweltering in the entry hall to the Calvert Street rowhouse. Hodges' name was not on any of the doorbells, but there was an E. Darner on one. He assumed that was for Elizabeth. He pushed that button. A girl's voice came through the speaker asking who it was.

"I'm Detective Sergeant Maury Antonelli, investigating the murder of Rory Crawford. I would like to talk with Carl Hodges if he is here."

"He's here, I'll buzz you in." she said.

A brown-haired girl, wearing only white shorts and a very thin t-shirt that didn't hide her erect nipples, opened the door. The front room was hot, but Antonelli felt cooler air coming from the rear room, and he heard the whirr of a window air conditioner. Hodges came out of that room, buckling his belt. A good-looking dark-haired guy, he wore only a pair of jeans, showing off muscular arms and shoulders. Betsy retreated to the cooler room.

"Sorry to be bothering you like this," Antonelli said, "but something has come up in the murder of Rory Crawford, and I think you might be able to help me."

"Anything I can do, I hope you catch his killer," Holmes said. "Sit down. Can I get you something cold to drink?"

"No thanks, this will just take a minute," Antonelli said.

"A re-examination of the post mortem on Mr. Crawford now indicates he had used the drug mescaline the day before he disappeared," he said. "Were you aware of his drug use?"

Hodges looked away, and didn't say anything.

"Don't worry, I'm not looking to get anyone in trouble with the narcs," Antonelli said. "I just need to know about his drug use, not anyone else's. You understand?"

"OK, yeah, he had just started using that drug. It's not illegal, but it's not easy to get. He liked it, and he was supposed to get some more so we could try it."

"Yes, do you know who is was going to get it from?"

"Don't know the guy's name. Never saw him, but it's someone from around here, not too far away, because Rory walked to his place."

"Do you know where his place is?"

"No, but somewhere close."

"Do you know anything about this person who supplied the drugs? Is he a drug pusher?"

"No, he wasn't Rory's pusher," Hodges said. "Since mescaline is legal, the pushers don't sell it. Apparently they can't make enough money on it. I think Rory met his source through Karen. He said the guy was a friend of hers."

"He claimed the guy was some kind of scholar, and he did some experimentation with drugs. He gave the mescaline to Rory on condition that Rory keep notes on how he reacted to it."

"On the night Rory disappeared, do you know if he was going to meet this guy and get some more mescaline?"

"I'm sure he was. He was planning to have a good time with Karen that night. He said the mescaline would really loosen her up. Rory said it heightened perception and experience without the bad trip hallucinations of LSD."

"So, he had an arrangement ahead of time to get them?"

"I don't know for sure, but I think so. I only know that because he told me he'd save some for me and Betsy."

"Do you know anyone else who knew about this?"

"Rory didn't make any secret of using pot and coke, but I don't think anyone knew about this."

"You say this man was not Mr. Crawford's pusher," Antonelli said. "Do you know the name of his pusher?"

"I don't know his name," Hodges said. "I've seen him around. He wasn't Rory's pusher anymore. They had a fight. Rory was pissed. He said he got some bad stuff from the guy and he wouldn't pay him."

"What can you tell me about the pusher? Could you recognize him if you saw him again?"

"Sure, I'd recognize him. He's an asshole from the art school, you know the one down in the old train station. He's a painter. I went down there with Rory back in the winter when Rory was having that fight with him. I was there to provide Rory with some protection. The asshole didn't show. I don't think Rory saw him again after that. While we were waiting, Rory pointed out one of his paintings hanging there. It was weird, man, a completely naked girl, all blue except for her blonde hair."

"Your name is not on my list of people we interviewed right after the murder. Didn't you talk with the police then?"

"No, nobody asked me to," Hodges said. "I never talked to any cops. I wondered why no one asked me anything."

Antonelli had planned to spend the night at his apartment for the first time that week. But what Hodges told him changed everything. He went back to the Southern District and checked the files. Sure enough, there was no interview with Hodges. Apparently no one told any of the police investigators about Crawford's best friend. Or one of the investigators forgot, and didn't put his name on the list for follow up. Whatever happened, Antonelli thought, may have cost Laurie Waslewski her life.

Now, he thought, we have a real suspect. It was about 9:00 PM and he and Meador, backed by a tactical team, were getting ready to pick up Blodgett, when two patrolman brought a naked blonde girl, wrapped in a blanket, into the station.

Chapter Twenty-Three

Almost Another Blue Girl Murder

Patrolman Jake Wells came into the interrogation room and said a naked young woman ran up to their patrol car next to Sam Smith Park a few minutes earlier. She said she had just escaped from a man who had a can of blue paint and a big meat cleaver. Would he like to question her? He said he had radioed the dispatcher to send units to the neighborhood to search for her abductor.

Cynthia Baker, a pretty twenty-year old blue-eyed blonde, seemed remarkably composed, considering what she had just gone through. Antonelli pulled a shirt and a pair of pants from his bag and after she put them on, she called her mother, who arrived at the station with some more clothes a few minutes later. They lived only four blocks away.

Her mother, also an attractive blonde, sat next to her, and held her hand, while she told her story. Her father, the captain of a merchant ship, right now was somewhere in the Atlantic.

Baker, a Penn State student home for the summer, told Antonelli and Meador that she was jogging through the park that evening around 8 PM when she was grabbed.

"This big man came out from behind a bush just as I made a turn and grabbed me. He moved so fast he caught me off guard and I couldn't fight back. He put duct tape across my mouth and tied my arms behind my back. He didn't say a word, or make any noise. He then put what looked like a pillowcase over my head and carried me to a car where he put me in the trunk. He taped my legs together, and put duct tape around the pillowcase and tightened it around my neck. I thought he was going to kill me right then."

"We only drove a short distance, maybe a block or two. It sounded like he drove up an alley. I could hear him drive over stuff that wouldn't be on a road. I thought I heard a glass bottle pop. He then got out of the car and I heard a door opened. It was a garage door. He drove the car into the garage, and shut the door. He lifted me out of the trunk and he carried me. I had the sensation of going down.

"He laid me down and he taped my arms and legs down. Then he left. I discovered I could move a little and I began rocking against the tape. I was able to loosen it so I could turn my body a little. I knew that with a little force I could get off that table. Just then I heard him come back

"When he came back, he took the pillowcase off my head, I was on a table in a basement. He was wearing a black cloth mask that covered his entire head. I could see the skin of his neck and his arms. He took out a knife, like a carpenter's knife, and he cut my clothes off. He did it very carefully and didn't cut me."

"He ran his hands all over my body, sort of massaging me, while he mumbled something in language I couldn't understand. I know some Spanish and it wasn't Spanish. He touched me everywhere, but he was gentle."

"Was he wearing gloves?" Antonelli said.

"Yes, surgical gloves like a doctor uses in an examination," she said.

"He didn't say anything to you?"

"Not a word. He kept mumbling, almost singing, but I couldn't understand anything he said. It sounded like he might have had an accent like those accents you hear in commercials for vacations in Jamaica, or the Bahamas."

"He was a Negro?"

"At first I thought he was. He did have dark skin. But now I think it was dark like a Puerto Rican's. He wasn't as black as an African," she said.

"So he could have been Hispanic?" Jenkins said.

"I think he could have been," she said.

"Or Indian, an American or South American Indian?" Antonelli said.

"That also is possible," she said.

"So then what happened?"

"He left me there for a few minutes and left the basement. When he came back he had a meat cleaver, a can of paint, a screwdriver and a paintbrush. He put those down on the floor by the table. He also had a syringe, and a large flashlight, that he put on a small table next to me. He put the paint can down on the floor, and got down on his knees with his back to me, and took the screwdriver to open the can. That's when I made my move."

"How did you do that?"

"I tore off the tape," she said. "I'm a lot stronger than I look, and I can move fast. I grabbed that flashlight from the table and hit him solidly on the head. That sent him sprawling, and I ran out of there. I looked around, but there were no lights on in any of the houses. I just kept running up the street to the next block. He couldn't have caught me if he had tried. I'm a championship runner."

"And swimmer," her mother said.

"I saw the lights of the park and ran as fast as I could towards them. I didn't see the police car until I almost ran into it. They were very nice. They gave me the blanket."

She continued to chatter. Antonelli thought she probably was suffering a little shock, and soon would wind down. He thought she did not fit the profile of the other victims. She was thinner, and had less of a figure. Her hair was shorter, like a swimmer's. She had a fresh-faced, athletic look, not the sultry, curvy, movie star looks of the other victims.

"We're so very happy that you are OK," he said. "Please don't go out jogging by yourself like that again."

"She won't, believe me," said her mother, who had tears running down her cheeks.

Antonelli left the interrogation room and went to talk to the desk sergeant, who made some calls on the radio. He returned to report what heard.

"Police officers have gone through every house in that block," Antonelli said. "They're all empty, some of them undergoing renovation," Antonelli said. "They didn't find anyone. We've got our Crime Lab people coming to go through the houses again. Maybe they will find something."

"I hit him pretty hard with that flashlight," she said. "I bet he bled. I know he didn't move very fast after I hit him."

"We're going to keep extra patrol cars in the area for the time being," Antonelli said.

Crime Lab technicians found a bloodstain and some hair in the basement of one of the houses. A patrolman found her cut-up clothes in a trash can three blocks away. By midnight, the chatter on the police radios, overheard in newsrooms across the city, brought more than two dozen reporters and photographers to the Southern District. It was too late for the Sunday papers, but the story would dominate radio and television news all day Sunday.

Antonelli did not believe that the man who did this was the same man who killed the others. In addition to Cynthia's differences from the other victims, there was a small difference in the MO that Antonelli considered enormously important. He did not subdue Cynthia by injecting her with drugs. If he had, she probably would be dead today. He did have a syringe, but there was no way to know what was in it, or what he was going to do with it.

All the basic elements of the earlier murders that were publicly known were present. The use of drugs to subdue the victims was never reported publicly. That there were no drugs used convinced Antonelli that this was a copycat.

Lt. Rauch agreed with Antonelli but decided to be a bit deceptive when he held a news conference at 11:00 AM on Sunday. He told the media that it appeared the attacker's MO was very similar to that in the murders. He did not say it was exactly the same, and he said nothing about the attacker not using a drug to subdue Baker. Reporters were kept away from Cynthia and her mother.

"We don't know if this was the same person who killed the others," Rauch said, "but it might have been. When the Crime Lab completes its analysis of what we found in that basement, we may have a better idea of who this person is."

While Rauch was holding his news conference at police headquarters, Antonelli and Meador, with a backup tactical team, arrested Victor Blodgett at his apartment, and took him to the Southern District station. Crime lab technicians began another search of his place, and his car.

Chapter Twenty-Four

Victor Blodgett Under Questioning

They held Blodgett on suspicion of drug trafficking and homicide, and the Crime Lab technicians found several dozen packets of marijuana and cocaine, but no mescaline, in his apartment and in his car. Antonelli let Blodgett sit in a holding cell at the station for more than an hour before he began the interrogation. Blodgett was agitated from the time they picked him up, and he paced the holding cell for the entire hour he was held there.

The Supreme Court was about to rule on a case that involved the right of a suspect to an attorney, and to refuse to talk to the police, as Antonelli had mentioned to Meador earlier. He did not want to jeopardize this case by not giving Blodgett every right possible. So before he began the questioning, he said to Blodgett:

"I want you to know that you are suspected of drug trafficking, and of multiple homicide. You don't have to talk to us. You can have an attorney. If you don't know of an attorney, we'll get one for you. There are lots of them around. If you do choose to talk with me, I can use anything you say against you. Do you understand this?"

"Yeah, I understand. I don't need an attorney. I didn't hurt anyone."

Antonelli put a paper in front of Blodgett.

"This says you have waived your right to an attorney, and are talking to us of your own free will, and that we can use anything you say against you in court. Sign it. The date is June 27."

He signed the paper, and dated it.

"Look, I deal some drugs a little," he said to Antonelli. "It's just for spending money. It's not a big deal. You can see that I don't have a lot of money. I don't want to go to prison. I haven't hurt anyone, I swear."

"Tell me about Rory Crawford," Antonelli said. "You and he had a fight over some drugs you sold him that he didn't pay for. Isn't that true?"

"Yes, it's true," Blodgett said, "but he made a bigger deal out of it than it really was. I got screwed on this. I got some marijuana that was crap. Maybe half of it was something else. I sold a bunch of it to Crawford. The next time I see him, he asks me for some cocaine. I give him some and he refuses to pay. He said the marijuana was shit, and since he paid me for that, he wasn't paying for the cocaine. The cocaine was $500, a lot more than the marijuana, and I told him I never would sell to him again if he didn't pay."

"You didn't threaten him?"

"Well, I might have said a few things to try to get him to pay me, but it was all bullshit. Look at me. I'm not someone who frightens anyone. I don't own any guns. But him not paying me put me in a real bind. I needed that money."

"I understand you were to meet him one day to resolve things, but you didn't show up," Antonelli said.

"I was watching from where he couldn't see me," Blodgett said. "He brought muscle with him, a big guy. I split. I never saw the creep again."

"You didn't kill him?"

"Hell no," Blodgett said. "I didn't want anything more to do with him."

"OK, tell me where you were on Friday the 17th," Antonelli said.

"I was in portrait class in the morning, and off in the afternoon," he said. "I hung out with some of the other students for a little while, and then came home. I stayed home all evening."

"Can anyone verify that?"

"I don't think so," he said. "I didn't see anyone."

"Did you know Laurie Waslewski?"

"The girl who was murdered last week, the receptionist at the Walters?"

"Yes, that's the one."

"I knew who she was. I went to the Walters sometimes. It was hard to miss her. She was a very good-looking girl."

"Did you ever talk to her?"

"I might have," Blodgett said, "yeah, sure, I talked to her. It didn't do me any good. She didn't have any interest."

"You offered her some drugs?"

"Yeah, I guess I did. She didn't like that. She wouldn't talk to me after that."

Antonelli put Blodgett back in the holding cell to let him stew for another hour. Again, Blodgett paced the floor, which was not a good sign. Antonelli knew that innocent people usually were far more upset about being held in a cell than people who were guilty. Another hour of questioning resulted in exactly the same answers.

The search of Blodgett's apartment and car turned up nothing that could link him to any of the murders, no police uniform, no blonde hair in the car, no tempera paint. They could charge Blodgett with drug possession, but Antonelli didn't have the case to charge him with the Blue Girl murders, at least not yet. He decided to release Blodgett, but to keep him under periodic surveillance.

Antonelli wanted to know more about mescaline, so he consulted a detective he knew in vice, Detective John Keever.

"Tell me about mescaline," he said. "Is it used much? Is there much trafficking in it?"

Keever explained to Antonelli that mescaline is the active ingredient in peyote, which comes from a cactus, and is widely used in Native American and Central American Indian religious ceremonies.

"It is a mild hallucinogen, and it's not very popular, probably because it is so mild, by comparison with others. It's not even classified as a drug. It's a chemical. It's not illegal, so it is sold by mail order by various companies. Since it can be purchased legally, and relatively inexpensively, the drug pushers usually don't sell it. There's no profit in it. Some people think it should be illegal, although I really don't know why. I think it's pretty harmless."

.

Chapter Twenty-Five

Nick and Maury Have Dinner at the Antonelli Family Restaurant

The Blue Girl murders were back on the front pages on Monday, and Nick tried repeatedly, without success, to track down Antonelli. He drove over to the police headquarters, only to be told that Antonelli, and all of the detectives assigned to the case, were not available. He left messages that he had the photos that Antonelli wanted, but no one called him. He tried to find the Baker girl by using a directory of addresses. But when he went to her address, no one answered the door.

That evening Lieutenant Rauch was a guest on the John Sterling show on WCBM, the city's major radio talk show. Caller after caller expressed concern about the safety of blue eyed, blonde women. Rauch tried to assure listeners that the police were confident they would catch the killer. At the same time he asked for help.

"Please call us if you see anyone suspicious in your neighborhood, anyone you are not used to seeing, especially if that person follows you."

Nick felt overwhelmed. The amount of news coming out of Baltimore right now was more than his small operation could effectively cover. His hours were getting longer and longer. Antonelli finally called him on Wednesday morning.

"I'm sorry again for being slow calling you back," Antonelli said. "This has been a hell of a week."

"I can imagine," Nick said. "Any developments?"

"I really think we are close to cracking this case, but we're not there yet, and please don't quote me saying that," Antonelli said.

"I have those photos, and quite a few more, if you still want them," Nick said.

"Thanks," Antonelli said. "Why don't you let me buy you dinner, at my father's restaurant, Antonelli's in Little Italy."

"Thanks," Nick said. "What time?"

They met at 7:30. The maitre d' led Nick to a corner booth, elevated two steps above the others on the floor. Antonelli shook his hand. He already had ordered an antipasto and a carafe of wine.

"Nice booth," Nick said, looking around the room.

"It's the family booth. No one who sits here has to pay for a meal," Antonelli said. "But, believe it or not, this is my first decent meal in almost two weeks. I've been going around the clock on this case."

"I brought my girlfriend here a few weeks ago," Nick said. "We liked it a lot." He handed Antonelli a large envelope. The detective opened it and took out the photographs. They all were in color. He looked through them while sipping his wine and picking at the antipasto.

"Sorry, I forgot," he said. He waved to a waiter. "We need to order our food. My dad's working tonight and he makes a great veal marsala. So that's what I'm having."

"That sounds terrific, I'll have it, too," Nick said. The waiter smiled and walked away.

"These photos are something," Antonelli said. "I have been trying to learn a lot about the Mayans pretty fast. I read a book, *The Ancient Sun Kingdoms of the Americas*, that had a long section on the Mayans. It was really interesting. I never knew anything about them before. They had an incredible civilization."

"I've been learning a lot about them as well," Nick said. "The man who took these photos is a friend of mine, and he is quite an expert. He just got his masters at Hopkins in anthropology. He took these photos for a book he is trying to get published. It is on the Mayan culture. It was his Masters thesis."

"What's his name?"

"Dewey Coughlin," Nick said. "He's a legend around Hopkins. He comes from an old and wealthy Baltimore family, and he has spent more than a dozen years as a student off and on at Hopkins. I think he finally ran out of courses to take. They gave him a BA and an MA this year."

"The name rings a bell," Antonelli said. He tried to remember why, but couldn't.

"He works in the circulation department at the *News American*," Nick said. "Why he does, I don't know. He inherited a fortune from his parents, both of whom died a couple of years ago. He says there isn't much cash in the estate and he needs money."

"I'd like to meet him," Antonelli said. "Maybe I could learn something about the Mayans from him."

"I'm sure he'd be happy to help in any way he can," Nick said. "He's an amazing person in many ways. He speaks the Mayan language, among other things. My girlfriend and I had dinner with him, and his girlfriend, at his house on Friday night. His talents include being a great cook. He showed us some blue powder he brought back from a Mayan site in the Yucatan in Mexico. Archaeologists found a 14-foot thick layer of the powder at one site where human sacrifices were done for hundreds of years. It's beautiful, but really creepy, being the combination of the paint they used on their victims, and the decayed remains of those they threw into a deep well, usually alive."

They chatted for a few minutes more before their meals arrived. Nick found the veal to be wonderful, and the great food quieted them for a short time.

"People are always commenting about me being so young to be a bureau manager for UPI, but you seem very young to be a detective sergeant," Nick said. "You must be the youngest one on the force."

"I guess I am," Antonelli said. He told Nick a little of his background, and his love of solving mysteries.

"I am determined to solve these Blue Girl murders. I have to solve them. I do wonder if the blue paint and the beheadings were done just to confuse us. I don't believe these really were human sacrifices. I don't see how that is possible. I think someone went to that exhibition at the Museum of Art, and got the idea. What has become very important in these cases is why? What is the motive?

"Believe it or not, motive usually is not a big deal in a murder investigation," Antonelli said. "It is a big deal on television shows, and sometimes it is important in a trial, but normally it isn't very important to solving the case. Most of the time, if the murderer isn't obvious, we catch him because there either are witnesses, or there is physical evidence. In these cases we don't have either. It's pretty remarkable that he's pulled off three of these without leaving any useful physical evidence, and without any witnesses. It's diabolical.

The guy is smart, and very careful. So, I'm trying to find motive. Maybe that's hidden in this Mayan stuff."

"That's fascinating," Nick said. "This is the first time I've ever covered a murder case in any detail. I didn't realize how little I knew about crime investigation. At UPI we don't have beats like the newspaper reporters. We report all the news, as well as sports and weather. We're an electronic newspaper, and a broadcaster, except we don't serve the public. I don't get much time to devote to any one story."

"I don't know much about your business," Antonelli said. "Most of the time I'm trying to avoid getting my name in the paper, and trying to keep details of my investigations out of the paper. Some of the reporters seem to be OK, but most of the time you all are a pain in the ass."

"It's a natural conflict," Nick said. "Our jobs are completely different. Our job is to get those details for the public that you don't want publicized.

"Sometimes I think I'd rather be doing what you are doing," Nick said, "or maybe I should get into politics, or government. As a journalist I'm more or less just watching from the sidelines. I'm a spectator providing information to others who can't even be spectators. I wonder if it would be more satisfying to be a player, causing things to happen, rather than just watching them."

"It's only satisfying when you succeed," Antonelli said, "and you have to succeed most of the time. It is hard to have a normal life. The job becomes your life. Right now I am living..." He stopped himself. "I'm sorry, but I almost told you something I can't tell you."

"Something about the case?"

"I can't say," Antonelli said.

"Look, I'm not the kind of reporter who will betray a confidence to get a story. I won't report anything you tell me that is confidential."

"I appreciate that, but I just got carried away there," Antonelli said. "I've enjoyed our dinner. It's been interesting, and I really appreciate you getting me these pictures. When can I meet your friend?"

"I'll probably see him tomorrow, and I'll ask him to call you," Nick said. "For the next several days I'm going to have the CORE convention to cover, so I'm going to be buried. I'm sure he'll be happy to talk to you. He likes to talk."

Chapter Twenty-Six

CORE Attempts to Integrate a Bar

"Now that King's going to be here, the CORE convention will be have a Who's Who of the civil rights movement," Nick said to Marsha, who was working the morning shift. Nick was looking through materials provided by CORE, including Wednesday's announcement by Floyd McKissick, National Director of CORE, that Dr. Martin Luther King, Jr. would be a speaker.

"We're going to get some extra help," Nick said.

"What do you mean?"

"Stan Scott will be here shortly," he said. "He's UPI's national civil rights reporter, and he was the first Negro to work for UPI. He was there when Malcolm X was assassinated. I hear he's very good."

"I guess he'd have to be," Marsha said. "I know what it's like to be the first woman here."

Nick laughed.

"Oh, come on, I'm not any tougher on you than I am on anyone else."

"No, you're not, but I have this feeling that the guys are just waiting for me to fuck up."

"Don't be paranoid," Nick said. "You already are on a better shift, but it's not because you are a woman. It is because you are doing a good job, and the clients like your work."

Just then a tall black man with closely cropped hair walked in the door. He looked to be in his 30s and had an intense, energetic aura. He wore a charcoal gray pinstripe suit with a white shirt and an elegant regimental tie, a combination that Nick guessed cost more than his entire wardrobe.

"Hi, I'm Stan Scott," he said. "I presume someone told you I was coming."

"Yes, I heard from NX yesterday," Nick said, using the UPI code for the New York bureau. "I'm Nick Prescott. This is Marsha Golding." They all shook hands.

"What can I do to help you?" Nick said.

"I talked to Floyd this morning, and I've got all the basic information. Will it be possible for you to go with me? I don't know my way around, and I'd rather not drive."

"Sure," Nick said. "I was planning to cover the convention. It's going to be big, with King coming."

"I don't think he's coming," Scott said.

"McKissick just put out a news release, saying he's coming," Nick said.

"I talked to Martin yesterday. He's heard that there's going to be a move at the convention to endorse Black Power. He's opposed to that, and he doesn't want to be associated with it. Floyd has been trying to negotiate something less than that, but he may not be able to. There's a big split going on in the Civil Rights movement."

"I've got a couple of white friends who work for CORE as organizers," Nick said. "What does this Black Power thing mean for them?"

"Well CORE used to be half white," Scott said, "but after this convention, the number of white members probably is going to drop a lot. The movement's going to be different from now on."

Dewey Coughlin came in while Scott and Nick were talking, and dropped the early edition of the paper on Marsha's desk. He nodded to Nick, and started reading the wires, as he usually did. Nick turned over his desk to Scott, who said he needed to make some phone calls, and walked over to Coughlin.

"Detective Sergeant Antonelli was very happy to get those photos," Nick said. "Thanks. He'd like to talk with you. He's trying to learn more about the Mayans. He isn't convinced of the connection to these murders, but he's following every possible lead. Will you call him?"

"Sure, I'll be happy to. Give me his number."

Nick took a sheet of newsprint from slot desk, wrote Antonelli's name and number and handed it to Dewey.

"Who's that?" Coughlin said, motioning towards Scott.

Nick told him.

"Your outfit is the wave of the future," Coughlin said. "Negroes and women are coming into the business in a big way. In a few years we white guys will be outnumbered."

"I guess you'll be tied up this weekend," Dewey said.

"Yes, this convention's a big deal," Nick said. "I think Susan is covering it as well."

"Yeah, I know. We probably won't see each other until it's over. She won't exactly blend in, will she?" Coughlin said with a grin.

"Not quite," Nick said.

When Scott was finished his telephone calls he told Nick that there was going to be a demonstration at a bar late that afternoon, one of the bars that legally could refuse to serve Negroes. "Some of the CORE delegates are in town early, and they want to make some noise. So they're going to try to integrate one of your bars."

It was a dive of a bar on a corner of Guilford Ave., about three blocks from North Avenue, in the declining north central section of the city, a bar that almost certainly none of the CORE members ever would have entered if it didn't refuse to serve Negroes. Four of the CORE members, three men and a woman, all blacks, went into the bar, sat at the counter and demanded service. Nick, and a half dozen other reporters, followed them in. Stan Scott had skipped the protest to meet with McKissick. The four were dressed well, Nick thought, especially for this bar. The men wore sport coats and slacks, and the woman wore a dark blue suit.

The small bar's principal attraction appeared to be the color television at one end of the wood bar. Otherwise it was dim and dull-looking. Six men were seated at that end, drinking bottles of National Bohemian, a local Baltimore beer. There were eight Formica-surfaced tables along the wall, but no one was seated there. The six men just stared at the visitors. The bartender, a balding middle-aged man, apparently expected the protest. He had copies of the city ordinance that exempted his bar from the public accommodations law.

"Your beef is with the city, not us," he said, "and we've got none with you. We're complying with the law. We can legally refuse to serve you, and that's what we're doing. You can sit there as long as you want, and if they change the law while you're here, then I'll serve you."

About fifty CORE members, half of them white, picketed the bar outside. Most of them were young, dressed in t-shirts and blue jeans, but a young Negro, wearing a suit, seemed to be leading the protest. An equal number of police formed a line that separated the demonstrators from everyone else, although few people were paying much attention to the protest.

Nick went outside and saw a radio newsman he knew standing on a corner, talking to a cop. He heard the cop say, "it's not like the old days, Eddie, when we could take them into an alley and beat the shit out of them."

The protest ended after about an hour without any incidents, or arrests. Several CORE members said they would have more protests later. However, that didn't happen. Major Harris hosted a welcome party by the city for the CORE delegates that night. The free food and drink, as well as the air conditioning, diverted the delegates from organizing any protests in the heat that evening.

He kept the bar open until 2 AM, when all the bars in the city had to close.

"Now you can go integrate another bar," he said to much laughter.

Chapter Twenty-Seven

Stokely Carmichael Speaks at the CORE Convention

The CORE delegates met in an un-air-conditioned Masonic temple in a black section of the city. The temperature that afternoon nearly hit 100 degrees and Nick thought it must have been 90 inside the auditorium. Black Muslims, never before welcome at CORE events, handed out copies of their *Muhammad Speaks* newspaper to everyone entering the building. The auditorium filled with people electric with the feeling they would witness a historically important event.

About 400 sweating people were in the hall when Stokely Carmichael, the 25-year old head of the Student Non-Violent Coordinating Committee, walked to the podium to begin his keynote speech. Carmichael took off his jacket, loosened his tie, and turned up the heat.

As the leading advocate of "Black Power," of which a key component was criticism and rejection of integration, Carmichael opened by saying, "the extremists in this country are not us. They are the ones who forced the Negroes to live in the conditions they are now in."

In response to shouts of "Black Power, Black Power," from the audience, he said it was time for Negroes to take control of the movement,

"This is not a movement being run by the liberal white establishment, or by Uncle Toms. What have you been doing all the time is letting them define how we are going to fight."

The mood and the priority for the convention were set. It was not a comfortable moment for the whites in the crowd. A white nun in the crowd said to a reporter, "This is the Congress for Racial Superiority."

Nick saw his friends Stuart Epstein and Rachel Kohn in the audience and went over to talk to them about Carmichael's speech. They did not seem to be very happy with it.

'We've given a lot of ourselves to the movement, and he doesn't seem to appreciate it," Rachel said.

"I think I understand what he means, and maybe he's right," Stuart said, "but I think he could have said it differently."

Carmichael had an energizing effect on the younger blacks in the crowd. Nick went to the restroom in the basement and found the small room crowded with young black men. Some muttered as he stood at the urinal. One young man said to another, "You know my great granddaddy was a slave. What do you think about that, white boy?"

Nick zipped up, turned and looked at the young man. He knew what he wanted to say, that his great granddaddy was in the Union Army and was killed at Fredericksburg, helping to free the kid's great granddaddy, but he said nothing. He nodded to the young man and walked out. He heard laughter in the men's room. As he went back up the stairs, he could feel his heart beating hard, and some sweat on his forehead. Things definitely were changing.

When he got to the top of the steps he heard some shouting. He ran into the auditorium and he found a crowd of reporters and cameramen yelling at Stan Scott. A *Sun* photographer who did stringer work for UPI lay on the floor, rubbing his chin. Susan stood off to the side.

"What's going on?" he said to her.

"That black guy, whoever he is, just punched that photographer, knocking him flat on the floor."

"Why'd he do that?"

"Carmichael and McKissick were having a press conference, and I think the photographer bumped him with his camera, hit him in the head with it, jostling for position."

Scott saw Nick and came over.

"Son of a bitch," Scott said. "He hit me in the head, and they're all yelling at me for punching him. That's what we do to photographers like that in New York. You let them get away with that here?"

"Yeah, we do, especially when the guy is working for us," Nick said. "That's Michael Lampkin. He's our stringer. He was covering this for us."

"Oh shit," Scott said. "I guess I better help him up."

Scott went and bent over Lampkin. He then helped him to his feet, apologizing profusely. That seemed to pacify the reporters, who wandered away. Lampkin saw Nick and marched over.

"I get something extra for this, don't I?" he said.

"Sorry, Mike, he didn't know who you were."

"Yeah, well I didn't mean to bop him in the head, but he didn't have to punch me. So he's one of your big name writers? Was he like this before he heard Carmichael start the race war tonight?

"Who is he?" Susan said motioning towards Scott.

Nick told her, and introduced her a couple of minutes later. She seemed impressed by the handsome and volatile Scott. He chatted with her for a few minutes, but seemed distracted. He excused himself and pulled Nick aside.

"Look, I've been invited to a private gathering tonight. It's all off-the-record, but it will give us some good background for what's going to happen in the next couple of days. Thing is, it's just me. I can get a ride back to the hotel. I'll meet you at the bureau in the morning, say around 9?"

"That's fine," Nick said.

"That blonde is hot. You got something going there?"

"No, she really is just a friend."

"Sure, and I'm the Grand Dragon of the Ku Klux Klan. Good luck. I'll see you tomorrow."

The delegates to the CORE convention adopted "Black Power" as the slogan and philosophy of the organization, rejecting integration, and the term "Negro." Responsibility for advancing the causes of the civil rights movement from now on would be in the hands of blacks. The goal would be to have blacks gain positions of power wherever they could. While white support was welcomed, white leadership was not. CORE now clearly was at odds with the NAACP and the Southern Leadership Conference. The media viewed the change in direction that CORE adopted in Baltimore as a watershed, as the direction the entire civil rights movement eventually would go.

Scott wrote the national stories and won the national logs by a large margin. Nick supplemented his stories for the state broadcast wire. He also got to know a couple of the local black newsmen who worked for black radio stations in Baltimore.

Scott and Nick had breakfast together at the Hilton Hotel on Sunday morning. Scott was in a philosophical mood.

"Do you know what this slogan 'Black Power' really means?" he said.

Nick wasn't sure what he meant by the question, and given that he responded, "I'm not sure I know what you mean. Doesn't it speak for itself?"

"No, really it is sort of an unfortunate choice, but it's done and there's nothing we can do about it," he said.

"What this really is about are rights that everyone has, rights that are not limited by skin color, sex, race, etc. but are possessed by all human beings, those inalienable rights that are in the Declaration of Independence. These are rights that no one gets to vote on. No one gets to grant, or deny them. No one can give them up. We all have them. At least, we all should have them."

Scott sat forward in his chair and looked right at Nick.

"But black people have not had them," he said. "We were enslaved. The Jim Crow laws discriminated against us. All kinds of laws still discriminate against us. I can't walk into a bar in Baltimore and be sure I will be served. That's wrong. You know it's wrong."

"Of course," Nick said. "But it's ending, the times really are changing."

"Things are changing, but they are changing according to the will of white people," Scott said, "according to how fast they are willing to change.

"Think about that for a minute," he said. "We are the only people in America whose inalienable rights have been alienated. Now that we are demanding the right to exercise the rights that everyone else has, we have to wait for white people to adjust to the idea. They don't have the right to control our rights. No one does. We are not going to wait any longer for the white man to give us our rights. This is what 'Black Power' is all about. We are now asserting our rights, demanding our rights, and saying that white people no longer are in control of our rights. Does that make sense to you?"

"It does," Nick said. "I understand, but practically speaking, things just don't change overnight. You are asking for people to change their attitudes very suddenly. That's not human nature."

"True, it isn't," Scott said, "and we know things are not going to change suddenly. There's a long struggle ahead, but it is time for us to stand on our own and to prove ourselves. That's what Stokely was saying, and I think he speaks for his generation, and for many others."

"You, too?"

"I think I took that step a while ago," Scott said. "I made myself a free man. I compete in the white man's world, and I do it reasonably well, but I'm my own man. I'm doing it on my terms. I'm just the beginning. Millions are going to follow, maybe not right away, but in your lifetime I think you will see it happen. And I didn't punch that photographer because he was white. I have a temper. Sometimes I can be an asshole like anyone else. Every man has that right. I'll punch anyone who interferes with my body, or my rights. Race has nothing to do with it. That is the fundamental principle."

Nick talked by phone with Stuart Epstein.
"So what are your plans?" Nick said.
"We're leaving CORE," he said. "It's time for whites to get out of the movement. They've got their own leaders now. They don't need us anymore. We're going to move over to the antiwar movement. I think that's going to be huge before long."
Nick thought he probably was right. Protests against the war were increasing in number and size, along with the number of casualties, mostly of young men who were drafted.

Two days later, the news director of black radio station WEBB, Eric Blair, with whom Nick spent some time during the CORE convention, invited Nick to ride with him in the inner city, to get a feeling for what it was like. They spent two hours driving around sections of the city that Nick, and most white people, usually didn't go into, and knew little about. His station was a daytime-only operation, so that night he had WWIN on the radio, with the city's most popular black disk jockey playing rhythm and blues and soul music. It was hot and there were hundreds of people on the sidewalks. Music was blasting from everywhere, and a low rumble from the bass and the heavy beat echoed from the buildings into the streets.
Nick did not feel threatened by the crowds and the raucousness. Much of it was good natured and friendly. He could feel the energy. Wilson Pickett's rousing "Mustang Sally" and his haunting "In the Midnight Hour," were reverberating from radios around them, with the crowds moved to the music. But in that he also felt the potential of danger.

Some on the sidewalks waved to the car, marked with the station's call letters. Blair stopped periodically and chatted with people who walked up to the car.

"There's a lot of tension in the community," he said. "Folks are fed up with those white power rallies. There could be a problem if they continue."

"They've indicted some of the leaders, but they haven't been able to stop them from holding the rallies yet," Nick said. "If they get convicted, they'll get sent to prison. That will stop them."

"There are rumors on the street about some brothers who have a machine gun in a panel truck," he said. "It's probably not true. But you can't be sure. There is talk about retaliating against those white supremacists. People won't tolerate that here for very long. This isn't Alabama or Mississippi. So it's possible there is something to the rumors. If you go to another one of those rallies, be careful. The situation is dangerous, especially as hot as it is."

"It's ten o'clock and it's 90 degrees in the city," said the disc jockey, followed by James Brown belting out "This is a man's world."

Chapter Twenty-Eight

Antonelli Reveals His Secret to Maria Conseco

Antonelli heard some grumbling about the CORE convention, and their adoption of the slogan, "Black Power," from some of his detectives, but it added little to the anxieties he already felt. The pressure to solve the Blue Girl murders got worse every day, and if it were not for Maria, he would not think of anything else.

With the racial situation in the city close to explosive, he found himself wondering more and more what it was like to be a Negro, or to be considered a Negro. He about 25% Negro and he didn't look like one. But from what he had read, that percentage was enough for many to consider him a Negro. Sometimes he had the strongest sensation of wanting to talk to some of the Negro activists in CORE to find out how they would view him.

He also really wanted to talk to his father about how his family might react if he were to reveal the truth. So far, he had been unable to do that. How would they react in Tony's Bar, just down the street from his apartment building, where he often had a drink after work in the days when he went home after work. Would they refuse to serve him? He could not avoid doing something soon. His relationship with Maria depended on it.

They started going out on formal dates after classes ended in May, and after Antonelli met her parents and asked her father for permission to court his daughter.

He told her parents about his family and their restaurant, and explained his position in the police department. He said he wished to call on their daughter regularly, and that his intentions were entirely honorable. Antonelli thought her parents seemed both surprised and pleased that he not only understood this custom, but also carried it out with the proper respect. Of course he did. There still were families in Little

168

Italy where similar customs were practiced, including his own. Only a month ago, the boyfriend of the older of his two sisters made a similar appearance before his father and stepmother.

Maria's father, Roberto Conseco, did all the talking. Her mother, Angelina, smiled gently, and embraced him when it was over. Conseco appeared to be about 50 years old and quite physically fit. Clean-shaven, with streaks of gray in his jet-black hair, and wearing slightly tinted glasses, he seemed almost military in his bearing. He spoke English quite well, with only a slight accent. He questioned Antonelli about his work as a detective. He seemed quite knowledgeable of police work, and made Antonelli promise to keep Maria away from his work, and not expose her to any danger that he might face.

They were going out twice a week, and abiding by her father's condition that they not be alone in his apartment, or anywhere else. They went to movies, had dinner, and went to concerts. They made out in his car. There was no chance of any sex except for some heavy petting. He did get to fondle her firm and ample breasts, but knew that anything more than that could not occur until they were formally engaged, if then. That was fine with him. He thought it was a good custom, even though it seemed so much out of date.

Maury knew he was serious about Maria and he was very tempted to play it safe, and say nothing about his mother. But it felt cowardly and wrong. Sitting in the family booth with Maria on Saturday night of the 4th of July weekend, he decided to tell her.

"I have a secret I am going to tell you," he said, "but you have to give me your solemn promise that you never will reveal it to anyone else without my permission. Regardless of what happens between us, you must promise on your family's honor, never to say anything. Can you do that?"

She looked at him quizzically, concern in her eyes.

"It's nothing illegal, immoral, or criminal," Antonelli said. "It is a family secret."

"Yes, then I make you that promise."

"Say it, it's important," he said.

"I promise I never will reveal your secret without your permission," she said, smiling.;

"My mother was from Jamaica. She was half Negro. That makes me about 25% Negro."

He waited to watch her reaction. She blinked her eyes.

"That's the secret?" she said.

"Yes, my father told everyone in the family that my mother was Sicilian. No one knows she was Jamaican and part Negro."

"And if they knew?"

"It would be a disaster," Antonelli said. "It could tear the family apart. It probably would kill my father. I probably couldn't come here again."

"Really? They hate Negroes that much?"

"Some do, but most would regard it as shameful, as embarrassing. It would be threatening to their whole world."

"I have some Negro blood," Maria said. "My great grandmother was a Negro. It's not a big deal to us Cubans."

"It doesn't bother you?"

"Not at all. Some say it makes a man more macho, maybe more virile," she said, and laughed. "Maybe one day I can find out if that is true."

"I hope you can find that out with me," Antonelli said. "I love you, and I want us to get married. Will you marry me?"

Her smile vanished into a very serious look.

"I didn't expect this," she said. "I love you, also, but this is very fast. I would have a difficult time with my parents. I think we have to wait a little while longer."

"If I have to, I can wait," Antonelli said. "I just want you to know that I am sure about this. I want you to be sure, also. I can wait until you are ready, but I hope that is not a very long time."

"Let's wait until the fall," Maria said. "If we then still are sure, then you can ask my parents."

"Well, I think we should celebrate now." He waved to the waiter and ordered two glasses of champagne.

"Since we are sharing secrets, I have one I think I have to tell you, now," she said. "You have to make the same promise to me. You will not reveal it to anyone without my permission."

"I make that promise," Antonelli said. "I never will reveal any secret of yours to anyone without your permission."

"My name really isn't Conseco," she said.

"What is it?"

"I can't tell you now," she said. "Maybe if we do decide to get married, maybe then I can tell you. Maybe then I will have to tell you. But right now, I cannot."

"Why?"

"My father was an officer in the Cuban Army, a special unit of the Army that provided protection to Battista and his family," she said in a low voice, after looking around. "He got his military training in the U.S. He is a graduate of the Virginia Military Institute."

"That explains why his English is so good," Antonelli said.

"Yes," she said. "He became disillusioned with Battista, and he went over to the rebel side. He joined Castro in the mountains, and was with him when they went into Havana. Castro made him a Colonel in his security force. However, when Castro embraced communism, and the Soviets, he arranged to defect to the U.S. We went on a family vacation to Mexico, and there we met some people, probably CIA. We got new identities, including all the papers, and were set up here in Baltimore. We all became citizens last year."

"So why the secrecy about your real name?"

"Because he is viewed as a traitor by both sides, my father believes we would not be safe if anyone knew our real name."

"Well, your secret is safe with me," Antonelli said. "I think the next thing I would like to do is have your parents meet mine. We have a tradition of a Sunday dinner for the family at home. It is too late for tomorrow, but how about I arrange an invitation for next Sunday?"

"That would be wonderful," she said.

Chapter Twenty-Nine

Antonelli Interviews Coughlin

Homicide detectives had interviewed nearly 1,000 people concerning the Blue Girl murders, including nearly every man they could identify who ever had dated any one of the girls. As it turned out, Dewey Coughlin was the exception. He was on three lists, but no one had talked to him.

After Nick told him about Coughlin, Antonelli checked the names on the various lists the team had assembled. There was a list for each victim, including all their relatives and known friends, people they had dated, people they had worked with, and anyone else possibly connected to them. For Barlow, because her murder occurred just after the Mayan exhibit concluded at the Baltimore Museum of Art, there was a list of Museum of Art members and contributors. For Waslewski there was a similar list of Walters members and contributors. Dewey Coughlin's name was on both museum lists. He also was on a list of men who had dated Karen Billingsley.

Now Antonelli wondered why no one had talked with Coughlin. He was to blame for missing him on the Museum of Art list. He had interviewed fewer than half the people on the list before he turned it over to the team following the Crawford-Billingsley murders. A note from another detective indicated a visit was made to his house, but no one was home. There was no follow up.

A similar note was on the list of men who had dated Billingsley. Two visits were made to his house, but there was no follow up. He had not yet been overlooked on the Walters list because the detectives doing those checks had not yet gotten to him.

Antonelli received a call from Coughlin shortly after noon on Monday.

"Nick Prescott told me you would like to talk with me, that you are trying to learn more about the Mayans," Coughlin said. "I'll be happy to talk to you at my house after 7:00 PM any evening except Saturday when I work at night."

Antonelli said he would come by that evening.

Antonelli and Meador arrived at his house exactly at 7 PM. Antonelli was fanatical about being on time. Coughlin answered their knock within moments.

Coughlin immediately impressed Antonelli as the stereotype of the Baltimore society guy. He was light haired and blue eyed, a medium build, with a gracious but not intimate style, keeping just a little distance from someone outside his social circle. However, as the evening progressed, he realized that his first impression fell far short of reality. He turned out to be far from a stereotype.

Coughlin invited them into the kitchen, and as they walked through the house, Antonelli quickly glanced around and thought it appeared quite bizarre, with its unusual doors and windows, and other interior architectural features.. There were several wooden crates in the front hall, and in what looked like a large library. Antonelli sensed that Coughlin noticed his reaction.

"Come outside," Coughlin said. " I need a cigarette, and I don't smoke in the house."

They sat at his patio table. Coughlin took out his pack of Gauloise. "Either of you interested in a French cigarette?"

"Those are the ones that smell like horse shit, right?" Meador said.

'That's what some people think," Dewey said. "They taste better than they smell."

"I'll stick to my Winstons," Meador said.

Antonelli already had his Marlboros out.

All three of them lit up.

"My father collected architectural features from old houses, especially windows and doors," Coughlin said. "Every door and window in the house has a story. And right now, things are a mess. I just got deliveries of things I bought in Mexico last month. I haven't had a chance to unpack them."

"What kind of stuff?" Antonelli asked.

"Some art, some sculpture, some books, all legally purchased and properly processed through Customs, I can assure you."

"Not our business," Antonelli said. "We're here to talk about the Blue Girl murders, and whether there is any relationship to Mayan human sacrifices. Mr. Prescott told me about you, and I thank you for those photos."

"I think Nick had it right in his story," Coughlin said. "Whoever is doing this probably is just copying some aspects of the sacrifices, those that are generally known."

"The sacrifices were part of their religion, weren't they?" Antonelli said.

"Yes, they were conducted by their priests," Coughlin said. "The priest class was the highest and most powerful class in their culture, other than their kings. I have an explanation of what we know about their religion, as well as their class structure, in my Masters thesis, which I am trying to get published as a book. I made a copy of it for you."

"Thank you," Antonelli said. "That was very thoughtful."

"The Mayans used some of the drugs that have come into recent use here, didn't they?" Antonelli said.

"You mean peyote, mescaline, mushrooms, etc.?" Coughlin said.

"Yes," Antonelli said. "I think they even had a version of what we know as LSD."

"That's true," Antonelli said. "They did, and they extensively used, a variety of both types of hallucinogenic drugs."

"Both types?"

"There are some, like mescaline, which is the active ingredient of peyote, that just enhance perception of existing things," Coughlin said. "There is a hallucinogenic experience, but it is just of things around you. Colors are brighter. Some things change shape slightly. Pleasurable experiences are heightened. You don't see things that aren't there. You don't go on mental trips.

"Peyote probably was used by Mayan priests, and maybe by large numbers of the population. It's very easy to grow the cactus. I have some inside. But the peyote tastes terrible, and so it's never become very popular. Mescaline is a powder extract that is taken like a pill. It's not illegal. It doesn't seem to have any harmful effects.

"Aldous Huxley, you know the author of *Brave New World*, where drugs were used to control the population, has written probably the best known book about mescaline, *The Door to Perception*. He describes the experience of using mescaline in Mexico in great detail, and generally, very positively.

174

"Then, there are the other kind, the drugs that not only alter perception of existing things, but introduce things that aren't there, the drugs that sometimes cause bad trips, and terrible nightmares. These are chemicals extracted from mushrooms and toads, and, of course, LSD. The experience of using these drugs is much more unpredictable, and can be dangerous. It is possible these drugs may have both beneficial and harmful side effects. We don't know enough, yet."

"You sound like you have had some experience with these drugs," Antonelli said.

"Of course," Coughlin said. "I have done quite a bit of research on them, and have consulted others. I have kept records of my experiences, which you will see in my chapters on Mayan religion. At least I've kept records up to a point. With that second group of drugs, it isn't always possible to remember the effects. Some combinations of those drugs, particularly the extract from the toads combined with the mushrooms, can cause blackouts that may last quite a few hours."

"That doesn't sound beneficial," Antonelli said.

"On the contrary," Coughlin said. "I suffered a brain injury several years ago while surfing, and periodically I still have problems, mostly in the form of severe, blinding headaches. I have found that some of these drugs seem to ease the pain, and not just momentarily, but for extended periods of time after use. I've been trying to get medical researchers interested in looking at them, so far, without success."

"Have you used these drugs recently?" Antonelli said. "Do you have some here?"

"I haven't used any really recently," Coughlin said, and then smiling slightly, he added, "Of course, I only keep controlled drugs here for which I have prescriptions. Right now, I don't have much of those.

"I am not what you might call a recreational user of drugs," he continued. "For enjoyment and relaxation, I prefer wine. I only use them for research, and for medical experimentation. I used some for headaches I suffered last month. I used some others when I was in Mexico as part of my research. They are easier to obtain there, and there are not the legal technicalities we have here." He smiled again when he said that.

"I'm not from Vice," Antonelli said. "My interest is in trying to learn as much about what might be involved in the

Mayan sacrifices to see if there is any thread I can follow that will lead me to the killer. You said Mayan priests used peyote and mescaline. Do you know anyone around here who uses those?"

"I've used them, as I said, for research, not regularly, and not recently. I don't currently have any mescaline. I have gotten mine through mail order. Other than some very occasional contact in the past, I really don't know anyone around here who uses mescaline regularly. I think people who use drugs want a more exotic experience than mescaline provides. They want to go on trips, even if it means an occasional bad one. There's also no social enjoyment in its use, like there is, say, with the smoking of marijuana.

"I knew two of those girls," Coughlin said. "They were nice girls, and quite beautiful. What happened to them was horrible. I hope you catch the guy soon. I'll try to help you in any way I can."

"Who did you know?" Antonelli said.

"The Billingsleys and my family were close for many years. My father and her father both worked at Alexander Brown. I danced with her at her coming out at the Cotillon three years ago, and we dated briefly.

"What was the nature of your relationship? There was some difference in age, I believe," Antonelli said.

"You mean what was I doing dating someone 11 or 12 years younger?"

"Something like that."

"My father was to blame, to tell you the truth. He liked the idea of a match between the families. Her parents seemed to like the idea, too. I was OK with it. As I said, she was very pretty, and I had sort of run out of girlfriends. The only problem was she didn't like the idea. At the insistence of her parents and my father, we went out a few times. It always was awkward. Nothing developed between us. Then my father died, and I broke it off, much to her relief. I didn't date her again."

"When was that?"

"Just about two years ago," Coughlin said.

"And who was the other one you knew?" Antonelli said.

"Laurie Waslewski," Coughlin said. "She was the receptionist at the Walters. I used to see her when I went there. She was a knockout, and, like Karen, also very nice, but also like Karen, not interested in me."

"You tried to date her?"

"Sure, who wouldn't?" Coughlin said. "She was diplomatic about it, but she made it fairly clear that I was too old for her."

"By any chance did you know Candy Barlow?"

"The stripper who was murdered just like Karen?"

"Yes."

"No, I don't go to strip joints," Coughlin said. "I've never been out with a stripper."

Coughlin intrigued Antonelli. He wanted to know more about his experiences with drugs. He wanted to know more about his relationships with the two girls. He wasn't sure he believed that the Waslewski girl would have rebuffed Coughlin like that. Coughlin was a handsome man, from a good family, and worth a large amount of money. He would seem to be a good catch for a girl of modest means and background like Laurie.

He decided to take the questioning a little further.

"We have been talking to all the people who knew the victims, or had some connection to them, and even without Mr. Prescott, we probably would have gotten to you eventually. So, if you don't mind, I'll ask you the questions we are asking everyone."

"No, I don't mind at all," Coughlin said.

"First, can I assume that you don't know anyone who might have committed these crimes, or anyone who might have had a grudge against either of these girls?"

"Absolutely," Coughlin said. "Who could? They both were nice girls. There was nothing complicated about either one. I don't know anyone who had anything against either of them."

"Do you remember what you were doing when the first murder occurred?"

"Not for sure because I don't know that I know exactly when it occurred," Coughlin said. "I know when her body was found, but it had been there for a while."

"We think she was taken on a Friday night, Jan. 30," Antonelli said. "Do you remember what you were doing then?"

"I don't have a clear memory. I'm having some problems remembering a lot of things because of those headaches. I started having them again during the winter. One of my doctors thinks I might have a tumor. I'll be getting some tests soon."

"I hope everything is OK," Antonelli said. "Can you remember anything?"

"If it was a Friday night, then I probably was here," Coughlin said. "I often have dinner parties on Friday nights, but I didn't have any around that time. That also was when the big snow came in. I don't think I had any companion here then, either. I hadn't had a regular girlfriend in a while."

"Can anyone vouch for you being here?"

"I doubt it. I stick to myself quite a bit. I don't remember anything, or anyone, that could vouch for me then."

"What about the second murders. Where were you on that Saturday night?"

"That's easy, and there are a number of people who can vouch for me. I work at the *News American* and always work Saturday nights. I handle the distribution of the Sunday paper, getting the papers loaded onto the right trucks, setting up the correct routes, and all that. I haven't worked a Saturday since before I went on vacation, but I was there on that April Saturday night until after midnight."

"What about Friday, June 18th?"

"The night Laurie was killed?"

"Yes," Antonelli said. "I'm sorry, but these are just routine questions we have to ask."

"I understand," Coughlin said. "No problem. I was here that night. I had a terrible bout of headaches right after I got back from Mexico. I took off work almost that entire week. That's what got me to go back to the doctor."

"Can anyone vouch for that?"

"I don't remember that Friday at all, so I can't say," Coughlin said. "I know I did talk with my girlfriend by telephone some time during that week, and I saw her on the weekend. I was feeling somewhat better, and we had dinner here on Sunday."

"What's her name?"

"Susan Fanning," he said. "She also works at the *News American.*"

"Well, thank you for your time," Antonelli said. "I really appreciate you helping me with the photos, and with your thesis. I will start reading it right away."

"It probably will be a good antidote to insomnia, if you suffer from that," Coughlin said as they walked back into the house. He took them into the library, and handed Antonelli a large package.

"You might find this interesting, also," Coughlin said. He handed Antonelli a small mason jar containing a bright blue power.

"Mr. Prescott told me about this," Antonelli said. "I'd like to compare this color to the paint used on the girls."

"Go ahead, but I'd like it back," Coughlin said. "It's not something I'm likely to get again."

Chapter Thirty

The Coughlin Family History

Coughlin intrigued Antonelli. He had not thought of Coughlin as a suspect when he went to see him, and there was nothing suspicious in his manner, or in the way he answered questions. If it were not for some interesting coincidences, there would be no reason to give him any more thought. Coughlin knew two of the three girls; he was an expert in Mayan culture; he had no alibis for two of the three murders; he had used mescaline and could have been Crawford's source; and until early May he owned a 1972 dark green Buick.

A check with the Department of Motor Vehicles produced the record of the ownership, but also showed that the license plates were returned in early May, usually the sign that a car has been privately sold. The sale must have been to an out of state buyer because the car had not been re-registered in Maryland.

Antonelli sent two detectives to interview employees of the *News American* who worked in circulation, and on the loading docks. They verified that Coughlin was there on the Saturday night when Crawford and Billingsley were kidnapped. However, there was a two-hour period, from approximately 9:30 to around 11:30 P.M., a slack period between editions of the Sunday paper, when he was not seen.

Two more detectives were assigned the task of developing background information on Coughlin and his family. The basic facts were relatively easy to obtain. Coughlin descended from two of Baltimore's oldest families, the Bains and the Coughlins, dating to the 18th Century. He also was the last of the line of both families. His father was an enormously successful and highly influential investment banker. He had a brother and two sisters. One sister died from Polio. Another died in a small plane crash. His brother was killed in the Korean War. His mother, Angela Bain Coughlin, committed

180

suicide two years ago, and his father died of a heart attack shortly afterwards. He inherited a multi-million dollar estate, comprised primarily of valuable real estate, as well as what was believed to be a very large portfolio of stocks and bonds.

Antonelli knew there had to be a lot more to the story. He wanted to know why Coughlin's mother committed suicide. First, he wanted to make sure it was suicide. He found the file on her death. Suicides quite often are investigated by Homicide to make sure they aren't murders. Brad Jenkins was the primary. He remembered the case.

"It definitely was a suicide," Jenkins said. "An overdose of sleeping pills, for which she had a prescription. Her husband found her when he came home from work. He said she did not leave a note. Obviously, she might have and he took it. But I had no reason to challenge him. I talked with her doctor, and with her psychiatrist. She suffered from severe depression, and other problems. She spent some time at Sheppard Pratt back in the 1930s, and again in the early 50s. Her husband, who was extremely distraught by her suicide, said she was mentally ill all her life, but it had been kept under control in recent years with some of the new drugs.

"Mr. Coughlin said he believed she killed herself because she thought she was losing her looks," Jenkins said. "He said she started complaining about losing her looks three years earlier, and she just became more despondent about it.

"He showed me a colorized photograph of her in their bedroom, taken when she was a debutante in the late 1920s. She was an incredibly beautiful blue-eyed blonde. She had looks like Marilyn Monroe, but even better. And dead, she still was good-looking, and still had a very good figure. Great tits. She still was proud of them, and made sure that they got noticed. After taking the pills, she positioned herself on their bed, stark naked, with a red rose between her breasts. That's how her husband found her, and how I saw her.

"Then two months later, Mr. Coughlin dropped dead of a heart attack. Because of how he reacted to his wife's death, I really wasn't surprised."

"Did you meet the son, Dewey Coughlin?" Antonelli said.

"I talked to him briefly," Jenkins said. "He was a self-described professional student at Hopkins. Apparently he had been going to classes there for years. Clearly, he didn't have to worry about making a living. He lived in what had been a Hopkins fraternity house over on Guilford, not far from Union

Memorial. Unlike his father, he didn't seem to be particularly upset by his mother's death. He said she was gone during much of his childhood, and he wasn't close to her."

Antonelli showed Jenkins the photos of Barlow, Billingsley and Waslewski. "How do these girls compare to Mrs. Coughlin?"

"I only saw that photo once," Jenkins said, "but they're all similar, and not just because they are blondes. It's their type of look, like I mentioned, sort of like Marilyn Monroe, sexy, sultry, maybe almost voluptuous, but a little more refined. Of course, unlike Monroe, she was a natural blonde."

"These women were as well," Antonelli said. Jenkins stared at their photos.

"This one," he said, pointing to the photo of Candy Barlow, "looks the most like Mrs. Coughlin. Remarkably similar."

He looked at Antonelli.

"If I were you, I'd find out a lot more about Mrs. Coughlin."

That did not turn out to be very easy to do. The detectives Antonelli assigned to research the families came back with copies of newspaper clippings from the *Sun's* files that didn't reveal very much. The most interesting story was an obituary of Angela Coughlin's father, one of Baltimore's most prominent businessmen, in 1934. The story said he died of gunshot wounds suffered in a hunting accident on his Green Spring Valley farm. The obit said there would be no public viewing, and that funeral services would be private. Antonelli thought that curious for a man so prominent.

The detectives found no newspaper stories mentioning the Coughlins after that obit until the late 1950s when their names appeared in several society columns and stories about Baltimore society. There was one photograph of Mr. and Mrs. Coughlin at a charity event in 1959. They were a handsome couple, Antonelli thought.

The obituary of Angela Coughlin did not list a cause of death, just that it came after a brief illness. Her funeral also was private. The Sun's story of her death provided some history of her illustrious and wealthy family that included a clipper ship captain and a Revolutionary War hero. Without being specific, the story said a series of illnesses had forced her to live abroad for extended periods during the 1940s and

50s, but in recent years she had been active in Baltimore society, and in charitable activities.

Mr. Coughlin's funeral was not private. There was a long obit of him in *The Sun* that focused on his reputation as being one of the most influential investment advisers to Baltimore's wealthy society families. During World War II he became one of the primary managers of the government's war bond sales. After the war he moved to Alexander Brown as a senior partner. He had a reputation for getting results, but taking no prisoners in the process. He was said to aggressively help his friends and punish his enemies. In the 1950s he helped to finance many new ventures, and as well as the expansions of older ones. He particularly was active in the financing of suburban developments around Baltimore and Washington. His influence was said to be so pervasive that his opposition to a project, or an investment, would kill it.

There was another story about the huge turnout for his funeral. Antonelli wondered how many of them were there to make sure he really was dead.

A line in the obit, quoting an unnamed associate of Coughlin's, caught Antonelli's eye, and raised his curiosity.

"Mr. Coughlin knew more about the financial status of Baltimore's wealthiest families than anyone, and probably took many of their secrets, along with some of his own, to his grave."

He didn't know how it possibly could relate to the Blue Girl murders, but Antonelli wondered if maybe some of those secrets didn't go with Coughlin to his grave. Maybe some of them still are in that bizarre house. Now he also wanted to see that photograph of Angela Coughlin.

Chapter Thirty-One

Sunday Dinner with the Antonellis and Consecos

There were four guests at the Antonelli family Sunday dinner, including the boyfriend of Maury Antonelli's oldest half-sister, Stella. The other three were Maria Conseco and her parents. Serge and Anna Antonelli assumed the tradition started by Serge's parents, but instead of hosting the meal in the restaurant, as his parents had done, Serge chose to do it at home. He did not want to be at work on Sundays.

The standard fare every Sunday was the spaghetti, made in the old fashioned Italian mother way: a huge pot of various meats, tomatoes, onions, wine and spices cooked for hours. Serge always cooked one of the classic entries from the restaurant. Today it was his Veal Marsala. Loaves of bread, pitchers of olive oil and a big bowl of salad were the only additions. Desserts came directly from the restaurant. Bottles of Pinot Grigio and Chianti provided most of the liquid refreshment.

The Antonelli home consisted of two formstone-faced three-story rowhouses with portions of the connecting walls removed, and one central staircase replacing the two that originally went up either side of the connecting wall. The standard floor plan of a living room, dining room and kitchen was converted to a large eat-in kitchen adjacent to the dining room in the rear, a living room, and a family room, which opened to the kitchen. The section containing the living room and dining room only was used on Sundays, or when there was company. With Serge now more active in politics as the Democratic Party precinct captain, the living room was being used almost every night. Some people were promoting him as a candidate for the City Council in the 1967 city elections.

Today the modest-sized living room was full. Antonelli, who prided himself on his ability to read people, carefully watched his family, and the Consecos, as they were

184

introduced, and began interacting. The roots of the two families may have been geographically far apart, but they were not culturally. Antonelli thought that sometime in the past, maybe 1500 years ago, they could have shared a Roman ancestor. They had far more in common, than differences. It did not take long for the bonding to occur that Antonelli hoped would guarantee his marriage to Maria.

He could see that Maria's parents were nervous, as was his mother. His father was himself. He was the one person Antonelli could not read. Serge smiled broadly, shook hands, and hugged, like they were old friends. He cast a very admiring look at Maria, and then winked at Maury. Everyone laughed. It took the edge off, and from then on, everyone was family. Antonelli could see his father in politics.

Maria and Antonelli sat beside each other on one side of the table. His sister and her boyfriend sat on the other side. There were rounds of toasts to both couples, and to both sets of parents. Following several toasts, the big dinner was served, and it was a huge hit. Antonelli never tired of the great food his father routinely produced. Antonelli squeezed Maria's hand under the table several times. He was ecstatic, and she beamed beautiful happiness. This was what he wanted for his future.

After dinner the men went to the basement to shoot pool, smoke and drink something harder than the red wine served with dinner. The women cleaned up the dishes and sat in the living room briefly before calling the men back for dessert. Just as that happened, Antonelli received a call from Meador.

"I just got a call from Mike Withers, who came on duty late this afternoon," Meador said. "There is a report from the Western District. A woman's body, pained blue, was found in an alley, her head a few feet away. The big difference is she was a Negro."

She also was a prostitute. It only took the detectives about two hours to identify her as Violet Washington, 22, who worked some West Baltimore bars, and was in the stable of one of the more notorious pimps, Junior Johnson. The identification was easy because her purse and wallet, minus any cash that might have been in it, were found just a few feet away from the body.

Unlike the blue girls, she had been severely beaten and raped before she was killed, which was easily determined by the preliminary examination by the Medical Examiner's staff at the scene. There also were cigarette burns in numerous places.

"She was tortured before she was killed," said Joe Burns, one of the ME staff.

"And her killer sent a message by doing this," Meador said. "This wasn't a copycat. This was his way to make sure everybody heard what he did to her. I wonder what she did to earn this?"

Detectives rounded up three other prostitutes, two runners for Junior Johnson, and the man himself. By 8:00 PM they had eyewitnesses describing what happened to Washington, and the address where it happened. She had tried to get away from Johnson and go with a different pimp. That man now was missing. One of the runners suggested the police look in Leakin Park, infamous as a dumping ground for murder victims.

Presented with the physical evidence and eyewitness claims, Johnson said he would confess if he got the right kind of deal. Antonelli refused to give him anything, and let him spend the night in jail.

While at the police headquarters, Antonelli called his father, as well as Maria, to tell them what had happened, and to hear their reactions to the family gathering. Maria told him she had a wonderful time, and loved his family. She said her parents could not have been happier. Serge told him that he would be proud to have Maria as an addition to the family.

Chapter Thirty-Two

Dewey's Stroke

Nick heard "Wild Thing" playing on the radio as he walked down the hall to the bureau on Monday morning. Marsha waved at him from the slot desk while talking on the telephone, typing notes with her other hand, and tapping her feet to the heavy beat of the song, which had just hit number one on the Top 40.

"Triple fatal accident on 301," she said when she hung up the phone. "Susan Fanning is looking for you, and NX wants a follow up on that blue girl attempt yesterday."

The bureau called Nick late Sunday afternoon when the story broke of the murder of the prostitute. The copycat nature of the murder caused the blue girl story to get back into the news. Nick had to do a follow up story this morning. He decided to talk to Susan first.

"Dewey spent yesterday at Union Memorial Hospital," Susan said. "He didn't call me until late last night. He says they think he might have suffered a small stroke. He had planned to come in today, but he told me a little while ago he doesn't feel well enough to drive."

"Oh my God," Nick said. "We need to go see him, but I can't do it right now. I've got to work on the blue girl story. I can go out there this afternoon. Can you come with me?"

"Yes, I will," she said. "I feel terrible. I think I might have caused this."

"Why?"

"We went out to dinner together on Saturday night, but I declined his invitation to spend the night at his house, and I did not invite him to my apartment. His feelings were hurt. I am trying to break things off as gently as I can, but sometimes it just doesn't work."

"He thinks that since you haven't gotten an offer in Boston that his relationship with you can continue," Nick said.

"A part of me wishes it could," Susan said. "But I know the best thing for both of us is to get the breakup over with as soon as possible. I realize I can't have the kind of relationship with him that I wanted, and he can't have the kind of relationship with me that he wants. So it has to end."

Nick called the homicide department, but as usual he had to leave a message for Antonelli. The detective returned his call a half hour later.

"I want to look into the blue girl murders in greater detail," Nick said. "My editors in New York want a feature story that goes behind the scenes. I want to see how the case is being investigated, and why it is taking so long to catch the killer."

"We don't allow access to such information," Antonelli said. "It might compromise our investigation."

"This is not for immediate use," Nick said. "It's a feature that would be done for Sunday newspapers, probably for publication in August. So I'm not looking for hard news, just background and color."

"Well, maybe we can do something for you there," Antonelli said. "I'm working all the time, whenever you want is fine."

"I'd like to do it after 6:00 PM. In fact, I'll buy you dinner if we can eat somewhere inexpensive."

"Better yet, come to my father's restaurant and neither one of us will have to pay," Antonelli said.

'That's a deal," Nick said.

Dewey didn't answer the door, so Nick and Susan walked around the house to the rear patio where they found Dewey dozing in a chair, a half-full cup of cold coffee on the table next to him, the remnants of a burned out cigarette on the ashtray. Nick took the cup and went into the kitchen. He took two clean cups from the cupboard, emptied Dewey's cold cup, and filled all three with still-hot coffee from the coffee maker. When he returned to the patio, he found Dewey and Susan talking quietly, with her holding his hand.

"Oh, Nick, where'd you come from?" he said.

"I heard you had a rough time yesterday, and since you didn't call me, I brought Susan by to see if you still were alive," Nick said.

"I'm alive," Dewey said. "Actually, I feel quite a bit better than I did earlier. Those pills they gave me work pretty well, but they make me sleepy."

Other than looking a little sleepy, Nick thought Dewey looked close to normal. Dewey wasn't having trouble pronouncing his words. His eyes seem to be reasonably bright.

"Tell us what happened yesterday," Nick said.

"I don't remember driving home from our dinner Saturday night," Dewey said, looking at Susan. "I woke up yesterday morning with the worst headache I've ever had. I tried every painkiller I had. Nothing worked. So I took a cab to the emergency room. I was afraid to drive."

"They think I might have had a small stroke," he said. "One side of my face was drooping. It's better now, but it feels a little odd. They wanted to keep me and put me through a battery of tests. But I didn't want to do that. I just wanted them to get the pain to go away so I could think. They basically did that, and they gave me a prescription for some codeine."

"I still feel a little dizzy," he said. "I guess that could be from the painkillers. They gave me morphine intravenously."

"You've got to get some help," Nick said. "According to what you told Susan, the hospital would have kept you and given you some tests. Why didn't you let them do that?"

"I don't know," Dewey said. "It didn't feel right. I was in so much pain, I didn't want to make any decisions."

"They must have given you some follow-up information," Nick said. "Where is it?"

"All the information is in a folder on the kitchen table. You're welcome to look at it."

It took Nick a while to figure out the medical forms, and the handwritten notes of the doctors and nurses. They clearly believed Dewey had suffered some kind of brain abnormality, most likely a mild stroke, but the doctor also said a tumor should be considered as a possibility. It was recommended he receive a complete examination, including X-rays.

Nick returned and summarized for Dewey and Susan what the report said.

"I thought you were going to have some tests, and then a surgical examination of your brain," Nick said. "What's happened with that?"

"I put it off," Dewey said. "I didn't think I needed it, and I didn't want to do it right now."

"Which is it," Nick said, "you don't think you need it, or you don't want to do it right now?"

"I'm really concerned about my relationship with Susan," Dewey said. "I fear I am losing you," he said, looking at Susan. "I want so much to figure out how we could stay together in some way. You know how much I love you."

"If you want a relationship with me, you have to take care of yourself," Susan said. "I am not a nurse. I am not a person who likes taking care of other people. You just have to accept that about me. If you aren't strong enough to face up to your problems, then you aren't strong enough to be my mate."

Dewey was quiet for a few moments.

"That makes sense. I understand. Finally, I really do understand," he said. "I'll do it. I'll have the surgical exam."

"Very good, Dewey," Nick said. "Don't change your mind. In fact, let us know your schedule for tests, and for the exam, and we'll make sure you go through with them."

Susan kissed Dewey as she and Nick got up to leave.

"Take care of yourself, and things will be better," she said. Dewey just smiled.

When they were in the car, Nick turned to her. "Did you really mean that?"

"I don't know," she said. "I'm confused. I'm torn. But I do want him to get the care he needs. So maybe I did mean it."

"I hope so," Nick said. "It only gets worse if you don't."

Chapter Thirty-Three

Antonelli's Warning

Antonelli arrived before Nick and, like the last time, ordered a carafe of Chianti and an antipasto plate. He had agreed to talk to Nick about his idea for a story not because he had any interest in the story, but because he wanted to learn more about Dewey Coughlin. His impression of Nick so far was that he was a cut above most reporters he had encountered, smart and mature for his age.

Nick showed up about ten minutes late. They briefly chatted before Nick made his pitch for his story, basically an inside look at the homicide department at work.

"I don't have a problem with that," Antonelli said, "but I'll have to clear it with my lieutenant, and he probably will have to clear it with the captain, and the captain may have to go higher. I have no idea what will happen.

"Complicating your proposal is that you will be calling attention to the fact we haven't cleared the Blue Girl murders. Now we've got pimps painting their whores blue before killing them. If we don't solve these murders soon, I'll be walking a beat somewhere very unpleasant."

"It's amazing to me that someone could kill three people like that, and not leave any physical evidence, and not be seen by anyone," Nick said, "that something by now hasn't surfaced."

"The murders were carefully planned and expertly carried out," Antonelli said. "The killer is very smart."

"It's just so bizarre," Nick said. "The killer has to be insane to kill those women that way. Can an insane person be that careful, that smart?"

"Sure can," Antonelli said. "But usually killers like this start to get careless, or they actually want to get caught so they can enjoy the notoriety. That hasn't happened with these. There's a purpose behind these killings that we have not been able to identify."

"And you have no suspects?"

"This is off the record," Antonelli said. "We do have one suspect. We've questioned him several times and searched his apartment twice. He looked good for the murders early on, but I'm less enthusiastic now. Still, we're keeping an eye on him.

"Do you think that girl getting away from the killer is having any effect on him?"

"Again, off the record, that wasn't the killer. That was a copycat," Antonelli said.

"Really?"

"The killer is white, that guy was dark-skinned," Antonelli said.

"How do you know the killer is white?"

"Once more it's off the record, we have a witness who saw him with Laurie Waslewski," Antonelli said. "We have a partial description, enough so that we know he's white. We also now know how he got close to all the victims, but I'm not telling you that."

"You are keeping a lot of information away from us journalists," Nick said.

"We have to," Antonelli said. "I don't think the public, if they knew, would want us to tell you things that compromised our investigations. We hold back information to make sure that only us, and the killer, know certain things. We use that knowledge to verify a suspect, or a tip, and to invalidate the phony ones, as we did with the attack on Cynthia Baker. There was something that guy didn't do that was done in the other three attacks, and it had a significant impact on the outcome. We haven't revealed that piece of information, and so the copycat wouldn't have known to do it. Also, this guy didn't use the method of getting close to Baker that was used in the other murders."

"Fascinating," Nick said. "You will tell me all these things when you catch the guy, won't you? It will make a great story. That's assuming it doesn't leak out like the blue paint did."

"That was really unfortunate," Antonelli said. "I still don't know how it happened, or who the leaker was. I've taken steps since then to limit the flow of information. There are some things that no one outside my team knows, that I'm not even telling my lieutenant. If there's a leak of any of that information, it won't take long to find who did it.

"By the way, thanks for getting me with Dewey Coughlin," Antonelli said. It was time to start probing Nick for information. "He's quite an interesting man."

"He is," Nick said. "Unfortunately, he's having some problems. I fear that he's got something seriously wrong in his head, maybe a brain tumor."

"He mentioned something about that to me," Antonelli said. "He said he had been having a lot of problems with headaches. Is there something new?"

"Yes, they're getting worse," Nick said. "He spent Sunday in the emergency room at Union Memorial. They think he either had a slight stroke, or has a tumor. He's going to get some tests now."

"He mentioned something to me about getting some tests, but I got the impression they weren't a high priority with him."

"As soon as he feels better he postpones getting the tests," Nick said. "This time I don't think he will. He needs the doctor to prescribe the drugs he needs to control the pain.:

"He seems to know a lot about drugs, legal and illegal," Antonelli said.

"He does know about the hallucinogenic and psychedelic drugs, the drugs the Mayans used, but he's not a real user himself," Nick said.

"Yes, he told us he wasn't a recreational user, but did use them for research purposes."

"That's probably true," Nick said. "I've never seen any drugs when I've been with him. I don't like them, and I don't do them, and he knows that. It's not even a subject he brings up very much, other than in connection with his Mayan research."

"So he never said anything about mescaline?"

"Mescaline, that's an odd one," Nick said.

"It came up in my conversation with him," Antonelli said.

"I think he might have mentioned it at some point," Nick said. "He kidded me, saying that it was my kind of drug, enjoyable but harmless, also not illegal."

"Did he ever give you any?"

"No, he knows better than that," Nick said. "I'm serious about not liking them. It's bad enough that I smoke. I'm addicted to nicotine. I don't want any other addiction."

"Supposedly mescaline and some of these other drugs aren't addictive," Antonelli said.

"Yeah, he told me that, but I'm not taking any chances," Nick said. "Besides, I just don't feel the need for any artificial enhancement of my senses. They're pretty damn good, now. I'm not going to have some drug that people don't know much about fuck around with my brain."

Despite his aversion to talking to the press, Antonelli found himself liking this young reporter. He particularly liked his attitude about drugs. Tonight Antonelli ordered Spaghetti Diablo, a spicy pasta with hot Italian sausage that was a house specialty. Nick ordered the conventional sweet Italian sausage and peppers.

"How long have you known Mr. Coughlin, and how well do you know him?" Antonelli said.

Nick told him how he met Dewey during fraternity rush, how they had become friends, and how Dewey had arranged his blind date with Joan.

"We saw each other occasionally, but this year we have gotten much closer. His girlfriend, Susan Fanning, is a friend of mine. I introduced them. My girlfriend and I have spent a lot of time with them. We spent a weekend together at his beach house in Rehoboth Beach. I guess I could say the four of us have developed a very close relationship."

"I bet," Antonelli said. "And in the time you have known him, you never have seen anything about him that concerned you?"

"I'm not sure what you mean," Nick said, "Sometimes he's an odd duck, no doubt about it, but he is a really nice guy. He's very lonely. As you probably know, all his family is gone. He lives alone. He craves love and friendship, and he tries hard to be a good friend."

"Did you ever meet his mother and father?" Antonelli said.

"No, I never did," Nick said. "When I met him, he was living in his fraternity house. I never saw his family house until after he moved back there following the deaths of his parents."

"Do you know if there is a photograph of his mother in the house now?"

"There's a great framed photo of her in what was his parents' bedroom," Nick said. "Dewey says he has left that room the way it was before they died. It is a hand-colored photograph of her at her debutante ball - they call it the

Bachelor's Cotillon - in 1928. She was very beautiful. Also, according to Dewey, she was insane."

"Really? He used that word, 'insane?'" Antonelli said.

"Oh yes, he said she was in Sheppard Pratt in the 1930s the same time Zelda Fitzgerald was there."

Antonelli's face must have given away the fact that he didn't know who Zelda Fitzgerald was.

"You know, the wife of the writer, F. Scott Fitzgerald. They had a famous tempestuous relationship," Nick said, "apparently not all that different from what Dewey's father had with his mother. Dewey didn't get along with her at all."

"When did you see that photo?"

"In April when my girlfriend and I were there for dinner. He took me on a tour of the house. It is very unusual." Nick said.

"Sort of weird, I think," Antonelli said, "with all those different doors and windows. Did she remind you of anyone?"

"Now that you mention it, she definitely did," Nick said. "Dewey's girlfriend, Susan, could be his mother's twin sister. The resemblance is incredible. I thought his mother also reminded me of someone else I had seen, but I couldn't remember, and until now, I hadn't thought about it again."

Antonelli hesitated momentarily. He did not expect Nick's answer. He did not know Susan Fanning, and did not know she was a blue-eyed blonde. That made things even more interesting. He took a business envelope out of his jacket pocket.

"What about these?" Antonelli said. He put photos of Barlow, Billingsley, and Waslewski in front of Nick.

Nick was quiet for a few moments.

"My God, they all look like his mother, and Susan," Nick said. "It was Barlow I was thinking of, but couldn't remember, when I saw his mother's picture. It didn't hit me when I saw all three of these photos how much they all looked like Dewey's mother, and Susan. What an unbelievable coincidence."

"Yes, it is unbelievable, isn't it?" Antonelli said.

"No, you can't possibly think that Dewey's involved in these murders," Nick said.

"I'm not saying that," Antonelli said. "I honestly don't know. I just don't like coincidences. I think there is some kind of connection between the killings of these women and the Coughlin family. Mr. Coughlin's father was a very important man. He knew an awful lot of intimate information about very wealthy and powerful people in this city. He had a reputation for being very tough, and, as a result, he had some enemies."

"So you think it is possible that someone could be doing these murders because of something they think Dewey might know?" Nick said, "as a warning to him, or maybe to implicate him?"

"Or it is something he possesses, maybe something he doesn't even know he possesses" Antonelli said. "Or possibly it is revenge for something his father did. Or it all could be coincidence. But I doubt that. There's some kind of connection. I know there is.

"I haven't had a chance to ask Mr. Coughlin about all this, but I will. I would appreciate it if you said nothing to him about our conversation tonight."

"No, I won't" Nick said. "He hardly needs anything else to upset him right now."

"What's he upset about?"

"His relationship with Susan Fanning is very tenuous," Nick said. "He's madly in love with her, and would marry her in an instant, if she would agree to it. But she won't. She doesn't want a complicated relationship. She is one of those 'liberated' women we are hearing about now. She is on her way to being a big name in journalism. She isn't interested in marriage, or family."

"So why is she seeing Mr. Coughlin?" Antonelli said. "From what you are saying, that seems to be what he wants. It would make sense. He is the only one left of his family, so almost surely he wants to keep it going by having a family of his own."

"I'm sure you're right," Nick said. "The problem is, neither Susan, nor myself, for that matter, understood Dewey when this all started. Susan is attracted to him because she likes him and he is a good lover. They have a very good sexual relationship. That is pretty much all Susan is looking for in a man. Dewey, however, wants more. It is the reverse of the normal situation. She wants the sex. He wants the family."

"So what is going to happen between these two?" Antonelli said.

"I wish I knew for sure, but Susan's trying to get a job in Boston," Nick said. "She desperately wants to go back there. I don't think she wants company when she does. So I suspect it's not going to turn out very well."

"This episode with the severe headaches that sent Mr. Coughlin to the emergency room, did it occur after some problem between the two of them?"

"Yes. That's a remarkable deduction," Nick said.

"Well, I am a detective, after all," Antonelli said. "Tell me about it."

"It happened after Susan refused to spend the night with him as she had been doing on weekends. She told me she was trying to wind down their relationship."

"He told me that he started having severe headaches early in the year, and that they come and go," Antonelli said.

"Yes," Nick said. "He seems fine for quite a while, and then he has problems."

"When was the last time before this one?"

"Right after he got back from a trip to Mexico in June," Nick said. "He missed nearly a week of work, and then he recovered. He had seemed fine until this past weekend."

"Did anything happen prior to that last episode of headaches, anything with Miss Fanning?"

"Yes," Nick said. "God, yes. Right beforehand, she told him in a long telephone conversation she didn't want him moving to Boston with her."

"And the time before that, when he had an episode before that?" Antonelli said.

"I have to think about that," Nick said. "I really wasn't aware of his problem much before that. I think the June headaches were the first he had since meeting Susan in April."

"Try to think if you recall anything," Antonelli said. "You don't have to do it now. Just let me know if you remember anything."

"I'll try, but nothing comes to mind," Nick said.

Antonelli wanted to ask more questions, but his instincts told him to ease up. Even though he liked him, Nick still was a reporter and a close friend of Coughlin's. He also felt he was flying blind about Coughlin. He didn't like asking questions when he didn't know the answers. So he went to the men's room, and when he came back, he started a new subject.

"When are you getting married?" Antonelli said.

Nick smiled.

"Joan is also one of those liberated women," Nick said. "She wants to live on her own for a while before we get married. She plans to go on to graduate school, so it is possible that it may be a while. Are you married?"

"No, but I think I will be engaged soon," he said.

"Congratulations," Nick said. "When will the wedding be?"

"Next summer, after we get our degrees. We're both taking courses at the University of Baltimore. That's where we met."

"It must be tough, doing your job and also being in school," Nick said.

"It's taken me longer than I thought it would when I started," Antonelli said. "I'm going to try to go to law school. I don't know if I'll be able to manage that."

"I thought about doing that," Nick said, "but I got a part-time job in the news department at WCBM a couple of years ago, and sort of got sucked into journalism. I didn't plan it."

"You seem to like it, and you seem to be doing well," Antonelli said.

"I love it," Nick said. "There's something new almost every day. It's exciting. I just wish it paid better."

"I have the same problem," Antonelli said. "I love being a detective, and I'm doing well - except for not solving the Blue Girl murders yet - but the pay isn't very good."

"So that's why you want to go to law school?"

"Not really," Antonelli said. "I don't think I want to practice law. I think it will help me move up in the department."

"What is your major?" Nick said.

"Just general liberal arts, a little of this, a little of that, whatever seemed interesting to me at the time," Antonelli said. "I especially like history and political science, but I've taken courses in almost every area. I like learning about things I don't know much about. I don't like not knowing things."

"Me too," Nick said. "I was a political science major, but I took a lot of courses in other areas."

They went on to talk about some of their courses. They had many interests in common.

Antonelli enjoyed talking with Nick, who was the first man near his age, not a member of his family, or a cop, who he had attempted to get to know. While their backgrounds were quite different, they were alike in a number of ways.

He wondered if they really could become friends. That made him realize he had to go back to their discussion of Coughlin.

"One more thing about Mr. Coughlin," he said. "I think it's important that he gets those tests. Until he does, you might consider warning your friend, Susan, to be careful about what she says to him."

"Do you think she is in danger?" Nick said.

"Someone is," Antonelli said, "maybe both of them."

Chapter Thirty-Four

Nick Tells Susan about Antonelli's Suspicions

Nick took Susan to lunch the day after his dinner with Antonelli, and told her of the detective's theory of some kind of connection between the murders and the Coughlin family. He had stayed up late the night before, thinking about the conversation with Antonelli, and realized what the detective didn't say was more revealing than what he did.

Antonelli intrigued Nick. He came from a much different world, but he found they had some similar interests. They were ambitious young men holding highly responsible positions, especially for their ages. They shared the same kind of intellectual curiosity. They wanted to learn, to improve themselves, but also for the pleasure of knowing more. As Antonelli said, they didn't like not knowing things. Neither of them was particularly materialistic. They loved their work even though neither job paid very well and didn't promise wealth in the future.

Antonelli differed from him in one important respect: he was devious. While he did reveal some things off the record, he also held back. While he talked about Dewey's expertise in drugs, and his knowledge of Mayan culture, he did not discuss the obvious: the Blue Girl murders apparently being made to look like Mayan human sacrifices. Instead, he talked fairly vaguely about the possible connection of the Coughlin family to the murders, because of the similarity in appearance between the victims and Dewey's mother.

Antonelli clearly wanted to know much more about Dewey than he let on. He probed some, but then backed off. This thought kept Nick awake until the early morning hours. This was all entirely new to him. Never before had he been this close to a murder investigation. Even more unsettling was the thought that he might be close to a murder suspect. He decided to talk with Susan about Dewey.

"Have you and Dewey discussed the Blue Girl murders?" Nick said.

"A little, some casual talk, but nothing of any substance," she said.

"I'm sorry to be so nosy, but I'm surprised, considering he knew two of the victims, and is so involved with Mayan history and culture," Nick said. "What do the two of you talk about?"

"Most of the time he is just like what you have seen when you have been with us. He tells stories about himself and others, but he really doesn't talk about himself. I never get much of an idea of what he's really thinking, or feeling. He also doesn't ask personal questions of me. We may be sexually intimate, but otherwise, we're not intimate. It's one of the reasons he has a hard time understanding me. Do you think they suspect him?"

"Antonelli is the kind of person who suspects everyone," Nick said. "He's also very careful about what he says. He didn't tell me he suspects Dewey. If anything, he seemed to avoid the subject. So, yes, I think he suspects Dewey, but I think he also believes it is equally possible, maybe more so, that someone is trying to implicate Dewey."

"Why would anyone do that?" Susan said. "So far as I can tell, Dewey's never done anything bad to anyone, other than what he told us he did in Mexico." Her eyes got big. "I wonder if that is it? Maybe someone from Mexico is getting revenge on him, by making it look like he is the killer."

"It would have to be someone who knows a lot about him," Nick said. "How would they know these women who were killed? Has he ever mentioned anyone he works with down there with whom he is particularly close?"

"No, no one," Susan said.

"I think we need to ask him," Nick said. "Also I'm concerned about his headaches. They seem to be getting worse, especially since he started seeing you. Have you noticed?"

"You think his headaches are related to our relationship?" she said.

"I don't know enough to reach a conclusion," Nick said, "but the last two major episodes of headaches occurred after conflicts with you, when he was worried the relationship was breaking up."

"I hadn't thought of that," she said. "He was having headaches before he met me."

"Yes, but not as frequently, or as severely, at least as far as I know," Nick said. "Each time he's thought your relationship was in danger he's had a bad episode of headaches. It happened when he came back from Mexico, and it happened again after your dinner with him on Saturday. I think his fear of losing you triggers the headaches. What I don't know is what triggered them before he met you."

"He has to get those tests," Susan said. "We both have to keep after him. Also, I guess it probably would be a good idea for the time being for me not to talk about going back to Boston."

"Yes, there's no reason to make a big deal of it now. Let's see what happens with his tests and with Antonelli's investigation."

"In other words, I should just string him along," she said, reminding Nick of his concern about her when they were in Rehoboth Beach.

"Touché," Nick said.

Susan came into the bureau at midday on Wednesday and told Nick the police were going to question Dewey that evening. He had called her and asked her to be present during the questioning.

Chapter Thirty-Five

The Photograph and the other Blue-Eyed Blondes

Antonelli had worked almost around the clock after the dinner with Nick, digging into the background of the Coughlin family. He talked at length with Karen Billingsley's father, who had worked with Coughlin at Alexander Brown. The FBI provided some information from its dossier on John Coughlin, begun during World War II and updated in the late 1950s when he briefly was considered for a high level Treasury Department appointment.

The FBI file proved to be very revealing, but it also raised more questions. He decided to try to get more information from Coughlin while he still could question him without having to give him the Miranda rights dictated by the recent Supreme Court decision. Such rights only applied when the subject of questioning was a suspect. They also did not apply if the individual was questioned in his own home. While he didn't think Coughlin was the killer, he believed he knew more than he had let on in their previous discussion. Now he knew more questions to ask.

Antonelli and Meador arrived at Dewey Coughlin's house promptly at 7:00 P.M. Coughlin took them into the kitchen and introduced them to Susan. Antonelli immediately understood Coughlin's obsession with her. Seldom did he see women as beautiful as she was. He also saw the resemblance to the Blue Girl victims.

"I hope you don't mind," Coughlin said, "but I would like Susan to be present during our discussion."

"I have no objection," Antonelli said, "but before we sit and talk, I wonder if you and Miss Fanning would mind showing me the photograph of your mother?" Antonelli said. "I have heard about it from others, and I think it is important to our case."

"Really?" Coughlin said. "Sure, follow me."

The picture was everything Brad Jenkins and Nick Prescott had described. Angela Bain, at 18 was one of the most beautiful young women Antonelli had ever seen, either in person, or in a photograph. After looking at the photo intensely, he turned and looked at Susan.

"Stand by the photo," Antonelli said. She walked over to it.

"Truly remarkable," Meador said.

"Is there any possibility that you are related to her?" Antonelli said.

"I see the resemblance," Susan said. "It's a little unsettling. She could be my twin sister. But I can't imagine there is any family relationship unless it is way back in England several hundred years ago."

Coughlin was silent, but kept looking back and forth between his mother's picture, and Susan. Finally he spoke.

"Susan has much nicer eyes," he said. "In part, because she is a much nicer person. She also is quite sane. My mother was a bitch, and she was insane. I think the coloring used on the photo hides the real look of insanity in her eyes. I remember the look. I hated it. I didn't much like her, either. Maybe I should burn this photo."

"Oh, no," Antonelli said. "It is a critical piece of evidence. In fact, I'd like to borrow it. I don't want anything to happen to it."

"Take it," Coughlin said. "I don't want it. I get upset every time I look at it. But why is it evidence?"

"Come back into the kitchen and I'll show you," Antonelli said.

Back at the table in the kitchen, Antonelli took out his envelope of photos of the three murdered girls and spread them out on the table.

"Can you see why it is evidence?"

"My God," Susan said. "They all look like your mother, and like me. I never noticed that before."

"They do have the same type of look," Coughlin said. His face suddenly showed concern.

"You're not thinking that I killed those girls, are you?"

"No," Antonelli said. "I think someone may have killed them trying to make it look like you did."

"What?" Coughlin said. "Why would anyone do that? I am not aware of anyone who would hate me that much. In fact, I don't know anyone who hates me. I've never done anything to generate any hate, not like my parents."

"That's the point," Antonelli said. "I think it is very possible that whoever is doing that has a grudge against one, or both, of your parents, and they are getting revenge against you."

"Look, my father was a very successful and important man," Coughlin said. "He was successful because he was a real bastard. He didn't care if he hurt someone if he got his deal. I am sure he left a lot of bodies in his wake. I wouldn't have been surprised if someone had sued the estate, but they didn't. I've never heard a peep out of anyone. This seems way beyond reason. I just can't believe it."

"Well, it could have been your mother as well," Antonelli said. "From what little I have heard, she was no angel, either."

"No, as I said, she was insane. She was totally self-absorbed, narcissistic, and exhibitionistic. Do you know what she did when she killed herself?"

"The homicide officer who investigated told me," Antonelli said. "Do you know if the red rose had any particular meaning?"

"I don't know for sure, but I think it might have, but only to my father," Coughlin said. "He seemed particularly upset by it, but he never told me why. You'll notice if you walk around the property that there are no rose bushes. My mother hated roses. That's why her leaving that rose was so mysterious."

"I want to go through several other things with you," Antonelli said.

"Go ahead," Coughlin said.

"To whom did you sell your 1962 Buick?"

Coughlin stared at Antonelli for a couple of moments, and there was a momentary, but noticeable change in his eyes - a darkening - and then it was gone. Without looking away, Coughlin said, "That's the damndest thing. I know I sold it. I put an ad in the classifieds. Somebody came here and got it and paid cash because I found a wad of cash in my kitchen and the registration was gone. However, I don't have any memory of making the sale, and I have no receipt for it. It was during one of those times when I was having severe headaches."

Antonelli wanted to tell Coughlin exactly what he thought of that story, but there were too many other questions he wanted to ask to risk a confrontation now. But this made him very suspicious of Coughlin. He tried hard not to let that show.

"How widely known is your expertise in Mayan culture?" Antonelli said.

"It certainly is known among the people with whom I have had contact in recent years," Coughlin said. "I started going to Mexico years ago, and I sometimes gave gifts to people of items I brought back. So yes, it is widely known."

"You also brought drugs back from Mexico, drugs used by the Mayans, isn't that correct?"

"I did," Coughlin said. "I used them to discover their effects, and I described those effects in my thesis. Aside from the research, I had no other purpose in getting them."

"What about mescaline?"

"I bought it from a pharmaceutical company," Coughlin said. "It's legal and readily available."

"In the Appendices to your thesis, you have a chapter where you discuss the effects of mescaline, and you compare the reactions of two researchers, which were similar in most respects. Correct?"

"Yes," Coughlin said.

"I presume you were one of the researchers. Who was the other one?"

"OK, it was Rory Crawford," Coughlin said.

"And you supplied Rory Crawford with mescaline?"

"So you lied to me the last time we talked about who might have supplied Crawford with mescaline?"

"Yes, I wasn't myself that night, and I didn't want to get any more involved than I had to. I know it's a poor reason."

"When did you give him mescaline?"

"Several weeks before he was killed," Coughlin said.

"You didn't give him any on the night he was killed?"

"No, I was at work," Coughlin said.

"Your fellow employees at the *News American* cannot verify you were there between 9:30 and 11:30 that night," Antonelli said.

"That's the time when everyone takes their lunch hour," Coughlin said. "I went over to Burke's and had a hamburger and some of their German potato salad."

"Can anyone verify that?"

"I don't know," Coughlin said. "I picked up a *Sun* on the way and sat in a booth and read it."

"Do you know of anyone else who might have supplied Crawford with mescaline?"

"Not specifically," Coughlin said. "As I said, I bought it by mail order from a pharmaceutical company. Once I tried it, I didn't have any reason to buy any more. I only use drugs as part of my research. I think I told you before, I don't use drugs regularly."

"He's never used them around me," Susan said, "for whatever that's worth."

"It's important to think about this, Mr. Coughlin," Antonelli said. "Crawford's best friend told me someone was going to give him some mescaline that Saturday night, someone who lived in the neighborhood, and who was a friend of Karen Billingsley."

"I have no idea who it might be," Coughlin said. "I had little contact with Karen after we stopped dating. Rory and I had become friendly during the past year. I gave him some of the drugs I was researching for my thesis, and he wrote reports on their effects. I compared his experiences with mine."

"Getting back to your parents, what can you tell me about your mother's associations? I understand she was away from Baltimore for extended periods of time."

"There were times when she went off the deep end, and wound up at Sheppard Pratt, and at other institutions," Coughlin said. "I don't know the details. My father kept them from all the children. Then, in the 1950s she started to get better. I think it was some of the new drugs she was prescribed. But she still went away for months at a time.

"My father bought her an apartment in Paris not long after the end of the war. She spent a great deal of time there. He never went there. I inherited it. I'm probably going to sell it."

"Did she have affairs with other men?"

"Oh sure, men and women," Coughlin said.

"Did she break up any marriages?"

"None that I know of," Coughlin said.

"I have to ask this," Antonelli said, "but did she abuse you, or any of the other children?"

Coughlin was silent for a few moments, almost as if he never had considered the question before.

"Honestly, I am not sure," he said. "I don't think I was abused. I have no memory of it. My younger sister had polio

210

and died right after World War II. I am not sure about my older brother and sister. Both of them had serious problems when they were older. My sister fought with my mother all the time, at least she did when my mother was here. My brother drank heavily when he was a teenager, and always was getting in trouble. Of course, both of them were killed, my sister in a plane crash, and my brother in Korea."

"Do you know the circumstances of those deaths?" Antonelli said. He knew because the FBI file had the details.

"Not the detailed specifics," Coughlin said. "I enlisted in the Army when I was 18, late in 1952. I was in basic training when my brother was killed. My sister was killed six months later, when I was stationed in Germany. So, I didn't hear much of the details."

"I didn't know you were in the Army," Susan said. "You've never mentioned it before."

"There's never been a reason to mention it," Coughlin said. "I enlisted to go to Korea like my brother, but instead they sent me to Germany. I was in Armor, and, other than getting to see parts of Europe, it was very boring. They wanted me to go to OCS, but I'd had enough of regimentation. At the time I thought I wanted to be a doctor, so I went to Hopkins. I changed my mind after a couple of years."

"Your sister took out your father's plane by herself before she was licensed to fly solo. At the time she was getting flying lessons. The plane crashed into the Bay. Because of her inexperience, it was ruled an accident, but there was some opinion she did it on purpose."

"Obviously, you know more than I do," Coughlin said. "She had a terrible temper. I later heard from the housekeeper that before she left, she had a fight with my mother. She was a lot like our mother. I remember them screaming at each other. She could have done that."

"Your brother was killed in Korea when he crashed a jeep into a tank," Antonelli said. "He was quite drunk at the time."

"I didn't know that," Coughlin said. "How did you find that out?"

Antonelli just shrugged.

"I'm not surprised," Coughlin said. "He had several drunk driving incidents here."

"I need you to think about people you heard about, or knew, when you were growing up, especially anyone who might have had a reason to hate either of your parents,"

Antonelli said. "If there is anyone you can think of, please tell me as soon as possible."

"I still don't get it," Coughlin said. "If someone had such a tremendous hatred of us that they would kill these poor girls, why didn't they just kill me? I live alone. I don't have a dog. Someone could have come in here and killed me and walked out and no one would have noticed."

"I don't know the answer to that," Antonelli said. "Perhaps it is someone who wants you to suffer greatly, more than you would from just being killed. We're going over your father's affairs very carefully to see if we can find that person. Meanwhile, think hard. Try to remember anyone who might have any kind of grudge."

"I can't think of anyone, but I'll try," Coughlin said. "I just have a hard time believing this. I just don't see how these murders relate to me, or my family, just because the victims look like my mother. They also look like each other, and like many other beautiful blondes. I think it is just a coincidence."

"And the blue-painted bodies?" Antonelli said.

"Anyone who went to the BMA's exhibit on the Mayans could have gotten the idea there," Coughlin said. "You really need to rethink your theory."

"Believe me, we are looking at every conceivable possibility," Antonelli said.

"I'm sure you are," Coughlin said. "Are we about done? I need to go to the john."

"Go ahead, Dewey," Susan said. "I'll see them out."

Susan walked with the detectives out to their car.

"I agree with Dewey," she said, "but you know a lot more about this case than I do. Do you think I am in any danger?"

"I think it is possible," Antonelli said. "You should take some precautions. We think the killer posed as a policeman to get close to his victims. He then injected them with a tranquilizer, which enabled him to control them. You should avoid isolated areas, and you must avoid close contact with anyone you don't know. If a policeman approaches you, demand to see his identification, not just his badge. If he keeps coming at you without doing that, run and make a lot of noise."

"Do you suspect Dewey?"

"Right now we have no suspects," Antonelli said. "Do you think we should suspect him?"

"No, I don't," she said, "but you are scaring me."

Chapter Thirty-Six

A Discovery at Alexander Brown

The Coughlin interview left Antonelli dissatisfied. He thought Coughlin knew more than he let on about his family and about Rory Crawford. Even his admission of lying earlier about Crawford seemed too easy. He came away from the session even more convinced the murders were linked to the Coughlin family. He needed to know more about them.

Three two-man teams of detectives were sent to interview members of the Baltimore society, prominent and not-so prominent people whose names were taken from the "Blue Book," which listed those considered "society" in Baltimore. Their purpose was to find out as much as they could about John and Angela Coughlin.

Antonelli went to Alexander Brown on Thursday and met with the managing partner, Robert Penrose.

"We are looking into the deaths of both John and Angela Coughlin," he said. "Information has been discovered raising the possibility of foul play in one, or both, deaths."

"It did seem rather remarkable that they died in such close proximity to one another," Penrose said. "She supposedly committed suicide, but he was, what 59, or so, and very vigorous."

"We need to look at business deals in which he was involved where someone else got hurt, or didn't get an opportunity they thought they should have gotten - anything that might have led to someone holding a grudge. I also need to find out if Mr. Coughlin had any affairs that might have caused some very hard feelings."

"Most of what we do is highly confidential," Penrose said.

"If you wish, I guess I could get a search warrant, but I'd prefer to keep this informal and quiet."

"So would we," Penrose said. "Assuming you will agree to certain non-disclosure and confidentiality requirements regarding our company and its activities, I'll have some files pulled for you. However, we will not let you see the files of our customers."

"I'll have the State's Attorney review your requirements," Antonelli said. "Also, the FBI. They are lending us some forensic accountants."

"We worked in separate areas of the company, and I had just become Managing Partner shortly before he died," Penrose said. "Thus, I did not know him very well, and I knew nothing of his personal life. However, he had an assistant for many years, Virginia Moorhead. If anyone knows anything, she is the one. She retired after he died and moved to the Eastern Shore. I can give you her address and phone number."

The State's Attorney and the FBI agreed to the non-disclosure and confidentiality restrictions Alexander Brown required, and began examining an extensive collection of files of the financial transactions managed by John Coughlin.

Antonelli and Meador traveled to the pretty little town of Chestertown, on Maryland's Eastern Shore, where Virginia Moorhead now lived in a very beautifully restored early 19th Century house.

"This is where I wanted to live, and John made it possible," said Moorhead, an attractive and still fine-figured brunette with big brown eyes.

"I've gone back to college, at Washington College here, to get my B.A. Degree. It's wonderful. I love being a middle-aged college student. I don't have to work. John made sure of that. So I do some volunteer work for the college, and I've made a number of friends in the area."

Antonelli explained he was looking into the deaths of both Angela and John Coughlin, because some indications of possible foul play had surfaced.

"I've always been mystified by John's death," she said. "He was a very healthy and vigorous man. I saw his medical reports. He didn't have a weak heart."

"I think, from what you are telling me, I can assume your relationship with Mr. Coughlin was more intimate than what is normal between an executive and his assistant," Antonelli said.

"Yes, you can assume that," she said. "We were lovers for many years. In most important respects I was more his wife than Angela. I was the person with whom he shared his secrets, his fears, his innermost thoughts."

"Then why did he stay married to her?" Antonelli said.

"She had something on him, something so compelling, she frightened him," Moorhead said. "People thought he was infatuated with her. In reality she was the only person in the world he feared."

"So there was no love in their relationship?" Antonelli said.

"Not for a long time, but in the last few years, amazingly, they got along better, and were closer. Her suicide disturbed him tremendously."

"He had a reputation for having relationships with many women," Antonelli said. "How true was that?"

"There was a time quite a few years ago when he had numerous short term affairs," Moorhead said, "nothing lasting more than a few months, most just a few weeks. But I don't think he had any in the past ten years or so, except with me, of course."

"Did his wife know about these affairs?"

"I think she knew about some," Moorhead said. "She didn't care. If anything, she encouraged them. She had her own affairs, many of them in those days."

"What about more recently?"

"Like John, I don't think she had any in the last few years of her life."

"How did you feel about Mr. Coughlin's affairs?"

"At the time they were going on, our relationship really had not developed into what it became, and so I was just one of a number," she said. "But I think I am the only one who loved him. He eventually figured that out, and he stopped having affairs."

"What do you think Angela Coughlin's hold on him was?"

"Honestly, I don't know," Moorhead said. "I tried to find out so many times that it angered him. He just kept telling me to forget about it. He said it was something that happened long before we met, and there was nothing anyone could do about it."

"Do you know of anyone who had a grudge against him for something he did in his work, a really serious grudge that might cause them to seek revenge?" Antonelli said.

"There were two aspects to John's business," she said. "Early in his career at Alexander Brown, especially in the 1950s, he raised capital for companies and large projects. In that role, he sometimes was controversial and combative. But it wasn't the kind of business that really harmed anyone.

"Later, he shifted into being a financial adviser to wealthy families and individuals," she said. "That's all he did in his last few years. He was very successful. He helped his clients make a lot of money. I don't remember any client who lost any substantial amount of money because of his advice.

"But there was one occasion, involving one of his earliest financial advisory clients, when the client didn't follow his advice, and made an investment John had recommended against," she said. "It failed, and the customer took a terrific loss, basically losing his entire family fortune. The man committed suicide. His widow thought John had recommended the investment and she made quite a fuss. There was a lawsuit that was thrown out."

"Can you find, or direct me, to the specifics on that one?" Antonelli said.

"Funny thing you should ask," she said. "John told me he thought this one would come back to haunt him some day. He gave me a copy of a file to hold for him, just in case."

Chapter Thirty-Seven

A New Suspect

The man's name was C. Johnson Smelt, typed on the label at the top of the file. There was a six-page document at the front inside that summarized the case, and then numerous other documents, including a lengthy prospectus for an oil and gas limited partnership. Antonelli read the six pages.

Smelt, who was 42 at the time, committed suicide in 1954. At the time he was running a family real estate business catering to wealthy society families. He listed only a handful of houses at any one time, and they usually were expensive and in exclusive neighborhoods. Although he didn't have to sell very many to make a comfortable living, the file indicated he was selling very few, and his listings were diminishing in number.

His family was old Baltimore society, but not enormously wealthy. He had slightly more than $500,000 in stocks and bonds, managed by John Coughlin at Alexander Brown. This was a period of good growth in the stock market, and his investments were doing quite well, but not well enough for him. To make up for declining revenues from his real estate business, Smelt began to withdraw capital from his Alexander Brown account.

He took a prospectus to John Coughlin for an oil and gas limited partnership in Texas. The projected returns were enormous. The Texas oil industry was booming. Fortunes were being made almost overnight. As Antonelli read the file, he recalled the movie, "Giant," that involved a woman from Maryland and a wealthy Texas rancher/oil man. Coughlin talked to a number of his contacts in the oil industry in Texas. He gave Smelt a negative recommendation on this venture.

In his letter to Smelt, Coughlin said, "This venture is exploring land outside the areas generally known to contain substantial oil reserves. The opinion of numerous experts is that it is highly unlikely this land will yield any substantial amounts of oil, and, most likely, none at all. There is a very substantial risk that you could lose your entire investment."

Smelt decided to proceed with the investment and he took nearly all the money out of his Alexander Brown account. Within a year, the venture failed. No oil was found and all of Smelt's money was lost.

His widow apparently did not know that Coughlin had recommended against the investment. In fact, she said that her husband told her that Coughlin had approved of it. When he showed her the letter he sent to her husband, she accused him of forgery. She then sued him and Alexander Brown. The suit was thrown out on motions before the trial.

The next day, back in the office, Antonelli discovered the widow died in 1964, leaving a son, Michael, now twenty-four years old, and living in a rowhouse apartment on Maryland Avenue south of the Johns Hopkins Homewood campus. A check with the DMV revealed he owned a 1962 dark blue Buick that he apparently inherited from his mother. She was listed as the previous owner.

He had no criminal record and a clean driving record. He had been drafted into the Army when he was 18, and assigned to the military police. He was honorably discharged in 1962 as a corporal, and had gotten a job as a security guard at the Homewood campus of Johns Hopkins shortly after returning home.

Antonelli was excited. A security guard could look like a policeman. He had a car like the one seen picking up Crawford and Billingsley. He could have a grudge against Dewey Coughlin.

Antonelli and Meador went looking for him that afternoon.

This area south of Hopkins was a little dicey. The houses were run down. There was trash on the streets and Antonelli and Meador received furtive looks of recognition from several of the young black men hanging around the intersection.

"They made us immediately," Meador said.

"They've had lots of experience," Antonelli said. "And besides, that antenna on the car might as well be a neon sign."

Smelt's house had an enclosed porch across the front, probably originally intended to catch the breezes, but today it was like an oven. There were three doorbells, including one with Smelt's name. No one answered. They rang the others. A buzzer sounded and they pushed the door open. A white youth who appeared to be in his late teens, or early twenties, was at the top of the stairs.

"Who are you?" he said.

"We're police, we're looking for Michael Smelt," Meador said.

"He's at work," the youth said. "He's a security guard over at Hopkins. You probably can reach him through the security office there."

Michael Smelt sat in the interrogation room at headquarters for nearly an hour before Antonelli and Meador began questioning him. They found him at Johns Hopkins and told him they had some questions to ask concerning John Coughlin and his dealings with his father. They asked him to go with them to headquarters and he readily agreed.

While in the interrogation room, he sat silently at the table, almost as if he had been through this before.

Detectives were sent to pick up Walter Ostrowski, who had seen a man he thought was a policeman with Laurie Waslewski. Smelt's security guard uniform, seen from a distance, could have been mistaken for a police uniform. Antonelli planned to put Smelt in a lineup.

News of a possible breakthrough in the Blue Girl murders spread through police headquarters generating an air of excitement and curiosity. First, the Captain stopped by, followed before long by a Colonel. Lt. Rauch tried to keep them away from Antonelli and his team. Antonelli wrote a summary of what linked Smelt to the crimes and thought about his questioning strategy.

With the recent Supreme Court Miranda decision regarding the questioning of suspects and the right to an attorney, police departments all over the country were scrambling to implement guidelines for their police forces. The major issue was that the right to be advised of the right to an attorney, and the right not to say anything only applied when someone was a suspect. It did not apply to potential witnesses. There was a large undefined area of what exactly made someone a suspect.

Antonelli consulted with the assistant State's Attorney about Smelt. At this point he couldn't say the man was a suspect, but he couldn't say that he wasn't. He needed to question him before he could decide that. He was advised to tell Smelt his rights and try to get him to waive them.

Antonelli decided on a slightly different course. He and Meador went into the interrogation room with a cup of coffee for Smelt.

"I'm sorry to have kept you waiting like this," Antonelli said. "No sooner did we get back here and we got hauled into a meeting with our lieutenant about a problem with another case. We couldn't break free until now." Without giving Smelt a chance to say anything, he continued.

"We brought you down here today because information came to us that raises questions about you, and your involvement in the murders of three women and one young man." Smelt tried to say something, but Antonelli held up his hand. "Wait, you'll get a chance to talk, let me finish.

"We've got a witness who says he saw you with one of the victims just a few minutes before she disappeared and was killed. We have another witness who saw you in your car picking up Rory Crawford and Karen Billingsley the night they were killed. This eyewitness testimony is pretty compelling. It's the gas chamber for you."

Smelt at this point had turned dark red and he started yelling, "Stop, stop, you don't know what the fuck you're talking about. I didn't kill anyone. I've never killed anyone."

"Look, before you say anything, you have to understand. I am going to read you your rights under the recent decision of the U.S. Supreme Court. Once I read these rights to you, you have a choice. You can stop talking to us and wait for your lawyer, or you can waive your rights, and keep talking to us. If you decide to stop talking, then we are done. We charge you with multiple first-degree murders, and we're done. You'll go to trial on those charges.

"However, if you waive your rights, and you talk to us, and tell us what happened, then maybe the death penalty is off the table. Maybe some deal can be made. But we can't make any deal if you don't waive your rights."

"Fuck that," Smelt said. "I didn't kill anyone. I'm willing to talk right now. I'll waive my rights."

Antonelli handed him a document and pointed out where he should sign and date it.

"OK, now tell me your story," Antonelli said. He was flying high, feeling good. Maybe the Blue Girl murders were about to be history.

It didn't take long for Antonelli to realize it wouldn't work out that way. Antonelli and Meador questioned Smelt for two hours. He didn't have verifiable alibis for any of the murders. He readily admitted having a grudge against John Coughlin.

"That man screwed my father and caused him to lose all of our money," Smelt said. "He wrecked our lives. We had a good life and he wrecked it."

Antonelli showed Smelt the court record.

"There is proof here that Mr. Coughlin opposed the investment. Your father did it over his objections, not because of his recommendation."

"That's a damn lie. That letter is a forgery. My father never would have done that on his own."

"How do you know that?" Antonelli said. "You were only 11 or 12 at the time."

"My mother told me," he said. "Her life was ruined, and she said it was all due to John Coughlin."

"But she was wrong," Antonelli said. "This letter isn't a forgery. Look at all these other documents. Mr. Coughlin tried to warn your father, but he acted on his own."

Smelt looked through the documents, and read several of them.

"Shit, I've never seen any of this," he said. "I believed my mother, but I can see she was wrong. She was so unhappy, feeling that my father had been double-crossed."

"Your father probably couldn't admit to your mother that he made the investment against the advice of Coughlin," Antonelli said. "But he did admit it, by hanging himself."

Tears ran down Smelt's face.

"I see that now," he said. "How in the world could he have been so stupid?"

"From what I can tell from reading the file, he was desperate because the real estate business was failing. Huge amounts of money were being made in Texas oil, and he got sucked in."

Smelt was silent.

"Do you know Dewey Coughlin?"

"The son of John Coughlin?"

Antonelli nodded.

"I've never met him," Smelt said.

"You didn't feel some hostility towards him because of his father?"

"No, it never occurred to me," he said. "My mother was the big hater of his father, but she never said anything about him. She was consumed with his father, and when his father died it seemed to take something out of her. She had been fighting cancer for quite a while, and holding her own. It was like she kept living because of all that hate. She declined rather rapidly after his death, and died about three months later."

"And you didn't feel any resentment towards Dewey Coughlin?"

"No, I haven't even thought about the Coughlins since my mother died," he said. "I might not be able to say this the right way, but my mother's death sort of freed me from the past. I didn't have to listen to her anymore about how our family was destroyed. I no longer had to feel the shame I knew she felt about me having to work as a security guard. Once she was gone, I could be my own person. That's what I have been trying to do since then, and while it's tough now and then, life has been getting better.

"I'm trying to do something with my life," he said. "I've got a decent job and because they cover much of the cost as a benefit, I can get a degree through the Hopkins night school eventually. I don't even think about what happened to my parents now. What happens to me now is up to me."

Antonelli canceled the lineup. He gave Lt. Rauch the bad news.

"He's not our guy, not even close," he said.

"Are you sure he's not playing you," Rauch said. "He's had some training, you know."

"I know, but he's not the one," Antonelli said. "He's not hiding anything. It's a waste of our time. We just have to start over and look for someone else."

"The FBI doesn't seem to be coming up with anything," Rauch said.

"I know. We're hitting dead ends everywhere."

Chapter Thirty-Eight

Racial Tensions and Politics

By early August the Blue Girl murders once again had faded from the news. The police department did not issue any official statements after mid-July. Nick talked with Antonelli several times, and knew from him, as well as from Susan and Dewey, that he still believed in his theory of the case, but no progress towards solving the case had been made.

Despite all the reforms underway in the police department, opening it up to close scrutiny by a reporter had no appeal, especially with a new Police Commissioner just starting out. Nick's proposal for an in-depth study of the investigation of the Blue Girl murders was rejected.

Donald Pomerleau, the man who headed the study released early in the year that labeled the Baltimore police department one of the worst in the nation, became permanent Police Commissioner, replacing Gen. Gelston. He immediately said all the reforms instituted by Gelston would continue under him, and would be expanded. Pomerleau visited black neighborhoods and pledged to have a police force that served all the people. Foot and vehicle patrols were stepped up in black areas. However, racial tension remained high. There were riots in several major cities, including Chicago and Cleveland.

"I'm sorry it took so long to get you an answer," Antonelli said over the telephone, "but with the new Police Commissioner, and many internal changes resulting from that, the timing just isn't right."

Nick wasn't about to give up, and decided to try a different tact. He had gotten four box seat tickets to an Orioles game, with the intention of taking Joan, Susan and Dewey. But now he had a different idea.

"Are you a baseball fan?" he said.

"I love the Orioles, of course. Who doesn't this year?"

"I've got four box seat tickets to the game Friday night. I'm taking my girlfriend, but I don't have plans for the other two tickets. You can have them, if you are interested."

"Thanks. I would enjoy that. I tell you what, I'll bring my girlfriend, and maybe the four of us then could have dinner at my dad's place."

"Sounds good," Nick said.

The Beatles tour of the U.S. drew large crowds, and Nick thought about their music, driving into work on a Tuesday morning the second week of August, with "Yellow Submarine" blaring from the radio, a song with a different sound that also came with a different message. To Nick it signaled a shift, in the music, and in the culture, even though Frank Sinatra had a hit with "It Was a Very Good Year." Despite its seeming zaniness, Nick didn't think "Yellow Submarine" really was humorous, or innocent. Something ominous was in the air. Drug use, especially marijuana and LSD, seemed to be expanding rapidly. The coming fall college term promised increased antiwar activity and upheaval. The era of California girls, surfboards, the jitterbug, and holding hands had passed. The times had changed.

There was no summer slack time in the news. Racial tensions were extremely high. Desegregation activities by CORE diminished in late July, but the National States Rights Party announced it would hold a rally in Sam Smith Park in mid-August. In addition to the racial tension, the Democratic Party's gubernatorial campaign heated up. With just a few weeks to the September 13th primary election, Nick spent almost every evening covering appearances by the candidates around the state, and some days did not go into the bureau until midday. Baltimore's top officials worked hard to prevent the racial tension in the city from exploding into violence. Mayor McKeldin kept himself visible in the city, riding around in his black limo, stopping and getting out to talk with people on the street corners.

The previous Saturday, on a visit to the city's famous Lexington Market, Nick saw the Mayor's car pull up to a red stoplight on North Howard Street. The rear window rolled down and an arm came out. People on the sidewalk walked over and shook hands with the mayor. "Mr. Mayor, Mr. Mayor," they yelled. McKeldin stuck his head out of the car window to reach more hands.

There only had been three Republican governors of Maryland in the 20th Century, and McKeldin was the only one to serve two terms. First elected Governor in 1950, he became nationally famous at the Republican Convention in 1952 for his rousing speech nominating Dwight Eisenhower for President. Unlike conservative Republicans, the few remaining liberal Republicans like McKeldin favored government action to solve social and economic problems. McKeldin was far more liberal and dedicated to social change than the 100% Democratic City Council, which refused to change the city ordinance permitting racial discrimination by bars. Even with his powers limited by lack of support from the Council, McKeldin was helping to keep the peace through force of personality and enormous energy.

With the Charles Center project rebuilding a portion of downtown Baltimore, rapidly expanding suburban developments around Baltimore and Washington, Maryland faced rapid growth and change. Plans for a subway system for Baltimore were underway. Even though the Governor's position in Maryland government was stronger than in many states, state government still operated on a relatively small scale, with functions divided between Annapolis and Baltimore. Governor J. Millard Tawes, now finishing his second term ran the state with the low-key and casual manner of his Eastern Shore upbringing.

One Saturday morning *The Sun* reported the Governor was about to endorse a candidate in the primary election, something he so far had refused to do. Nick called the State House in Annapolis, hoping to find someone from the Governor's staff working on a Saturday. A gruff voice answered the phone.

Nick explained he was trying to reach the Governor to talk to him about the *Sun's* story.

"This is Governor Tawes, what would you like to know?"

That the Governor would be in his office on a Saturday morning in August and would answer the phone impressed Nick as quaint and refreshing. He wondered if any of those now running for Governor would do the same.

Every prognosticator expected the winner of this year's Democratic Primary to easily defeat the little known and colorless Republican candidate, Baltimore County Executive Spiro Agnew, who Nick had gotten to know, and to like. Agnew gave Nick the number of a phone that only he answered, and Nick frequently called him to get comments on various news stories. Agnew had a gentle sense of humor and seemed genuinely amused by the fracas in the Democratic Party.

George Mahoney, a perennial candidate who never had won a primary, exploited the racial tension in the state by basing his campaign on the slogan, "Your Home is Your Castle - Protect It." He appealed to blue collar and lower middle class whites feeling threatened by open housing laws and the "blockbusting" of traditionally white neighborhoods. Those who had predicted an easy win by liberal Congressman-at-Large Carlton Sickles were worried.

Chapter Thirty-Nine

Antonelli Presents a Conclusion

On the morning of the Friday when Antonelli and Maria would be going to the Orioles game with Nick Prescott and his fiancé, he conducted a review meeting of the Blue Girl murders. While he conducted periodic working meetings, he had a bigger purpose for this one. It had been a very difficult analysis, and he was unhappy with his conclusion, but he was sure he now knew the identity of the Blue Girl killer. To proceed further, he needed to make his case.

In addition to his team of five detectives, present were Lt. Rauch, FBI Special Agent in Charge of the Baltimore Field Office, John Walters, Assistant State's Attorney Robert Samuels, and representatives of the Medical Examiner and the Crime Lab. He also asked Lt. Rauch to invite his boss, Captain Roger Carling, the head of Crimes Against Persons.

"It's time for us to summarize the Blue Girl murder cases and make some decisions about where we are headed," he said. "We have reached a point in the investigation where I believe we can focus on a specific suspect. I have reached that conclusion after exhaustive investigative work by my team of detectives, as well as by the FBI."

Antonelli had positioned large displays along one wall, including photos of the crime scenes and of the victims pinned to a bulletin board. Enlarged photos of the victims were arranged around photographs of Angela Coughlin, one published in the Sun in the late 1950s, and the other one, the portrait photo from Dewey Coughlin's home. He walked to the photos that showed the crime scenes.

"I'm going to review what we know about the crimes, and some of the details of our investigations. I think you will see everything we know leads to one conclusion, but I want you to see why.

"All three murders of the women were committed inside buildings, almost exactly the same way. They were injected with very fast-acting sodium thiopental, also known as sodium pentothal, which gave the killer almost instant control. A second injection later would completely disable them. Barlow and Billingsley also had LSD in their systems. Waslewski did not. The Medical Examiner says it is impossible to determine if any of the victims was conscious when she was killed. Is that not so?" Antonelli said, looking towards the assistant ME.

"Yes, that's true."

"Their bodies were painted with the same blue tempera paint, probably from the same mixture," Antonelli said, standing in front of, but not looking at, the photos of the victims before they were moved. He still found it very difficult to look at the pictures, particularly the one of Billingsley.

"Their heads were cut off from the front with an extremely sharp knife. There is little evidence of the crushing of tissue or bone that would have occurred if an axe, or cleaver, had been used. Basically, the heads were sliced off. As you can see, the bodies and heads were in nearly identical positions. The women were not physically or sexually abused.

"Very basically, these killings were done in the style of a Mayan human sacrifice, but we have no reason to believe they were intended as human sacrifices," he said. "We have consulted with a number of authorities who have advised that probably not enough is known about the ancient Mayan rituals of human sacrifice for a real one to be carried out today. The Mayans conducted human sacrifices for a period of maybe 1,500 years, ending with the Spanish conquest. No written records of their rituals survived the Spanish conquest.

"Clearly, there is a reason why the killer did the murders this way, but we don't know what it is. We have operated on the theory that it probably was done either to confuse us, or to point us in a certain direction. We do know, however, that there is a direct link between the Mayan-style deaths and our suspect.

"Rory Crawford was killed simply by garroting with a sharp wire. We wondered whether he might be the principal target, with the women killed to hide that. We haven't found any evidence to support that theory, although he did have a conflict with his drug pusher, an art student who paints blue nudes, Victor Blodgett, who we have questioned extensively, and are certain is not the killer.

"On the night of his killing Crawford was supposed to meet someone who would give him more mescaline. Crawford had mescaline in his system when he was killed. Blodgett did not sell mescaline, a legal drug available by mail order, and thus not of much interest to drug pushers.

"The only witnesses we have found for any of the murders are a woman who saw Crawford and Billingsley get into a 1962 Buick near his Johns Hopkins fraternity house, and an old man who saw Laurie Waslewski walking towards the Pagoda in Patterson Park, with what he thought was a policeman. In the first case the killer was not seen. In the second, not much of him is remembered, except he was dressed as a policeman. We believe the disguise may have enabled him to get Crawford and Billingsley into his car, and to approach Barlow in the alley behind the strip club. However, if the killer was the mescaline provider, he would not have needed the police disguise for Crawford and Billingsley. Keep that in mind.

"We have looked very carefully into the backgrounds of all the victims to try to find links among them. We didn't find any. They didn't know each other. They lived in separate worlds. As far as we can tell there is not a single individual all three of the women knew.

"However, we did discover there is one characteristic shared by all three women," he said, walking over to the photograph of Angela Coughlin. "They were blue-eyed natural blondes with the Marilyn Monroe type of sexy, sultry, curvy look, as opposed to the thin, model type of look. And all three strongly resemble another woman, the late Angela Bain Coughlin, this woman." He pointed to her 1928 portrait.

"The resemblance to our victims is incredible," he said, pointing to the enlarged photos of each of the victims.

"Now to add to this link," he said, "Dewey Coughlin is an expert on ancient Mayan culture, and periodically travels to Mexico to work on archaeological digs, and to obtain drugs.

"Because of the similarity in appearance of the victims to Angela Coughlin, and because of Dewey Coughlin's expertise in Mayan culture, we have exhaustively investigated him and his family. However, anyone who attended the Mayan exhibit at the Baltimore Museum of Art that ended early this year could have learned everything he needed to know to stage the murders as they were done. The fact that Coughlin is an expert in this field might not be so important if it were not for similarity of the victims to his mother. Consequently, we have

230

been operating on the possibility the killer intended to implicate Dewey Coughlin, and could be someone he knows, or at least has a link to the Coughlin family.

"We have questioned Dewey Coughlin extensively. He knew two of the victims, Karen Billingsley, a long time friend of his family, and Laurie Waslewski. He briefly dated Billingsley, but says he did not attempt to date Waslewski. Coughlin denies ever going to the strip club, or knowing anything about Barlow. His name does not show on any customer, or credit card list. He does not match descriptions of men who were known as big fans of Barlow. None of the bouncers or bartenders recognized Coughlin when we showed them a number of photos. But, for comparison, they weren't able to identify as customers two of our detectives who went to the strip club undercover on two occasions each, when the club was reasonably busy. So, it is conceivable Coughlin could have gone to the strip club on a busy night and not have been noticed.

"With one exception, he has not exhibited any behavior we normally associate with the guilty. In my first interview of him he did deny knowing Rory Crawford. In our second interview he readily admitted knowing Crawford and providing him with mescaline. Other than that, he has answered all our questions, and we haven't found any other inconsistencies. He seems to be a person of good character. In addition to being extremely wealthy, he also is said to be quite brilliant. He now works in the circulation department at the *News American*, but until recently he was a professional student. He went to Johns Hopkins off and on for years. This year he got both his BA and MA degrees.

"He is suffering from some kind of ailment that causes severe headaches. He suffered a brain injury several years ago. He has undergone tests for a possible brain tumor, but the results were inconclusive.

"We cannot find any motive he might have for these killings. He also says he is not aware of anyone who would have a grudge against him. He knows very little about his father's activities. He was not close to either of his parents, although he does not have the hostility to his father that he has towards his mother.

"It is important to note that Dewey Coughlin currently is involved in an intimate relationship with Susan Fanning, a feature writer for the Hearst Headline Service, located at the

News American. But to add to the mystery here, she resembles Angela Coughlin so closely that she has said she could be mistaken for a twin sister. She has been made aware of our theory of these crimes and advised to take appropriate precautions.

"Detective Meador will review what we know of the Coughlin family," Antonelli said.

Meador reviewed the history of the Bain and Coughlin families, including its social and financial prominence, and that Dewey Coughlin was the last of both families.

"Because of the strong resemblance of his mother to the victims, we dug further into her background," Meador said.

"Mrs. Coughlin, who committed suicide with an overdose of sleeping pills in 1964, suffered from mental illnesses, with several stays in psychiatric facilities. During the course of her life she engaged in infidelities and other questionable behavior. She ignored, and probably mistreated her four children, but we have found no evidence of sexual abuse. She was alienated from her son, Dewey, maybe from all her children. Dewey describes his mother as 'insane.'

"Angela's father, an extremely successful and wealthy businessman, was shot to death in 1934 on the family farm in Baltimore County," Meador said. "It was reported as a hunting accident. No charges were filed. Shortly afterwards, Angela entered Sheppard Pratt, where she stayed for 18 months. We think she may have shot her father, but we don't know the circumstances. We checked Baltimore County records, and there aren't any. They were a very prominent and powerful family, and I think whatever happened was hushed up very effectively."

Meador sat down and Antonelli resumed.

"Despite all this, her husband, John Coughlin, was believed to have worshipped her," he said. "Dewey Coughlin believes that. He blames his mother for his father's death. However, John's longtime mistress, his administrative assistant, claims otherwise. She says Angela had something on her husband that was extremely threatening to him. We have been unable to find out what it was.

"Angela's suicide does have some mystery," Antonelli continued. "She positioned an old dried up red rose between her breasts that Dewey says was an important message to his father, but his father never said what it was. Dewey says it caused his father considerable agitation, maybe even his fatal heart attack. Dewey says his parents hated roses and never allowed any in the house, or on the property. We have not been able to find out the significance of the rose.

"Now, I'd like Special Agent in Charge John Walters to give us some background on John Coughlin, and the results of the FBI's investigation into him," Antonelli said.

Walters handed out a stapled set of papers.

"This is biographical information we assembled on Coughlin," he said. "He was from old Baltimore society family, and was a powerful and highly influential investment banker, and financial adviser to many of Baltimore's wealthiest society families. He left an estate of real estate, stocks and bonds to Dewey worth many millions of dollars.

"John Coughlin had three careers," Walters said. "In the 1930s he rose to a senior executive position with an import/export firm that closed at the beginning of World War II. During World War II he worked for the Treasury Department as one of the primary managers of war bond sales. After the war he joined Alexander Brown as a partner, and he was one of their most successful investment bankers and financial advisers. At the time of his death he was a senior partner.

"Given his prominence, we thought he might have a number of enemies," Walter said. "We haven't found any. We can't find any case where we can identify a potential suspect for these murders. We talked to many people, and checked thousands of pages of records. We came up dry."

"In the course of questioning John Coughlin's mistress, we identified a possible suspect," Antonelli said. "He is a security guard at Johns Hopkins. His mother blamed Mr. Coughlin for her husband losing the family fortune on an investment, and then committing suicide. The truth is that Mr. Coughlin recommended against the investment, but the man never told his wife that.

"We interviewed this individual at length and we do not consider him a suspect," Antonelli said.

"At this point, we have not been able to identify a single person who might have a motive, as well as the capability, of carrying out these crimes in an effort to implicate Dewey Coughlin. I think we must consider the possibility that no one is trying to implicate him, and either the links we have found between the murders and the Coughlins are entirely coincidental, or, in fact, Coughlin is the killer.

"Up until now, we have not considered him a suspect, but we have investigated him," Antonelli said.

"Coughlin has no verifiable alibi for the Barlow and Waslewski murders, and there is a two-hour gap in his alibi for the Crawford-Billingsley killings. He claims to have been in a downtown restaurant, but we were unable to confirm that.

"Rory Crawford had traces of mescaline, a scarce drug in this area, in his body. Coughlin has used mescaline, and said he did give Crawford some several weeks before he was killed. He denies meeting him on the night of the murder. Crawford's source was said by his best friend to be an individual in the neighborhood, not a pusher, and a friend of Karen Billingsley. However, mescaline is not illegal, and it can be purchased by mail order. Coughlin's use and knowledge of drugs apparently is fairly well known. Crawford's use of drugs was known among his fraternity brothers. He also obtained drugs from the art student, Blodgett, a small-time dealer, but Blodgett says he did not deal in mescaline. Our experts in drug trafficking confirm that pushers generally do not offer mescaline because it is legal, and thus not profitable

"Since Crawford had arranged to meet his supplier of mescaline that Saturday night, and since Coughlin was known to Crawford, he would not have had to use the police disguise, something that would have added to the time, and complexity, required for the abductions to have taken place during the two hour period when he says he was on his break. We talked with the restaurant's staff, and no one remembers Mr. Coughlin being there that night. Two of the waitresses said they knew him from other visits, and they said they thought they would have remembered him being there.

"Finally, Coughlin had a 1962 Buick matching the description of the car Crawford and Billingsley were seen getting into near the fraternity house on the night they were murdered. He told us he sold the car for cash in early May, but says he kept no record of the sale. We did verify he advertised the car in *The Sun* and the *News American* in late April. The license plates were returned to the DMV, but the car has not been re-registered in the state.

"It must be noted that dark green and dark blue Buicks from the period are among the more common cars in the area. The art student, Blodgett, has one, as does the Hopkins security guard we recently interrogated.

"As of this moment, unless someone has a different idea, I think we have to consider Dewey Coughlin as our principal suspect. There just are too many coincidences, and we have explored every reasonable alternative. I would like to do a search of his house, and bring him in for extensive interrogation. Bob, do you think there is enough circumstantial evidence to get a search warrant?"

"It's dicey," the Assistant State's Attorney said, "but I will try."

"Let's do it early next week," Antonelli said. "That will give you time to go over our investigation in detail, and develop your very best argument."

As the meeting broke up, Capt. Carling pulled Antonelli and Rauch aside. He looked at Antonelli and smiled.

"Very good presentation," he said. "I think you are correct. I'll talk to Samuels and make sure he approaches this with the right attitude."

"What's really bothering me," Antonelli said, "is that Dewey Coughlin seems like a really nice guy, not a killer. I like the guy. Everybody likes the guy. I haven't been a homicide detective for very long, but I've encountered quite a few killers. He doesn't fit. I don't think I'm wrong, but I think there is a whole lot to this that we don't know."

Chapter Forty

Antonelli Tells Prescott

"Things they do look awful c-c-cold (Talkin' 'bout my generation)
"Yeah, I hope I die before I get old (Talkin' 'bout my generation"
- The Who, My Generation

As he sat in Memorial Stadium that evening with Maria, Nick Prescott and his fiancé, Joan, Antonelli could not keep his mind on the game. He worried about what he had set in motion. While he was sure he was right, there was so much he didn't know. It was like that dream, walking towards that light, not knowing what he was going to find when he got there. And there was danger. Not to him, but to others, especially to Susan Fanning who looked so much like Dewey Coughlin's mother. He had to make sure she was not the next victim, that there were no more victims.

He wanted to warn Nick, but he knew he shouldn't. He didn't know for sure if the search warrant would be granted. He didn't know if he would find anything incriminating if it was. He still did not feel comfortable saying much to a reporter, even though Nick had shown himself to be trustworthy.

At one point, Maria whispered to him, "Are you OK? You seem a million miles away tonight." He smiled, and squeezed her hand.

"I'm fine," he said. "I had to do a big presentation today, with the Captain present, the first time I've done something like that. It's hard to get it out of my mind, but I'm trying."

But he couldn't. Halfway through the Oriole game, he said quietly to Nick, "Let's go out to the concession stand. There's something I need to tell you." Nick gave him an odd look, and then said to Joan, "Maury and I are going to get us some beers. We'll be back in a few minutes."

Out in the walkway that curved around the outside of the stadium, the noise of the crowd and the public address system receded enough so they could talk without yelling.

"There's been a major development in the Blue Girl murder case," Antonelli said. "I think I have to tell you about it, but I don't want to talk about it in front of the girls. Also, it's something you can't report. You have to promise me that you won't report anything until I say you can."

"Sure," Nick said. "No problem."

"We think your friend, Dewey Coughlin, is the killer," Antonelli said.

"No! That can't possibly be true." Nick said, an alarmed look on his face.

"It took me a long time to reach this conclusion," Antonelli said. "It wasn't easy, but I'm quite certain. There's much I don't know yet, and we're not ready to charge him. That's why you can't report anything. You can't say anything to him, either. I know you're his friend, but you cannot say anything to him. Understand?"

"Yes, I understand, but I just don't believe it," Nick said.

"Believe it," Antonelli said. "It all adds up. I need you to do something that I can't do," Antonelli said.

"What's that?"

"If I'm right, and I'm sure I am, Susan Fanning could be in danger," Antonelli said. "You might be in danger as well, but I think she is in greater danger."

"Because she looks like his mother?"

"That has to be it," Antonelli said. "I don't understand it, but that has to be the link among all the murders. She could be the next victim."

"He loves her," Nick said. "He wouldn't harm her."

"Maybe not while they are together, but you told me she is trying to get away, to go back to Boston. It could be dangerous for her to break off her relationship. I don't really know. It's just my gut instinct. She needs to be warned, and I can't do it."

"So, you want me to do it?" Nick said.

"Yes, but you have to do it in such a way that she doesn't panic, and neither of you can say anything to Coughlin. We're going to search his house next week, and he can't have any warning in advance. You understand how serious this is?"

"Yes," Nick said. "I think you're wrong, but I'll talk to Susan this weekend. I'll figure out some way to do it. She's very levelheaded. I don't think she'll panic."

"Good, let's get back to the game before they come looking for us," Antonelli said.

Having warned Nick made Antonelli feel a little better, and it became possible to enjoy the rest of the evening. After the game they went to his father's restaurant and had a leisurely meal, with some good wine, and much talk, mostly by the two women. He and Nick were quiet. He could see Nick thinking, while trying to be attentive.

While their backgrounds were quite different, Maria and Joan seemed to like each other enormously. They shared a positive, optimistic view of life, different from the darker view of life that Antonelli had from being a homicide detective. He so much enjoyed just sitting there, watching and listening to these two bright and attractive young women, and to be with someone like Nick, who had such enthusiasm and idealism, again something he didn't see on a daily basis. He soaked it up. Even though he was only a couple of years older, he felt ancient compared to the three of them. Somehow, he thought, he missed the period of life that they were experiencing.

Chapter Forty-One

Nick Warns Susan

It was nearly 1:00 A.M. when they left the restaurant, too late to take Joan back to his apartment, so Nick drove Joan directly home. On the way he told Joan what he had learned from Antonelli, and what Antonelli wanted him to do.

"My God," Joan said. She was silent for a minute, and there were tears in her eyes. "I just can't believe Dewey is the killer. There's something really wrong with their investigation."

"I think so, too," Nick said. "I don't see how we, and Susan, could be so wrong about him. There's got to be something they are missing."

"So how are you going to tell Susan?"

"I want to do it tomorrow, at my apartment, before she sees Dewey again. I think he is spending the night at her apartment tomorrow night. I'd like you to be there when I talk with her. I'll call her in the morning and let you know."

Nick would have enjoyed the evening a great deal more if Antonelli had not dropped that bomb on him at the game. During the dinner he tried to pay attention to Joan and Maria, but found his mind drifting. He could tell that Antonelli's mind also was elsewhere. The two women did most of the talking while he and Antonelli tuned in occasionally, and the rest of time tried to appear interested.

The enormity of what Antonelli wanted him to do sank in during the course of the evening. This was much different than covering a story and writing about it. Now he was involved in someone's life, and he had to be very careful.

He studied Antonelli during the evening. He was only two years older and hadn't gotten through college, yet he had the power, and position, to destroy a man's life by accusing him of multiple murders. It awed Nick that he could do it so calmly and confidently. It made Nick feel puny in his world where life mostly was ephemeral, one story after another, each soon forgotten and replaced by a newer one, hardly any of them having much importance. Never in his life had Nick had to make a decision as tough as the one Antonelli had made that day. He respected the man, even though he thought he was wrong.

Now it was his turn to make some difficult and potentially life-altering decisions. He had spent a good share of the dinner trying to imagine Dewey as the killer. If Dewey was the killer, then everything Nick had ever thought about him was wrong. He would be the most duplicitous, and the most dangerous person he had ever known. On top of that he would have to be insane, more insane than his mother, and far better at hiding it. The more he thought about it, the more he found it impossible to believe Dewey was the killer. Still, he had to make some decisions knowing that it was possible.

He felt responsible for Susan, and her relationship with Dewey. If it had not been for him, Susan probably would have succeeded in breaking off the relationship. Of course, if Dewey really was the killer, then keeping the two of them together may have protected her. He didn't want to think of it that way, but it made him feel a little less guilty.

Now he had to suggest a way to Susan to keep her relationship with Dewey stable while the investigation played out. Nick thought through the murders, and could see that if Dewey was the killer, it may have been because the girls rejected him, like his mother rejected him. Barlow refused to do some of the things the other strippers did. She didn't date any of her customers. Karen Billingsley and Dewey broke off. Laurie Waslewski might have refused to date him. Thus, if Susan suddenly were to pull away from him, she could be in real danger, unless she went far away, like back to Boston to stay.

It was good that when Antonelli thought the killer was someone trying to implicate Dewey, he had warned Susan that she might be in danger. That caused her to have her overnights with Dewey at her apartment. Unless Susan decided to bolt, to get as far away from Dewey as possible, she would have to continue that practice, and to try to avoid being alone with him anyplace else. Assuming Susan stayed, Nick decided that he and Joan would have to spend much more time with Dewey until the investigation was completed.

He called Susan Saturday morning and set up a meeting at his apartment at 1:00 P.M. He then called Joan and told her what he had in mind.

When Susan came into Nick's apartment, she said to Joan with a smile, "You should know that this is my first visit to Nick's apartment, and I know I wouldn't be here if you weren't here."

"Nick is very proper," Joan said, and then after a pause, added, "and very careful."

Nick blushed, and they all laughed.

"He still blushes," Susan said. "After Rehoboth Beach, I didn't think I'd ever see him blush again. Dewey keeps lobbying me to get the two of you to spend another weekend there. He wants to see Joan and me in bikinis."

"Why bikinis?" Joan said. "He's seen us very close up with nothing on."

"He thinks it would be sexy," Susan said with a smile.

"I think it would be sexy," Nick said, but he didn't smile. "Maybe sometime, but that's not why I brought you here today. It's something far more serious. Detective Antonelli believes Dewey is the Blue Girl killer."

Susan's smile faded into a shocked look. Her eyes got very dark and serious. Nick could see tears forming in the corners of her eyes.

"Oh, Nick, this can't be true," she sobbed, but then she added, "but I think it could be."

"What?" Joan said. "You think Dewey is the killer?"

"I never thought that before this minute," Susan said, "and I'm not saying now that I believe it. I just think it's possible. I've seen some things in Dewey that disturbed me."

"Such as?" Nick said.

"I thought I mentioned this before, but maybe I didn't," she said. "I've seen it a couple times when we had some tough conversations, one of them involving me moving to Boston, and me not wanting him moving with me. The other one was when I tried hard to get him to tell me more about his mother. I know he had a tough time, and I thought it might help for him to talk about it. He did a little, but then shut up. When I tried to get him to talk some more, he gave me a look that was chilling. It was only momentary, and he shook it off. Literally, he shook himself, and then apologized. He said his mind had wandered to a time when he was very unhappy, and he didn't want to think about it."

"Describe the look," Nick said.

"Very hostile, very different. It wasn't a loving look. I swear it seemed predatory. It was just momentary, and then he was back to himself. It shook me each time. Each time he apologized, and was super sweet afterwards."

"I think you were on the right track, trying to get him to talk about his mother, but please don't do it again when you are with him by yourself," Nick said.

"If there is any reasonable possibility that he is the killer, then is it safe for Susan to be with him alone at any time?" Joan said.

"I don't know. It's up to you," Nick said, looking at Susan. "If he is the killer, then you could be in great danger, particularly if he thinks you are going to dump him, and he already is worried about that. You might be better off just going back to Boston now."

"You mean I should just quit my job and go hide," Susan said. "If he is the killer, he'll come after me. With his money he could find me anywhere. I'd never be safe. I can't do that. I won't do that. I can keep things stable with Dewey for the time being, certainly long enough for police to determine if he is the killer."

"You're sure you want to do this," Nick said. "You're going to be with him tonight. You can't let on a thing."

Susan stared at Nick and blinked her big blue eyes.

"I think I am perfectly capable of keeping his attention focused on other things," she said. "Don't you?"

"I have no doubt," Nick said, and then he smiled. All three of them laughed.

"Meanwhile, Joan and I will spend much more time with the two of you, so you are not with him alone very much at all. There's not much we can do about tonight, but I'm assuming this will come to a head this coming week."

"Are they going to arrest him?" Susan said.

"I don't know" Nick said. "They are going to search his house, and probably question him at great length. We won't know anything until those are done."

Chapter Forty-Two

Dewey's Fraternity House

The very thought of Dewey possibly being guilty of the Blue Girl murders changed Nick's perception of Dewey, and how he felt when he was around him. He would have to work hard Monday morning to be as friendly as he had been, and that made him feel bad.

On Sunday, Nick remembered Dewey saying something about renovating his old fraternity house, so he drove past it in the 32nd block of Guilford, only three blocks from his apartment. It was a large rowhouse, with a big covered front porch. The front of the house looked like all the rest of the houses on the street. There didn't appear to be any activity inside.

Suddenly Nick had a strong compulsion. He wanted to see that house. He thought about it, and realized that he should tell Antonelli about the house. However, he thought, it wouldn't hurt to see it first. He wanted to give Dewey the benefit of the doubt.

When Dewey came in Monday morning, Nick engaged him in a conversation about campus life at Hopkins.

"I'm thinking of getting a larger apartment in one of the new buildings downtown," Nick said, which was true. "I'd miss the atmosphere around Hopkins. It's become a part of me. I lived in my fraternity house for a couple of years. I really like it around there."

"I do, too," Dewey said. "As you know, my old fraternity house isn't far from your apartment. I had a good time there. I had the entire second floor to myself. I never had that much room to myself before then. It was great."

"I'd love to see that old house again," Nick said. "I stopped by my fraternity house the other day. It was fun."

"You really want to see it?" Dewey said.

"Sure," Nick said.

"I'm off at four today. If you want to see it, I'll meet you there at 4:30. If I'm late, just wait on the porch."

But he wasn't late. He was five minutes early. Nick knew that because he was ten minutes early.

The house obviously was in the process of restoration. Its old plaster walls were being repaired. Some walls now were smooth, with the lighter color of the new plaster showing. Others still were nicked and dirty. The hardwood floors creaked.

"The floors will be repaired and resealed once everything else is done," Dewey said.

He showed Nick the kitchen, which consisted of just the plumbing, electrical wires, and gas pipe.

"I'm having an entire new kitchen put in," he said. "I had it specially designed to fit this space. It will be here next month."

The kitchen connected in the rear to a portico in the fenced-in rear yard that led to the one car garage. "I can't get my Bronco in the garage. It was built for smaller vehicles," he said.

"What are you doing with the basement?" Nick said.

Dewey walked over to the door to the basement, which was under the front stairs, and opened it, and headed down the stairs. Nick followed. It was very dark. Nick felt a little trepidation, which surprised him.

"I'm replacing the lights down here, so it's pretty dark now, but you can see our old bar," Dewey said. "It still looks great."

Sure enough the brick and stone bar that he remembered when Dewey tried unsuccessfully to get him to join the fraternity, with the fraternity's seal painted on it, was still there. Stacks of hardwood flooring and bags of plaster were on the floor. In the corner were numerous paint cans.

"The contractors aren't going to do any more work until it gets cooler," Dewey said.

The second and third floors were completely clear and appeared ready for painting. Nick saw nothing suspicious in the house.

The only space he didn't see, and he couldn't figure out a way to ask to see it without raising suspicion, was the garage, but he could tell that Dewey was correct. It barely was large enough for a conventional car, and definitely wouldn't handle his truck.

Dewey had passed this test as far as Nick was concerned. Still he called Antonelli when he returned to his apartment that evening and told him about the fraternity house. He had talked to Antonelli on Saturday, following his conversation with Susan, but had not spoken to him since.

"You went there this afternoon?" Antonelli said.

"Yes, after the Orioles game," Nick said. "I know I probably shouldn't have done that, but it was a spur of the moment thing."

"Please don't do anything like that again," Antonelli said. "He could have killed you there, and no one would have known."

"I really don't believe he's the killer," Nick said.

"I know you don't, and I understand," Antonelli said. "You just have to trust that I know a little more than you about murder, and murderers."

"I'm sure you do," Nick said. "But I know Dewey is my friend."

"Well, I appreciate the call," Antonelli said. "I'll have the fraternity house added to the search warrant. We'll have the warrant tomorrow morning, and we will serve it when he gets home from work."

"I think it would be a good idea for Susan, Joan and me to be there," Nick said.

"It will tip him off that you knew in advance," Antonelli said. "You don't want to do that. Furthermore, we're going to haul his ass down to headquarters and put him through the ringer. Unless he lawyers up, and I bet he won't, we'll be with him all night, and maybe all day on Wednesday. We'll have to see how it goes. If he doesn't confess, and it would be a miracle if he does, and if we don't find any evidence in our searches, he'll probably be released Wednesday afternoon. He'll need some sleep, and then some company."

Chapter Forty-Three

Dewey Coughlin's Interrogation at the Police Station

As Antonelli expected, Dewey Coughlin waived his right to an attorney and said he would answer any questions they had. This was after they left him in the interrogation room alone for four hours, allowing a couple of bathroom breaks, and giving him some coffee. During much of the time he alternated between pacing the floor and sitting at the table, tapping his fingers. At times he talked to himself in a voice so low that he couldn't be understood.

Antonelli brought in Walter Ostrowski, the man who had seen "the pretty girl and the policeman," and put Coughlin in a lineup. Ostrowski did not recognize anyone in the lineup.

The team from the Crime Lab that searched his house came back with bottles of various drugs, some of which were not readily identifiable. Of those that were, the cocaine and marijuana clearly were illegal. The toad and mushroom extracts required a discussion with the DEA. They did not find any mescaline, LSD, or sodium thiopental, or even any syringes.

Other than the drugs, nothing was found in the house that implicated Coughlin in any illegal activity. Nothing implicated him in the Blue Girl murders.

Much the same was true of the fraternity house. The cans of paint were checked, but none was a blue tempera. The garage was empty.

It was about ten o'clock in the evening when the interrogation began.

Antonelli and Meador took turns, each questioning Coughlin for about a half hour, then taking a break.

Once again he denied ever hearing of Candy Barlow, and of ever being in her strip club. He readily admitted dating Karen Billingsley, but said their breakup didn't leave him with any hard feelings. This time he admitted he wanted to date

Laurie Waslewski, but she turned him down. He said his feelings were hurt, but not so much that it left any lasting negative feelings.

"Look, I've dated many girls in my life, and one more or less is no big deal," he said. "There always are more."

He once again admitted that he had given mescaline to Rory Crawford, but said he did not meet him on the night he was murdered.

They repeatedly asked him about his relationship with his mother. Did she abuse him? No, he had no recollection of any abuse. She just ignored him. What about his brothers and sisters? He wasn't sure. It was possible.

At midnight they brought in a pizza and cans of Coke, and the three of them shared everything. Antonelli was astonished at Coughlin's good humor. He didn't complain about the way they were treating them. He continued to answer questions without any reservations. Of course, nothing he said implicated him in any of the murders.

It was about two o'clock in the morning when Antonelli decided Coughlin was not going to break. He felt himself beginning to doubt his own judgment. He found it increasingly hard, despite all the coincidences, to believe Coughlin guilty of the murders.

They drove him home at 3:00 A.M. Antonelli went to his apartment and slept for four hours. At 8:00 A.M. he was back in the office to listen to the tapes of the interrogation. Before he began that, he called Nick.

"We had him here all night, and he never admitted anything. We didn't find shit at his house, or at the fraternity house. We can't charge him with anything except possession of some illegal drugs, and we're not going to do that. I am sure that he is the killer, but I have no fucking idea how I am going to prove it. So right now he is loose. Be careful. I am not giving up. We will be all over him."

Chapter Forty-Four

Dewey Asks for Nick's Help

Nick called Susan and Joan and told them what Antonelli told him. Nick said they should wait to have any contact with Dewey until he called someone, unless no one heard from him by late afternoon. Then, he said, Susan should call Dewey. However, Dewey called Susan at 3:00 that afternoon and told her what had happened. She called Nick.

By agreement, Nick and Joan met Susan a block from Dewey's house and picked up some pizzas and beer. The four of them spent most of the evening sitting around the patio table listening to music and smoking cigarettes. Dewey was quiet, but did not seem to be overly agitated. In fact, he seemed to be deep in thought most of the evening. Around 10 P.M. he became more alert.

"They think I killed those girls, and they are going to try to prove it," he said. "They no longer think it was someone trying to frame me, so they won't be looking for anyone else. The only way I am going to get out of this is to figure it out myself. The problem is, I can't do it by myself. I need some help."

"What do you need?" Nick said.

"The secret to all these killings is my mother," he said. "It now seems obvious. Somebody killed those girls because they looked like my mother. He wants me to die in the gas chamber because of my mother. What the fuck did my mother do? Somebody got hurt very badly by her, maybe more than one. My problem is that I barely knew my mother. I have virtually no memories of her from when I was a kid. Somebody must know a lot more than I do. I need you, Nick, to find that person, or persons. I need to know what my mother did that caused this horror."

"It's sort of out of my line of work," Nick said. "I'm not a detective."

"You are a reporter. You know how to dig up a story. Take
that approach here. There is a big story here, but it has to be
dug out of the past. You have to find people who knew my
mother years ago, and knew what she did, maybe even people
who were her lovers. I'm sure there still are some around.
They'd never talk to the police, and they probably won't talk to
you as a reporter. But they might talk to you as my friend.
You'd have to tell them you are helping me, that I need to find
out everything I can about my mother."

"Why not do it yourself?"

"It would be unseemly, not proper," he said. "It is more
proper for me to have someone do it for me, someone who has
discretion and judgment, and would know how to filter what
is found. I don't need to know, and I don't want to know,
every salacious detail. But you have to get them because
buried among them is the truth about these murders."

"I am really jammed right now," Nick said. "I can't do a
lot until after the Primary."

"That's fine," Dewey said. "You can do some digging, you
can make some phone calls. It may take a while anyway. But
tell me you'll get started. I need you to do this for me."

"I might need some help, someone to do some of the
digging, like a private detective," Nick said.

"Fine. Whatever," Dewey said. "Money's no object.
Whatever you need. Just make sure it is someone who is
discreet."

OK, before I hire anyone, I'll see what I can find out,"
Nick said.

"I can help, also," Susan said.

"No, Susan," Dewey said. "I appreciate you being willing,
but I don't know what is going to be found. I'd rather that only
Nick know, initially. There may be things I don't want you, or
anyone else, to know. I hope you understand."

Nick had expected to be tied up with racial unrest in the
city for the rest of the month. However, the racial violence
that had occurred in several other cities did not spread to
Baltimore. Nick thought that maybe the great season of the
Orioles had something to do with it, with Frank Robinson
having what could be an MVP season, but racial tension in the
city seemed to ease as September approached.

The National States Rights Party held a rally in Sam
Smith Park in South Baltimore, but hardly anyone noticed.
The prosecution of the NSRP officials for the Patterson Park

riot moved towards trial, and no more rallies were planned. CORE's activities were easing as many of the volunteers headed back to college.

The Democratic gubernatorial campaign reached a fever pitch with only two weeks to primary. Polls showed the race to be very close between Sickles and Mahoney. The Sickles people were worried and kept promoting all the endorsements he had received from prominent Democrats. Mahoney had none. President Johnson expressed concern about the Mahoney campaign's tactics.

On Saturday night of the last weekend of August Nick got four box seat tickets and took Dewey, Susan and Joan to an Orioles game. The last place Red Sox were making their final appearances at Memorial Stadium for the season. It was a treat for Susan, a fanatical Sox fan. The Orioles now were 12 games in first place, but the Sox had some promising young stars, and one of them, Jim Lonborg, would be pitching that night.

It was a tight game, and Susan annoyed the Oriole fans around them by cheering for every Sox batter. Lonborg pitched very well, and the Sox had a 3-0 lead into the bottom of the ninth. The Orioles scored two runs and had a runner on third when Don McMahon struck out Frank Robinson to end the game.

They went to Sabatino's in Little Italy that, like Antonelli's, offered very late night dinners. They went through three bottles of wine in the course of a lively meal. Nick thought Dewey was the most cheerful he had been since the Rehoboth Beach weekend. Nick's agreement to dig into his mother's past had lifted his spirits.

Chapter Forty-Five

Nick Finds Someone to Tell Him About Angela Coughlin

Nick learned from a conversation with Dewey that one of his mother's ancestors was a captain of a Baltimore clipper ship. Nick called a reporter he knew at the *The Sun*, and arranged an introduction to the paper's society editor. He told her he was working on a feature story about the families of Baltimore's famous clipper ship captains, who were, or became, socially prominent, and were listed in the *Blue Book*, the official list of Baltimore's society.

He did some research before going to *The Sun* and had names of several ship captains, along with several other prominent Maryland family names. Dewey's mother's maiden name was Angela Rosemont Bain. Her great grandfather was Captain Millard Bain, who upon retiring from the sea started an importing business that over the next two generations made the family quite wealthy.

The society editor provided him with some historical information, and leads to more, including people who knew more than she did. She also let Nick look through her collection of *Blue Books*. Nick wanted to find at least a couple of women who were about the same age as Angela Bain, possibly debutantes with her. He found the list of debutantes from Angela's 1928 Cotillon, and then cross-referenced them to marriage lists. It took about two hours to find six women from the 1928 Cotillon who the society editor knew were alive and living in the Baltimore area.

Nick had telephone conversations with three of the women, and left messages for the other three. The three who talked to him did not want to meet in person. All three said they were not personally friendly with Angela Bain Coughlin, and that they only knew one woman in the area who was, Marjorie Talbot.

Nick left four messages on her answering machine during the week before the Primary, leaving both his office and home numbers. She finally returned his calls on Sunday, two days before the primary election.

"It took me a while to reach Dewey," she said. "I wouldn't have called you back, otherwise. So Dewey wants you to find out everything about Angela?"

"Yes."

"He wouldn't do it himself?"

"He didn't think it was proper."

"He would think that, and, of course, he's right," she said. "He says he trusts you to be discreet. You're not doing this to write a story, correct?"

"Correct," Nick said. "I'm doing this entirely for Dewey. He's a good friend."

"Well, if you can stay on a horse, come out next Saturday morning, around nine A.M. We'll ride around my farm, and I'll tell you everything about Angela."

UPI took over the *News American*'s radio-TV department next door on primary election night, and Nick hired three of that department's editors to help collect the results. Joan, and two Johns Hopkins students, both fraternity brothers of Nick, also were in the room, answering the phones. Nick had stringers at the election boards in every county, and in the city, to call in results as they were posted.

The returns soon indicated how effectively Mahoney's "Your Home is Your Castle" motto resonated with blue-collar whites. The liberal, Congressman Carlton Sickles, was in trouble. Results from Baltimore City showed that the party machine did not deliver the vote to Thomas Finan. Mahoney ran well in white precincts. By midnight the race was too close to call. Mahoney was ahead by about 1,500 votes when Nick sent everyone home at 2 AM. He stayed in the bureau overnight by himself to take the calls with the results of the last precincts to be counted.

Mahoney's victory, by just 154 votes, stunned the Democratic Party establishment. Party leaders, including most elected officials, appeared less than enthusiastic about the result. Few embraced Mahoney as the party's standard-bearer. The more liberal and likable Spiro Agnew, unopposed for the Republican nomination, suddenly looked like a possible winner in November. When Nick talked with Agnew on Wednesday, the Republican seized the moment and started saying the right things to attract the liberal Democrats who could not abide Mahoney.

On Thursday the *Boston Globe* formally offered Susan the columnist position, and she immediately accepted it. Her column, to be oriented to women's issues, would first appear in the Globe on January 1, with her due to report to work at the *Globe* on December 1. Nick was the first person she told, almost running into the bureau that afternoon, her eyes shiny with tears that told him what had happened.

He hugged her.

"Congratulations. I'm so happy for you, but I will miss you."

"You and Joan will always be welcome at my place in Boston," she said. "I mean that with all my heart. I hope you will take me up on it."

"So what are you going to tell Dewey?"

"I don't know. It's funny. I thought I knew. I've been thinking about it for weeks. Now that it's happened, what I thought I would say doesn't sound right. I need to think about it, and maybe you and Joan can help me. Maybe I should tell him at our dinner with him on Friday night." Dewey was hosting one of his periodic Friday night dinners, and had told Nick that morning he was planning something special.

"Dewey's got something special planned for Friday night," Nick said. "It would be cruel to say anything to him then. You don't have to say anything yet. You don't have to give your notice right away, so no one else will know unless it leaks out of Boston."

"It won't," she said. "They're not going to announce it until the end of the month."

After she left the bureau, Nick called Antonelli to tell him the news.

"Keep in close touch with me, and let me know when he is going to find out," Antonelli said. "We'll then put surveillance on him, and Miss Fanning."

Dewey's special for Friday night was Beef Wellington. Nick could only remember having it once before, and it was at some large affair. He remembered the dough being soggy and the beef overdone. Dewey's was quite different. It was one of the best things Nick had ever tasted. The dough was light and crispy. The beef was medium rare. The foie gras and truffles were sublime. He served it with a 1945 Lafitte Rothschild, one of the great vintages of the century.

Dewey smiled as each of them praised his production.

"My God, Dewey, you could be an executive chef at a world-class restaurant," Nick said.

"I know it's getting close to the time when Susan will find out if she's getting that columnist job in Boston," Dewey said. "I'm sure she'll get it. I wanted to show her what she could be missing if, well, you know."

Nick could see that Susan was having a hard time responding. He broke the momentary tension.

"I think the two of you will become very used to the Boston shuttles," he said.

Everyone laughed. Dewey turned to get another bottle of wine. Susan mouthed "thank you" to Nick.

"Let's drink to that," Dewey said, having refilled everyone's glasses. They clinked the glasses and drank their second bottle of the ethereal wine.

"This has to be the best wine I've ever tasted," Nick said. "How many more bottles of this do you have in your cellar?" Nick said.

"I think there are six more," Dewey said. "My father bought a couple of cases of it years ago at an auction."

"Good," Nick said. "We'll look forward to finishing them off."

Again, everyone laughed. They then adjourned to the patio to have coffee and smoke.

It was going to be a difficult night for Susan, Nick thought. There was no way she could avoid spending the night at Dewey's house. Joan went to help Dewey get the coffee and it gave Nick a chance to talk briefly with Susan.

"Are you going to be OK tonight?" Nick said.

"I'm going to give Dewey the night of his life," she said. "It's the least I can do."

Chapter Forty-Six

The Story of Angela Coughlin

"What a drag it is getting old."
- The Rolling Stones, Mother's Little Helper

Nick remembered how sore he was when he took a few riding lessons several years ago. His girlfriend at the time rode horses almost every weekend, and insisted that he try to learn. He learned enough to stay on the horse and get it to start and stop when he wanted. If he had to do much beyond that this Saturday morning he would be in big trouble.

Marjorie Talbot lived on a huge horse farm in the rolling hills of Green Spring Valley north of Baltimore not far from the Vanderbilt-owned Sagamore Farms. It had the same kind of white board fencing, and beautiful horses strutting around the paddocks.

A teenage girl met Nick in the driveway and directed him to the stable. As he approached, he saw two saddled horses tied up outside, and a woman standing by one of them. He knew Marjorie Talbot was fifty-five or fifty-six years old, but she looked much younger in her figure-hugging riding pants and blouse. With bright auburn hair and a creamy white complexion, she still was a striking-looking woman. Nick wore blue jeans and the riding boots his girlfriend talked him into buying four years ago. They still had their original shine.

They shook hands and he felt her eyes appraising him. She noticed the boots.

"I guess you have done this before," she said. "I wasn't sure from your answer."

"It's been a while, so take it easy on me. I'm not ready to do a cross country course," he said.

She laughed and shook her hair before pushing it up to put on her riding helmet.

"I'm past that now, myself. I've had enough broken bones," she said. "We'll just take a short ride around the farm, and then we'll sit on the patio and talk."

They followed a trail that took them around the edge of the farm, and up and down several hills. Nick slipped around a bit on the flat English saddle, and felt his legs growing stiff by the time they returned to the stable. He knew they would be very sore later.

They sat on a patio that overlooked the pastures. A maid brought coffee and tiny sandwiches. Nick didn't think he'd ever been in a more idyllic location.

"Is this your family farm?" Nick said.

"No, I bought it at an auction ten years ago. My husband died the previous year, and I didn't want to stay in the house where we had lived."

"You didn't remarry?"

"No, one husband was enough for me," she said. "I like my freedom."

"There seems to be a lot of that going around now," Nick said.

She gave him an odd look.

"I have a friend, a woman friend, who says the same thing. She is trying to avoid marrying a guy who is crazy about her."

"You?"

"No, not me, just another friend."

"Does she love your friend?"

"I'm not sure. She likes him a lot, but she's a career woman and doesn't want to be tied down with a husband, or family, at least right now."

"Smart woman," she said. "I wouldn't have married Ryan except he was worth a fortune, and he wasn't very needy in other ways."

Nick smiled.

"Do I shock you?" she said.

"I think I'm getting immune to being shocked," Nick said. "I'm from Pittsburgh, and we're a little more backward there. However, I'm catching up fast."

"I bet you are," she said.

"So, what can you tell me about Angela?" Nick said.

"How much time do you have?" she said. "You aren't doing this to write about it?" she said. "I'll deny everything and sue you if you quote me."

"Honestly, I promise. This is not for publication."

"We were born in 1910, and didn't really notice the war," she said. "We reached puberty during the Roaring Twenties, and as much as our parents tried to control us, it was futile. Despite Prohibition there was plenty of alcohol and many wild parties. We were so filthy rich that even the Crash and the Depression didn't bother us much.

"Angela and I were like sisters in many respects," she said. "We were very close from the time we were little. We could have anything we wanted, and we were used to getting it. We shared everything, including some boyfriends later. We knew everything about each other."

She sat there telling her story, looking off at the fields, not at him. He thought it was a story she really wanted to tell, and she was going to do it with style. He sat back and listened.

"Her father was Robert Bain, the president and principal owner of Bain Imports, which at the time was a major import/export company, and very successful. He also was extraordinarily handsome. All the girls thought so. Her mother was Mary Hamilton, probably the most beautiful young woman in Baltimore at that time. Good looks run in this family. All the women were gorgeous, and the men were pretty good looking as well.

"In 1912, two years after Angela was born, her mother was crippled in, of all things, an auto accident. She spent the rest of her life in a wheelchair. She also couldn't have any more children. Angela grew up to be even more beautiful than her mother, and the apple of her father's eye."

"I've seen a colorized picture of her from the 1928 Cotillon that Dewey has in his house. She truly was a spectacular beauty," Nick said.

"I remember that picture, and I can tell you it didn't do her justice," Talbot said. "She was even more beautiful than that. She also was very troubled. She started having sex with her father when she was 13. Truthfully, I am not sure who initiated it, but they still were doing it after she was married. That's why he was killed."

"He was murdered?"

"Yes, I'll get to that," Talbot said, apparently irritated by the interruption.

"John Coughlin married her, knowing she was pregnant by another man. At that time he didn't know it was her father.

John was involved in international finance and spent a lot of time in Europe. When he was away, Angela's father continued to have sex with her. A number of people suspected that her father abused her and she let them believe that. I was the only one who knew the truth, that she enjoyed having sex with him. Even after she was married she invited him to her bed when John was away. She had such a manner, and such looks, that no man could resist her.

"John returned from a trip unexpectedly early in 1934, not long after Dewey was born, and found them together in bed. There was a fracas, and John killed Bain, shot him twice with a revolver. Other than those two, I am the only person who ever knew this. She persuaded John to let her tell people she killed her father in self-defense. That was the story told to the police and to friends and family.

"It was publicly reported that Robert Bain died as the result of a hunting accident. The Bain and Coughlin families had enormous influence to go with their wealth, which enabled them to get the authorities to go along with this story, especially since Angela agreed to spend 18 months at Sheppard Pratt."

"Dewey told me his father was devoted to her all their lives," Nick said. "Now I know why."

"He wasn't devoted to her. She had him by the balls. He murdered her father and would have gone to prison if anyone found out. Even his wealth and influence could not have prevented that. She held that over him their entire lives. It enabled her to get away with anything. He put up with some terrible things, most of the time without complaint.

"She returned home a year and a half later, and she was wilder than ever," Talbot said. "I think it was partially due to feeling guilty about her father, but also because of something that happened to her while she was in the hospital. She definitely was different. She started taking on boyfriends, more than one at a time, also, some girlfriends, and held orgies in and around her swimming pool at her house when Coughlin was away. She liked to take her clothes off in front of people, and many days didn't wear any at all. She told me her father liked to watch her undress. It became a ritual between them. It would end with him giving her a single red rose."

"A red rose, really?" Nick said. "When she committed suicide, she was found with a dried up red rose between her breasts."

"Angela was very dramatic," Talbot said. "Didn't you ever read Blake's poem, "The Sick Rose?"

"No, I can't say that I have," Nick said.

"Well find it, and read it. It is Angela's story. It's a poem about illicit love."

"So why would she put that old dried up rose between her breasts when she was committing suicide?"

"She was reminding John of what had happened, and that she never got over it," Talbot said. "It was her way of zinging him even in death. She was a nasty piece of work."

"So in the late 30s, she was having wild parties?" Nick said.

"The wildest," Talbot said. "She had her last child during this period. The girl was a brunette. She was the one who died from polio. Like Angela, Coughlin was blond. John found out about the parties, and he had the pool filled in."

"How do you know about the parties?" Nick said.

She gave him an odd look, and then laughed.

"What does it matter now," she said. "I went to some of them. I guess I was almost as wild as she was in those days. Angela and I were very close, very intimate friends. Does that shock you?"

Nick smiled. He had not blushed. Maybe he had reached the point where he wouldn't any more. He didn't show it, but he felt very sad for Dewey.

"Did she strip at these parties?"

"What the hell," she said. "Of course. We both did. Then everyone did. That was the idea."

"Do you know if any of the children ever saw what was going on, maybe saw their mother strip like that?"

"I don't know. Quite frankly, it could have happened. She wouldn't have cared. She was a lot of things, but a responsible mother she was not. Hell, she was naked half the time. It probably was no big deal to her."

"It might have been to the kids," Nick said.

"That's true. I never thought of that," she said. "I wasn't very responsible then, either."

"Did you have children?"

"A son and a daughter, one born in 1934, the other in 1936. And that was it. I didn't want any more."

"Where are they now?"

"My son works on Wall Street. I hear from him at Christmas. He just got married two years ago. His wife seems nice. I barely know her. My daughter lives in Ruxton with her husband, who works for McCormick. She's pregnant. I see her all the time."

Nick was silent for a moment. He couldn't help but wonder if her daughter was like her.

"Now tell me what happened next."

"The war came. John got a job with the Treasury Department in Washington selling war bonds. He rented an apartment in Washington and stayed away from Angela a lot of the time. It was a difficult time for everyone. Wild parties were sort of frowned on, so it became more subtle. We spent some time together, but we also had other relationships. She and John drifted far apart.

"After the war she insisted that John buy her an apartment in Paris. For the next few years she spent at least half of every year in Paris. She developed a group of lovers there. I lost touch with her during this period. When Angela was away John told people she was getting treatments at a hospital, or at a spa, or at a resort, some place different every year. I think I was the only other person who knew what really was going on. Angela and I remained friends, but we didn't see each other to speak of for the last ten years."

"Do you know if Angela abused any of her children?" Nick said.

"I don't know that she did," Talbot said. "She didn't like having children. She didn't like the ones she had and didn't want much to do with them. She was quite cruel to them. So it's possible, I guess. I never saw any of it. Come to think of it, I doubt she did. I don't think she cared enough about them to even bother abusing them."

"How was she cruel to them?"

"She ignored them. She punished them for things most parents would ignore. She'd lock them in their rooms for long periods of time. That's about all I know."

"The information is very limited about the deaths of Dewey's brother and sisters," Nick said. "All I know is that one sister died from polio. The other was killed in a plane crash, and his brother was killed in a jeep accident in Korea. Is that all true?"

"Partially," she said. "The one younger sister did die from polio right after the war. His older brother was a deeply troubled young man, well on his way to being an alcoholic when he joined the Army. He was the result of the incest between her and her father, and maybe he knew it. I guess it also is possible that she abused him. He certainly acted like he was damaged in some way. He was killed in Korea when he got drunk and crashed a jeep into a tank.

"Dewey's other sister did die in a plane crash, but one of her own making," she said. "John used to own an airplane, and she was taking lessons. One day, after a fight with her mother, she went to the airfield, took out the plane, and crashed it into the Bay. No one knows if it was on purpose, but I always suspected it was. She looked a lot like her mother, and I think was a lot like her. Now that I think of it, it is possible that her mother made her do some things that she couldn't live with."

"Jesus," Nick said, "This is a horror story. It's a wonder Dewey survived."

"If you could have seen Angela when she was young, you would have an even better idea of it. She was beautiful and seductive, but very poisonous. No one who got close to her came away unharmed."

"Other than her husband and children, was there anyone on whom she might have inflicted a lot of pain, or someone whose life, or family, was damaged, or destroyed by her behavior?"

"Other than me?" Talbot said. "Why do you think I married a man much older than me, a man I didn't love? I was ruined in the eyes of every man my age I knew. None of them would marry me. They'd fuck me, but they wouldn't marry me.

"Let's face it, and I say this as someone who once loved her in every sense of the word," Talbot said, "She was a bitch. She was totally hedonistic. She was sadistic. She enjoyed inflicting pain on people she didn't care for. She didn't care for John, and she made his life very painful. She didn't care for her children, and they had unhappy childhoods. Nothing mattered to her except her own pleasure. But other than me, I don't know of anyone whose life she really damaged except for members of her own family."

Nick called Joan at home from his car as he drove away from the farm. He needed to cleanse himself, to absorb some wholesomeness.

"I need to talk with you," he said. "Right now. I need to be with you."

They went to his apartment. What he wanted to discuss he wanted to do in absolute privacy. He made a pot of coffee and they sat at his kitchen table.

"This is one of the most incredible stories I've ever heard," Nick said. "I told Mrs. Talbot that I thought it was a horror story. The more I think about it, the more I am convinced of that."

He told Joan the entire story, reading from his notes, but at times just repeating from memory what Talbot had said.

"Poor Dewey," she said, when he finished. "It's a wonder he isn't stark-raving mad."

"See, that's what bothers me," Nick said. "What if he is? What if he is as insane as his mother, maybe more so? What if he is killing these women just because they look like his mother?"

"I don't believe that," Joan said. "You can't possibly believe that. I have no idea how a murderer acts, especially an insane one, but I know that Dewey has never acted like one around us. He is a great guy. Yes, a little weird, but still not criminally insane."

"I know what you mean, but don't you see? We may now know what the trigger was, what set off these killings. What if Dewey somehow saw a picture of that stripper who looked so much like his mother? What if he went and saw her? Is it possible that it brought back some terrible memories of his mother stripping, and doing other things, maybe even to him for all we know? What if he tried to see her outside of the club and she refused. According to what I heard, she didn't do things like that."

"And he killed her just because she rejected him?"

"I know it doesn't make sense," Nick said. Then he remembered something.

"I saw something in Dewey when we were in the hot tub and Susan did her little stripping routine. For a moment Dewey had a very strange look on his face, not a happy look. It passed quickly, but something bothered him. Now maybe I know what it was."

"The stripping reminded him of his mother?"

"It's possible. But the actions of an insane person may not make sense to us. And almost certainly there's more we don't know."

"But why bring attention to himself by killing the Barlow woman the way she was killed, making it look like a Mayan human sacrifice?" Joan said.

"Maybe it was the part of him that is decent," Nick said. "Maybe it was his way of making sure he got caught."

"And why did he kill the others?"

"It's possible that once he started, every girl who reminded him of his mother, and who also rejected him, like his mother did, became a target. Karen Billingsley rejected him, and I suspect Laurie Waslewski also did."

"If that is true," Joan said, "It may mean that if Susan breaks things off to go to Boston, she could be his next victim."

"Yes, if all that is true, then she could be in mortal danger."

"It's just too crazy," Joan said. "I don't believe it. Are you going to tell Antonelli?"

"For Susan's safety, I think I have to," Nick said. "I feel really bad about it. I was trying to help Dewey. I didn't do this to get him in more trouble. But what if he really is the killer? What if Antonelli has other information he hasn't told me that, when combined with what I have learned, proves he is the killer? I don't see how I can take the risk of not telling him."

"I think you have to tell Antonelli," Joan said. "If Dewey really is the killer, it might be dangerous for you to tell him what you have learned. You have to be careful. You shouldn't do it by yourself. You don't know how he might react."

"Maybe another Friday night dinner with all of us," Nick said. "I could take him aside and talk to him."

"And maybe Antonelli should be close by, just in case," Joan said.

"This is not what I had in mind when I got involved in this," Nick said.

Chapter Forty-Seven

Nick Tells Antonelli the Story of Angela Coughlin

Nick called Antonelli on Monday morning and gave him a brief summary of his session with Marjorie Talbot and asked for a meeting. They decided to meet that evening at the family restaurant.

Antonelli arrived at the restaurant a half hour before their agreed upon time, which gave him time to say hello to his father, who was in the kitchen, and to joke around with the staff, many of whom he had known for years. It had not taken very long for word to get around, and they were congratulating him, patting him on the back, and shaking his hand. He and Maria had picked out her ring on Saturday. They planned to make the formal announcement of their engagement on her 21st birthday in October. The wedding would be next July, after both of them completed their bachelor's degrees. He had signed up for extra courses so he could catch up to her.

He usually took Maria out on Friday and Saturday nights, unless he was working then. They went to movies, concerts, and dinners, and she came to the Sunday family dinners every other week. He had dinner at her house several times. He became increasingly convinced that they were perfectly suited to each other. They still did their kissing and petting in his car. A part of him envied Nick's sex life.

The Blue Girl case continued to haunt him. He had been able to overcome not closing them by closing so many other cases, but it still was a black mark against him that they remained open. If he could just find a little bit of evidence making it possible to charge Coughlin, he could close them. It would be a huge boost to his career. That evidence, any evidence, remained elusive, even after a complete review of everything his team had assembled on all of the murders.

Nick arrived at 7:00 PM and found Antonelli in his usual place in the family booth, with his usual carafe of wine, and antipasto platter. Just after they finished ordering their entrées, another waiter came over and congratulated Antonelli on his engagement. Nick shook his hand and toasted him.

"Being engaged is nice," Nick said. "It's even better for you because you've picked the date for the wedding. We haven't done that, yet. I am sure your family must be happy. Maria is a beautiful addition."

"Yes, they are, but if they only knew," he said, suddenly realizing that he had spoken out loud what had been bothering him for the last several days.

"Only knew what?" Nick said.

"I shouldn't have said that," Antonelli said. "I have this little problem, a family secret, that I'm trying to figure out how to resolve."

"I seem to be deep in family secrets," Nick said, "so tell me yours. Maybe I can help."

"My mother was Jamaican, not Sicilian, as my father always has told the family. She was half Negro. On top of that, Maria has Negro blood in her."

"And that's a problem with your family?"

"A big problem," Antonelli said. "My father and I have kept it from them, but I don't know that I should any longer, especially now that I am going to marry Maria."

"You have a big family and I assume everyone is very close, very supportive," Nick said.

"Yes, it's hard to fit everyone into anyone's house on the holidays," Antonelli said. "It's great. It's comforting to have a big family."

"Yes, I'm sure it is. I wish I had one, myself," Nick said. "For what it is worth, I wouldn't do anything to fuck that up."

"You wouldn't tell anyone?"

"Not a soul," Nick said. "Why do it? What difference does it really make? You're not going to become a Negro. You are who you are. Maria is who she is. No one needs to know anything else, at least not for at least another generation. Maybe things will change for your kids, but right now, don't say a fucking word. Why screw up your family?

"Look, I've just heard the most incredible story about a family about as fucked up as it possibly could get. It's a sad, tragic story, and it continues to have terrible consequences. If they had had what you have, what an incredible difference it would have made. And some lives would have been saved.

"No, accept your family for who they are, warts and prejudices and all. Having that family is the most important thing in your life and the most important thing you can pass on to your kids. I have just learned that, myself, after hearing the story of the Bains and the Coughlins. Maybe after you hear it, you'll understand what I mean."

"Tell me," Antonelli said.

Nick proceeded to relate Marjorie Talbot's story. The entrées arrived as he completed the story. Telling it again did not make him feel any better about it. He took a long sip of his wine, and sat back in his chair.

"That's quite a tale," Antonelli said. "They certainly led very different lives from us."

"It was a different world, and they were very rich," Nick said. "But they weren't very happy. It's like a cliché. All that money didn't buy them happiness. Look how sad and lonely Dewey is, not having had a loving family. Really, you don't want to screw that up."

"You have given me something to think about," Antonelli said. "I appreciate that. Truthfully, I haven't wanted to say anything, but I thought I should, that it was the right thing to do."

"The right thing to do is to protect your family, to keep it together," Nick said.

"There also are some pressures on me in my job. There, being part Negro now might be an advantage."

"The price of that advantage is too high," Nick said, "if it means wrecking relations with your family. Furthermore, you don't need it. You're too good not to get ahead just on merit. You've already made sergeant much faster than most. You'll probably be a lieutenant in a couple of years, and maybe a captain by the time you are 30."

"I doubt that," Antonelli said. "Advancement in the police department is slow."

"If this new Commissioner turns out to be everything we've been led to believe that he is, I suspect there'll be some speeding up of advancement as he cleans out some of the dead wood. You'll do fine."

"From your lips to God's ears," Antonelli said, as he raised a glass of wine and clinked glasses with Nick

"Now, the most interesting part of your story is Angela Coughlin doing strip teases for her guests," he continued. "If Dewey saw her, it could have been traumatic, especially if he saw some of the other things that went on. Then, this year he sees Candy Barlow, and it brings back all those memories. To him, it might have been like seeing his mother again when she still meant something to him. Maybe that drives him nuts for a period of time. Maybe he inherited some of that insanity from his mother, and seeing Barlow is the trigger that starts everything in motion."

"Except, if that is true," Nick said, "he doesn't remember. Not only doesn't he remember what his mother did, he doesn't remember what he did. It's the only explanation for how he feels now. I am convinced that he believes he is innocent. Of course, I want to believe that as well. That's why I'm trying to help him. But this story about his mother stripping has made me think that I could be wrong. He might be the killer. I still don't know how he did the killings, with all the preparation beforehand, and the careful concealment afterwards, without any memory of it, unless he is the greatest liar I've ever seen."

"I know what you mean," Antonelli said. "The longer we interrogated him the less convinced I became of his guilt. It wasn't that he told us anything that got him off the hook. It was his manner and the way he talked. Like you, I became convinced he was sincere in denying his guilt. But, he's still guilty. I'm even more convinced of it now. But I still don't have the evidence I need to charge him."

"I've made arrangements to tell Dewey what I have found out at a dinner at his place on Friday night," Nick said.

"What about Miss Fanning?" Antonelli said. "When is she going to tell him that she is going to Boston?"

"We're going to do this is two steps," Nick said. "First, I am going to tell him what I have learned. We then will see how he reacts. Susan isn't going to tell him until just before she leaves for Boston."

"If anything is going to set him off again, Miss Fanning's departure is it," Antonelli said. "You have to keep me informed. We'll keep both of them under surveillance after she tells him."

"You really think he will go after her?"

"I think it is very possible he will," Antonelli said. "I'm worried because he is so smart. He may not do things the way we think he will. He could outthink us. We're going to have to be very careful."

Chapter Forty-Eight

Dewey Gets a Double Dose of Bad News

Dewey put on another elegant dinner Friday night with such enthusiasm and warmth that it made Nick feel very sad about what he was going to do. As usual Dewey tried to charm them with both the quality of his cooking, and his conversation.

The weather was very comfortable, and after dinner they all went out to the patio to have coffee and to smoke. Nick didn't sit down. Instead, he walked out into the yard, which was surrounded by stone walls, and featured a formal garden in the center. Dewey followed him.

"This garden must be about where the swimming pool once was," Nick said to Dewey, who gave him a quizzical look.

"How did you know about the swimming pool?" he said. "I barely remember it, myself."

"Marjorie Talbot told me about it," Nick said. "It was a centerpiece of some of your mother's activities when you were a child."

"Really," Dewey said, not appearing to be terribly interested as he looked at one of the plants.

"Do you remember any of what went on here?" Nick said.

"Once in a great while, usually in a dream, something comes to mind, but it isn't pleasant, and I think I block it out," Dewey said. "For most of my life I haven't wanted to remember anything. If it weren't for these murders, I still wouldn't want to. But I think I have to. That's why I asked for you help. Let's go sit down, and you can tell me what went on here."

"Are you sure you want me to tell the story in front of Susan and Joan?" Nick said.

"I thought about it," Dewey said. "Susan should know everything, and I trust Joan, so sure, go ahead."

They sat with Susan and Joan at the patio table, and poured some wine all around.

"Dewey wants me to tell this story, so here goes," Nick said. He sat so he faced Dewey. "It is the story of your family, which you may be hearing for the first time.

"Once upon a time, Angela Bain, the young woman who later became your mother, was the most beautiful debutante Baltimore had seen in a generation, at least since her mother's coming out. That photograph taken of her in 1928 for the Cotillon is proof of that. However, I have been told that the photo hardly paid justice to her, that she was even more remarkable looking in person.

"She also came from one of the wealthier families in the area, but tragedy stalked this family. Because of an auto accident two years after Angela was born, her mother was condemned to spend the rest of her adult life in a wheel chair. Her father, the powerful head of Bain Exports, could not have sex with his wife, and a few years later, when Angela was 13, she became the object of his affections."

"That's not true," Dewey said.

"It is true," Nick said. "Except her father's attention may not have been unwelcome to Angela. Their sexual relations continued through the time that photo was taken, until she became pregnant with her father's child, your brother."

"No, that's a lie." Dewey said.

"I wish it were, Dewey, but check the dates," Nick said. "I did. Your brother was born six months after your parents were married, and he was not premature. He weighed nine pounds. Your mother was pregnant when your father married her.

"In those days your father traveled a great deal," Nick said. "He was home long enough to get your mother pregnant with you, but not long after you were born, he was off again. While he was away, Angela's father came calling again, at your mother's invitation. This was not abuse. She liked it. She wanted it. And when they were finished, he gave her the single red rose he always gave her after sex."

"The dried up rose," Dewey said. "She must have saved one."

"Yes, and it recalls a poem by Blake, 'The Sick Rose,' that is about illicit love, like incest," Nick said. "Do you remember it?"

"No. I never heard of it," Dewey said.

"I'm surprised," Nick said. "Since you took about every course at Hopkins, didn't you take Wasserman's course on the Romantic poets?"

"No, I passed on most of the literature courses," Dewey said. "Anyway, why does it matter?"

"According to Marjorie, your mother knew the poem. It's last two lines are, 'And his dark secret love Does thy life destroy.'

"Jesus Christ," Dewey said. "She was reminding my father of something, wasn't she?"

"In 1934, about six months after you were born, your father came home unexpectedly early and found Angela with her father. An altercation resulted, and your father shot and killed Angela's father."

"My God, did Marjorie tell you that?"

"Yes, and they decided your mother would take the blame because they knew the authorities wouldn't prosecute her. She had let people believe her father was abusing her, even though it wasn't true. All she had to do was to say she killed him in self-defense. That, and the influence of the families, did the trick. She just had to spend some time at Sheppard Pratt.

"That was the hold your mother had over your father," Nick said. "There's no statute of limitations on murder. I bet that dried up rose was the rose her father gave her that night. I'd be willing to bet she kept some other evidence as well. It wasn't love that kept your father bound to your mother. It was fear."

Dewey didn't say anything. He just stared at Nick.

"She came back from Sheppard Pratt a somewhat different person," Nick said. "For the next six years she lived a wild life, with multiple sex partners of both sexes, nudist parties by the swimming pool that used to be here, and strip tease shows she put on for her friends."

Nick saw Dewey's eyes change expression.

"You remember that, don't you, Dewey?" Nick said. "You were a little boy, but you saw your mother, didn't you? You watched her take her clothes off, and then, maybe you saw her do other things. Do you remember now?"

Dewey's eyes darkened. The expression completely changed. He started to say something with a voice that Nick did not recognize, but stopped. He seemed to be struggling with his emotions. Suddenly, he just sobbed, and his eyes changed expression again, back to their normal look. He spoke again, this time in his normal voice, but somewhat choked.

"I remember something," he said. "I didn't before."

"It had to be extremely traumatizing to a little boy to see all this, especially since this little boy craved affection from his mother, but never got any. She gave it freely to others, but not to you, or to your brother and sisters."

"I don't even remember my mother kissing me," Dewey said. "I don't think she ever did. She didn't like me. She didn't like any of us."

"So then sometime early this year, or maybe late last year, could you have happened to see a beautiful young woman, a woman who looked very much like your mother, take her clothes off, do a strip tease?"

"I have no idea what you are talking about," Dewey said. "The only women I have seen without clothes on in the past two years are Susan and Joan here, and Joan only when we were at the beach house. I haven't been with any other woman. I haven't seen any other woman take her clothes off."

"This doesn't jog your memory?" Nick said, taking the strip club flier promoting Candy Barlow out of a file folder. Dewey looked at it.

"I never saw this girl in person," he said. "This flier is all I've ever seen of her. This was in the paper after she was killed. I didn't kill her. I didn't know her."

He said this with intensity and the same sincerity that Nick had seen in him all along when he denied being the killer.

"Each of the girls who was killed rejected you," Nick said.

"I just told you, I never knew the stripper, never saw her. How could she have rejected me?

"I've talked with Detective Sergeant Antonelli at great length about each one of those murders," Dewey said. "He's wrong about me. I couldn't kill these girls. I'd have no reason to do it. Two of them were girls I knew and liked."

"But like your mother, they rejected you," Nick said.

"So what, the vast majority of girls I have known rejected me, but some didn't," Dewey said. "If I killed every girl who rejected me, there'd be a hell of a lot more than two or three. The same would be true of almost any man. Why would I kill just these two? His allegations just don't hold up."

"What about the mescaline?"

"OK, I gave Rory Crawford some mescaline. Big deal. I didn't kill him. I had no reason to do that."

"You've said you didn't see him on that Saturday night, but that is a lie, isn't it," Nick said. "You did see him, both of them."

"OK, yes, I did see them." Dewey said. "I lied about that because I was afraid they would seize on that as evidence that I killed them. I didn't kill them. I had promised him some more mescaline, and I had a little left. I agreed to meet him outside the fraternity house at 10:30. They got in my car. I gave them the drugs. I then dropped them off in the next block. They told me they were going to go back to the fraternity house. That's everything I did. I then went back to work."

"But Dewey look at all these coincidences," Nick said. "They all tie together, and all tie in with you, no one else."

"What's going on here, Nick? I thought you were my friend. Now you think I am a murderer," Dewey said. "I am not the one, and there is no proof that I am. If there were, they would have charged me. With as much pressure as Detective Antonelli is under, if he had even the tiniest piece of evidence, he would have charged me. I'm not the killer."

"God, I hope that is true," Nick said. "I really do."

What about you, Susan," Dewey said, turning to look at Susan, who had not said a word. "Do you think I'm a killer?"

"I don't want to think that, Dewey, I really don't," she said. "What Nick found out is very hard to reconcile. It doesn't look good at all. Maybe it all can be explained. Maybe it points to someone else. I don't know. I hope so. But right now, I'm scared for you."

"What does that mean for us?" he said.

"Dewey, I am on your side," she said. "I am scared for you, but I'll do whatever I can to help you, to support you."

Dewey looked at her in what Nick thought was a pure worshipful look, a look of total love. It made him feel sick to his stomach. He began to doubt he could do everything he had planned.

"Don't worry," she said. "I'm sure this is going to work out."

"Will you stay with me tonight?"

"Of course," she said.

"Nick, are you going to tell Detective Antonelli what you have learned?" Dewey said.

"I have to tell him some of it," Nick said. "I don't know what he knows. Maybe, as Susan just mentioned, this information will point to someone else. I hope that's the case."

Dewey gave Nick a look that was not friendly. His eyes darkened. He was quiet for a moment. Nick felt his stomach tighten. He and Dewey no longer were friends. He could see that Dewey felt double-crossed, and not without reason. Nick knew he had betrayed his friend, but also knew that he had to do it. He had crossed a line and there was no turning back. Now he realized what it was like to be Antonelli, to have power over another man's life.

"I think I want to be alone with Susan now," Dewey said. He didn't look at Nick.

"OK," Nick said. He, Joan and Susan stood up. There were tears in Susan's eyes.

"I'll see them out," she said.

The three of them went out to the driveway.

"Are you sure you want to do this?" Nick said.

"I'm sure," Susan said. "I still don't believe he's guilty. He loves me. He's not going to hurt me."

"Well, there will be police nearby, just in case," Nick said.

He used his mobile phone to call the police dispatcher to pass on a message to Antonelli.

"This is Nick Prescott. Detective Sergeant Antonelli is expecting a call from me. Please tell him we have just left after doing what we planned."

Chapter Forty-Nine

Dewey Challenges the Police to Produce Evidence

Antonelli took Dewey Coughlin into custody for questioning once again on Saturday morning, Coughlin did not seem surprised to see Antonelli, and he raised no objections to going downtown to police headquarters. In keeping with the new guidelines, he was advised of his right to have a lawyer, and his right not to answer questions without an attorney present. At the interrogation room, he signed the paper waiving his rights.

Antonelli went through his list of coincidences with Coughlin, updated with Coughlin's admission to Nick that he gave mescaline to Rory Crawford the night he was murdered, and Nick's information about Angela Coughlin.

"There is a clear pattern here that could fit no one else," Antonelli said.

"Why don't you charge me with the murders?" Coughlin said. "Let's get it over with. I'll take my chances with a jury."

"It would go so much easier for you if you just confessed," Antonelli said. "I have been authorized by the State's Attorney to tell you he will take the death penalty off the table if you confess."

"So then I get to spend the rest of my life in prison for crimes I didn't commit," Coughlin said. "I think I'd rather be executed."

"If you are alive and in prison, and if by some strange circumstance someone else really did these crimes, and was caught, you could get your life back. You couldn't do that if you were dead."

"What incentive would you have to look for anyone else if I confess?" he said. "Of course, I am not going to confess. The person you are looking at here, right now, is not guilty of these crimes, and he is not confessing."

They spent six hours going through all the material that Antonelli had put together to building his case against Coughlin.

At five o'clock PM, Coughlin said, "Look, by now you know my position. It is not going to change. Either charge me with a crime, or let me go. I've had a very tough 24 hours. I found out things I didn't know about my mother, which were very hard to hear. Someone who I thought was my friend has betrayed me and thinks I am a murderer. I feel like shit, and I'd like to go home and get very drunk."

"We're going to be keeping an eye on you," Antonelli said.

"I assumed that. It's OK. I don't have anything to hide," Coughlin said.

Antonelli had a patrolman drive Coughlin back to his house. He called Nick at home and told him what had happened.

"He's in a state of confusion right now," Antonelli said. "It may take him a while to decide what to do. He knows we're watching him, so he's going to be super careful."

"Are you keeping surveillance on Susan as well?"

"We're keeping a patrol car near her at all times. She knows to let us know if he contacts her, or if she goes out by herself."

Dewey did not stop in the bureau on Monday, or Tuesday. Nick learned from the newspaper's personnel office that he had called in sick. However, on Wednesday morning, he came in with the 8 star edition of the paper almost as if nothing had happened.

"I was going to stop out at your house today if you didn't come to work," Nick said. "I was getting concerned about you."

"I did some heavy drinking, and then some heavy thinking," Dewey said. "My life is a wreck, and it's no fun being suspected of being a murderer. I came by to thank you for what you found out about my mother. You found out things I didn't know, and I now understand a whole lot more about my childhood. I am sorry you went behind my back to the police.

"Until the real killer is found they are going to keep suspecting me," Dewey said. "But still there is no real evidence, and I am not hiding anything. I gave up the right to a lawyer. I've answered every factual question. I can't think of anything more I can do to prove my innocence. Fortunately, I don't have to prove it. They have to prove me guilty, and they can't do it because I'm not guilty." Then he walked out of the bureau.

Nick found it very hard not to believe Dewey. There was no guile in his face, or his eyes. If he was lying he was the best liar Nick had ever seen.

Chapter Fifty

What Happens When Susan Ends the Relationship with Dewey

The *Boston Globe* decided to announce Susan's appointment as a new columnist on Sunday, Oct. 9. She gave her notice to the Hearst Headline Service and reached an agreement that she could leave as of that date. Now, the question was how she would tell Dewey she was leaving. They had continued to see each other, and did not talk about Boston, or the murder investigation.

The Baltimore Orioles would be playing the Los Angeles Dodgers in the World Series beginning on Oct. 5 in Los Angeles. The third and fourth games would be played in Baltimore on the weekend of the eighth and ninth. Susan told Nick she would be leaving for Boston on Monday the tenth. She said she wanted to tell Dewey at his house on Friday night.

"I want you and Joan there when I tell Dewey," she said. "I want to get Dewey to host another dinner for the four of us. I will tell him how badly you feel about what happened, and that I'd really like to get the two of you back together. I think he'll go for it."

"And then he really is going to feel betrayed," Nick said. "It's going to be very cruel. Are you sure you want to do it this way?"

"He's really given me no choice," Susan said. "Despite saying he could accept a limited relationship, he's become more dependent on me. He calls me every day. He wants to see me every evening. I've become an obsession. It's not good. I have to end it, but I can't do it by myself. I am so looking forward to getting back to Boston. Have you heard "Dirty Water," by the Standells?"

Nick said he hadn't.

"It's about Boston. I love it," she said. "I guess it probably doesn't get a lot of air time here in Baltimore."

The Orioles surprised the baseball world by winning the first two games in Los Angeles, defeating Sandy Koufax and Don Drysdale. Jim Palmer, at age 20, became the youngest pitcher ever to pitch a complete game shutout in the World Series. Nick spent Friday with the UPI sports reporters at Memorial Stadium, but begged off going out with them that evening. Instead, he picked up Joan and they went to Dewey's house.

Dewey was cordial, acting as if nothing had happened. He barbecued rib steaks, and served them with baked potatoes and a salad. As the wine, he selected a Chateau de Beaucastel, which he described as one of the greatest of the Chateaneuf du Papes, a big and luscious wine that stood up nicely to the grilled steak.

As usual after dinner, they moved to the patio table so they could smoke and drink coffee.

After some brief chatter about the dinner and the Orioles, Susan spoke.

"I got the job with the *Globe*," she said. "I have given my notice, and I will be going to Boston on Monday."

"And me?" Dewey said.

"Dewey, you need to stay here, and get your situation cleared up," Susan said. "And you promised to undergo that procedure to see if there is a tumor. I want everything to work out for the best for you. I know you're innocent, but you can't live with this cloud hanging over you, and neither can I. I need to focus on my new job right now.

"If everything works out for the best, as I sure hope it will, then maybe we can see each other occasionally. But until it does, I think we have to stay apart. I just don't feel comfortable right now. I can't see you until things are cleared up."

It looked like someone had just punched Dewey in the stomach. He turned a little whiter than normal. He shook a little. His eyes teared up.

"I understand," he said in a sort of croak. "I'm not the killer. That will be proven eventually."

"I hope that happens, and I hope it happens soon," she said.

"I think I want to be alone now," Dewey said.

Susan stood up. There were tears running down her cheeks. She started to bend over to kiss Dewey, but he waved her off, and turned away. She ran into the house.

Nick and Joan walked into the house, leaving Dewey at the table. Susan came out of the powder room looking pale. She had lost her dinner. They went out to the driveway. Susan got into her car and left. Nick and Joan followed in his Mustang.

He called the police dispatcher and left a message for Antonelli.

Nick followed Susan to her apartment building, and after she drove into the garage, he headed for his apartment.

Memorial Stadium was packed with 54,000 fans when Wally Bunker pitched an incredible 1-0 shutout in the third game on Saturday, setting up the Orioles for a possible sweep on Sunday. Nick spent the evening with the UPI sports team. Joan and Susan went to dinner together at Obrycki's. Susan wanted to have crabs one more time before going back to Boston. She told Joan she would pack her apartment Sunday afternoon, and then finish cleaning out her office at the *News American* in the evening. Joan told Nick and he told Antonelli. Surveillance was set up for Susan and Dewey.

Nick had two assignments for the two games in Baltimore. He had to interview Oriole shortstop Luis Aparicio after each game and write a story to be sent to Venezuela where he was a national hero. UPI had its national sportswriters to do the game and principal color stories. His other assignment was to sell what was left of the block of tickets to the Series that UPI automatically purchased each year for promotional use.

He bought four of the tickets himself and gave two of them to Joan and her father, and the other two to Antonelli. In return Antonelli invited Joan and Nick to have dinner with Maria and himself at the family restaurant after the game on Sunday.

Triple Crown winner Frank Robinson hit a solo homerun Sunday afternoon for the Orioles who shut out the Dodgers for the third straight game, winning 1-0, and sweeping the Series. The crowd erupted and the stadium shook. Brooks Robinson leaped into the arms of the winning pitcher Dave McNally.

286

It took almost two hours for Nick to do his interview with Aparicio in the celebrating locker room, and get back to the Press Box where he typed it and gave it to a UPI teletype operator for transmission to New York. Joan joined him in the Press Box, using press credentials he gave her before the game. It was after 7:00 P.M. when they finally left.

They drove south on St. Paul Street and then east on Baltimore Street toward Little Italy. Downtown Baltimore was hopping. Traffic was jammed on Baltimore Street. When they got to "The Block" they knew why. Some of the strippers from the bars were performing on the sidewalks. Some bands were set up outside. Huge crowds were milling around, yelling and drinking. If there were any police around, they also were celebrating.

One girl wearing nothing but a "G" string and no pasties over her nipples as required by the city ordinance, came up to their car and shook her breasts, laughing loudly.

Nick called the bureau and dictated a brief story about the celebration going on. He said he would stop in later to do an overnight story.

Little Italy was hopping just like The Block, except half naked girls weren't dancing on the sidewalks. The restaurants were packed. Nick and Joan had a great dinner with Maria and Antonelli. Serge fixed them a special veal scaloppini and came out of the kitchen to sit with them for a while.

It was about ten o'clock when Nick decided he had to leave to write his overnight story.

"You should see Miss Fanning at the newspaper," Antonelli said. "I checked with the dispatcher a half hour ago, and she was there."

"What about Dewey? Any word on him?"

"He seems to have settled in for the evening. He parked his truck in his driveway yesterday, and it still was there a half hour ago."

"Good," Nick said. "We'll follow Susan back to her building tonight, and that should be it. She's leaving for Boston in the morning."

"We'll continue to check on Mr. Coughlin through tomorrow," Antonelli said.

He and Joan then left the restaurant and went to the bureau. When Nick drove into the parking lot, Susan's GTO was one of just a couple of cars parked there. They didn't see Susan when they walked through the City Room on their way to the bureau. The door to her office was open, and her notebook was on her desk. There were three empty boxes by her desk. There was no one on the city desk at that hour, but Nick saw sports editor John Steadman in the sports section. He introduced Joan to Steadman, and asked him if he had seen Susan.

"I saw her about 45 minutes ago," he said. "I passed her in the hallway. I think she was on her way to the cafeteria to get some coffee from the machine in there. I haven't seen her since, but I've been busy."

Nick opened the bureau door and told Joan he was going to find Susan. He walked to the cafeteria, but it was empty. He went back to the bureau, and asked Joan to check the restrooms. She came back a few minutes later and said they were empty. He then walked back towards the cafeteria until he got to the door to an internal staircase. He noticed a damp spot on the floor. He opened the door and saw a coffee cup on the stair, along with some wadded up paper towels, stained with coffee. They still were damp. A chill went down his spine. He ran back to the office.

"Call Antonelli at the restaurant," he said to Joan, "and tell him I think something has happened to Susan here, and he needs to get here as fast as possible. Tell him to go up to the old city room on the fifth floor." He looked around and grabbed a pair of scissors.

"What are you doing?" Joan said.

"I hope to God I'm not too late," he said. "I'm going up there."

Nick ran up the stairway until he reached the entrance to the fifth floor. The light was out in the hallway. He stopped to catch his breath and listened. He heard nothing, but could feel his heart beating. He opened the door slowly to try to see if anything was on the other side of it, something that might serve as an alert if the door was opened.

He heard a slight noise, and looked through the crack of the opening. On the other side of door, leaning against the door, was a four-foot long fluorescent bulb. Nick remembered there was a stack of boxes of them in the old city room when he was here that day when Dewey talked about the death of newspapers. He opened the door a little more, pushed his hand through the opening, and grabbed the bulb as it began to slide faster. He put the bulb down on the floor and started walking towards the old city room.

It was very dark on the floor, and he moved slowly. Lights from the streets below provided some illumination, which improved as his eyes adjusted. He heard a sound coming from the area of the old Hearst office. As he got closer the sound was more distinct. It was a voice, but the words were not clear. When he reached the door he realized that it was some kind of rhythmic chant in a language he did not understand. He could see the flickering glow of candles through the smoked glass of the door. He broke out in an enormous sweat from the fear of what he was about to find.

He turned the handle and slowly, and silently, pushed the door open. He saw the figure of a man on his knees in front of the large desk. He had something on his head that was covered with feathers. His eyes moved to the desk where he saw her blue naked body.

"No!" he screamed, and holding the scissors like a weapon, he charged. The man reacted so fast, and with such agility, that Nick ran right past him, and slammed into the desk, only a foot from her head, which in that second he saw still was attached to her body. Now he was facing a crouched man who wore a painted wooden mask, and had what looked like a knife in one hand.

The man pulled off the mask. The face behind the mask was Dewey's, at least it resembled Dewey's, but the look on his face was not anything he had ever seen on Dewey's face, and when he spoke his voice was not Dewey's.

"You have interrupted a sacred ceremony, and I will have to kill you," he said. The voice was rougher, deeper in tone, and with an accent much different from Dewey's. It was hard to see his eyes in the dark, but they looked different. They looked predatory.

"Dewey, Dewey, it's me, Nick," Nick said. "You have to stop this right now."

"I'm not Dewey," the man said. "Dewey isn't here now. My name is Robert Corrigan. I am Dewey's protector. I know who you are, and as the protector, I have to kill you. Dewey will be very sad, but it has to be done. The Paal Kaba has to complete the ceremony."

"What is a Paal Kaba and what is the ceremony?" Nick said, trying to buy time. Just as he charged into the room, he saw the flashing lights of a police car outside.

"He is a high priest of the Mayans. He is here to perform the ancient sacrifice to the God, Ahau Chamahez, the God of Medicine," he said. "If the God is pleased with the sacrifice, he takes away the pain for a while."

"Is the pain bad again?" Nick said.

"Very bad, unbearable, but soon it will be better," he said.

"What has happened to the Paal Kaba? Where did you come from?"

"He is here," Robert said, pointing towards his head. "He will return once I kill you. The sacrifice must be completed."

"Is Dewey in there, also?"

"Yes, but he won't be coming out for a while. Not until after the ceremony, and after we return to his house. He won't remember your death, or the sacrifice. He just will feel better tomorrow."

"I can't let you do this," Nick said. "It is wrong. Dewey would know it is wrong. He would not want Susan hurt."

"She won't feel anything. She won't be hurt. The Paal Kaba says her spirit will be transformed and will move to another plane. He does not kill her, he frees her to be in another world."

"That's bullshit," Nick said. "This is just primitive savagery. You know it, Robert, you don't believe it, do you?"

"I don't have beliefs," he said. "I have a job. My job is to protect them, both Dewey and the Paal Kaba. That's all I do."

"Dewey does not want your protection," Nick said. "Go away, I want to talk to Dewey."

"He won't come here. I won't let him," he said. "Now it is time for you to die." He started moving towards Nick, and then he jumped. The man had tremendous strength and speed, and he pinned Nick against the wall with his body, and swung his right hand, holding the blade, towards Nick's throat.

Nick freed his right hand, still holding the scissors, and jammed them into the man's stomach, driving them in as hard as he could, and then, taking advantage of the shock of that, he used all his strength to push away from the wall and slip from the man's grasp. Robert held one hand to his stomach, his shirt rapidly darkening from the blood, but it only slowed him momentarily. In a flash he had Nick backed up against the wall again and slashed at Nick's neck. Nick deflected the thrust with his left arm, and an enormous gash opened the length of his forearm. Blood spurted over both of them. Nick swung and hit Robert in the face with his right fist and then kneed him in the crotch.

Robert rammed his body against Nick and said, "It's time to die."

"No it isn't, drop it or you die," a loud voice said behind Robert. He turned his head and Nick saw Antonelli and other policemen rushing them. Antonelli grabbed Robert from behind, and with strength out of proportion to his size, pulled him off Nick and threw him against the wall. Two other policemen grabbed Robert from both sides and rammed him down to the floor. Robert said nothing.

Antonelli glanced at Nick.

"Let me help you get that shirt off, we have to use it as a tourniquet to stop the bleeding."

With Antonelli's help, Nick got out of the bloody shirt. Antonelli wrapped it around his upper arm and kept turning it until it tightened so much that it hurt. But it stopped the bleeding.

"Get him to the hospital now," Antonelli said to one of the policemen.

"Not just me," Nick said. "We have to get Susan and Dewey to the hospital as well."

Antonelli felt for a pulse on Susan's neck, which was streaked with blue paint.

"Her pulse is strong," Antonelli said. "She's probably just drugged. She'll be OK."

Nick looked at her lying on the desk, her beautiful blonde hair spread out from her head, her breasts, except for the nipples, painted blue. He watched her chest rising and falling from her breathing. Suddenly a feeling of enormous relief rushed over him, and it quickly centered itself in his bowels, which he came close to emptying into his underwear. He became very dizzy, and felt Antonelli steady him.

"Put something over her," Nick said. "Don't let everybody see her like this."

"You're on the way to the hospital right now," Antonelli said. "I'll take care of her and I'll be there as soon as I can."

"What about Joan?" Nick said. "She's downstairs."

"No I'm not, I'm right here," he heard her say. "I'm going to the hospital with you."

That was the last thing he remembered.

Chapter Fifty-One

Nick is the Hero and Antonelli Gets his Man

When Nick passed out he fell against Antonelli who grabbed him and gently lowered him to the floor. Joan cradled his head in her lap until the ambulance crew arrived a few minutes later. They wrapped Susan in blankets and put Nick and her on stretchers. They found Susan's clothes and purse under the desk and put them on her stretcher.

Just as they were getting ready to leave Antonelli noticed a pool of blood under the prisoner, who sat quietly in a corner of the room, staring into space, his hands cuffed behind him, with two patrolmen standing in front of him. One of the patrolmen held a plastic bag containing his wallet and three sets of keys they took from his pockets.

"You're wounded!" Antonelli said. He bent over the prisoner, who was getting very pale, and pulled up his shirt. He could see the puncture wound in the left side of his stomach spurting blood.

"This is bad, you've got to get him to the hospital as well," Antonelli said to the emergency crew. They said they didn't have another stretcher, but two of them picked up the wounded man and carried him out. Antonelli followed.

"Dewey Coughlin, you are under arrest," Antonelli said, as he began to read his rights while walking beside the men who were carrying him.

"I'm not Dewey Coughlin," he said. His voice was weak, but deeper and flatter than Coughlin's normal voice. Antonelli recognized it as the voice and speaking manner that Dewey Coughlin had when he was interviewed the first time.

"What do you mean you're not Dewey Coughlin."

"My name is Robert Corrigan," he said. "Check my wallet. You'll see my driver's license, issued by the State of Delaware."

Antonelli opened the wallet and found the driver's license, along with an American Express card and a Hutzler's charge card, both in the name of Robert Corrigan. There also was about $200 in cash, and a stub from the parking garage next to the *News American* building.

"Whatever your name is, these are your rights." He proceeded to go through the list and finished as they reached the elevator.

"I want an attorney," the prisoner said. "I don't waive any of my rights, and I will not answer any questions."

"Do you have an attorney?" Antonelli said.

"No, but I want Michael Rosen. I want to call him right away."

They reached the first floor lobby and headed for the ambulance about the time more police arrived, including Detective Meador and Lieutenant Rauch, who came directly from home.

"Our killer is Dewey Coughlin, but he's calling himself Robert Corrigan. He's badly wounded and has lost a lot of blood."

He said to Meador, "Go to the hospital. Get his fingerprints and run them through the system. He hasn't waived his rights. He wants to call an attorney as soon as he gets there. He may not be in good enough shape to do it. If he isn't, make the call for him. He wants Michael Rosen. You know who he is?"

"Sure, the biggest name criminal lawyer around," Meador said. "I guess he can afford him."

Antonelli looked at the three sets of keys, and motioned to another patrolman.

"These are keys are to a Buick in the parking garage next door. Call the Crime Lab and get them down here right now. Then find the car, but don't touch it. Wait there for the Crime Lab."

There now were about a dozen police cars outside the *News American*. Two more Homicide detectives had arrived. Lt. Rauch told Antonelli he was bringing in more. Antonelli handed another set of keys to one of the detectives.

"I think these are the keys to Dewey Coughlin's house," he said. "Go there and check it out. There's no time for a search warrant, so don't touch anything. I just want to make sure there aren't two of him."

The detective gave him a quizzical look.

"Just do it," Antonelli said. He then walked over to the security guard at the reception counter and showed him the third set of keys.

"Do you recognize these?"

"They look like keys to the building," he said, and separating one of the keys with his fingers, he looked at Antonelli and added, "This key opens the door on the loading dock."

"That's how he got in without being seen," Antonelli said to no one in particular.

They took Nick and Dewey into surgery almost immediately. Nick's surgery was brief and he was in a room in the trauma center an hour later, very groggy. He was aware of Joan holding his hand, and speaking to him, but he had trouble making out the words. His mind slowly cleared and he saw her. He raised his right hand and touched her arm.

"Where am I?" he said.

"You're at the hospital, you're going to be OK," she said. "It was a close call. You almost bled to death."

"What about Susan?"

"She's here, too," Joan said. "They told me she'll be fine once the drugs are out of her system."

"And Dewey?"

"I don't know yet," she said. "I think he's still in surgery."

"He called himself Robert Corrigan," Nick said. "He said Dewey wouldn't know what happened. When I got there he was wearing a mask. He was about to cut off her head. He said he was a Mayan priest. What in the hell is going on?" He felt dizzy and dozed off.

Antonelli went back to the fifth floor office and made sure it was blocked off. He then went in and carefully looked around the room. Everything used in the previous Blue Girl murders was here. There was a can of blue tempera paint, a paint brush, a screwdriver to open the can, a wooden painted mask festooned with feathers of several different colors, a large sheet of black plastic, a syringe and several vials of liquids, a roll of duct tape, a towel and a wet wash cloth, a plastic trash bag, a box of surgical gloves, and an extremely sharp knife made of obsidian.

A team from the Crime Lab arrived about twenty minutes later and they proceeded to dust the room for fingerprints and to photograph from every angle. They also went to the parking garage where the patrolman had found the Buick.

The Buick found in the parking garage had Delaware license plates, and a Delaware auto registration card in its glove compartment, listing Corrigan as the owner, with an address in Rehoboth Beach. However, its VIN was the same as the Buick Dewey said he had sold. The Crime Lab found a policeman's uniform, badge and ID in the trunk, along with two more cans of tempera paint, a box of vials of chemicals and syringes, another Indian mask, and duplicates of most of the items found in the Hearst office. The car would be towed to the Crime Lab to be examined in microscopic detail. It was about 3:00 A.M when Antonelli broke loose to go to the hospital.

Nick and Susan still were in the trauma area, but a nurse said they were in the process of being admitted to the hospital. The prisoner was just getting out of surgery. The scissors had hit the large intestine and the emergency room doctor told Antonelli there was danger of massive internal infection.

Susan was asleep. Antonelli found Joan also asleep in a chair next to Nick's bed, but Nick was awake, and he waved. That woke up Joan.

"How are you?" Antonelli said.

"I think you saved my life," Nick said. "They told me that if you hadn't put that tourniquet on my arm, I wouldn't have made it."

"Boy Scout training," Antonelli said with a smile. "How's the arm?"

"Stings a bit, but it's all stitched up now," Nick said. "They say I shouldn't have any lingering problem, but that I'm going to have quite a scar."

"The mark of a hero," Antonelli said. "You saved Miss Fanning's life. I think you got there just in the nick of time."

"Yes, when I got there, he was kneeling in front the desk, chanting something, and he had that knife in his hand," Nick said. "Do you have any idea what's going on with Dewey? Is he OK? I stabbed him pretty hard with those scissors."

"You ripped his large intestine open," Antonelli said. "He had to have emergency surgery. I think he just got out. I don't know how he is"

"He told me his name was Robert Corrigan," Nick said. "When I asked him where Dewey was, he pointed to his head. He said Dewey would not know anything of what happened."

"Well he was still claiming to be Robert Corrigan when I charged him," Antonelli said. "He has a driver's license and some credit cards in that name. We found his car, a Buick, in the parking garage, with a policeman's uniform in the trunk, along with other materials that have been used in the killings. The car is registered in the Corrigan name with an address in Rehoboth Beach."

"Rehoboth Beach, really?" Nick said. He then remembered the address of the beach house and told Antonelli, who took out his notebook.

"Yes, that's it," he said.

"So Dewey has been using two names?" Nick said.

"If it is Mr. Coughlin, and not someone who assumed his identity," Antonelli said.

"You really think that is possible?"

"Right now, I'm barely thinking," Antonelli said. "I'm just reacting. We're running his fingerprints through the system. We have a previous set of Mr. Coughlin's fingerprints on file, and the FBI has them from when he was in the Army. We'll compare all the prints and see what we have."

"Has he explained what this was all about?"

"Not a thing," Antonelli said. "He won't answer any questions, and he's hired a big name criminal lawyer."

"I've got to call this in to New York," Nick said. "This is one hell of a story. Joan, I need to get to a telephone."

"Don't use his name," Antonelli said. "We're not giving out any names until we know who he really is."

Nick's first person account of the capture of the Blue Girls killer was the biggest story in the country on Monday morning. With Nick in the hospital, and a central character in the drama, UPI sent two reporters and a photographer from the Washington bureau to take over the coverage. Dozens of out of town reporters were in the city by late morning.

Police Commissioner Pomerleau cut off all contact between Homicide detectives and the media, putting his public affairs officer in charge of all information releases. Very little was released during the morning, which kept Nick's story as the primary source of information. Pomerleau held a news

296

conference at noon. He had Antonelli, and his entire chain of command, standing nearby, but did not allow them to talk.

"As you know, we captured the man we believe is responsible for what have become known as the Blue Girl murders," Pomerleau said. "We are not releasing his identity because he has used more than one name, and we have not yet determined his real name. I can tell you that he is a white male in his mid 30s or so. He has not yet been arraigned and formally charged because he is in critical condition at the University of Maryland Hospital.

"He was captured late last night when he attempted to commit another murder like the previous ones. His intended victim was Susan Fanning, a columnist for the Hearst Headline Service, who worked in the *News American* building. She was working late last night when the building was nearly empty. He gained entrance to the building through a door on the loading dock. He apparently grabbed her in a corridor and injected her with a disabling drug in very much the same way the other victims were disabled.

"He then took her to an unused area of the top floor of the building, where he prepared to kill her in the same way the other women were killed. From what we have reconstructed, he was about to cut off her head when Nicholas Prescott, the Baltimore bureau manager of United Press International, attacked him. Detective Sergeant Michael Antonelli, who had been alerted by a telephone call to the crime in progress, arrived moments later with other police officers and subdued and arrested the killer."

He went on to tell how Nick learned that Susan had gone to get some coffee, and that he had discovered the spilled coffee, and then went up the stairs and found the killer and Susan in the old Hearst office.

"During the fight between Mr. Prescott and the killer, both were seriously injured. Mr. Prescott suffered a severe cut to his left arm that resulted in so much blood loss that he nearly died. The killer suffered a life-threatening stab wound to his abdomen that penetrated his large intestine. He underwent emergency surgery at the University of Maryland Hospital early this morning. He is expected to survive, but he still is in critical condition. Miss Fanning suffered no injuries and has recovered from the drug that was injected into her."

Pomerleau then enumerated the charges that were filed. He said the man's identity would be revealed once it was clearly established. He praised the work of the Homicide department, particularly that of Antonelli.

Chapter Fifty-Two

Dewey Coughlin Explained

The fingerprints definitely were those of Dewey Coughlin, and when he woke up after the surgery, he no longer claimed to be Robert Corrigan. He told the nurse he was Dewey Coughlin and he asked her how he got hurt and wound up in the hospital. When she told him his attorney, Michael Rosen, was waiting outside the room to talk with him, he said he did not call Rosen. He said he had no reason to hire an attorney.

The nurse said all this to Rosen in the hall outside Coughlin's room. Antonelli and Assistant State's Attorney Robert Samuels were standing nearby. The three met at the hospital right after Pomerleau's news conference, and had been waiting for an hour. During that time, Antonelli learned that Rosen, a short, thin man around 50 with thinning gray hair and thick glasses, taught criminal law and procedure in the University of Maryland's night law school. Samuels took both courses from him and he and Rosen were very friendly to each other.

Samuels told Antonelli that Rosen not only was one of the top criminal lawyers in the state, he also was acknowledged as probably the leading scholar of Maryland criminal law.

"He's written a number of law review articles and most of the materials used in the continuing education programs for lawyers. And despite his reputation, he's a very nice guy."

Because of the chaotic situation the night before, Coughlin's critical physical condition, and the uncertainty about his identity, Samuels decided that Antonelli should go through the formal arrest and Miranda warning procedure again. Rosen insisted on being present for that.

After the nurse described Coughlin's reaction, Samuels and Rosen talked quietly, and Rosen went into the hospital room by himself.

"Coughlin's probably in a very confused state," Samuels said to Antonelli. "I thought it best to let Rosen talk with him before we do. Since you caught him in the act, the only way he's going to get off is if we make some mistake with his rights. We're not going to do that."

After about five minutes they could hear Coughlin yelling, but could not understand what he said. It lasted just a few minutes, and then things were quiet. Rosen came out of the room about 25 minutes later. He showed a document to Samuels.

"He has retained me as his attorney," Rosen said. "He's very confused. He doesn't understand what has happened. I acknowledge his arrest on his behalf and concede that he has been given all his rights. There is no need to charge him again. I also would like to hold off his arraignment until he is in better condition to answer some of my questions.

"I'd sure like to know who Robert Corrigan is," Antonelli said. Samuels gave him a disapproving look.

Rosen smiled. "Have you seen the movie, 'The Three Faces of Eve?'"

Antonelli said he had not. He looked at Samuels. Samuels shook his head.

"Well, you both are soon going to get quite an education," Rosen said. "I think I know what we're dealing with here. I am going to have him examined by a psychiatrist. You probably will want to get your own in here as well. I'll call you later to make arrangements."

"You're not really planning an insanity defense, are you?" Samuels said.

"Not the usual one," Rosen said.

"What do you mean?"

"When you get back to your office, read up on multiple personality disorder," Rosen said. "That's what we're dealing with here. It's very rare, especially like this case. I've seen it in convicted felons, but I've never seen it in a defendant before. It's very interesting. Once you're more familiar with it, we'll talk."

Antonelli had been up for more than 24 hours and there was little prospect of sleep in the near future. Before going back to headquarters, he went to the Pratt Library. He wasn't going to wait for Samuels to tell him about multiple personality disorder.

He discovered that the movie, "The Three Faces of Eve," in which Joanne Woodward played the lead part, and for which she won an Academy Award, tells the story of a real woman who had three different personalities, the one she was known by, a bad one who tried to kill her daughter, and a third, a good one who eventually took over.

What information he could find explained that the disorder, which was not officially recognized as a psychological disorder, appeared to result from severe trauma, most often sexual and/or physical abuse, to the individual at a very early age. The person's personality literally "split," apparently as a defensive reaction. In many cases, the fully developed alternate personality did not appear until adulthood, and new alternate personalities could appear over many years. As many as 100 different personalities were reported in one case, but most of the time it was just a few. One of the physical symptoms of the disorder was the frequent occurrence of severe headaches.

In all cases reported, the original personality did not appear to be aware of the other personalities, who usually were aware of each other and conscious of what the original personality experienced. Alternate personalities could be dramatically different, sometimes being left-handed when the original personality was right-handed, sometimes speaking with different accents, sometimes exhibiting a radically different cultural background. Some personalities were animals, or babies. Some were violent.

There did not appear to be any cure for the disorder. Sometimes the personalities just disappeared later in a person's life. Occasionally, one of the alternate personalities took over, as in the case of Eve. Hypnotism and psychiatric therapy seemed to help. Electro-shock therapy seemed to worsen the condition.

There were cases of horrific crimes committed by alternate personalities, but Antonelli could not find any case where the disorder was used as an insanity defense. From what Samuels told him about Rosen, this might be the first.

The description of the disorder seemed to fit what Antonelli knew of Coughlin. He had severe headaches. He apparently had trauma in his childhood. He may have been abused. He always had been completely believable in denying any knowledge, or involvement, in the murders. That would be consistent with the disorder if the killings were being done by the alternate personality of Robert Corrigan.

Antonelli was upset. Coughlin could get off. Rosen was the right attorney to develop the disorder as an insanity defense, and his client could pay whatever it cost.

Chapter Fifty-Three

Dewey Coughlin's Offer

Samuels called Antonelli the next day to tell him that Rosen intended to try to use the disorder as an insanity defense. He said Rosen was going to have Coughlin examined and tested by a number of internationally prominent experts.

"He thinks that at the least he can prove that Dewey Coughlin, through no fault of his own, was not in control of his body when the crimes were committed, and thus cannot be held criminally liable, especially to a first degree murder charge. He thinks he can prove there was no premeditation, no intent, whatsoever."

Antonelli groaned. "I was afraid of that," he said.

"You have the perfect combination in this case, a great lawyer who likes to break new ground, and a client with virtually unlimited resources. I think I can hold my own against him in the courtroom," Samuel said. "After all, I learned from him. But we can't match the resources he has to spend. He could bring in every expert in the world and bury us."

"So does he want a deal?" Antonelli said.

"I really don't have much to offer," Samuels said. "I'm supposed to get him into the gas chamber. Much less than that, and I'm out of a job."

"Coughlin told me one time that he'd rather die in the gas chamber than spend the rest of his life in prison," Antonelli said.

"Apparently, he doesn't want to do either," Samuels said. "So it looks like we're in for one hell of a battle."

To prepare for that battle, Antonelli started his team on a detailed review of each of the Blue Girl murders. Each murder had its own file, and each of those files now filled a file drawer. They took over an interview room and started from the beginning. Now with the physical evidence recovered from the attack on Susan Fanning, they could reconstruct each murder. A narrative would be prepared, backed by exhibits, to present in the trial.

Nick felt much better on Tuesday. He sent Joan home Monday afternoon to get some sleep. She had classes on Tuesday, but said she would be in late in the afternoon. He was dozing lightly when he sensed a presence. He opened his eyes and saw Susan sitting next to his bed. She smiled radiantly, stood up, and bent over to kiss him on the cheek. Then he saw tears in her eyes.

"Thank you, Nick," she said. "You saved my life. I don't know what to say."

"I'm so happy to see you," he said. "You look great, especially considering what you have just been through."

"They're going to release me today," she said. "I'm going to be around for a while. The prosecutor wants to talk with me at length. So maybe I'll take turns with Joan looking after you."

"I'm feeling better today, but it is hard to do things with just one arm," he said.

"I'll stay here as long as you need me," she said.

"Have you heard anything about Dewey?"

"All they will tell me is that he is in satisfactory condition, and recovering from his surgery. I don't know anything else. It's so horrible. I can't believe it. I only saw him for a few moments in that hallway, and I didn't recognize him until just before I passed out. He didn't look the same. He looked like a different person. His voice was different. His manner was different."

"I know," Nick said. "I don't understand it. Clearly, he is insane, but way different from anything I've heard of."

"What do you think they will do with him?"

"I guess if he is found insane, then he'll be sent to a mental institution, one of those facilities for the criminally insane, but I'm not really sure. Antonelli told me he would stop in sometime today. Maybe he can tell us what's going on."

Antonelli stopped in shortly after noon and found Susan sitting near Nick's bed, reading a magazine. Nick was asleep, but woke up when he heard the two of them talking.

"I just told the Detective Sergeant that you are going to be released tomorrow," Susan said.

"That's good news," Antonelli said. "You must be healing quickly."

"It's stinging some," Nick said. "It will be nice to get out of here and get back to work. This is the story of my career, and I haven't been able to write anything."

"The media is clamoring for interviews with you, but we've kept them away," Antonelli said. "You're going to be a celebrity for a while."

"I didn't think of that," Nick said. "That does make things a little complicated, doesn't it?"

"I don't think you're going to be writing much very soon," Susan said. "Not with one arm, and the medication you are going to have to take."

"What's happening with Dewey?" Nick said.

"He's hired the top criminal defense attorney in the state, and it looks like they will use an insanity defense based on him suffering from multiple personality disorder."

"You mean like Joanne Woodward in that movie?" Susan said.

"You've heard of it?" Antonelli said.

"Of course," she said. "It's a great movie. Is that the problem Dewey has? He has more than one personality?"

"That's what his attorney believes," Antonelli said. "He's going to get extensive examinations by psychiatrists. The problem with his defense is that this disorder is not officially recognized, and a defense based on it has never been tried before. The judge might not even allow the defense."

"And if it isn't allowed, what happens?" Nick said.

"Then he probably gets convicted and gets the gas chamber," Antonelli said.

"Oh God," Susan said. "I don't think that's right. I know he tried to kill me, and he killed those others, but now I understand. It wasn't Dewey. It was a different person inside his body."

"That's the theory, but there's a lot of controversy about it," Antonelli said. "Some people don't believe it at all."

"I saw him as Robert Corrigan," Nick said. "That was a different person, as Susan just said, inside Dewey's body. That was no act."

"I know," Antonelli said. "I saw him, too. I don't think it was an act, either. But I do think someone has to atone for those murders, even though it may be unfair. The lives of those four young people were snuffed out, and consciously, or

306

unconsciously, Coughlin was responsible. There has to be some justice for the victims. In some way, he has to pay."

Samuels called Antonelli on Wednesday morning to tell him that there would not be an insanity defense.

"Coughlin wouldn't let him," Samuels said. "He has proposed his own plea deal that we're considering. It's bizarre, and we're not sure it's legally possible, but we're trying to see if we can do it. Basically he pleads guilty and gets life without parole."

"There's nothing bizarre, or illegal, about that," Antonelli said. "I'm surprised your boss would consider that."

"He's going to create an irrevocable trust of nearly all of his assets for the benefit of the families of the victims. That is going to amount to millions of dollars."

"So he is buying himself out of the gas chamber," Antonelli said.

"Yes, that's pretty much it," Samuels said. "The bizarre thing is that it's not going to be the person we know as Dewey Coughlin spending the rest of his life in prison. It's going to be the person you know as Robert Corrigan. Coughlin apparently believes that he can make the Corrigan personality take over from him permanently. So the Dewey Coughlin personality theoretically will commit suicide, and the victims will inherit his property. We have to agree to send him to the penitentiary as Corrigan, not as Coughlin. The Coughlin name will stay in the court records, but they will have to be sealed. The public would not be told his real name."

"Can we do that?" Antonelli said.

"My boss is talking with a judge today to see if it can be done, or how it could be done," Samuels said. "He still hasn't been arraigned, and so there are no formal charges against Dewey Coughlin."

"I wonder if he really can change personalities permanently," Antonelli said.

"We really don't care," Samuels said. "He's in for the rest of his life. What does it matter what he calls himself? Personally, I think it is bullshit. I don't believe in the whole multiple personality disorder idea. I think it's an act. But so what? I'm for the deal because of what it does for the families, especially that family out in West Virginia. They're very poor and they still have little kids."

Antonelli wanted to tell Samuels that he did believe the multiple personalities were real, but didn't. He thought the differences between the personalities had to be seen to know they were real, and that Samuels would see that for himself when Coughlin became Corrigan again.

Chapter Fifty-Four

Nick gets offers and Dewey's goodbye

Nick returned to work on a part-time basis two weeks later, after his celebrity status subsided, and returned to fulltime duty the night of the general election. With the support of many liberal and middle-of-the road Democrats, Spiro Agnew defeated George Mahoney for Governor of Maryland. Nick got some good quotes from Agnew that evening and won the logs on the story. He still couldn't punch the Teletype tape fast enough to keep up with the transmitter, as he had been able to do previously, but he could type well enough to write stories.

Nick met with reporters once shortly after leaving the hospital, but had not granted any private interviews. He answered questions about his role in the capture of the killer. He did not say anything about his involvement in the investigation prior to that night. He said he saved Susan simply because of a hunch he had when he couldn't find her and saw the spilled coffee.

"I knew about the abandoned space on the top floor and just thought I should check it out," he said.

He stayed in his apartment for a week after leaving the hospital. With his arm immobilized, he frequently needed assistance. Susan stayed with him during the days when Joan was attending classes. Joan spent every night with him.

"If I don't, Susan will," she said. "It's a good thing for me she has to get to Boston."

Nick laughed, but he knew there was some truth to that. Susan was more openly affectionate towards him than she previously had been. Even after she went to Boston, she called him every day. Two weeks later he received a job offer from the *Boston Globe* for more than twice what he was making with UPI. Susan denied having anything to do with it, but he didn't believe her.

He had four job offers, including the *Globe*'s. UPI's management seemed intent on keeping him. Managing Editor, H.L. Stevenson talked to him about going to the New York general desk. Grant Dillman, UPI's Washington news editor, talked to him about moving there. He said he wanted to stay in Baltimore at least until next summer, after Joan's graduation.

Susan and he received solicitations to write longer features about the Blue Girl murders. A literary agent suggested that if they wrote a book together, he could market it to Hollywood. They declined, saying they needed time to get their lives in order. Nick and Susan had agreed never to reveal what they knew about Dewey and the murders.

One of Nick's fraternity little brothers dropped a record album by his apartment, with a note, "You must listen to this, it's very cool." The album was titled "Freak Out," and it was by a Baltimore group called "The Mothers of Invention," but the principal was a young man from East Baltimore, Frank Zappa. Nick listened to the album and while he didn't like some of the songs, he thought they were highly original. He also thought they reflected the dramatic change in the culture that he already had sensed. He particularly liked "Trouble Every Day."

Nick and Joan became closer friends with Maury Antonelli and Maria Conseco. They were invited to the announcement in October of their engagement, and they had gone out together several times since. Nick became fascinated with crime detection and the criminal mind and starting reading books on those subjects.

The Blue Girl story itself was huge news for several days, but died fairly quickly after the announcement that a plea agreement had been reached. The killer finally was identified as Robert Corrigan, 36, of Rehoboth Beach, Delaware. He would be going to prison for the rest of his life. Described as a single reclusive man with a substantial inherited estate, he had no living relatives, or close friends. The State's Attorney said Corrigan got the idea for human sacrifices from seeing the Mayan exhibition at the Baltimore Museum of Art. He actually believed, when he committed the murders, that he was sacrificing the women to a Mayan god who would relieve intense pain he suffered from headaches. In return for not suffering the death penalty, Corrigan agreed to provide substantial financial compensation to the families of his victims.

Nick and Susan both had asked to see Dewey several times, but always were refused. Each received a short note from Dewey apologizing for refusing to see them, but saying he preferred to remember them from that weekend at Rehoboth Beach. He hoped they would remember him the same way. He also said he would give them a fuller explanation soon.

Michael Rosen called Nick on the Monday after the November election and invited him to lunch. "I am bringing a detailed communication from Mr. Coughlin."

When Nick drove to the Chesapeake Restaurant, WCAO played "Good Vibrations" by the Beach Boys. Nick loved the song. They met for lunch at the Chesapeake Restaurant. Rosen immediately ordered a bottle of an expensive Burgundy, and then asked about Nick's condition and inquired about Susan. He was not Nick's idea of the typical criminal lawyer. He was polite and relaxed and very attentive, as if he had nothing else on his mind.

After they started drinking the wine, he took a thick envelope out of his inside breast pocket and handed it to Nick. "This is Mr. Coughlin's communication to you, Susan and Joan. You may share it with them, but no one else. In order to do that, you must sign the confidentiality agreement on the first page. There are separate agreements for each of them."

Nick read the three-paragraph agreement, which forbad him to ever disclose any of the information that followed, unless compelled to by a court order. He signed his document and handed it to Rosen. The next document was a letter from Dewey, addressed to Nick, Susan and Joan, and dated five days earlier.

Dear Susan, Joan and Nick,

This will be my last communication with you. By the time you read this the person you knew as Dewey Coughlin will have ceased to exist. By agreement with the State's Attorney and the Court, the person known as Robert Corrigan, will have pleaded guilty to the Blue Girl murders and will have been sentenced to life without parole in prison. Robert Corrigan has replaced Dewey Coughlin as the dominant personality. In effect, I have committed suicide. I have done this willingly, in full possession of my senses, because it is the right thing to do. It is the end of a trail of violence and evil that at least three generations of my family left behind.

Bobby was my childhood imaginary friend, or so I thought. In actual fact, he was Robert Corrigan, an alternate personality of mine who split off from my personality when I was six years old and was about to be sexually abused by my mother. This second personality also calls himself the "protector." His purpose is to protect me. He has no other purpose.

I will not go into the details that I have learned from Bobby in recent days, but my older brother and sister were sexually abused and my turn was coming. When my mother made her move, Bobby took over my personality. He was much older and stronger. He told my mother not to ever touch me. He said if she did, he would get a knife when she was sleeping and cut off her head. Now you know where the idea for cutting off heads came from. He so frightened my mother that she never came near me again. I, of course, did not know what had happened. All I knew was that my mother hated me, and gave me no love, ever. That hurt me deeply. Bobby felt that hurt, but he did nothing about it until this year.

I always had headaches fairly regularly, but late last year they became much worse when I was in the Yucatan. That's when I began using some of the Mayan drugs. I thought they were helping me. I don't think so now. One day we - I mean Bobby and me - saw a flier about Candy Barlow. It didn't register with me, but it did with Bobby. She looked just like our mother. Bobby came out and went to the strip club. He looks a little different from me, as you probably know, which probably explains why no one there remembered me being there.

He approached her and had a drink with her. He watched her act. She reminded him so much of our mother that he began to think of her as our mother. He tried to get closer to her, but she rejected him, just like our mother rejected me. Bobby knew of my great pain from what our mother did, and also from my headaches. He had learned the Mayan religion with me, and he induced another personality to develop, a Mayan priest. The priest told Bobby he could cure my headaches by sacrificing a human to one of the Gods of Medicine. Bobby and the Mayan priest carried out the sacrifice of Barlow.

Bobby next became fixated on Karen Billingsley, who also reminded him of our mother. He knew she had rejected me when her parents and ours tried to get us together. I was seeing Rory Crawford occasionally and giving him mescaline. I also saw Karen. So did Bobby. My headaches were bad and getting worse by the day. Bobby and the Mayan priest then went after those two so they could sacrifice Karen.

The killing of Laurie Waslewski was close to a spur of the moment thing. I had gone to the Walters the day after Nick and I had lunch at the Maryland Club, when I was feeling very badly about my relationship with Susan. Nick basically had told me that I could not have the kind of relationship with her that I wanted. I saw Laurie, who I had seen many times, but this time something made me pursue her. I asked her out, and while she was polite about it, she turned me down. She also reminded Bobby of our mother, and shortly after that, Bobby came out again, and he and the Mayan priest killed her.

Things stabilized with Susan, and I was very happy for a while. Also, the medications the doctor was giving me for the pains in my head worked well for a while. I didn't have headaches for several weeks. They returned

314

when I realized that Nick suspected I was the killer. I was hurt. I didn't understand it. I felt betrayed. Then the headaches became unbearable when Susan broke off with me that Friday night. Bobby came out the next day, and he went after Susan.

Bobby's only purpose is to protect me. He will protect me from the humiliation that a conviction of these crimes would cause me, and from the pain of incarceration. So by the time you read this he has become the dominant personality. The personality of Dewey Coughlin has been extinguished.

Meanwhile, I have enclosed an obituary of Dewey Coughlin. Sometime in the next few weeks I would like Nick to have this published. I have made several telephone calls to neighbors and friends in which I have told them that I am at the Mayo Clinic receiving treatment for a difficult cancer, and that I have asked Nick and Joan to look out for my house. They will not be surprised by this obituary. Meanwhile, you can check on my house, and use it as you wish.

I have created a trust to hold nearly all of my assets. A copy of the trust is enclosed. The trust is entirely for the benefit of the families of the Blue Girl victims, except that its existence is to be kept secret. The families can be told the money came from the estate of Robert Corrigan. They cannot be told anything about me. I have appointed Nicholas Prescott as the Trustee. Compensation is provided for this service. I hope you will accept the position, Nick. You will allocate the funds to individual members of the families as you see fit, but in a way that will do the greatest possible good. I know you will handle this responsibility with a high degree of ethics. If, for some reason, you are unable to carry out the responsibilities, Nick, then Michael Rosen shall be the trustee.

I retained Michael Rosen as the attorney for the trust. You may fire him, but I urge you not to do so. I have paid him a retainer sufficient to cover his services for at least 20 years, if it takes that long to close the trust.

I kept four properties out of the trust, my book on Mayan culture, the beach house in Rehoboth Beach, my mother's apartment in Paris and my father's wine cellar. I give the beach house to the three of you to use, or to sell, as you wish. The weekend we spent there was the happiest time of my entire life, the only time when I truly was happy. I thank all three of you for that special time.

Michael Rosen has been retained to market my book to publishers. If it is successfully published, I would like any profits to be donated to the School of Arts & Sciences of The Johns Hopkins University, in my memory. Nick, as compensation as trustee I am giving you the apartment in Paris so that you will have to place there when UPI makes you the Paris bureau manager. In the meantime, you can enjoy the rest of those Lafite Rothschilds and all the rest of the wine in my father's collection.

Finally, Nick, when the announcement of my death has been published, please collect the photograph of my mother from the police and burn it in my backyard and bury the ashes as if they were mine. No one else should ever see her again. That will truly end all the pain and tragedy that she caused.

I am deeply sorry for what Bobby did. I hope you realize that it was devastating for me to find out the truth. I could not live with it. Nick, I thank you for putting an end to the horror of the killings. Your courage and friendship are rare. Joan, I hope that Nick and you will always take care of each other and treasure what you have together.

Susan, I hope you can forgive me for what nearly happened. I have loved you more than you can know. I hope you have a good life, and find someone you can love.

I love all three of you and I hope your lives are happy, healthy and fulfilling.

Dewey

Afterword

The entire story of the Blue Girl murders is fictitious. Most of the characters in the novel also are fictitious except for the public officials, including Spiro Agnew, Theodore McKeldin, Major "Box" Harris, and Maj. Gen. George Gelston. Some of the newspaper personalities are real, including *News American* City Editor Eddie Ballard and Sports Editor John Steadman. Bob Bradley is a fictional composite of that newspaper's outstanding crime reporters.

The incident on Franklin Street, when CORE blocked traffic, and Gelston refused to arrest them, essentially is true. The dialogue is my invention. The attempt to integrate the bar is true, as is the story about the party thrown by Major Harris that night. Some of the details are fictitious, but not what the policeman said to the radio reporter, which I overheard.

I think I have accurately portrayed Stokely Carmichael's speech at the CORE convention. I have a copy of the press release announcing prematurely that Dr. Martin Luther King would speak. Stan Scott was UPI's first black reporter. I invented all the dialogue involving him, including the discussion of "black power."

The "white power" riot in Patterson Park actually occurred. I was there as a reporter for UPI. Joe Carroll, who had great speaking ability and charisma, and might have achieved greater political influence eventually, was convicted of inciting to riot, and served a prison term. That ended his "white power" activity, and the potential threat it represented. He was murdered after he was released from prison, but it had nothing to do with his political activities.

In 1970, about the time the "War on Drugs" began, mescaline and peyote, from which it is derived, became illegal. There was litigation over the use of peyote by various Indian tribes for religious practices. The issues never have been completely resolved.

Multiple Personality Disorder now is called Dissociative Identity Disorder. It still is controversial and not universally

318

accepted, although it now is recognized officially as a disorder. Many more documented cases have been reported in recent years. In 1966 it was barely known, and then mostly because of the movie, "The Three Faces of Eve." It wasn't until 1987 that a criminal defendant successfully used the disorder as an insanity defense to win an acquittal. It still is not accepted in all states as a valid insanity defense.

I have used the term, "Negro," because that was the popular term of the time. Even black-oriented radio stations used that term. The use of "black" replaced "Negro" fairly rapidly after the CORE convention, and that organization's adoption of the term "Black Power."

Knowledge of the Mayan culture in 1966 was not nearly as extensive as it is today. The hieroglyphics now can be translated, and many more sites have been excavated. The Mayan religion is much better understood today. There is a very active Internet community devoted to Mayan culture, archaeology and history.

The *News American* closed in 1986, and the building was torn down. The abandoned fifth floor city room actually existed, and there was an office in a corner like the one in the novel. I was told when I worked there that Hearst had used it. I thank Jacques Kelly, of the Baltimore *Sun* (and earlier, the *News American*), who saved the building's first floor directory, for helping me recall the various newspaper operations on the right floors.

I became the bureau manager for UPI in Baltimore at the end of 1966, succeeding Joel Shurkin, who had hired me early in the year. An outstanding journalist, he later won a Pulitzer Prize as a member of a Philadelphia Inquirer team that covered the Three Mile Island nuclear meltdown. I apologize for eliminating his role as bureau manager during the period of this novel. The character of Nick Prescott is not intended in any way to represent him, nor does he represent me. I was not nearly as cool as Nick is, nor was I ever able to rescue a damsel in distress, but I did have a beautiful Goucher College girlfriend who was my wife for nearly 47 years until her death in 2014.

The 1960s were an amazing time of enormous events, fascinating characters, and cultural upheaval. The Nick Prescott-Maury Antonelli mystery saga, set against the events of this time, will resume shortly after this one ended, at the beginning of 1967.

Made in the USA
Charleston, SC
20 December 2015